# City on the

# Heights

Joseph J. Cox

Published by Big Picture Books

Modiin, Israel

Note: In this book, the English transliteration of the Arabic name of G-d is used. Because this is a name of G-d as recognized by Jewish tradition (and because this book has been written by a religious Jew), it is not fully spelled out. Rather, in respect of that name and to prevent copies of it from being placed in the garbage or otherwise disrespected, that name is written with a dash in it. It is written as All-h.

Cover Photography from Shutterstock.com

Cover Calligraphy and Map by Veronika Váňová

Edited by Richard Crasta

Feedback from many friends & associates – you know who you are!

www.JosephCox.com

Dedicated to my wife Rebecca.
You are a blessing from G-d.

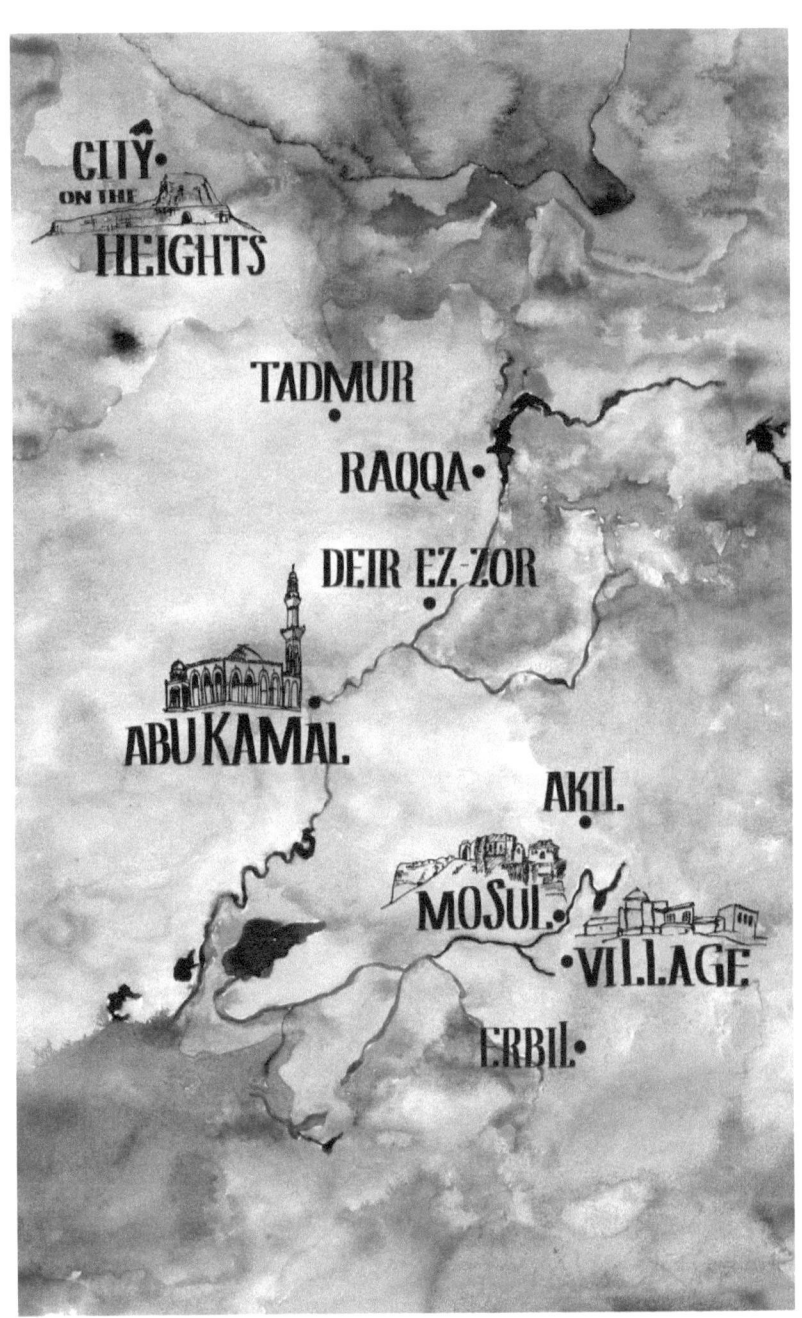

*Map of the Region*

# The Explosion

*October 1, 2014, Golan Heights*

It is 3:38AM, October 1ˢᵗ, 2014. The moon's light is choked by a massive sandstorm that has engulfed the Golan Heights. Against all public health recommendations, Steven Gold is outside. He is sitting on a lawn chair behind his trailer. He is drinking a beer.

His world is in shambles.

Eighteen months earlier, Steven had been living in a well-appointed Colonial home in a leafy suburb of Washington DC. He'd had a respected and secure position. He'd had influence and he'd had the ability to help so many in need. He'd had everything he'd worked for. And then, he'd invested everything that he had in a belief, a belief that he could reinvent a society he'd never been a part of.

Now, as he sits in the polluted darkness of that night, reality is destroying him. All of his efforts have been for nothing.

When he sees the flash of the explosion piercing the sandy air, he is not surprised. Nothing surprises him anymore. By the time the shock wave hits him, he has already accepted the reality of the explosion.

But then, he is surprised. Because, instead of taking another drink of his beer, he finds himself standing up from his chair and dusting off his sand-covered clothing. It is time to get back to work.

In a way, his life has been saved by the bomb that almost killed him.

--

Mohammed al Hassan is awake. As he lies down on his cot, Mohammed sees the faces of those who have died for his people. He sees the faces of those who have been sacrificed by his actions.

But, for the first time in years, their spirits are not torturing him.

He knows, finally, that he will give their lives meaning; their sacrifices will help overcome crushing and devious forces.

For that brief moment, he is content.

But when the sound of the explosion ruptures the night air, Mohammed is both shocked and surprised.

He fears, already, that this bomb will undermine the gifts of those who have already given everything.


--

I, Maryam al-Mosuli, step into the communal bathroom. A harsh fluorescent light burns into me, replacing the darkness I've emerged from. Outside, the wind and the sand have been brutal, but I've overcome both. I've prepared everything as well as I could manage.

Now, my success lies in the hands of All-h.

I place my hands on the sink and stare at the filthy aluminum surface that serves as a mirror in this dismal place.

And I wait.

I wait for the explosion.

"Any second now," I tell myself, trying to will a different reality.

I grip the counter, tightly.

But nothing is happening.

I step outside, back into the darkness and the sandstorm, so that I can pray.

But there is no answer from All-h.

Reluctantly, I begin to walk back to my tent. I begin to walk back to my crippled brother.

Perhaps it is time for us to run, again. Perhaps we can find a new place to hide. Perhaps we can find some other way to evade the terror that surrounds us.

I glance up towards the target, almost regretfully. I can't actually see it through the sand. But then, a moment later, there is a massive burst of light that pierces even the dirty fog that surrounds me. Moments later, the sound wave hits me with a thud.

I step back in shock and surprise.

And in joy.

My prayers have been answered.

G-d is great.

Hope endures.

# Maryam: The Beginning

*Oct 28, 2008: Mosul, Iraq*

I hated being woken up in the morning. That's probably why my father seemed to take particular pleasure in doing exactly that. He was an unusual man. While others mourned their predicament and cultivated their anger, he seemed to feed off of his own endless wellspring of joy. He was always smiling, and it wasn't an act.

He was tremendously happy, even though he had no sons.

Somehow, he always found, or made, the happier path. Others might insist it didn't exist, but he always proved them wrong. Others would see a desert mirage, but he would see water. And because *he* was the one looking, the water would materialize.

Of course, my father didn't wake me for school. Only a few schools were open. They were madrassahs and built like fortresses; even children weren't off-limits when it came to violence. But those few schools that were open were only for boys. There was nothing for girls. There used to be, my father told me, but the dangers had become far too great.

That's why my father taught me. In the afternoons, we'd read and talk. He could discuss everything – and he spent an enormous amount of time filling my head and then testing me on topics as random as physics, the Koran and biology.

But that was only in the afternoons.

The core of my education started in the mornings. It started when he woke me – despite my protests.

5

As soon as I had a single eye open, he would hurry me along as I slipped into a dress. He'd time me as I did a few pushups and sit-ups and some jumping jacks. He called that spurt of early morning exercise "coffee for kids," but I called it torture. And then he'd rush me out of the house and into his Land Rover.

There would be some breakfast there, waiting. Most often, it was hummus and some pita.

And then we'd drive somewhere in the city; going to do *something*.

He never told me what we were going to do, or even why. And I knew not to ask. Figuring out the answers was part of my education.

I did ask him once why he wouldn't just tell me what we were up to. But he just smiled, like he always did, and said, "What do you think?"

The answer annoyed me. I'd wanted a real answer, not another mystery. Nonetheless, I noodled over his reply for months. And then, finally, it came to me. I went to him and announced, without any sort of introduction: "Because if I figure it out for myself, I'll never forget the answers."

Somehow, he knew what I was talking about. It was like we were just continuing the earlier conversation, and there had been no months-long break.

He was like that.

But even then, he didn't respond. He just smiled.

It was as close to a confirmation as he ever gave me.

I never forgot that answer – or any of the others.

He was right, figuring it out for myself was the surest form of education.

That particular morning, my father seemed even more chipper than usual. He was barely suppressing an extra-wide grin as I moaned myself into consciousness. I really didn't want to get up. I felt even more tired than usual. But I knew I had no choice.

I lifted my head and noticed that it was still dark outside.

"This early, ab?" I asked plaintively. I *was* more tired than usual.

He just grinned even wider.

I didn't like going out in the dark. Everybody knew it was dangerous. Trucks driving at night were more likely to be deemed suspicious by any one of the four major forces operating in the city.

But my father didn't seem to notice these things. He'd always insisted that nobody would kill him.

But, as with most things, he never explained how he knew this.

It was my job to figure it out.

I didn't like this kind of puzzle. I knew he was right, of course. Nobody ever tried to harm us. But when I saw the darkness outside, all I could think of was the horror stories of people who left their homes at night and were blown to smithereens by drones, kidnapped by Al Qaida, torn apart at checkpoints by machine-gun wielding federal soldiers, or summarily executed by the Kurdish secret police.

I suppose most nine-year-olds might have been ignorant of what was going on, but most nine-year-olds didn't have my father.

My father, despite everything that was going on and everything he told me, was still smiling.

He was smiling like he expected me to learn his joy, despite knowing why I should not be happy.


Reluctantly, I climbed out of bed and got dressed and did my exercises. And then, as always, he rushed me out to the truck. I barely caught a look at my pregnant – and worried – mother before we escaped out the front gate of our house.

We lived in the Althaqafa district of the city, on the left coast of the Tigris. I'd seen every nook and cranny of the city, and I can assure you that ours was the nicest. The homes were large and surrounded by high walls. The ancient ruins of Nineveh were only blocks away. And our neighbors were all important people.

I got the sense my father was also important – but he was different than them. Whether they were politicians, imams, priests, or criminals, they all seemed to keep themselves away from the physical dirt of the city. Whether they wore suits or robes, their garments were always spotless.

But they seemed to wash themselves in another kind of filth.

My father wasn't like that. He was Mosul's municipal handyman. That's why, most days, when we went out, we'd find ourselves wading through sewage, wrestling with pipes or securing downed power lines. And he was a good man.

The neighbors were different in another, critical, way. They all had their own people. They were leaders of particular slices of our society. But my father had everybody. Arriving at an overflowing berm, my father could assemble a work crew in minutes. Sunnis, Shiites, Assyrians, or Yazidis – people who had become incompatible through the long years of ethnic conflict and war – all of them would come out, together, when my father asked.

He used to joke that that's how our family earned its name: Al-Mosuli. The city was pulling itself apart, but we still belonged to it and it to us. We were Mosuli, first and foremost.

As we drove, the streets were dark. Power was intermittent, despite the massive electrical dam that continually threatened our lives. The dam was, predictably, poorly maintained. The street was roughly paved, and so our headlights bounced along the walls that bordered it. I saw, here and there, the one-eyed smiley face of the letter *nuun*.

It marked the houses as Christian – Nazarene. We weren't Christian. Nonetheless, it scared me.

Everybody, even other nine-year-olds, knew that Al Qaida had recently told the Christians of the city to convert or die. Thousands of homes had been marked. Over a dozen Christians had already been killed. By that dark morning, the dust that regularly blew through the city had collected around those houses' gates.

Every one of them had been abandoned.

At that moment, even my father wasn't smiling.

We drove past the University and headed north, across the Khosr river and then out of the city. We passed checkpoint after checkpoint with only a wave. Soldiers saw my father's truck and they let us pass. We probably passed roadside bombs with unseen people effectively waving us by as soon as they knew it was our truck.

North of the city, we passed a small village. I'd forgotten what it was named, but it seemed to be overflowing with people – extra cars were parked akimbo in the small spaces between the homes, and tents were pitched everywhere outside. The village was bordered, north and south, by checkpoints. The checkpoints weren't manned by Federal troops, but by scared-looking villagers. They were Christians. But when they saw us, they waved us through.

My father still wasn't smiling.

We kept driving north. The road narrowed to three lanes. We passed streams and farmland and more overflowing villages. The road narrowed to two lanes, divided from one another by a sandy strip.

There was no traffic.

We passed between low mountains and into an area covered with lush farmland. It had grown brighter, and I noticed, for the first time, that the sky was covered with clouds. I felt like I hadn't seen clouds in months. They almost looked false, like they had been painted above me as a joke from on high.

I looked up, watching them shift in the sky, as our highway widened to four lanes and we arrived at a major intersection.

We turned right, towards Mahad.

I'd never heard of the place.

About seven kilometers later, we reached the turnoff for Mahad itself. But instead of turning towards the town, my father turned in the other direction, and up a tiny dirt road.

Before long, we'd stopped – next to a massive arrangement of carefully cut and perfectly placed stone blocks. It was a ruin, but a sizable one.

My father stopped the truck. And without a word, he got out.

He was smiling again. The grin he was trying to suppress at our house had finally broken out completely. He was almost laughing with joy.

We seemed to be in the middle of nowhere. But I knew where we were.

It was the Jerwan Aqueduct. It had been built thousands of years before, in the days of Sennacherib. It was the oldest surviving aqueduct in the world. It was a massive 75-foot-wide water bridge. It was only a small part of the 90-kilometer water delivery system that Sennacherib had constructed. It had all been capped with a series of retaining ponds – intended to modulate the rapid flows from the spring melts.

The whole thing had been built for only one reason – to sustain the ancient city of Nineveh. It was built to sustain what we now called Mosul.

Just then, it began to rain.

As the water ran over and between the stones, and the musty smell of reinvigorated life filled the air, my father looked at me. And then he said, in a voice somehow both solemn and delirious with joy, "Maryam al-Mosuli, this is who we are."

A moment later, I answered the question he'd implied: "We exist to sustain the city of Mosul."

Somehow, he managed to smile even more.

And then I saw it, the unbroken chain of my family extending back through time.

We were the ones who sustained the city. Working on its water and its sewage, on its power and its streets, we were the ones who had spent countless generations intertwined with it.

Whoever came to rule Mosul recognized that we were the key to their success. It was why he was always safe. My father had no party or sect, he threatened no one.

He belonged to the city. And in a way, the city belonged to him.

As we stood in the rain and watched the flow of water over the broken stones of the aqueduct, I smiled. I smiled like my father did.

I knew who I was, and I knew why.

That day remains the fondest memory of my life.

At 1:29 a.m., a car bomb had targeted our house. It was the very first attack the Islamic State had launched on Mosul.

For the first time, my family had been a target.

My parents were killed instantly, and my five-year-old younger brother was struck in the head by shrapnel. He was alive but unconscious.

I remember grabbing a bolt of fabric to carry him with and slinging him over my shoulder and then running. I was panicked and scared. We left the city, heading north with other refugees. He became extremely heavy.

As we traveled further and further from Mosul, I realized just how lost we were. We existed to sustain the city, but we were no longer a part of it. I could imagine my father had set the whole thing up. I could imagine the questions he wanted me to answer.

The first was, "Who am I now?"

The second was, "Why had they tried to kill my family?"

And the third was, "How can you find joy?"


As we run, I try to hold the memory of my father's face.

But, gradually, all that remains is his smile.

# Steven: The Beginning

*April 3rd, 2013: Washington, D.C.*

When Steven Gold was five years old, his parents had brought him to a Phoenix Suns playoff game. It was a big year for the Suns – they made it to the NBA Finals. The excitement in the Memorial Coliseum was something Steven would never forget. The place was bursting with light. The crowds, made up of people who little in common with one another, were united in their support of their team. There was a fellowship there.

And then, the game was over.

The crowds filed out of the Coliseum that night, excited by the victory. And then they were thrust into the cool darkness of the night. As they went their separate ways, they tore at the bonds that had held them together during the game itself. Steven and his parents embarked on a longer walk than most. Officially, they disliked the traffic that slowed those who parked near the Coliseum. But, unofficially, they were cheap and didn't want to pay for parking. The neighborhood they parked in was filled with large warehouses. Before long, the last of their companions from the game drifted towards vehicles parked in other spots. Before long, they were almost entirely alone. As they walked, the streetlights lit the sidewalks unevenly. The city seemed to darken, and Steven's parents instinctively shifted to a close and protective formation. Steven felt their fear, peering out from between them.

As they walked, Steven noticed a misshapen lump lying next to one of the warehouses. At first, he thought it was simply a shadow, cast by the rickety-looking warehouse that rose above it. But as they drew closer, Steven realized it was not a shadow, but a woman. And his parents were ignoring her. But Steven couldn't. As they passed, Steven chanced a glance at her. She was young, probably a teenager. She was wearing layers of old and tattered clothing. A smell wafted from her body. And her eyes were open and unblinking.

Steven realized, with horror, that she was dead.

He didn't remember what happened next. But he did remember that, later, his father said the woman was homeless and had probably been crazy. He cursed a mental health system that was releasing the ill from long-term hospitalization. When he was much older, Steven realized that his father had been trying to create distance from the dead woman and her circumstances. Steven's father wanted to blame her death on something; something that didn't apply to him or his family.

But Steven wasn't like that. Instead of drawing away from the woman, he was drawn to her. If he could feel kinship with strangers at a basketball game, why not a woman lying on the street? Of course, he didn't know her. But as he kept remembering that evening, she developed in his mind. She became a victim. She became somebody who didn't need to die. As Steven imagined it, if others had drawn close to her, instead of being repelled, she wouldn't have ended up where she had.

That woman, whom he'd never met, defined Steven's life. It started slowly at first. Steven would reach out to the ostracized kids on the playground. But it snowballed as he grew older. Steven became the one who, even in high school, would invite street people over for dinner. He believed you could unlock the goodness in almost anybody. You just needed to understand them, instead of running away from them. His parents tried to set boundaries, but that wasn't his way. They told him

14

he needed distance in order to truly help those in need. But as he saw it, they were intellectuals, and they used their ideas to excuse their inaction. Failing to help gnawed at Steven. He needed to restore those who had no one else to turn to. He needed to bring life back to eyes of that homeless woman on a Phoenix street. When he was nineteen, Steven joined the Jewish Union of Charities. He joined, and he never left.

At first, he worked directly with those in need. It was intensely rewarding. He drifted away from his parents as his involvement deepened. But, before long, he realized that some of what his parents claimed was true. He could help so many more people from a position of greater responsibility and power. Reluctantly, he began to see how ideas and organization could be as important as personal interactions. He applied for, and joined, the management of his local JUC. At first, he hated the fluorescent lights, the ticking clocks and the unending meetings. But he came to know that this was where the real opportunities lay. He learned to find satisfaction, not through his personal efforts to help those in need, but from reports on the impact of the JUC across his region. Instead of finding joy in the faces of those desperate for help and human support, he found it in the faces of his staff. He helped them help others and saw success through *their* achievements.

Slowly, Steven climbed the ranks of the JUC. He was a truly gifted administrator. He inspired his people. And he helped them to inspire themselves. He met his wife there. She, like so many others, had been drawn to his dedication.

Finally, 27 years after joining the JUC, Steven Gold was offered membership on the National Executive Committee of the Jewish Union of Charities.

The night before his new role officially started, an energetic wisp of a woman came to his home. She'd introduced herself, in a clean American accent, as the Chief of Staff to the Israeli Ambassador. Her name was Tamar Rothstein. They had coffee together in his living room, and Steven realized the responsibilities of his new role were no longer just local or regional. They were international. While the thought burdened him, it also inspired him. The opportunities were immense.

The next morning, as Steven was still getting his computer account set up at work, a man had come to see him. He wasn't Israeli, or even Jewish. He was African, and he was lobbying for refugees from the Lake Chad region. Steven wasn't a politician – but the man figured he might eventually earn the ears of politicians. This went beyond the dreams he'd had. Steven's responsibilities had always extended a little beyond the parochial needs of the Jewish community, but this was something entirely different.

It was what he'd worked so hard to achieve.

The Executive Committee met daily. Thus, soon after his email was set up, Steven set off for his first meeting.

He was the first to arrive.

As Steven watched the other members of the committee arrive, he struggled to contain his excitement. The lighting in the room was harsh, the clock's ticking incessant, and the coffee poor, but he knew the people were superb. Each and every member of the committee was an accomplished community leader. Together, they could do tremendous things.

The Director of the JUC, a black-haired woman with sharp eyes and a reputation for even sharper elbows, called the meeting to order. The committee meeting started like so many others. Steven was introduced, and then he contributed as he could; but mostly, he listened. They discussed financial issues. They discussed various programs. And then, eventually, they got to a topic the Southwest Regional JUC would never have discussed: the war in Syria.

Steven watched as the conversation flowed around the room. He watched as proposals were floated and debated. Some suggested lobbying to bring more refugees into the United States. Others suggested aid to refugee camps. Steven suggested sending JUC representatives to work in the camps themselves. He suggested reaching out, directly, to help those in need. But as the conversation continued, Steven realized his joy was being replaced by something else. He realized that nobody was attacking the core of problem. Nobody was helping those caught in the war zone. Instead, they were dancing around the problems, speaking to symptoms instead of fundamental needs. And he was no exception.

At a pause in the conversation, Steven asked, "Can't we fix anything – ourselves?"

Maybe these people, these assembled experts, could find a way to do more.

"Fix?" asked a man named Ethan Cohen. He was a 20-something social media coordinator.

"I don't know." said Steven. "We keep seeing these wars. Lebanon, Iraq, Syria, Libya, Egypt, Yemen. I know most of the people fleeing Syria belong to ethnic groups that have decided to engage in ethnic conflict. I know they aren't just innocents. But can't we somehow interrupt their decision to fight? Can we stop just trying to deal with the war's exports and deal with the social problems that lie at the core of the conflicts?"

He was met with blank stares.

"We study genocide," said Rachel Samuelson, a specialist in Genocide prevention, "so we can spot the warning signs and can get the international community involved in preventing the worst."

"But does it work?" said Steven. "Have we actually stopped genocides? Have we fixed what's wrong in these societies?"

"Fixed?" Rachel asked, almost confused, "What do you mean?"

"Have we tried to change Arab society?" Steven asked. He realized, as soon as he opened his mouth, how horrible that sounded.

Ethan looked at him, almost stunned. "Um, Steven, Kipling's been dead a long while now. It isn't our job to bring civilization to the savages."

Steven backed off immediately. "I wasn't suggesting that. I just thought maybe we could do something other than accept the breakdown of their societies?"

The table went silent.

The Director spoke up, "It isn't our mission to change other cultures. In fact, we shouldn't do so. We just help those in need."

"But the whole Arab world is in need," said Steven. "And we work on culture all the time. We try to change our own communities. We may be subtle about it, but we try to improve on the values many of our communities hold. Why not do it here?"

"You want to send in social workers?" asked Rachel, incredulously.

"Maybe we could send in your Genocide experts," said Steven. "Maybe they could talk people down. I don't know."

"That isn't what they do," said Rachel. "They study what's occurred. And they work with world leaders to help spot the signs and prevent the next big catastrophe."

Steven felt like he was going in circles.

"The question is simple, for me at least... Is there anything we can do to strike at the causes of these wars? Can we repair the problems that are causing so much pain?"

Nobody said anything.

Steven continued. "Have you seen the beheadings? Have you seen the protesters shot down by snipers? Isn't there something we can do to help?"

Steven was almost desperate as he looked around at the committee members. They were the best and the brightest and the most capable. They were good people, all of them. And they had nothing to offer. They were doing what his father had done. They were distancing themselves from the suffering. But Steven couldn't do that.

The silence extended.

Eventually, the Director announced, "We'll table this discussion for now."

As the meeting continued, Steven felt a hopeless lethargy growing within him. When the meeting finally ended, he rose from his seat and walked from the office to the parking lot below.

His excitement had completely vanished.

As he got into his car and started to drive, Steven felt like a kid again, crying as he realized the dead woman on the Phoenix street was beyond help.

He realized that, even though he could find his way to his new home, he was completely lost.

# Mohammed: The Beginning

*September 5th, 1998: Abu Kamal, Syria*

Mohammed al-Hassan was six years old when his father returned. It was the fifteenth of the month of Jumada al-awwal.

There was a party, of sorts, that night. People started to come when the heat of the day had retreated. Mohammed could see them come. The full moon illuminated the land outside his house. Those who came were all men. They came and quietly paid their respects. Mohammed recognized many of them, but he did not know or recognize his own father. Mohammed's father was a stranger, a man Mohammed had never met – at least not as far back as he could recall. The celebration that day wasn't loud and raucous, although it felt like it wanted to be. People smiled in genuine and enormous pleasure on seeing Abu Mohammed, an honorary name for the father of Mohammed. They would walk towards him. As they moved, for reasons Mohammed could not understand at the time, their expressions would change. They would start with celebration. A few steps later, there would be confusion. Then as they drew near, there would be mourning. And, finally, as they bent over to kiss his cheeks in greeting, there would be terror.

Mohammed stood in the corner of his tiny house, watching the men stream out and then talk quietly amongst themselves.

They spoke of things Mohammed didn't understand. But one word came up again and again: "Tadmur."

After the party, Mohammed asked his mother about it.

She looked worried, very worried. Then she put her fingers to her lips and said, gently, "Never say that word again."

He never did, at least not to her. But he also never forgot it.


Mohammed's father screamed that night. Mohammed covered his ears and looked to his mother in fear. She looked back at him, not with reassurance but with confusion and fear of her own. Mohammed screamed then, suddenly unmoored. He would never again be more shaken then he was at that moment. His mother was helpless. He was helpless. The world was untethered. Abu Mohammed, his father, was screaming and lashing out in his terror. And no matter how they tried to comfort him, he heard nothing. Mohammed's mother pleaded with the terrified man, but he just hit her. Even as he did so, his eyes showed no malice, or even recognition. All they showed was fear.

In the morning, Abu Mohammed awoke. He had no memory of what had occurred.

He just sat quietly, in the corner.

That cycle continued, every night, from that day until the day he once again disappeared – ten years later – on October 26th, 2008.

Abu Mohammed was a shell of a man. The neighbors came to call him *bari*. It was a euphemism. It literally means "pure" or "guileless", but it also means "simpleton" – like a brain-damaged boy.

That first day, Mohammed's mother went to her husband and talked with him, briefly. And then she came to Mohammed himself.

"Nobody," she said, "can ever know what he does at night."

Mohammed nodded in frightened agreement.

A few weeks after Mohammed's father came home, a few men came to talk to Abu Mohammed. One of them had been there the night of his return. They came and asked questions in muted tones. Abu

Mohammed asked them to tell him more. Mother came and poured tea for the men. And then, eventually, he told them, "Come to me tomorrow and I'll tell you my answer." The following day, in a stuttering tone, he read them his answers – consulting the notes he held in his hand.

And they went away, satisfied.

He took many meetings after that. Many men came and asked him questions. Mohammed's mother would pour tea. And every time Abu Mohammed would say, "Come to me tomorrow and I'll tell you my answer." And every time, they came and went satisfied with what they heard.

It was confusing to Mohammed. The neighbors called his father *bari*, but the respected men of the town and even other nearby villages all came to him for advice. Little Mohammed didn't understand how both could be true.

Mohammed asked his father once, but his father just looked at him and said, almost like a robot, "Come to me tomorrow and I'll tell you my answer."

It took Mohammed years to understand.

Mohammed's father was a shell of a man. He hadn't always been so. He'd been a leader of men. He'd been a leader of the anti-Assad movement in his region. A Sunni Muslim, he resisted the heretical Alawites' domination of his people. He'd been arrested by them. He'd been sent to Tadmur, a prison so foul and evil that the guards themselves regarded serving there to be torture. The secret police bent and broke men. They played with their minds and their fears and their bodies. They electrocuted them. They beat them with clubs. For years, they never saw another face – even as they were shoved into cells with dozens of other men. Simply raising one's eyes to look at a guard or another prisoner could lead to execution.

In Tadmur, there was no conversation – other than the confessions the jailors had extracted through torture. The Assad family had worked out how to prevent the radicalization so common in prisons – they simply stopped the prisoners from speaking to or even seeing one another. It was a crowded isolation.

The most notorious incident occurred in 1980, when the dictator Hafez Assad's brother killed thousands of men in that prison in just a few minutes. Their worthless lives had been forfeited because their allies had tried to rise up in the city of Homs.

Mohammed's father was arrested in 1994. He was kept there for four years – under constant torture and in complete isolation. They never meant to kill him. They meant to break him and send him home, as a message to those he had once led.

That was what Mohammed had seen, that first day.

Men arriving to greet the returned hero: that had been their celebration.

Men seeing a man with same body, but a very different spirit; that had been their confusion.

Then, the men realizing that the man they knew was dead; that had been their mourning.

And then, finally, men coming close and kissing the shadow of a one-time leader; that had been their terror.

Assad and his men knew their trade well.

Mohammed didn't understand how his father, his simple and broken father, had once again become a leader.

Mohammed's mother sent him out, every day, to buy things in the market. People knew who his father was. Whether they regarded him as a martyr or as a leader, they treated Mohammed with respect. Even as a boy, he could buy without being cheated.

One June day in 2002 started like any other. Mohammed was ten years old then. He was drawing close to the shuk when he realized that something was terribly wrong. The normal bustle of prices being fiercely negotiated was simply absent. Mohammed stopped, nervously. He was still two blocks from the market. He peered ahead, hoping to see what was happening. And then he saw something. A man he knew, a man who had a small fruit stall, was being pushed into a van. He was being arrested by the Mukhabarat.

Mohammed turned calmly and walked back the way he had come.

Mohammed came home much earlier than usual. He'd intended to tell his father everything, right then and there. But when he walked into the kitchen at the back of the house, he heard his mother talking in a low voice. She was talking to his father. The sentences were simple and clear. They were instructions. They were the answers his father was to give to those who came to visit. As he quietly opened the door, he saw her handing his father a sheet of notes.

In a flash, Mohammed realized what was happening. Assad's men had done their jobs well, but they hadn't counted on Mohammed's mother. She was the reason his father always answered new queries the same way, "Come back tomorrow and I will tell you my answer." She told him to. And while they asked their questions, she would pour tea and wait on the men and listen to their questions and conversations. And then she would send Mohammed to the market. And while he was out, she would consider their issues and give her husband, Mohammed's father, the answers to the visitors' questions.

This was how he could be both simple and wise.

Mohammed wanted to confront her. She was not in her proper place. As a woman and a wife, she should have been submissive.

But this was not the time.

He cleared his voice and she looked up, shocked to see him. She was frightened of him.

"The fruit seller," Mohammed said. "They just arrested him."

In a moment, her fear was smothered. Calmly, she turned to Mohammed's father, who had been sitting peacefully, and she said one word, "Tadmur."

In a moment, Abu Mohammed's calm face became ripped with fear and confusion. The fear was so complete that he relieved himself, staining his pants and filling the room with a foul odor. With a word, he had been transformed from a simpleton to a blathering incontinent.

Mohammed was shocked, but his mother looked at him sternly and said, "You must, must, must ignore him. You must pretend that this is how he always is."

Mohammed did just that. He imagined his father was just screaming and lashing out, like he did every night, instead of shaking in place with eyes desperately seeking some sort of relief. His mother threw the notes she'd composed into the stove.

Moments later, there was a knock on the door.

A heavy-set man in a light jacket stood at the door. He had a mustache but was otherwise clean shaven. He had a round face and the thick hands of a street fighter. He was wearing slacks and a sweat-stained off-white shirt. He looked like the kind of thug who no longer had to fight for his food. He must have been 35 years old.

He saw Mohammed looking up at him almost curiously. And then he roughly pushed past the boy and into the living room.

Mohammed's mother looked up and saw him and put her hand to her mouth in an expression of fear and surprise. It almost seemed like she didn't know the man was coming, but of course she did.

Mohammed's father was paralyzed in the corner.

The man looked around the room. He saw Mohammed, he saw his mother, and he saw his father. After a brief period of consideration, he turned and left. He must have concluded that the living, breathing shell of a man who was there was more of a burden to the enemies of the state than any corpse would have been.

It took three days to bring Mohammed's father back to his normal, empty, self.

Nobody ever saw the fruit seller again.

Mohammed thought about confronting his mother as soon as the man left. But he couldn't fight her, not while his father was paralyzed with the fear of Tadmur. That's why he waited. And while he waited, he came to a new understanding. It was his mother's duty to be submissive, but it was also her duty to serve and satisfy her husband. He realized, over those three days, that that was exactly what she was doing. She was enabling her husband to live. She was enabling him to have honor among men. And, judging by the satisfaction of their visitors, she was making wise decisions.

The family's world began to change with the U.S. invasion of Iraq. The Mukhabarat withdrew from their village. And then young men started to arrive. The local people didn't know, at first, who they were. The Assads could not communicate with the leaders of their Sunni opposition, because they had already killed or incapacitated every leader they could identify. But before long, the men of the village understood what was needed. The young men were Sunni fighters. They had come to fight. They had come to martyr themselves. Their target was not the Assad family and their Alawite heretics, but the Americans in Iraq. The local Sunni leaders were expected to ferry these fighters across the border, and that is exactly what they did.

As Mohammed grew older, his mother began to discuss her thoughts with him, soliciting his advice. Mohammed came to realize that she was running Al Qaida's operations on the Syrian border with Iraq. She was in charge. And his father, the incapacitated martyr, was her figurehead. Mohammed's mother organized the movement of the martyrs across the border. She kept the records, paid the Bedouin smugglers, and ensured there was no action taken against the Assads. The war against the Americans was far too important to risk a second, simultaneous conflict.

Nonetheless, for all her energy and organization and focus, Mohammed's mother's efforts were not meeting with success. The martyrs were crossing and killing – but the Sunni forces of Al Qaida were being crushed. Mohammed didn't understand why, at least not yet.

When Mohammed was sixteen his family moved to a new warehouse that was being constructed in a poor neighborhood far from the river. The warehouse was a front, of course. Theoretically, it held building supplies, and his parents had been hired to guard it. The reason they were here was that the buildings here were larger than those in the green belt. They could move people through these buildings, and nobody would notice. Perhaps, with this scale of infrastructure, they could redouble and reinvigorate their efforts against the Americans.

But even as they expanded their operations, everybody knew it wasn't going to be enough. Even Mohammed could tell that they were losing their war. Not only were they losing, but they had actually played into the hands of their enemies – the Alawites and their allies, the Iranians.

Their Al Qaida forces were opposed to the democratically elected government of Iraq. They knew the Shia majority would oppress them with a dictatorship as harsh as that of the Assad's, so they had to resist. But the harder they fought, the more the Americans pushed against them. The Shiites were happy to enable the Sunnis, even if the Sunni forces bombed Shia markets and destroyed Shia holy places. The Shiites knew that every act of destruction was met with ever-greater American force. The Sunni tribes themselves began to bend to the will of the American forces. Mohammed's mother and her kind were playing into the hands of the Shia enemy. The Sunnis were being used to fight the Americans, and the Americans were being used to fight the Sunni. And the Shiites were winning both wars.

Mohammed's mother was a straightforward thinker. When the enemy lost, she won. For her to win, they must lose. It was a natural way to think, for a woman who grew up on the Euphrates. On the river, life is lived on a thread of green life. There are only two directions on the river. Upriver, or downriver. Sideways is the direction of death and irrelevance. In this one-dimensional world, you can win or you can lose, you can strike a bargain or you can be cheated, you can rise or you can descend, and you can serve All-h or you can blaspheme Him. There is never a third way – at least not one Mohammed's mother could understand.

The way Mohammed saw it, the Shia would win, and the Americans would leave, licking their wounds, but content in their victory. And the Sunnis would be crushed. Their defeat would be all the greater because they had fought so hard.

As this realization cemented in Mohammed's mind, he resolved to never accept one-dimensional thinking. Yes, there was victory and loss, but the path towards victory was not so straightforward.

By October 2008, it was clear to Mohammed that his family had outlived their usefulness. The Al Qaida forces in Iraq had been crushed. They had moved to the new warehouse, hopeful. But they all knew their time was short. They were intimately involved in a war only miles from their town. Despite the proximity of the fighting, they had never been caught up in the violence. And that was a reality that could not survive.

It was clear the Assad regime no longer needed Al Qaida.

Mohammed was at the market when the helicopters came. They were Americans. They came to call the attack the "Abu Kamal" raid. They killed seven people, including both of Mohammed's parents. When reporters asked, their neighbors said the Americans had killed a simple man and his wife, who had been hired to watch the warehouse.

They had killed a simple man, Abu Mohammed – otherwise known as Abbas al-Hassan. And they had killed a woman who was anything but simple.

Mohammed came home to the destruction, but even as he looked at his parent's bodies, he cursed them for their mistakes. Their fate had been sealed by his father's mistakes in the battle against the Alawites and by his mother's mistakes in the fight against the Shia and the Americans.

In the eyes of Mohammed, they deserved what had come upon them. They had been outthought by their enemies, and the precious lives of the Al Qaida martyrs had been used to undermine their own people.

Mohammed resolved to learn from his parents. He resolved to never make the mistakes they had made.

And he resolved to destroy his enemies.

# Flight
*June 4th, 2014: Mosul, Iraq*

I knew I had to leave Mosul. So, I did. I tied my injured brother to my back and began to walk.

My brother was tiny for his age, but he was still just over 30 pounds. Thankfully, I only had to go 9 kilometers to reach the edge of the city; despite having over a million people, Mosul doesn't occupy a large area.

I only had to go 9 kilometers before the world I grew up in vanished completely.

As soon as we left the charred ruins of our home, we encountered soldiers preparing for the fight ahead. They were in uniform, and there were tens of thousands of them in the city. But despite their density, I could see the fear in their eyes. The armies of All-h had swept through city after city. And while the soldiers might have had a numerical advantage against the attackers, the Islamic State had widespread support in Mosul itself. There were over a million citizens, a clear majority of whom were Sunnis. Eighteen months earlier, the Sunni Finance Minister of Iraq had been arrested on trumped-up charges. It was a consolidation of Iranian-style Shia political power in the central government, and it represented a disenfranchisement of one of the most important Sunni voices in the country. The population rose up, peacefully. But from that point on, the soldiers of the government were seen only as Shia occupiers. Their very presence was seen as a statement of the weakness of true Islam and the arrogance of Nouri al-

Maliki, the Shia Prime Minister. The soldiers, whose fearful eyes were now examining every passerby, were justified in their paranoia.

As I walked, I both heard and felt other massive bombs. My family had been the first target, but we were far from the last. With every explosion, the confusion and terror on the faces of the soldiers grew. They had established a perimeter around the city. They had dug in and reinforced themselves to the best of their ability. Every car bomb undermined their already shaky belief in their control.

We were passing the University when the largest of the bombs went off. It was initially an explosion like all the others – no larger. But then it just seemed to grow and multiply. The sky was lit up and the booms echoed off the walls around me. There was only a sliver of the moon visible, so every massive explosion seemed to illuminate the street, capturing in still-frames the terror on the faces of the soldiers and the joy on the faces of many of the citizens.

The armory had been attacked. In a few minutes of cataclysmic, explosive fury, the soldiers had been reduced to the guns in their hands and the bullets strapped to their bodies.

Despite everything going on around me, I still had my father's approach to conflict. I still believed the conflicts weren't mine. I still believed that somehow, my family was above it all. We adapted to the changes around us and stayed a part of the city. I had skinny jeans for some periods, and a niqab for others. I'd been wearing the niqab for 18 months. We could comply with anybody; nobody had ever wanted to hurt us, so long as we weren't aggressively disobedient.

I felt that way that night, even though I knew it was no longer true. Despite having been one of the first targets, I felt distant from the attacks. The conflict wasn't mine.

If the soldiers looked, they might have seen fear on my face. But in reality, all there was was shock. My parents were gone, in an instant. My tiny, harmless, and incapacitated brother was strapped to my back. And my belief in my family's neutrality had been shattered. And nothing had taken its place.

I desperately wanted to check on my brother. I needed to run, but first, I needed to make sure he was okay. I put him down on the street and knelt over him. I saw a dent in his skull – something had smashed him there. His eyes were closed, but his breathing was steady. He needed a hospital. Where was the nearest one again? I couldn't remember. My brother needed me, I thought. I couldn't panic. I forced myself to breathe slowly. And then, to think. Of course! The Alzarawi hospital was straight ahead. It was a tiny place, but it would be better than nothing. Most importantly, no detour would be necessary. I got up again and lifted my brother onto my aching shoulders.

When I looked up, I saw a soldier, shifting nervously from foot to foot. In the distance was the sound of automatic gunfire. He was clinging to his gun like a child to his safety blanket, his finger resting on the trigger. And then I heard a shot, very close by. I cowered instinctively. But the soldier just collapsed onto the street. I saw the blood pouring from a wound in his head. I looked up, but I saw no gunmen. Instead, the cry of "All-hu Akbar" emanated from every window.

I knew then, for certain, that the soldiers were doomed.

I lowered my head and walked past the corpse. I had to make it to the hospital.

We passed another soldier. His was in a hurry, removing his uniform as quickly as he could manage. Whatever confidence the army's numbers may have provided had vanished completely. The army was melting away. It wouldn't work, of course. Even in a city of a million people, these soldiers could find no place to fit in. When the city fell, they would be trapped within it – and then slaughtered.

I kept moving. Soon enough, I was at the small bridge over the Khosr river. I only had to travel a few hundred more feet to make it to the hospital.

I looked up, hopefully.

The entrance to the hospital was illuminated by a single dim streetlight. There was probably a generator within the building itself that was providing the power for the light. But underneath that light was a mob. They were shouting. There were five frightened soldiers standing guard outside the hospital. They probably had a compatriot inside. The crowd moved towards them, dangerously. They lowered the barrels of their guns in self-defense. The crowd kept coming. And, in desperation, the soldiers opened fire. The crowd fell back under the onslaught of bullets. But then, moments later, they surged forward in an ecstasy of anger, hatred, and violence. The first soldiers died moments later. The rest of the crowd swarmed into the hospital.

The light outside flickered and died.

I kept going.

The road to the outskirts of the city veered to the left. I was almost out.

A pickup truck roared by me, heading into the city. There was one man driving, and three riding in the bed, their guns pointed in every direction. They stopped just past me and dismounted – abandoning their vehicle. None were wearing uniforms. They were an advance group from the Islamic State, probably sent in to organize the neighborhood resistance.

I kept walking.

I saw a group of men ahead of me. I lowered my eyes and kept going. I just wanted to avoid them. But one of them stopped me.

"Look up, girl," he said.

I did. The man in front of me was in his thirties. His face was unshaven. He wasn't big. Physically, he looked almost puny. But his eyes were hard. In the dim light of the moon, they seemed almost black. He was dangerous.

As I looked up, he stared at the upper half of my face. It was all he could see, because of my niqab.

"What's your name," he demanded, angrily.

I realized, in that instant, that I could not be Maryam Al-Mosuli.

"Fatima," I answered humbly, "Fatima Hassan." I winced as I said It, Hassan was often a Shia name.

He looked doubtful.

"Where are your papers?" he demanded.

"I have none," I answered, truthfully.

"Why not?" he asked. And then, before I could answer, he asked, "What happened to him?" He was pointing at my brother.

Again, there was no sympathy, only suspicion.

"There was a car bomb," I said, "He was injured, and I fled without my papers."

"Where?"

I knew I had to lie, "Near the University," I answered, "There was an army post there, we lived nearby."

He nodded, like he knew the target.

I came from a secular family, but I thanked All-h that I had said something credible.

"You look like somebody else I know," he said, with a hint of challenge in his voice. I had no idea how he could tell – just from half my face.

"Who?" I asked, neutrally.

"Maryam al-Mosuli," he said. "Daughter of Ibrahim."

I looked at him blankly. I was scared that if I opened my mouth, the shakiness of my voice would come through clearly. Just maybe I could pretend to know nothing. I prayed to All-h that he'd doubt himself enough to let me go.

He just looked at me for a long minute. He was watching me carefully, examining my expression. And then, almost miraculously, the challenge disappeared, and he looked almost embarrassed at his own foolishness.

"Where are you going?" he asked, a hint of politeness and care creeping in.

"I was going to the Alzawari Private Hospital," I answered, "But it has been mobbed."

He nodded. He clearly knew this to be true.

"If you can wait a few days," he said, "The Islamic State will set up field hospitals. They have doctors with them."

"Thank you," I said, meekly, "I hope my brother will make it."

"Inshall-h," he answered. May it be All-h's will.

"In the meantime," he continued, "Get indoors. And cover your eyes!"

I was dressed in an all-black niqab. It had been enough the day before. Clearly, the City's new rulers demanded that women wear a screen in front of their eyes.

I tipped my head in submission and thanked him.

"Go along!" he ordered.

I moved off, filled with both relief and confusion.

I knew now that we had been intentionally targeted. There had been no mistake. The Islamic State wanted us dead.

But I had no idea why.

I kept walking.

As the predawn light began to fill the sky, fields replaced the buildings on my left. Up ahead was the army checkpoint at the entrance to the city. I glanced at it as I passed the small concrete square that marked the city's edge. There was blood on the inside walls.

I kept walking.

Was I walking into a trap? Were there more Islamic State forces ahead, or had they all moved into the city? Were they killing everybody who tried to leave? I strained my eyes to see. But there was nothing I could make out – other than the broad outlines of the predawn terrain.

Behind me, the bombings had stopped, and while there was the occasional burst of automatic weapons fire, the city seemed to have calmed down.

Around me, I heard the conversations of what seemed like a city of small animals, chirping and rustling in the underbrush. There was life in the land outside the city, and it somehow seemed unperturbed by the violence I'd just witnessed. I smiled for the first time – imagining myself enjoying their blissful and ignorant peace.

I wouldn't know it until later, but while it had taken the Islamic State only hours to achieve victory, it took four days to conquer the city.

I kept walking north. As the initial shock and fear began to recede, I realized I was growing hungry and thirsty. I'd taken nothing with me but my brother. I was regretting my haste. But I knew there was a Christian village about 10 kilometers ahead. Perhaps I could find food and even shelter there.

I kept walking.

I couldn't see any Islamic State fighters. Perhaps the whole force had infiltrated the city. Perhaps they were hiding until their moment of attack. I didn't know. But I was worried somebody would stop me. Despite my worry, I didn't look around. I didn't want to arouse suspicion.

The sun had risen now. Dawn was early in June. There were fields around me. With the light, the irrigated portions of the land began to distinguish themselves from their surroundings. Green patches separated from the nearly lifeless sandy brown that dominated the landscape. They were the signs of the human resistance to our natural limitations. I smiled at that too; finding myself oddly philosophical about the contrast between the fight for life represented by the green fields, and the terrible violence I'd just witnessed.

I heard a deep engine behind me. It was approaching fast. The occasional tank-like squeak of its moving parts told me, before I looked, that it was an armored Humvee. Its suspension and engine were straining under the weight of the armor. I looked back and saw it. In the dark, I couldn't see through the windows. But there were men on the roof, and I could see the tops of men's heads peeking over the back of the truck. It must have been packed tight with them.

The gunner had his big machine gun at the ready. He was scanning the horizon in every direction. The truck whooshed past me; spilling the smell of diesel behind it. They hadn't seen me as a threat. I watched as it continued down the road. It was only going about 50 kilometers an hour, but I envied its speed. I almost wished I'd checked the Land Rover to see if it still worked after the bombing.

The Humvee was maybe a mile ahead when I saw a light emerge from the side of the road. It streaked towards the Humvee and then the entire vehicle suddenly burst into flames; the sound of the explosion hitting me a moment afterwards.

I lowered my head and kept walking.

There were a few bursts of automatic weapons fire. And then, once again, silence.

I knew now that the Islamic State fighters were watching me.

There was nobody else on the road.

I felt like a thousand eyes and thousand triggers were examining my every move. It would only take one suspicious or malevolent thought for somebody to fire.

I was scared – scared like I'd never been before. At any moment, my life could end, and I would never see it coming.

I slowed my breathing again. I prayed to All-h. And I continued to put one foot in front of the other.

I caught up to and passed the burnt-out truck. Dead men were everywhere, and flames continued to flicker. There was a smell of burnt fuel and roasted flesh. I saw one charred figure move and moan in pain. But there was nothing I could do. I couldn't even put him out of his misery.

One step at a time, I passed the truck. It had been near a wadi – a seasonal creek that cut through the landscape. I suspected the Islamic State fighters had been hiding there. I didn't look.

As I passed the wadi, nobody stopped me. I suppose they didn't want to break cover. And no shots were fired; I suppose they had no reason to kill me.

I had walked almost 20 kilometers when I passed a power substation. It connected the power created by the massive Mosul Dam to the city itself. It wasn't humming with electricity. It had been shut down and it seemed eerily quiet. I looked back and saw the city. It

41

seemed silent and peaceful in the distance. I looked ahead and saw the Christian village. And then I truly noticed the silence.

With a shudder, I realized that the village itself was lifeless. I kept walking, worried that I was about to come upon a massacre. But when I got to the village, there were no bodies. The local people had fled. They had known what was coming.

I didn't want to stay near the road, so I continued towards the center of the village. The last time I'd driven past here was when I'd visited the aqueduct with my father. There had been so many tents that I hadn't realized how nice the homes actually were. The Christians here called themselves Assyrians – they had been here a long time, Nineveh being an ancient Assyrian city. I'd guessed their homes had benefited from the slow but centuries-long acquisition of wealth. Some of the houses were new, though. Under Saddam, and after him, the Christians had been pushed out of Mosul. The wealthier city dwellers had probably put some of their money into their homes.

Looking around, I selected the nicest looking of the houses. It was most likely to have food and water.

I tried the door, but it was locked. I wasn't surprised, but I wasn't sure what to do. If I broke a window, animals and insects would eventually devour everything in the house. If I didn't, I'd have to wander from home to home until eventually I found one which was open – which was unlikely.

I'd walked 20 kilometers and over eight hours with my brother on my back, and without food or water. I needed both if I was going to take care of him. So, I put him down, smashed a window, cleared the glass with a stick, and crawled through. A minute later, I opened the front door and brought him in.

The house was orderly and clean. The occupants had been expecting to flee. I lay my brother down on a couch in the living room. A quick survey revealed that a few of the cupboards had been swept clean. Canned food, I imagined, was what the owners had taken. But there was still food to be found. And there was water. I sat by my brother and ate and drank. And I watched his unconscious breath slowly.

I found a backpack and filled it with food and some water – so we could leave in an instant if we had to. I found some chlorine and packed it as well. With chlorine, I could purify water.

But I had no idea what to do for my brother. Would he choke if I tried to give him water? I couldn't risk it. I knew he could survive for a day or two without water. But probably not longer. I had to keep him cool, so he wouldn't sweat too much. I found a bed in the house and moved him to it. I put my emergency bag on the concrete floor next to the bed and I lay next to him and we slept there until the afternoon.

When I woke up, he was still lying there. He was breathing, but his breathing was a little more ragged. He was going to need water, and so he was going to need medical care. Erbil was the closest city, aside from Mosul. It was controlled by the Kurds and was unlikely to have been overrun as easily as Mosul had been. The locals wouldn't rally to the Islamic State flag.

I could go to Erbil, I thought. But I realized with dread that I'd fled Mosul by the shortest route, and so Erbil was in the wrong direction. It was east, but I was north of the city. Not only that, but it was at least 100 kilometers away. It would take me five days to get there. There was no possibility of making it there in time to save my brother.

I wondered, should I go back to Mosul? The man had offered medical care. But if he figured out who we were, we'd be dead anyway.

Was I truly out of options? Did I have to stay in this house until my brother died – probably from dehydration? There was a chance he'd wake up. But there was a chance he wouldn't, and I'd find myself watching helplessly as the last of my family died in front of me.

There had to be other options.

I decided to walk through the village and try to find one.

I left the house by the now unlocked front door, and I walked slowly through the village. There were no cars here. There were no tractors. Everything motorized had been used to carry the belongings of their frightened owners. While there were bicycles, they were all children's bicycles – far too small to speed my progress. This was not the kind of place where adults cycled. There were also a few two-wheeled carts with small car wheels. They were small – and too rickety to attach to even a tractor. I couldn't push one of them any faster that I could carry my brother on my shoulders.

There was nothing else with wheels.

I went back into the house.

Perhaps I could look up how to feed the unconscious? But I didn't have a cell phone. I'd left it behind. I doubted I'd have a signal, anyway, with the power station being down. Even if I did, using a phone was risky. The Islamic State used cell phones to communicate. A lone signal in an abandoned village could easily be made a target.

Of course, I realized ruefully, if I was in Islamic State-controlled territory, I'd be facing another obstacle. The Islamic State had been taking over the cell towers and establishing their own cell networks. They used the cell networks not only to communicate militarily, but also to tax and control the local population. To use their network, you needed one of their data plans. And I didn't have one.

Somehow, I had to use the bikes.

I checked on my brother. His breathing hadn't gotten much worse.

And then I sat there, thinking, until the germ of an idea finally came to me.

I went downstairs and unlocked the courtyard. I then roamed the village, looking for supplies. I found the best bicycle I could, which I grabbed. A few seat posts were taken from other bicycles. I also came across a decent two-wheeled pushcart that was the right size. It had small car tires and a metal frame. Finally, I searched for tools, cobbling together everything I thought I might need.

Going back to the house we'd borrowed, I set up my little shop.

Before long, the front wheel and seat had been removed from the bike I'd taken and I'd grafted the front of it to the back of the cart using bolts, metal plates and epoxy. I'd created a rickshaw of sorts. Trying it out, I verified that I could pedal the contraption. I could even turn it, using the frame of the cart as a steering wheel.

The seat was still too low though. This was where the extra seat posts came in. I jammed one of the thinner seat posts inside my bike's post. And then I found another that matched my bike's seat-post size and jammed it onto the other end of the thinner post. The effect was what I needed. The seat was extended, and my feet could be a good distance from the pedals. I added some more epoxy to it to reinforce it.

It wasn't beautiful, and it wasn't elegant, but it'd be faster than walking. And when I came to the hills on the edge of Erbil, I could get off and push the entire thing.

It was late afternoon now. I went out one more time and found every right-sized bicycle tire I could. I'd probably need spares. Finally, I found a piece of wood and brought it to the kitchen. With the drill and some screws, I patched the window I'd broken and then I locked the door.

I went back upstairs to my still unconscious brother. I picked him and the backpack up and brought them down to the cart. He, the wheels, and the supplies all fit – barely. I pedaled out of the courtyard and closed the gate behind me.

Erbil was 100 kilometers away. But I had food and water and I hoped I just might be able to make it by morning.

As the sun set over the small Christian village and the peaceful chatter of the desert nightlife began to break the day's silence, I headed east on a small sandy road.

My little brother's breathing was becoming even more labored.

And there was almost nothing I could do to help.

# Urban Renewal

*April 4th, 2013: Washington, D.C.*

"You're disappointed?"

Steven seemed almost dazed as he looked up. The room was dappled in the afternoon sun of a Washington DC springtime. He had a beer in front of him. It was sitting, a quarter full, on the dining room table. He saw Amy, his wife, standing over him.

"I, uh," he said, trying to clear the cobwebs from his head. He hadn't realized she'd be home. But her JUC-related job wouldn't start for a few weeks yet. She was still unpacking the house.

"Who is it this time?" she asked.

"What?" he asked.

"You've been promoted." she said. "And now, you've discovered some other group of people you can't help. Right?"

He thought about what she'd said, and then he nodded. He hadn't realized there was a pattern.

"So," she asked, "who is it this time?"

"Syrians," he said.

She sat down across from him.

"Syrians?" she said. "Seriously?"

He nodded.

"You're depressed about not being able to help Syrians?"

There was an edge of mockery. He didn't reply.

"Okay," she continued. "You know the Serenity Prayer?"

He nodded.

"You know the part about accepting the things you can't change?"

He nodded.

"This," she said, "is one of the things you can't change."

"People keep telling me that," he answered. He let out a twisted chuckle.

"And I love that you don't believe them," Amy replied. "It's why I married you. But you'll destroy yourself if you keep glomming on to causes you can't actually do anything about."

He nodded. Picked up his beer and drained it.

"Steven," Amy said, "let's do a bit of role playing."

"Okay," he said.

"Let's pretend that you're the President of the United States."

He nodded again.

"How would you help, then?"

Steven closed his eyes, trying to think. After a while, he opened them.

"I have no idea."

"Better answer than most Presidents," she said. She was smiling. "It seems to me the best they ever do is pick sides. And I don't think we really like *any* of the options in this particular fight."

"But I'm not the President," Steven said.

"So, you have even less power," said Amy.

"No," said Steven. "I just have different tools."

"Like what?" she asked.

"There's got to be a way to help that doesn't involve fighter jets and bombers."

"Like what?" Amy asked, again.

"It's a community problem," Steven said. "You've got to try to help the community."

"How?" said Amy. Her voice was patient. She would get him through this.

"Normally, we'd provide job counseling or other social services," he said.

"But you can't," Amy said. "Your social workers would get their heads blown off."

Steven looked around nervously.

"The kids are at school," Amy said, "We can talk about heads getting blown off."

Steven didn't have much to do with his kids. As he saw it, others needed his help more than they did.

He nodded.

"They would get their heads blown off," he agreed.

"What else?" she asked.

He sat there, silent for a long while.

"Mentorships?" he said. His voice was uncertain.

"You mean bring people out, talk to them about how white Europeans really get their issues and how they have all the answers and then send them back in?"

He shook his head. The idea was ridiculous.

But then, something else struck him. "Model families," he said, more strongly.

"Model families?" Amy asked.

"There was a program in Phoenix," Steven said, "We found families from poor communities that were already successful and stable. And then we helped them out, in terms of housing and food. In return, they hosted people from the area. They served meals, they had community events. That sort of thing. The important thing was that other people could see how they functioned, as a family. It worked pretty well, too."

"So, you'll buy the Assads dinner?"

"No," Steven said. "The point is that people could see a functioning family but made up of people from the community. We can create a city that does the same thing. A model city, populated by people from the area. People can see it, and it can serve as an example for the whole region."

Amy just sat there. As Steven watched her, his excitement began to grow.

And then she said, "Where would you put it? You can't exactly build it in Syria or Iraq."

"I don't know," said Steven. As he pondered a moment longer, he could almost taste the solution.

And then he smiled broadly and said, "I'm not on the Executive Committee of the Turkish Union of Charities, am I? And the Chief of Staff to the Israeli Ambassador visited last night. So how about Israel?"

Amy nodded, impressed.

"I think it's worth a shot," she said.

With that, the two of them got up and headed for the door.

# Patterns

*October 26th, 2008: Abu Kamal, Syria*

Mohammed stood at the front of one of three lines of mourners arrayed in the courtyard of the mosque. Behind them, a larger mass of men was gathered. And behind that mass, beyond the walls of the mosque, close to a thousand other men filled the narrow surrounding streets. Only hours earlier, Mohammed's parents had died.

While Mohammed had thought of them as simpletons, they were to be celebrated as martyrs. The weakness of his people and their failures in the face of the oppressors seemed to be revealed by this stark distinction. Somehow, Mohammed thought, the adulation of these crowds was a key to understanding the domination of the Sunnis by the tiny Alawite cult.

As he stood in the mosque, the smell of the place suddenly grabbed his attention. Even within the walls of the mosque, he knew he was in the belt of life that followed the path of the Euphrates. He could smell the green beyond the walls. It was such a contrast from where he had been living, and where his parents had died, in the sandy brown nothingness of the outlying districts.

But the difference was more than color and organic life. Those districts were defined by one of the ideals of human order: they were laid out in a grid. Another order dominated in the river district that lay along the Euphrates. It was defined not by the compass and the straight edge, but by something far more powerful. In Abu Kamal, the institutions and markets of the city were laid out to serve the residential neighborhoods. The residential neighborhoods, in turn, were laid out

51

to maximize access to the farming plots. The farming plots were laid out along the irrigation ditches. And the irrigation ditches were defined by the terrain and access to the river itself. The city had grown like the veins within a body: river to irrigation, irrigation – defined by terrain – to farm, farm to house, house to markets and institutions.

The city was defined by the lifeblood of the river; almost everything else was aligned around it.

The mosque was an exception. The mosque obeyed yet another system. It was not aligned with the angle of the street. If there had been a grid, the mosque would have defied it. Instead, it was offset from any human or natural sense of order. It, and the worshippers within it, were pointed towards the distant city of Mecca. The lifeblood of the mosque was defined by Islam – and Islam by All-h. It was oriented around the divine order.

There were three different systems, Mohammed thought as he stood before his parents: the human, the natural and the divine. And each governed in its proper place.

Mohammed's parents had been wrapped in shrouds. His father was closest, given the primacy of place. His mother was just behind her husband. None of the mourners, aside from Mohammed, knew what she had done. None besides Mohammed realized that she had defied the proper order of things.

She had lived and died beyond the pattern of man, nature, and All-h.

It was late October, and although it had not yet begun to rain, the weather was cooling. The mourners' clothing reflected this; sweaters and jackets were layered on top of the usual garb. Looking at the shroud-covered bodies of his parents, Mohammed thought for just a moment, "They must be cold." He wanted to place a blanket over their bodies. But he realized how silly the idea was. It was the thought of a child. But he was their child, wasn't he? And he loved them, didn't he? How could he not feel for the coldness that surrounded them in their simple shrouds?

To Mohammed's left, at the front of the center line of mourners, stood the imam himself.

He raised his hands. The assembled people copied him and together they pronounced the praise of All-h, "All-hu Akbar."

It was not a joyous or triumphant shout, but a statement of contemplation.

After a moment's pause, in a haunting and mournful chant, the Imam recited the Al-Fatiha – the seven opening verses of the Koran:

> *In the name of All-h, the Entirely Merciful, the*
> *Especially Merciful.*
> *All praise is to All-h, Lord of the worlds –*
> *The Entirely Merciful, the Especially Merciful,*
> *Sovereign of the Day of Recompense.*
> *It is You we worship and You we ask for help.*
> *Guide us to the straight path –*
> *The path of those upon whom You have bestowed*
> *favor, not of those who have evoked Your anger or of*
> *those who are astray.*

The assembled mourners responded, solemnly, "All-hu Akbar."

Immediately after his father had died, those who tended to the dead had prepared his body. They had cleaned it of the discharge of death, sutured and wrapped the bullet holes and covered the regions of modesty. All respect was given to the martyr. The preparers had removed the discharge, but his father's body was still caked with blood.

And then Mohammed himself had washed his father's body. There had been a wider family – of brothers and nephews – but Mohammed had insisted on doing this job alone.

Turning the broken man onto his left, Mohammed had poured warm water over his father's body. He poured slowly, starting at the head and ending with the feet. Mohammed watched as the many scars left by the torturers of Tadmur broke the smooth flow of the water. Mohammed rolled his father onto his right side and repeated the pouring of water. And then, with his father lying on his back, he poured water on him a third time. In adherence of tradition and law, Mohammed repeated the washing process. This time he used dish soap mixed into the water. Right side, left side, front. The familiar smell of the soap and its place in the sustenance of life contrasted with the stillness of the body in front of him.

Mohammed hadn't known his father, not as a whole man. All he had known, for ten years, was the broken man his father had become. Now, he was cleansing him of his pain and his wounds. His father would be complete with All-h; his brokenness would be repaired.

Mohammed repeated the washing process a third time, with camphor. The smell was strong, like menthol, but the body was finally becoming clean of its blood. It was not clean enough, though. He washed a fourth and a fifth time – both with the camphor. And then, the body was clean. He dried and perfumed it with rosewater, covering the early smell of death and the strong smell of the detergents.

And then they laid his father on the white shrouds of death. The first shroud, the shortest, covered his midsection. Mohammed folded over the sides, wrapping the body. The second came from over his head and covered his body. But there was a slit for the head itself.

Mohammed looked at his father's face for the last time.

It was the first time he had ever seen it at peace.

Mohammed closed his father's eyes and recited the prayer.

> *O All-h, forgive Abbas abu Mohammed and elevate his station among those who are guided. Send him along the path of those who came before, and forgive us and him, O Lord of the Worlds. Enlarge for him his grave and shed light upon him in it.*

The third shroud came first from the right and then from the left. And it completely encased the man Mohammed had never really known.

Finding calm in the repetition of the ritual, Mohammed wrapped the body with the wide belts of cotton cloth that secured the shroud itself. One for the center, one for the chest, one for the ankles, one for the feet and finally, one for the top of the head. The belts were tied to the side of the body.

And then, in front of him, lay a white outline of a man.

In death, he had become like any other.

It was the fate of all men, Mohammed thought. But he found himself angry with the corpse. His father's life had been given away for less than nothing. He had been a pawn of his wife, and his wife had been a pawn of their enemies. Mohammed vowed that he would follow a different path.

As he stood in the courtyard of the mosque and looked at his father's body, his anger finally began to dissipate. His parents were cold; they must be.

The Imam intoned, in that same haunting voice:

> O All-h, forgive him and have mercy on him and give
> him strength and pardon him. Be generous to him and
> cause his entrance to be wide and wash him with
> water and snow and hail. Cleanse him of his
> transgressions as white cloth is cleansed of stains.
> Give him an abode better than his home, and a family
> better than his family and a wife better than his wife.
> Take him into Paradise and protect him from the
> punishment of the grave and from the punishment of
> hell-fire.

As Mohammed listened to the words of prayer, he realized that his father would be rewarded for his sacrifice and his suffering. He would be given all that he had lacked. The white shroud represented the purity of his soul in death; released from the limitations of life. The Imam continued, uttering two more funeral supplications. And then he concluded with two simple verses of prayer.

> O All-h, your male slave and the child of your female
> slave is in need of Your mercy, and You are not in need
> of his torment. If he was pious, then increase his

*rewards, and if he was a transgressor, then pardon him.*

Together with the rest of the mourners, Mohammed pronounced, "All-hu Akbar."

The Imam turned to Mohammed himself and pronounced, in a quieter voice.

*Surely, All-h takes what is His, and what he gives is His, and to all things He has appointed a time...so have patience and be rewarded.*

Mohammed bowed his head and closed his eyes in contemplation.

With a final short prayer, and with another unified chant of "All-hu Akbar", the funeral prayers were complete.

A short time later, Mohammed's parents were buried in their shrouds. The traditional double graves had been dug. An inner, small grave, to serve as the home of the deceased; and a larger grave to encompasses the smaller. They were laid to rest on their sides, their faces forever facing the light of Mecca.

As the bricks were placed over the inner graves, Mohammed's parents disappeared.

He would miss his mother, he realized. And he did admire her. Despite her faults, she had been tactically brilliant. If the perverters of the faith had known how important she was, they would have interrogated her, not handed her to the Americans. The government had reduced his father to a drooling incompetent, but they had never considered his mother a threat. They had destroyed the one; and underestimated the other. And under their watchful eyes, his mother had formed a network whose leadership they had failed to discern.

As the grave was filled, Mohammed recognized that everything had its order. The human ideals of the grid defined the settlements beyond the reach of the irrigation, like the designs of an engineer. The flow of life-giving water defined the settlements along the Euphrates, like the veins of a body. And Mecca defined the holy, like shafts of light.

Perhaps, Mohammed thought, his mother's greatest strength had been that she had defied the proper order of things. That defiance had enabled her to accomplish what her enemies had never expected.

Her mistake, Mohammed realized, was that her violation had been a small one. Thus, her successes were turned against her by the far greater manipulations of the Alawites and the Shiites.

It was then that Mohammed realized his path. His violations of the patterns of man, nature and All-h had to be so great that they would redirect the schemes of his enemies.

His mother's life had taught him that it was only by defying the patterns of expectation that change could be accomplished. But great change – change that would return those who followed the true path of Islam to their proper place – would require a massive defiance of expectations.

As the last of the earth was filled in, Mohammed resolved to do the one thing his enemies would never expect.

He would join the forces of his parents' most feared enemy.

He would join the Mukhabarat – the Syrian secret police.

The 16-year-old orphan looked at his parents' graves one last time and uttered a quiet prayer on their behalf,

> *Oh All-h, forgive them and have mercy on them and*
> *given them strength and pardon them. Be generous to*

*them and cause their entrance to be wide and wash*
*them with water and snow and hail. Cleanse them of*
*their transgressions as white cloth is cleansed of*
*stains. Take them into Paradise and protect them from*
*the punishment of the grave.*

And then he turned, and without another glance, sought out the grasping tentacles of his parents' enemies.

# Night Ride

*June 5th, 2014: Northern Iraq*

As I biked along the gravel and sand road leading east, the sun slowly sunk behind me. It only took about a half an hour for me to pass through the first village on that road. That village – a collection of compounds – was empty. There were only shuttered houses and empty streets. I biked through it slowly and found my way to another path on its far side.

As I left that first village, stars began to poke holes in the deep blue blanket of the sky. To my left, a small mountain range rose up from the plains. Even as the vanishing of the sun darkened the patchwork of recently harvested farms that surrounded me, the last rays of that same sun illuminated those distant cliffs and the sky above them, creating a beautiful image of golden rocks enwrapped in a halo of azure sky.

And then, bit by bit, it all grew dark.

As the sun disappeared, I realized I had not been out of Mosul at night in six years. The last time had been that visit to the Jerwan Aqueduct. Then, we'd been driving a Land Rover and had spent the bulk of the trip on the highway. The noises that dominated had been the noises of the truck and of the road. The undulating plains, with their patchwork of farms and villages, had simply been a background blur on the way to our real destination.

But this night, on my makeshift bicycle cart, I felt like a part of the plains themselves. Aside from the labored breathing of my brother and the light squeak of my chain as the pedals pushed it around the chain ring, there was no sound but the sound of the plains themselves. There were small animals and insects clicking with their nocturnal calls. And with the electricity in the region shut down by the fighting, there was almost no artificial light.

Behind me, the sun was entirely replaced by the Milky Way, rising from the horizon like smoke from a distant fire. The clarity of the cosmos, on that dark night, was like nothing I had ever experienced – or have ever experienced again. The battle of Mosul was made more obvious by the peace and darkness of the plains. The occasional distant explosion to my right would remind me of what I was fleeing.

I wished my father had come with me from Mosul. I wished he was there to share in the beauty. I wondered what unspoken questions he'd ask me if he too had arisen for a nighttime voyage to Erbil. One time, we'd read the Christian story of Abraham and G-d's promise that his children would be as numerous as these stars. Now, for the first time, I could grasp the incredible majesty of that promise. I knew now why the Sumerians and the Babylonians and the Arabs had so valued the study of the stars.

I wanted to tell my father what I learned.

It took me a moment before I remembered that I could never do so.

I kept pedaling. My path was increasingly difficult to see. The moon was thin and not high in the sky, and it cast weak and deceptive shadows. I began to navigate by feel. When one of the wheels of my cart neared the edge of the path, it would sink a bit and my progress would slow. I'd pull the cart to one side or the other and continue. I had no way of measuring distance. I could not navigate by the stars. I did not know what the position of the moon told me of my progress. No cities or towns were visible – the plains were entirely dark. If the path turned, I would follow it, unknowing.

As I listened and felt the ragged breathing of my brother, I was spurred on. My pedaling grew ever more difficult. My legs weren't used to the exertion. But I kept pedaling, putting my mind into my physical pain. It was an escape from far greater pains, and far greater fears. I tried to stop myself from thinking. I desperately wanted to overcome my impossible need to somehow track my progress and to track what I had lost.

We passed through more villages. Some were just a few compounds. I could barely see their high walls in the dim moonlight; I knew they were there because they blocked out the majesty of the stars.

But they were all empty. The Christian residents of these villages had fled.

I imagined, high above me, some drone was tracking my progress. I felt like the only person in forever. A cart, slowly cutting its way down the paths between fields would certainly attract attention. But no soldier or militant would travel like I was traveling. I was safe from attack.

I found myself back on a paved road. But it was a narrow one – not wide enough for two cars to pass one another; unless one pulled to the side. And then I began to climb, which reassured me. Everybody knew Erbil was a mountain citadel. And then the moon disappeared, and I found myself thrust into near total darkness. I could not see the land, and while I knew there must be hills and mountains nearby, only the lack of stars told me where they must be.

Eventually, I heard the sounds of a river. The Great Zab River divides Nineveh and Erbil provinces. But this didn't sound like a great river. It sounded like the whitewater rush of a large stream. I tried to scan my mind, drawing a picture of the geography. I was trying to understand where I was and how far I'd come. Then I remembered the Nahr Al-Khazir – the Al-Khazir River. It was smaller and it rushed rapidly out of the mountains. It grew louder as I pedaled. But I couldn't see it. As I continued towards it, my path petered away. I strained my eyes and saw the reflections of starlight on the rush of flowing waters. It was only a few meters in front of me. For the third time in less than a day, I prayed. I prayed I was near a ford and that I could find it. And for the third time, my prayers were answered.

There was no bridge, and so there was no way I could cross with my cart. But there was a ford. I tied my brother onto my back using the cloth I'd taken from my parents' house. And then I picked up my backpack. I crossed the ford then, my tired feet carefully navigating the near-invisible slickness of the river rocks. I heard, as the sounds of the water grew more distant, the noises of a small village. Perhaps it was Christian. Perhaps, in crossing the river, I'd fled beyond the line of fear. But I had no way of telling if they would see me as an enemy. And I knew that I must be drawing closer to Erbil.

Before long, I came to a road. It was paved and it was wide. I walked along it – enjoying the smoothness of the asphalt. I wished I had my cart – the road was winding downwards. My progress would have been rapid.

Long before any vehicles approached, their engines broke the silence of the night. I heard the diesels from far away. I was afraid of everything, and everyone. So, I lay flat beyond the horizon formed by the shoulder of the road. I imagined myself a hidden IED – but instead of threatening the cars and trucks, they were a threat to me. And they passed by, all of them, without seeing me.

The vehicles that passed drove quickly. All were heading in the same direction I was: down the road. Most had no lights on. Soldiers or militants must have been riding within them, night-vision goggles guiding them on their invisible path. The lack of lights frightened me.

As I walked, I wished I could see beyond the edges of the road. I imagined a rippled countryside with faraway mountains and green fields. But I could see nothing at all.

I continued, putting one foot after another. There were more villages now, and even towns, but none were abandoned. I tried to be invisible as I walked. No one accosted me, so I suppose I was successful.

Eventually, I saw a faint glow in the distance. It was the glow of a city; electric power producing the halo that spoke of life and prosperity. I could not see the city itself, but I knew it was Erbil. My head began to fill with visions of walking to that city, my brother tied to my back. A hospital would take him there. They would get him water, so he would not die. I imagined him and I, after our convalescence, walking through that city and even visiting the famous citadel – the great round fortress that rose above the rest of Erbil. It was the oldest citadel in the world and, by all accounts, a wonder to behold. I'd never seen it. The Kurds extended their power to Mosul, but it was not a simple thing for those of us who lived in Mosul to visit Erbil.

But today, they would let me visit. I was an orphaned girl with a wounded brother. The Peshmerga would take me in. Perhaps I would only need to walk to the town of Kalak, where there was a bridge. Perhaps, then, some Kurdish ambulance would transport us the rest of the way.

I saw other lights soon after. They illuminated the river ahead of me; it was the slow-moving mass of the Great Zab. The lights were on the far side, the power coming from Kurdish-controlled Erbil, and not

Mosul. I walked on and began to see the outlines of two bridges. The one upriver was formed by a series of low arches that cut across the water. The second was a steel truss bridge with large and separated piers allowing boats to pass beneath it. The bridges had been built at narrow points in the river. But even at those points, the river was far too wide to ford. I would have to cross one of the bridges.

As I continued, I noticed something strange. There was no traffic on the bridges. It was midnight, but there had to be stragglers like me, trying to cross.

And then, as I watched, the scene in front of me exploded. A string of rockets lit out from the Nineveh side of the river and snaked out to smash into the Erbil side. Moments later, a massive volley of automatic weapons fire erupted across the water. I could hear small arms. Layered within them was the sound of heavier 50-caliber machine guns.

I saw an armored truck lumber onto one of the narrow bridges. It accelerated straight towards the Kurdish defenders on the other side. There *whomp whomp whomp* of heavy machine guns. And then, the truck slowed and then stopped – blocking the bridge itself.

My foreboding had been justified. The vehicles that had passed me on the road were carrying Islamic State soldiers and Islamic State equipment. They were rushing to the front. They wanted to attack Erbil before the Kurds could react. They were attempting to cross the river.

As I watched, I suddenly felt exhausted. I turned off the side of the road and walked into a dry meadow that overlooked the town. I could see down to the river. I could see it all so clearly. I could see the sides shooting at one another. I could see that neither was winning. Then, I saw a massive explosion on the Kurdish side of the river. A second later, the sound and the shock hit me. It must have been a car bomb, prepositioned by the Islamic State even before the attack on Mosul. The whole point of the truck trying to cross the bridge was probably to concentrate the Kurdish fighters prior to the bombing. My heart sank as I watched men move on to the truss bridge, behind where the truck had stopped. They began to rush across the river; this was their chance to overwhelm the best defensive position between Mosul and Erbil.

Nobody was returning fire.

Then, a machine gun positioned downriver, on the Kurdish side of the water suddenly lit up and strafed the bridge. I could see tracers drawing the path of the gunfire as it poured into the structure. I could even hear the clanging of metal as the 50-caliber rounds struck it. And I could see the bodies of the Islamic State fighters shattering as they were struck by the heavy ammunition. The fighters began to retreat. Soon enough, both sides settled in for an extended stalemate.

I closed my eyes and I sat down, laying my brother on the grass.

For a moment, I imagined myself to be the Prophet Mohammed, on his great night voyage. Except instead of traveling to Al-Aqsa, I was trying to reach Erbil. And instead of riding the great winged horse of Al-Buraq, my own body had been thrashed by the exertions of the night.

And instead of rising to heaven, I was struck down: my mission to save the only surviving remnant of my family brought low by the battle before me.

As the first light of the predawn sun was erasing the weakest of the stars, my brother's lips were dry. His mouth was slightly open, and his tongue was swollen. His breathing was shallow. I put my ear against his chest and heard his heart pounding. He needed water, desperately. I had water, in my bag, but there was no way for him to drink. I took some on my fingertips and gently rubbed his lips with it. It could do nothing, except, perhaps, relieve some small part of his pain.

And then I hugged my brother close. And I prayed, one last time.

I was exhausted, in every way.

As the sun rose over the battle lines below me, I fell asleep.

I was awoken by a scream.

# Embassy

*April 4th, 2013: Washington D.C.*

Steven sat in an unadorned conference room in the heart of the Israeli Embassy. There were no windows, and the air smelled faintly of floor cleaner. It was an uninteresting room, but Steven's heart was pounding. He was nervous. It had been a long time since he'd been a supplicant; or at least since he'd considered himself a supplicant. He'd certainly raised a lot of money for the JUC. But when he did that, he wasn't just asking for something. No, in exchange for cash, he was giving others an opportunity for meaning. And he knew he could always find other people to raise money from. This was different. He was going to ask Tamar for help. And he didn't have a lot of other options.

As Steven and Amy had driven to the Embassy, they had strategized and fleshed out their idea. They had agreed the ideal place for the model city was on the Israeli border with Syria. They would invite the Israelis to help screen the new citizens of the place. That rule, all by itself, would screen the most violent potential citizens from undermining the city. They decided to pitch the proposal as an answer to the Islamic State. Finally, they decided that Steven would go in alone. He could wear the hat of a JUC director, but Amy could not.

The Embassy was a surprisingly comfortable and modest-looking place. The Embassy of Ghana, next door, looked far more formal. And, as far as scale was concerned, both were dwarfed by the gargantuan office complex that made up the Chinese Embassy across the street.

Really, the Israeli embassy looked like an overgrown house or maybe a small synagogue. It seemed human.

After clearing security, Steven was guided to the conference room to wait for Tamar. The building had limestone walls inside and out, and the floors were of polished marble. There wasn't a carpet to be seen. Steven didn't have to wait long for Tamar. After only a few moments, she knocked and entered the room. She smiled, betraying none of the political calculation that Steven knew had to be core to her position.

"Mr. Gold," she said politely, "I'm pleasantly surprised to see you so soon after our last meeting. How can I help you?"

"Tamar," he said, as calmly as he could manage, "I have an idea I'd like to run past you."

"What would you like to share?" she asked pleasantly, and with some, at least feigned, interest.

Steven took a deep breath. He decided to jump right in, "I have a possible solution to the Islamic State."

Tamar looked slightly bemused. "Go on," she said pleasantly. But her interest was clearly dropping. Steven girded himself and then continued.

"The idea is simple," said Steven. "I want to establish a model city."

He was almost triumphant. But the interest he expected didn't appear. Instead she asked, "And what's a model city?" There was a hint of strained patience.

Steven was still confident his explanation could set things straight. "A model house can help people in urban areas see a better way of living. It is almost like embedding mentors in a community. A model city is the same thing, just on a larger scale. A model city can take in families and enable them to be an example to help reform Arab Society as a whole."

"And why are you here?" asked Tamar, flatly.

Steven thought back to his fundraising. He had to sell her something.

"I think it would be in Israel's interest to host such a city," he said, hastily.

She looked at him. Then she pursed her lips and said, "And what would you like from *me*?"

"Feedback," said Steven. It seemed the most he could ask for, given her resistance.

"Do you mind if I'm direct?"

"No," Steven answered, preparing himself.

"Are you sure?"

"Of course," said Steven. Then, as much to himself as to her, he said, "How else do ideas get stronger?"

"Okay," said Tamar. "To begin with, and this is intended as advice and not insult, I think you should stick to normal JUC business."

Steven hadn't expected the bluntness of her personal advice. It stung even more knowing that it wasn't delivered as an insult. But Tamar wasn't done.

"You need to understand, Israel isn't just a playground for people's ideas. We're a real state with real needs and real obligations to our citizens – random flights of fancy have no place. Part of Israel's reality is that it's a small country. We don't exactly have lots of space to spare for massive refugee camps. Next—"

Steven interrupted, "But you do want to do something about what's happening in Syria, don't you?"

"Once upon a time, yes," said Tamar. "But we've discovered that when we get involved with our neighbors, *nothing* is achieved. With the Gaza withdrawal, we learned that when we give them land, we get rockets and terrorism. With the first Lebanon War, we learned that when we try to strengthen our allies, we find ourselves involved in decades-long conflicts. None of this accomplishes anything. So, we have a simple policy. Leave us alone, and we'll leave you alone. Hit us, though, and we'll hit you back – twice as hard. And try to change the strategic balance, and we'll do everything we can to frustrate you. There aren't any grand ideas in this approach, just an honest assessment of our limitations. We no longer invest money, land, or blood in fixing things that can't be fixed."

Steven caught his breath. The woman sounded like so many others he had dealt with. She was happiest just disassociating from the world's problems. But he didn't know how to address her concerns. He wasn't ready for them. He'd hoped for better.

"Doesn't Israel exist to be a light and example?" he insisted.

"Maybe at some point," answered Tamar. "But right now, we're just trying to get by and provide peace and safety for our people. You're suggesting bringing in a bunch of people, the vast majority of whom will be violently opposed to Israel and Jews. All the nice words and presents in the world won't change their feelings. We've tried. And simply resettling them won't suddenly unlock a beautiful future. This isn't reality."

"Okay," said Steven, unsure how to continue. He was feeling like he'd had enough.

"Anyway," said Tamar, "The diplomatic corps doesn't make any of these decisions. To do this kind of thing, you'd have to find somebody in the Israeli political world who'd actually support it. The left wing doesn't believe in this sort of cultural colonialism and are quite weak anyway. The mainstream is sick of land-for-peace initiatives that end up becoming land-for-war initiatives. And the right wing would never support giving up territory. Whatever other merits you might imagine your idea to have, it isn't politically practical."

"Okay," said Steven, in a resigned voice.

Tamar brightened up, "I meant what I said about your normal work. I've heard brilliant things about your administrative and collaborative talents. I am really looking forward to working with you on JUC business."

She paused and then concluded, "Is there anything else I can help with?"

Steven's idea was stillborn. He knew he should feel embarrassed, but he didn't. Instead, he felt crushed. The situation was hopeless, but he still wasn't ready to accept that. Pleasantries were exchanged, and then Steven made as gentle an exit as he could.

Amy was waiting for him. She had an expectant smile.

Steven looked at her. He saw her hope. And he wondered what had driven him to try to solve major world problems at the age of 46? He had no experience in these areas. He had no education in this area. He had no network. There was nothing he could accomplish. Perhaps the JUC could start some little initiative, but the idea of a model city was ridiculous. He couldn't help *these* people.

Amy's face fell as she saw his expression.

"She didn't like it," he said. "She had some very real objections. She objected to the risks of meddling, of giving land to enemies, and of uselessly railing against thousands of years of culture. And she said it would be politically impossible."

He gave a helpless shrug, almost trying to hide how disappointed he was.

But Amy stepped forward and hugged him. He found himself being fortified by her.

73

"Pie in the sky," he said, in a resigned tone.

She stepped back. "What do you mean?" she asked.

"Well," said Steven, beginning to see an opportunity, "if somebody had come into my office looking for funding, but being about as prepared as we just were, I also would have kicked them out. I would have been embarrassed for them. And for their own good, I might have done it as bluntly as she just did."

"Okay..." she said. "Is that all? Was her problem really just about preparation?"

"The problem with preparation isn't that people aren't prepared. It's that they don't have answers to the hard stuff. I think, with some preparation, we can deal with the security stuff and the screening stuff. We can flesh that out and make it stronger."

"But?" asked Amy.

"But..." answered Steven, "it doesn't answer the big question: Can a model city actually change culture? If the answer's 'no', then there's no point in creating a model city."

"Can a model city change culture?" Amy asked herself, aloud. "I have no idea. I suppose I'd start by asking if it's ever happened before."

"Before?" said Steven.

"I mean historically," Amy said. "Historically, have model cities changed the cultures around them?"

Steven just looked at her.

Amy continued. "I mean, maybe something like West Berlin?"

West Berlin? He thought about that, it seemed like a good example. It didn't draw in a lot of people – the Soviets saw to that. But it still served as a potent example of what was possible without Communism. And it had a massive cultural impact on the territory around it.

"A good example," he said, "but not a great one. Communism isn't like Middle Eastern culture. It was quite young and not nearly as established."

"Hong Kong?" Amy said.

"Same issue," Steven said. "It did great things. But the competition was weak. We need something that tackles more established cultural problems."

"Okay," said Amy, "call your father."

Steven hadn't talked to him in years. They hadn't had a falling out or a fight. They had just drifted apart. His father was a retired intellectual history professor and a master of pulling away from the immediacy of human suffering. He was, in many ways, Steven's opposite. Somehow, Steven's begrudging acceptance of the importance of ideas just made him more resentful of his father. But Steven's father did know the past. He had immersed himself in it.

Steven cared too much to let his pride hurt those in need. Without another word, Steven pulled out his phone and then looked up and dialed the number. The phone was on speaker. After a few rings and a few forced pleasantries, Steven was ready to ask his question.

"Dad," he said, amazed that he still called his father that, "I'm looking for examples of city states that reformed the cultures around them."

"You mean like Athens impacted other Greek cities?" Now that they were discussing ideas, his father's voice was suddenly comfortable.

"Not exactly," Steven said. "I'm trying to develop an idea. I want to argue for an independent city state in the Middle East that can bring in people of all stripes and use their success to change their home countries. Like Hong Kong or West Berlin. But I want a more religious example – and one that went up against more established competition."

The phone was silent for a minute. Steven looked at Amy, and then Amy at Steven. Then, the answer came through. "Amsterdam."

"Amsterdam?" Steven asked, girding himself for a longwinded, but informative answer.

"Yes. Amsterdam," repeated his father. "Amsterdam had a sort of unofficial religious toleration during the Wars of the Reformation. At that time, the Protestants and Catholics were in full-fledged battle over who had control where, but not in Amsterdam."

"Why were they fighting?" Steven asked.

His father answer, "Because it was almost universally believed that social harmony and peace required the church and state to be in conformance with one another. This setup was, of course, key to salvation. You had to follow the true faith, and you saved others by bringing them to it."

"So, there were wars," Steven said.

"Oh yes," said his father, "and those wars had a lot in common with wars today. They were fueled by new technologies. In those days, the printing press enabled the sharing of ideas like social media does today. And there was the development of cannon, which undermined existing military defensive techniques – kind of like mobile-phone based IEDs and car bombs. And new techniques in removing water from mines opened up massive financial resources for Protestant Sweden, which added more fuel to the fire. High oil prices may well have done the same now."

"The wars couldn't compare with today's, though, could they?"

Steven's father chuckled. "You still lack perspective," said his father. "In those wars, about a *third* of Europe's population was killed. That is the equivalent of seven million dead in Syria. But to be a true parallel, *every other Muslim country* would have to be going through the same thing. We'd be talking about hundreds of millions dead. But, through it all, Amsterdam was different. They had a state religion, but they were willing to look the other way when it wasn't followed. Jews, Catholics, and all manner of Protestants went there. And the Dutch were extremely successful as a result. Their ideas of toleration, some of which were ideological and some practical, slowly changed the culture around them, and were eventually supplanted by more explicit versions of tolerance that were practiced in England and the Americas."

"So, it was a good example of how things can be better?" Steven asked.

"An excellent example," said his father. "It probably wasn't the goal of the Dutch to produce that sort of example. But their tolerance did become a part of their trade empire, and so it was quite profitable. Trade networks of every stripe, Protestant, Catholic, Jewish, and even Eastern, could all come together in Amsterdam. That unique openness made it a very successful place."

Steven's father paused. "You know there will be those who doubt whether Islam can do this?"

"Of course," Steven answered.

His father continued, "But, you have to remember that the religion has taken many forms. There have certainly been multi-religious and multi-ethnic Islamic civilizations. There was no doubt that they were *Islamic* civilizations, and they saw political and religious conquest as a glorification of G-d. One could argue that the religious desire for political control, especially where different faiths and versions of Islam are competing, produces wars. Of course, one could argue that the same need produced wars within Christianity, and against its neighbors. The theology is different, but there are still parallels. I don't think Amsterdam gives you definitive answers, but it's a good model."

"If a city is set up – to bring in Sunnis and Shiites and Yazidis and anybody else – do you think it could work?"

There was another long pause on the phone. "Yes," said Steven's father, "it could work. But you'd need to make certain the people there feel fulfilled by *something*. Otherwise, they'll return to domination for fulfillment, and you won't be able to keep a cap on it."

Steven nodded to himself. He'd have to think about that. But he was gaining hope in his idea. Amsterdam would do nicely as a historical corollary.

"Steven," said his father, "This doesn't sound like your usual work."

"It isn't," Steven answered.

"But you're *really* working on it?"

"I'm trying to," said Steven.

"Well," said his father, after a pause, "keep trying. And I hope you succeed. These are the kind of ideas that reshape the world."

Steven's father had always liked ideas more than people.

"Thank you," said Steven.

Then, after a few more uncomfortable pleasantries, he hung up.

"This has legs," Amy said, in quiet excitement.

"I think so," said Steven. "But it's going to need a champion – an influential champion. Tamar won't work."

"Who?" Amy asked.

"I don't have a name yet," said Steven. "But I have a profile. I need somebody on the right wing, just because they would be the most resistant. And I need somebody who has shown, even a little bit, that they would be open to this sort of idea."

"But it is a good idea," Amy said.

He nodded. But inside, he knew that didn't really matter.

People only tended to listen to things they already believed in. And he didn't know if anybody influential was ready for what he had to say.

This was what frightened him the most as they got in the car and drove back home.

# Mukhabarat

*October 26th, 2008: Abu Kamal, Syria*

Mohammed sat patiently in the tall but narrow brick building. He'd sent a text message to himself an hour before. Now, he was waiting for the reply.

He sat cross-legged with his hands in his lap. The building was several kilometers away from the river. It must have been over a hundred years old. It had no furniture or other adornment; it was as desolate inside as the desert that lay outside.

Like most people in Abu Kamal, Mohammed's relationship with the desert was complex. The desert was a part of his identity. But he rarely ventured into it; it was dangerous and unforgiving; it was the river that was the source of life. When he was a young child, Mohammed's mother had shown him pictures of Mars. He'd thought – at first – that she was showing him a photograph of the desert outside Abu Kamal. Growing up where he had, even the Red Planet did not seem entirely alien.

The building was quite a contrast to those of Abu Kamal. In newer buildings in Abu Kamal, the act of stepping indoors was a decision to leave the desert heat for something far, far, worse. With those buildings' small windows and thick concrete walls, it was clear their designers wanted to build fortresses against the heat. But they built ovens instead. The concrete of those buildings sucked up the heat of the desert like a brick oven collecting the heat of a fire. But this building, with its thin and high walls and empty spaces where windows would normally go, was somehow more pleasant on the inside than the desert outside. It was certainly cooler. Despite the lifeless dryness of the climate outside, Mohammed could even detect a slightly musty smell of life within the building itself.

Mohammed wondered, of course, why the building was there. No shepherd would venture this far out – or build something so tall and so permanent. No oil wells were located nearby. Had there simply been some hermit who'd built his home in the unforgiving desert? Perhaps it had been a Christian ascetic seeking perfect solitude? But the desert was so harsh that Mohammed couldn't imagine that to be true.

He had no answers, so he just sat and waited for an answer to his text.


After the funeral of his parents, Mohammed had just started walking. He started in the green belt and then walked to the warehouse his parents had last occupied. And then he just kept going – straight into the desert itself.

He had faced a conundrum. He couldn't simply walk down to the local Mukhabarat – or Secret Police – recruiting office. The Mukhabarat doesn't maintain a stall in the shuk or an annex attached to the mosque. And even if they did, just being seen in such a place would probably be enough to get Mohammed killed – by his own people. Traitors, in any culture, are not appreciated.

But Mohammed knew that, as a spy, he would be an incredibly valuable commodity.

In a tribal culture, a man can't simply walk into a village and be accepted as a member of the clan. It doesn't matter how good his backstory, or his records, are. He has to have family; not some made up family, but a real family whose place in the broader community can be verified. In a society made up of a network of personal relationships, you can't reinvent yourself with a few documents in a database.

In a society like this, spies are not placed – they are created.

The Mukhabarat, like Secret Police everywhere, look for those they can leverage. In some cases, they are lucky, and the leverage is found. There might be a sick child who *could* be saved, or a debt which *could* be repaid. Or there might be a threat to reveal a married woman's affair. In the culture of Abu Kamal, revealing such a secret would result in her death; she will have violated her family's honor and the laws of marriage.

But in most cases, leverage is created. An assessment is made of the target. The question is always the same: what does the target love? If it is family, children or loved ones may be temporarily kidnapped. If it is honor, men may be drugged and filmed performing indecent acts, or women may be raped. If it is money, thefts can be carried out with the target reduced to penury. If it is desire, he or she can be tempted with immoral acts.

The leverage only needs to work once. Once the mark shares a single secret – even a minor one – they are forever trapped. Such a betrayal is not only a betrayal of one's religion, but of one's community, tribe, and family. Once the target has spoken, just one time, the Mukhabarat has all the leverage they will ever need.

In this culture, the Mukhabarat found their targets and then made them into spies. Their spies did not find them. There were no ideological betrayals. Of course, spies who are found and then leveraged are not the most useful of sources. Every spilled secret represents an unwilling betrayal, and so they are forever reluctant to share. They only show the interrogator what the interrogator already knows to look for.

A willing spy, like Mohammed, would be a rare commodity indeed.

Of course, willing spies were so rare that there were no obvious ways for a young man like Mohammed to get himself recruited.

Thus, Mohammed just kept walking. He walked through the desert until he came to this odd building in the middle of nowhere. It was then that he realized *how* he could be recruited. He stepped inside the building, surprised by its coolness. Then he took out his phone and sent himself a text message.

It read, "Mukhabarat, I want to help you. I am a member of the Sunni Mujahedin. Meet me, secretly."

And that was it.

Surely, the Secret Police monitored all cell traffic. They would see a message with key words that referenced them and their biggest domestic enemies. They would find who'd sent the message. And they would find out where he was. And with no buildings for kilometers in every direction – they would find Mohammed himself.

It was simply a matter of time.

Of course, Mohammed didn't want to be a real spy. Instead, he wanted to earn the *trust* of his greatest enemies. Given time, he could find himself in a position to outplay the Mukhabarat at its own game. He could find an opportunity to use *misinformation* to drive a wedge between the Alawites, the Shiites, and whatever other allies they had collected along the way. He could play his enemies the way his mother had been played. And he could weaken them in ways they would never expect. The Sunnis made up by far the largest part of the Syrian population. With a little strategic manipulation, their enemies' weaknesses could be turned into their enemies' total defeat.

But he'd have to start now. They had underestimated his mother, and that had empowered her. For a brief period of time, Mohammed could also be underestimated. He was 16, he was from a provincial border village, and he was the recently orphaned son of an incompetent who had been unfairly targeted by the Americans. For a brief period, they might underestimate him just enough that he'd be able to manipulate the manipulators themselves.

Mohammed had been sitting for two hours when a man walked in through the gap that had once held a door. Mohammed watched him cautiously, without standing. The man was in his early 50s. He had intelligent, calculating eyes set in a deceptively soft face. He was wearing a suit and a tie. He was, Mohammed, realized, not the kind of field tough Mohammed had encountered before. He was a far more senior man.

The Mukhabarat was taking his offer seriously.

Mohammed waited, silently, and the man in the suit sat, cross-legged, across from him. The man was in excellent physical condition. But, Mohammed noted, with satisfaction, he was clearly uncomfortable. That was good. The Mukhabarat had sent a senior man who was willing to discomfit himself to please Mohammed.

They needed Mohammed more than he needed them.

"What are you doing here?" the man asked.

"Waiting for you," said Mohammed.

"I've been discreet," said the man, "Nobody saw me come. How can you help us?"

"They killed my parents," Mohammed said, letting an edge of both anger and sadness creep into his voice. Without warning, a wave of real sadness threatened to overwhelm his composure.

"Who?" said the man.

"You know who I am," said Mohammed, his voice shaking, "You know who killed them. The Americans did. Earlier today. I want revenge. My people sent them pinpricks. Little bombs that killed one or two of them at a time. I want to cause them a catastrophe. I want to cause them pain. I want to drive them out. You have the power to do this."

"Many people want to hurt them," said the man. "What can *you* do about it?"

"I can join you in fighting them."

The man smiled, "You're just an angry boy who wants revenge. Go blow yourself up and be satisfied."

It was a bluff. If the man thought this little of Mohammed, he wouldn't have come.

Mohammed changed the topic.

"You don't really know who my parents were, do you?"

"Your father, Abbas, was a part of an anti-government terrorist network. We captured and broke him in Tadmur. Your mother was his wife. Out of sympathy, they were hired to guard the warehouse the Americans attacked."

"No," said Mohammed, "my mother was not simply his wife. Nobody realized it, not even you, but she managed the entire Mujahedin network in this region. She managed the movement of fighters into Iraq. You thought my father was incapacitated, so you didn't watch him. But he wasn't incapacitated. His role simply changed. Instead of being a leader, he became her mouthpiece. She spoke through him. She ran everything. And you didn't look, because you knew he was a broken man."

Mohammed couldn't read the man's expression. Was he trying to suppress surprise? No, Mohammed realized: the man's expression was one of regret. This was the man who had turned his parents over to the Americans. He was realizing he might have made the wrong decision.

"How can you help?" asked the man. His question was harder this time, like he was considering recruiting Mohammed – but in the normal fashion. Mohammed felt a chill run over him as the danger of this conversation hit home.

"Your people can accomplish more than a few ragtag Sunni fighters, no matter how enraged and how dedicated we might be. I want to fight with you – on your side. I can become a force within the Mujahedin. I am well known, and I am smart. In time, I can coordinate their actions with yours, so we can drive the Americans away – each in our own way."

Mohammed knew the offer was silly. The Mukhabarat had already manipulated the Sunni into attacking whatever targets they wanted. As a bonus, the Americans were spending the bulk of their response on the Sunni forces rather than their hidden Shia and Alawite manipulators.

"And we'll be allies then?" said the man with a cold smile.

"Of course not," said Mohammed. "We'll simply work together until the Americans are gone."

The man rose, seemingly uninterested. Suddenly, Mohammed realized that he no longer had the upper hand. The man might well consider Mohammed a wellspring of information about the past. After all, he had overheard conversations and seen the men who had them. But if the man didn't believe Mohammed was also a resource for the future, then he could simply leave now and have his interrogators pick Mohammed up.

Mohammed would then be wrung dry, not developed and cultivated.

In a sudden fit of panic, Mohammed realized that he'd end up in Tadmur prison, like his father. And, like his father, he would accomplish nothing with his life.

He needed the man to need him. He needed the man to see the future possibilities.

"I *want* to help," he said, trying to keep the fear from showing in his voice. "You don't get many volunteers. So even if we only have a *hudna*, a truce, it is worth it. No? So, what do you think I can do?"

The man turned and looked down at Mohammed, still sitting on the floor.

"Do you know what this building is?" he asked.

Mohammed shook his head. "No," he answered.

"Do you know what a signal box is?"

Mohammed shook his head a second time.

The man sat down again and then spoke. "Over a hundred years ago, this building was constructed as a signal box by the Ottomans. There was a railroad here. It ran from Aleppo to Baghdad. At this place, the railroad had a spur – a sort of railroad tributary – that went to Abu Kamal. There was a man who lived in this building. And he would climb the stairs and watch for trains. And he would switch the tracks – sending some to Abu Kamal and some to Baghdad and some to Aleppo. Can you imagine, a railroad connecting all of these places?"

Mohammed had never seen a train before, except in pictures, and he had no idea a railroad had been here.

"No," he answered, surprised at his fascination.

"Do you know what happened to the railroad?" asked the man.

"No," said Mohammed, again.

"The Ottomans fell. And the British and the French and then the Americans all made their mark on this land. But they didn't do what the Ottomans did. These lands were *Ottoman* lands, and while their empire was both weak and corrupt, they still wanted to develop and tie together their lands. But the French and the British and the Americans just want our oil. They want us weak. They want us fighting each other, instead of building railroads and a powerful society. They play us off against one another. They defended Shia Iran against Sunni and Baathist Iraq in the days of the Shah. And when the Ayatollah came, they supported Saddam against the Iranians. And then when Saddam became too powerful and too successful – when he threatened their oil – they crushed him and replaced him with chaos. Instead of helping us develop this place, which was once the most envied of any in the world, they just want to keep us weak. Our own people, desperate for money and food, demolished the railroad, selling the tracks and the switches and even the stairs that used to be inside this building. They want to keep us weak. Do you understand?"

Mohammed nodded. Of course, he thought to himself, the Shiites and the Sunnis had been fighting long before the British had come.

"I am not Shia," the man continued, seemingly answering his unspoken question, "And I am not Sunni. I am an Alawite. We are a tiny, tiny part of this country's population. For years after the modern country of Syria was established in 1946, there was terrible fighting and confusion and dissent. Just like the West wanted. But the oil still flowed. When the Alawites rose to power behind Hafez Al-Assad, we had a single goal in mind. We wanted to the strengthen the nation and empower the people. We don't need Shiite or Sunni dominance – we aren't a part of that struggle. We just want to develop the country – like the Ottomans had tried to do in their own imperfect ways. Unlike them, we didn't want it to simply be a fiefdom to pay taxes to Viceroys in Damascus or a Sultan in Istanbul; we wanted it to be strong in its own right. We wanted it to serve the people under the Arab Socialist ideology of the Baathist Party. We wanted peace and prosperity and justice. But the West has always opposed this. They've opposed strong and independent Arab nations. They've opposed Socialism. They've opposed anything other than weak and dependent leaders who rely on the West for their survival. Because Hafez Assad was not weak and because Bashar Assad is not weak, they have consistently opposed us. They've fought the Alawites and their leaders. But we've remained strong, which is good for Syria."

Mohammed nodded, politely.

"You may not realize it," continued the man, "But the West sustains your terrorist movement. They support the Saudi royal regime – who are themselves imposters. The real Custodians of the Two Holy Mosques are the Hussain family, but they have been relegated to the backwaters of the Kingdom of Jordan. They have been kept weak. The Saudi family, in turn, funds Sunni terrorists around the world – especially those in Syria. But without backing from the Americans, the Saudi family themselves would fall. The West sustains whoever is weak. They pretend it is so that the weak can have justice. In reality, it is so they can keep us all weak. We need to fight them; we need to drive them away. But they are clever. Their efforts hobble us."

Mohammed couldn't stop himself from objecting. "You think being strong against the Americans justifies what you did in Hama and Homs?"

The story of these two cities burned in the collective consciousness of Mohammed's people.

"The Alawites are a tiny group," the man responded, "If we lose power for even a moment, our enemies in this land will literally exterminate us. And if we don't have power, the Sunnis or the Shiites will, and they will kill each other like they always have. We need to keep power so our wives and our children can survive. And we need to keep power so Syria can be strong. Yes, we've sometimes done brutal things. We crushed the rebellions in Hama and Homs in the 1980s. Tens of thousands died. You know this. What you don't realize is that, to a man, we regret what was done. But we also know, if we hadn't done it, that the West would win, and *our* ancient people would have ceased to exist. That's why Hama and Homs were necessary."

Mohammed, raised in a stew of hatred for the Alawites, had never known this perspective. It confused him, and he fought back the dissonance.

"Did you know," the man continued, "that the guards at Tadmur – where your father was – use drugs to get through their tours there? They hate what they do. They hate the torture and the deprivation and the horror. They aren't callous. They are family men who know their prisoners are family men. In a way, they too are prisoners. We rotate them through, in short stints. Nonetheless, many return to our society forever cursed by addiction and nightmares. The price of that prison is terrible. But it remains necessary."

"What do you want?" asked Mohammed.

"Simple," said the man, "We don't want to be your enemies. Our fear of what you will do drives us to do things we hate. If you struggle more mightily against us, I can assure you that there are no boundaries we would be unwilling to cross. But we don't want this. We want to develop this country and strengthen it. We want to push back against the Americans and the British and the French. We need to end the war with the Sunni Mujahedin. I doubt, however, that you can deliver this."

Mohammed knew what awaited him, if the man thought he was impotent.

"I can help," said Mohammed, before he could think of how.

"How?" asked the man, pressing the question.

Mohammed thought quickly.

"I have the background and intelligence to rise within the ranks of the Mujahedin. I can inform on them and weaken them and free up your resources. With your protection, I can act more freely and rise more quickly than those who fear arrest or assassination. I can't win the battle – but I can cripple the Mujahedin and thus free up your resources so that you can fight the Americans."

The man thought, regarding Mohammed carefully.

After a long pause, he said, "Why would you do it?"

"It is basic," said Mohammed. "The Americans are my first enemy. I need to see them driven away. I need to punish them. Perhaps, once that is done, I can come to believe in your vision of a strong Syria."

The man answered, "I will need to know that you're sincere."

"How?" asked Mohammed. He knew what was coming.

"I need you to give somebody up. Not some random woman or child – our enemies are not the Sunni people. I need you to give up a *terrorist*. As a show of sincerity."

This was a price Mohammed was expecting to pay. But he needed to be careful. He knew so many critical people within the Mujahedin. If he gave up too important a resource – as his parents had been – then the Alawites would have such a strong spy that Mohammed himself would become extraneous. They wouldn't send him to Tadmur, they would just kill him.

"What will you do to the man I give up?" Mohammed asked.

"Do you really want to know?" asked the man.

Mohammed realized that he did not.

"Omar bin Abdullah." He pronounced. Omar was a 19-year-old with a beat-up pickup truck. He was sweet-faced but dedicated to the cause with every fiber of his body.

"And who is he?" asked the man.

"He's a courier. He moves packages from drop site to drop site. There is a network of couriers. They pick up explosives or guns or sometimes messages in one location and they bring them to another. He is one of them."

Mohammed didn't mention that the couriers never met one another. He expected the man would know this. The only information Omar would have would be the locations of the drop sites and the signs that would indicate a package was ready for pick-up. As soon as Omar was arrested, the Mujahedin would make adjustments, and his knowledge would be made obsolete.

The man smiled. "You're a clever boy," he said, appreciatively. He knew the courier would be both a fine test of sincerity and a useless source of information.

"So," the man continued, "I'll tell you what we'll do. We'll pick up Omar. We won't bring him to Tadmur – he isn't valuable enough. We'll bring him to someplace more convenient. And then we'll disassemble him. We'll pull out his fingernails, one-by-one. Then we'll cut off his fingers, one-by-one. We'll make sure he is awake the entire time. Then we'll suspend him by his feet and let the blood slowly drip out of his hands. And then, while he's hanging, we'll flay his skin. The entire time, of course, we'll ask him for information we know he does not have. And in his panic, he will try hopelessly to satisfy us. He will seek any way out – like a rat caught in a trap. But there will be no way. And just before he is completely broken, we'll release him back into your community – hobbled and permanently wounded. You'll see him. And then, just as the briefest moment of hope lights up his eyes, an unseen assassin will fire a single bullet. And everybody will watch him die."

"Is this all part of being strong?" asked Mohammed, bitterly.

"Yes," said the man, coldly, "You chose a useless target so that you would not overly regret the consequences of your choice. But I need you filled with regret. It is a part of any commitment to a greater cause. And it is only with the regret of commitment that this can work. But I also need you to know that the death of Omar bin Abdullah will hover over your community for years. It needs to remain our secret; the secret I can use to undo you should you betray us. I need you to know that if you betray us, you will be discovered by your compatriots and you will not only die painfully, but your name will be erased. Unlike your parents, you will not be remembered as a martyr. You will be cursed by the generations who come after you."

Mohammed nodded. This was his reality, and he had chosen it.

The man smiled, warmly. "Mohammed bin Abbas," he said, "We will protect you. And you will help make Syria strong. And your own community will benefit immensely. Instead of death, we will build railroads. Instead of martyr's funerals, we will celebrate births and weddings. There will be peace and strength and justice. We will not only punish the Americans, we will build a new and better reality. You understand. You are not betraying your community – you are contributing to them in a magnificent way. You understand, yes?"

Mohammed nodded, reluctantly.

Inside, he was bursting with emotion. When he had his chance, a chance this conversation would make possible, he would turn the tables on this man and destroy him and his people.

"Good," said the man. He reached across and shook Mohammed's hand. And then he rose and walked out of the building.

After the man was gone, Mohammed bowed towards Mecca and prayed. He concentrated on the last three verses of the Al-Fatiha,

> It is You we worship and You we ask for help.
> Guide us to the straight path –
> The path of those upon whom You have bestowed
> favor, not of those who have evoked Your anger or of
> those who are astray.

He was only sixteen. But he was confident that All-h would support him. He was confident His guidance would be true.

His prayer complete, he rose and walked out of the desert and back into Abu Kamal.

As he entered the outskirts of the town, he knew that Abu Kamal was where he belonged. Everybody who saw him knew who he was and what he had suffered. Many stopped him and greeted him with the customary phase:

> All-h takes what is His, and what he gives is His, and
> to all things He has appointed a time...so have
> patience and be rewarded.

Some said it with a tone of congratulations for the son of the martyrs. Some said it in sympathy for the new orphan. The voices of others were strangely mixed with both emotions. But all said it to a brother who was beloved in his place.

In turn, Mohammed showed both sorrow and joy. But his emotions were deeper than those around him could ever be allowed to know. He was sorry for what he had done, and he was joyous at the opportunities it would create.

He was near the warehouse that he still called home when Omar bin Abdullah stopped him and greeted him. The young man had a bright smile and almost joyfully exclaimed,

> All-h takes what is His, and what he gives is His, and
> to all things He has appointed a time...so have
> patience and be rewarded.

Mohammed thought about warning him – but he knew that would serve no purpose.

Instead, looking into the bright face of the happy young man, Mohammed could only see his father's face – broken by torture and crushed. And then he saw him in his final moments to come; he saw him with the last embers of his hope crushed by a bullet.

Mohammed looked sadly at Omar and said, quietly.

> All-hu Akbar

His neighbors saw the son of martyrs. Omar saw the son of martyrs. They saw the regret of commitment.

But only the man from the signal box could conceive of how deeply that regret had already been etched into his soul.

Mohammed walked into the warehouse, closed the door – and immersed himself in the bittersweet, but simple, memories of his childhood.

# Peace

*June 6th, 2014: Northern Iraq*

The scream had been my brother's. His voice had been hoarse with dehydration, but it was unmistakable. I slammed open my eyes. The sun was glaring overhead. It was almost noon. And I was as relieved as I'd ever been in my life.

I gave thanks to All-h. We were still in a battle zone, so I didn't sit up. I just rolled onto my side and leaned over him. His eyes were frantic with fear and confusion, but when he saw me, he began to calm down. I breathed a sigh of relief. A moment later, I had a water bottle at the ready. He drank from it slowly, his parched lips and swollen mouth struggling to manipulate the bottle and the water that it held. But he drank.

My brother had slight features: a tiny nose, thin lips, and a disappearing chin. He seemed to blend into the world around him, always watching – but rarely being watched. He was still like my father in many ways. Even as a three-year-old, he could remember and maintain conversations over months. I would watch him and my dad swap discrete snippets of long-running interactions. I couldn't follow their conversations, but they could. Somehow, they always managed to.

Ibrahim couldn't talk. But I wasn't worried. His tongue was still incredibly swollen.

But I could talk to him, and that was something. I wanted to tell him everything. I wanted to cry with him and hold him and share the burden of everything that had happened.

97

But I couldn't. He was in no shape to deal with our reality.

"Ibrahim," I said, in an undertone, "We went out for a walk."

As I said the words, I realized he was the first person I'd spoken to since we'd left Mosul. His was the first friendly face I'd seen since our parents had died.

He nodded. It was an encouraging sign. He understood.

"You fell," I said, "and you hit your head very badly."

He nodded again.

"We're going to stay here a little while, until you feel better."

He nodded a third time.

His eyes were bright and clear. It seemed, then, that he might be okay.

I thought of my parents, singing little Ibrahim to bed at night and my eyes unwillingly filled with tears. I wanted them to sing to him, to make him feel better. But they weren't there. There was nobody there but me and him.

It seemed like there was nobody anywhere, but us.

And then, almost without thinking, I began to sing. I sang the Dillelul – a desperate lament of a lullaby in ancient Iraqi Arabic. It wasn't a happy tune; it came from a place of overwhelming pain. It wished for enemies to suffer in the distant desert as it spoke of the loneliness of a woman who has lost her loved ones. She mistakes the wind's banging for the arrival of those she has lost. In desperate sadness, she begs her child to watch after her in her helpless infirmity and endless pain. The child in the song sings one line – regretting that he has been brought to such a life.

Ibrahim watched me, silently. He had heard the song so many times before that he didn't recognize the truth I was sharing. For him, it was just a lullaby. But as I sang, I cried. I imagined myself suffering the pains of the old woman. I imagined that the sound of the river was actually masking my parents' approaching footsteps. And I imagined my suddenly orphaned little brother, lamenting the unfairness yet to come.

He smiled at the end, as if to reassure me. Then he drank some more, and then we both slept under the open sun.

When he woke again and had drunk again, he tried to speak.

The swelling in his mouth had receded some.

"Maryam?" he asked, in a hoarse and poorly formed whisper.

"Yes?" I answered him, expectantly. I was delighted to hear his voice. I was delighted to hear he could speak.

"Where are we?"

"Near the Great Zab River," I said, plainly.

He nodded and I smiled.

Then he asked, "Where are mother and father?"

He had always been very formal.

"Not here," I said, gently. "They aren't here."

He nodded again, gently accepting my answer. And then he closed his eyes and rested some more. When night finally came, I told him it was time to go. I didn't want to leave yet; he had undergone a tremendous injury. But we would run out of water and food if we stayed.

As he got up, I saw that his movements were labored, like he'd forgotten how to walk and had to think about every step. I held his arm and his shoulder and guided him into a standing position.

He leaned on me, coming up to less than half my height. Walking in that way would be slow. But I preferred the peace of it to the mad rush that had brought us here.

I thought about where to go. The standoff at the Kalak river crossings was unresolved. East was out. I imagined the same battle front I had encountered edged all the territory the Islamic State controlled. I didn't want to try and cross those lines of fire and I lacked the money to pay people smugglers, even if I had known how to find them. That's why I chose west. I chose to take my injured brother and myself – wanted enemies of the Islamic State – back towards Mosul.

I hoped to find an empty village where we might survive.

As we walked, we stayed far from the roads – I didn't want to be seen. But the going was difficult. Although the summer grasses in the recently fallowed fields were not high, they effectively hid the uneven terrain. My ankles would roll, and my feet would sink in unpredictable places. It was far harder for my brother. He lost his balance regularly. I held him, of course, but I felt his weight sag in unexpected directions at seemingly random intervals.

Despite all the difficulty, we were able to travel. That night, we reached the edge of the Al-Khazir River. My brother had been silent the entire walk, he looked like he was deep in thought.

I noticed that his walking had improved, just a bit, and that gave me hope. It was almost like his thoughts had been poured into relearning how to move. I refilled our water, dropping a small amount of chlorine in it to purify it. We drank, and I sang the Dillelul again. I didn't cry this time. Then, we slept.

The next morning, close to noon, we began to walk upriver in search of a place to stay. We found a ford and crossed. As the river wound back and forth, we wound with it – never wanting to be too far from the one path I could follow. We bypassed one bustling village full of people.

Then, not far from our path, I saw a tiny village on top of a gentle hill which overlooked the river. The houses were ramshackle and had been built – one against the other – like blocks dropped by a child. More importantly, I noticed that the fields around the houses were only partially harvested. Some had standing sheaves, drying in the sun. But some others were totally unharvested. The people who lived here must have fled in the middle of their work.

As we drew closer, my suspicions were confirmed. The village was completely silent.

The image of children's blocks was reinforced by the high walls that surrounded the houses. They looked like cubic concrete formations which had been scattered on the ground. I broke into one of the tiny houses as my curious brother watched. Like the house we'd stayed in near Mosul, it had a courtyard. But this courtyard was miniscule and the house itself had only one room. Unlike the house in Mosul, there were no beds or mattresses. I guessed that the owners probably slept on bedrolls. During the day, they would roll them up so the single room could be a workspace. And during the night, they would unroll them. We didn't have bedrolls. But the floor was dry and flat, so we lay down and slept.

The next morning, I found the pantry. There were some dates there, and some halva, as well as a small amount of badly milled wheat. But that was it. It was clear that the people in this town were not wealthy; they had taken almost everything they had with them. But at least we had something to eat.

As we sat to eat, my brother asked, "Where are we?"

"In a village," I said, "Near Mosul."

He nodded. Once again, that thoughtful and serious face showed how carefully he was listening.

"Where are mother and father?" he asked, again.

"Not here," I said. "They aren't here."

He nodded again.

I gave him a few of the dates. He split one open, staring at it intently before eating.

I wondered what he was thinking about.

Because I didn't want to consume everything all at once, we were still hungry when we'd finished eating. To take our mind off our hunger, and to plan for our next steps, we left the little house in order to explore the village.

The basic layout was easy to work out. The village had only twelve houses, and it was located on the border of the mountainous regions of Kurdistan. Tiny shards of those mountains seemed to thrust out of the landscape, while deep wadis sliced through it, created by the seasonal waters that rushed down to the nearby river. The fields themselves were shaped within this landscape – custom-formed to whatever flat terrain could be found between the shards and the crevices. As a result, the fields were not square; their pattern was almost as ramshackle as the village itself.

This land was not important or valuable. Some who lived on this sort of land were forced to spend their winters in the warmer climates downriver; the harvests weren't substantial enough to support them year-round. But this was not wintertime, and the partially harvested wheat and the leftover food spoke to the urgency of their flight.

It felt odd to seek refuge in a place they had sought refuge from.

But there was no better place for us to go. My parents didn't have a people, and there were downsides to that reality.

As we explored, I broke into the other houses one by one. Some had a bit more food, some had none at all. We wouldn't be able to scavenge for long in this village. Given the villagers' poverty, I felt bad about what we'd already taken; it was clear they didn't have a great deal to spare. And then I looked at the fields again and realized that they, at least, were filled with food. There was wheat there. The fields weren't large, but for two orphans, they could be an almost endless resource.

Every vehicle in the village had been taken. There were no tractors there. I suspected, given the size of the village and its fields, that there may never have been anything as large as a combine. Somewhere, there had to be other tools. Before long, I found a shed, broke in, and discovered what I had expected.

We might have been fundamentally urban people, but my father had insisted that I watch a harvest once. We'd also visited an oil field and the Mosul dam. He didn't say so, but I knew he felt it was important to understand a little of the world that supported our city.

The plains of Nineveh, which surround Mosul, are blanketed with wheat fields. Unlike many other places, these fields only yield a single crop a year; the climate does not lend itself to multiple cycles. Some try to force the issue, but nature does not give in to them easily. For most, there is one planting and one harvest.

In that light, the abandoned harvest around me was even more shocking. The harvest was the only opportunity for the people who had lived here to earn enough to survive the year. Their fear had been so complete that they had abandoned even that.

Nearer to Mosul, combines dominated the harvest. A single machine would cut the wheat, beat the grains off the sheaves and then separate the grains from the chaff.

In ancient times, a sickle – a short blade connected to the end of a stick – might have been used to cut the wheat. Then flails would have separated the grains from the stalks. Finally, strong winds and stronger arms would have separated the wheat from the chaff.

The two methods – ancient and modern – stood at opposite ends of a spectrum.

As I looked in the shed, I saw we were going to do something in between. Thankfully, there were scythes there, not sickles. They had long blades at sharp angles to the sticks that held them. You would hold and sweep the sticks in broad motions and the blades at the bottom – parallel to the ground – would mow the grain. Unlike the scythe carried in the images of Death, these had a sort of rake above the blade that would sweep the cut stalks to the side and leave them in orderly piles.

In addition to the scythes, there was also a threshing machine. It was a small contraption, about the size of a piano. It had a generator on the side. I wasn't sure how to use it, but I knew I could work it out.

As I looked over the equipment, it occurred to me that we might save the harvest for these unfortunates. We might collect their grain and leave it for them, in safekeeping. We'd eat some – of course. But we'd leave the villagers better off for having granted us their unwilling hospitality.

With that thought, I decided that we'd start harvesting right away. In the meantime, we'd eat what remained of the villagers' food until we had gathered enough to sustain ourselves.

I grabbed a scythe – there were no child sizes – and my brother followed me into the fields. He was still walking unnaturally.

"What are we doing?" he asked, pleasantly.

"We're going to cut the grain," I said, "I'll cut it and you gather it and tie it up."

"How should I tie it?" he asked.

"I don't know," I said, "Let's work it out."

He nodded.

I walked into the field and pulled the scythe along the bottoms of the first rank of the wheat. Some of it fell, but I was stopped long before

I'd completed a full sweep. It required an enormous amount of force to pull the scythe through the grain – far more than I'd imagined.

I brought the scythe back and tried again, pulling harder. I almost made a complete sweep before being brought to a reluctant stop. I tested the blade, it was sharp. This was just incredibly difficult work.

I made another sweep and finally brought down the first row of the stalks.

I called my brother over and we used some of the grain to tie the rest. It was our very first sheave.

I had showed my brother what to do, and he seemed to be following. That's why I was surprised when I made another sweep and he just stood there, watching.

"Gather it up," I said.

He looked at me, pleasantly, and said, "How?"

He had always been a kid who could concentrate. He could always remember. He would remember conversations over months. And yet here he was, forgetting something as simple as tying grain.

"You know how," I said, "I just showed you."

He looked at me blankly. Then he said, "What?"

I surprised myself when I shouted, "JUST DO IT!" I felt like he was being intentionally slow.

But when he looked at me blankly, and then he started to cry, I finally knew that something was fundamentally wrong.

I calmed myself and showed him again. And then I scythed another row of the grain. And then I showed him again. I realized I was doing both jobs, but I hoped, somehow, that he'd learn what he needed to learn. I kept scything, pushing myself as hard as I physically could. My progress was slow. I was harvesting grain, but I was also fighting, helplessly, against whatever was wrong with my wounded brother. The work was hard, and I removed my niqab from on top of my cotton pants and shirt. There were no men nearby.

We took a break in the early afternoon. We went down to the river and filled our water bottles – then chlorinated and drank. I had found some sesame flour that morning, and I mixed it into a paste. We ate it. It wasn't pleasant, but it was nutritious.

And then we got back to work.

It became almost routine. I would cut, putting all of my meager force into the action. Then I would stop and help Ibrahim gather and tie the grain. We repeated it, again and again. By the end of the day, we had covered an area of 100 feet by 5 feet. The rest of fields, which had looked so manageable earlier in the day, now seemed overwhelming. But we *had* made progress. We had harvested *something*. In the place of the even field, there were now little towers made up of the sheaves we had cut and tied.

We slept for the night. In the morning, I decided to try my hand at baking. My mother had never really taught me how to cook. I mixed some of the flour in one of the houses with water and kneaded it as I imagined it ought to be done, and then I baked it in a charcoal-powered stove. The result was somehow both lumpy and flat. But it was food. The effort of baking had taken all morning. In the afternoon, my tired muscles didn't feel like scything – it seemed like every thrust demanded all the energy I had at *that* moment. And each pass needed to be followed by another. I'd never done anything so exhausting.

Luckily, there were other things to do, so I headed for the fields once again.

"What are we doing?" Ibrahim asked, pleasantly.

"We're going to test the sheaves," I said.

"How?" he asked.

"We're going to find the driest sheaves we can, and then we'll put them in the threshing machine and see if the grain that comes out is okay."

"Okay," he said. His look was still intense – like he understood and was drawing in everything I said. But now I knew that it meant he *didn't* understand. The day before, I'd learned that when I said one thing at a time, it seemed to make more sense.

"Let's feel the sheaves," I said, "And see which is driest."

"Okay," he said, more brightly. He took off at an ungainly trot, though his running was still far from normal.

I hoped he would do better at this job. But it was obvious, almost immediately, that whatever sheave he touched last was the driest he'd ever found. He couldn't hold the comparisons in his head. We worked our way through the field in this way. He was happy as he ran from sheave to sheave, pronouncing each one of them the driest of them all. And I followed him, feeling and testing to see if perhaps he was right *this* time. I found, strangely, that I was happy too. We were going to make this work.

When we had finished our sweep of the waiting sheaves, I picked the one sheave Ibrahim and I had agreed was the driest of them all. The sheaves were waiting on a small crescent of land just south of the village itself. We gathered up a sheaf between us – they were larger than the sheaves we had been making – and we carried it back to the shed in the village.

I wheeled the threshing machine out of the shed. It said, "AMAR Industries" in bright red lettering. Beneath that, in equally proud letters, were the words "BOMBAY, INDIA." There was also a serial number – but that was it. There were no instructions of any kind.

I looked over the machine. It was about six feet on the face, three feet deep and five feet tall. Across the face of the machine, open to the top, were a pair of rollers. Directly opposite them was an exhaust. And below that, there was a grate. Finally, off to one side, there was a small ramp. I looked at it for a while before I worked it out. The rollers would crush the grain, a blower would send the chaff out of the back of the machine, and the ramp on the side would deliver the grains themselves.

Next to the whole thing, connected to the rollers by a wide rubber belt, was a two-stroke generator. That, at least, was familiar. It seemed like half of Mosul was powered by two-stroke generators.

I checked the oil and fuel, and then told my brother to stand a safe distance away. After he had moved, I pulled the cord on the generator as hard as I could. It started with a satisfying roar. The sound shocked me though. I hadn't realized, until that moment, just how quiet the empty village was.

But then, moments later, I heard another sound.

It was my brother, screaming.

I killed the generator, but he kept screaming. There was total panic on his face and fear in his eyes.

I tried to calm him down. But he wouldn't settle. I just sat there, repeating again and again and again, "Ibrahim, it is all right." I tried, once, to ask what was wrong. But that just made him worse. Somehow, the generator had set him off.

After what seemed like an hour, I asked him to follow me and we went back into the shed. And there, in the far rear, was another threshing machine. It was smaller – and in place of a gas engine on the side, it had a single pedal at its front. It looked like it hadn't been used in a dozen years.

We wheeled it out of the shed, together. I found oil and some tools and set to fixing the old contraption up. Unlike the AMAR machine, this machine's mechanical elements were obvious. The rollers would thrash the grain together, a manual fan would gently blow away the chaff, and the grain itself would fall through a grate in the bottom. All of it would be driven by the pedals.

It was already near the end of the day when I had the machine running smoothly. I would push the pedal, and everything would move in unison, and then as the crush-blow-collection cycle was completed, the pedal would rise to be pushed again. The motion was almost like biking, one-legged.

I stood in front of the machine, pushed the pedal, and lay the dry grain against the top of the machine. It worked beautifully and quietly. The grains were ripped off the ends of the stalks. The chaff blew out the back of the machine in a gentle cloud and – almost like mechanical magic – the grain itself emerged out of the chute. It was perfect.

Best of all, Ibrahim was smiling.

Over the next week, we alternated harvesting and gathering dry grain for threshing. My legs, torso and arms began to ripple with newfound strength. It felt both exhausting and physically exhilarating. Sometimes, I could even complete entire sweeps of the scythe in a single pass. Best of all, Ibrahim learned. He learned to gather the fallen stalks and tie them by himself. He figured out how to help me carry it. And he understood how to lay the grains against the rotors of the machine as they were thrashed. He couldn't plan – multiple steps were beyond him. But, with enough practice, he could repeat.

We were steadily consuming the village's meager food stocks. While I wanted to keep harvesting, we did need to eat. We needed to make flour out of the grain. This challenge was a very different one from extracting the grain itself. While farms like these would have equipment for threshing and winnowing, grinding was another matter. Grinding was an industrial process. There were only a few silos in the entire region. Farmers would sell their grain to the central government – at inflated prices – and the government would grind it into flour and sell it onwards at a lower, market, rate. It was one way in which Baghdad kept its influence in the north. But given the price of that grain – and the attention given to the subsidies behind that price – I couldn't imagine individual farmers would keep much of their product for themselves. It wouldn't have made any sense for them to do their own grinding. My exploration of the kitchens bore that out. We had used flour, but it had all come in bags with the flag proudly displayed on it. The farmers had sold the grain at inflated prices and then bought back the flour at a cheaper price.

Of course, the central government hadn't always subsidized the farms in this way. I thought that there must be some equipment left from an earlier era – just as the manual thresher had been. I dug through the shed, and then house after house, looking for something to grind the grain with. I needed, somehow, to make flour.

Finally, I found something that might work. It was a small hand mill. It had two stone rollers, both of which were connected to a single wheel with a crank. A hopper rose above them. Crank the wheel, and the stone rollers would rub against each other. Pour grain into the hopper, and it would fall to the point at which the rollers met. Keep cranking the wheel, and the grain would be pulled between the rollers, crushed and transformed into flour. The remarkable thing about the small device – after so much searching – was that it was in plain sight. It was mounted on a wall in the kitchen area of one of the small village houses. It was in excellent condition and hadn't been used that long ago; only a small patina of dust had gathered on its surfaces. I wondered why it had been in use, before the villagers had fled. And then I smelled it and I understood. It smelled of sesame. The people who lived here used it to make sesame flour from seeds. It wasn't intended for wheat.

I was worried it wouldn't work for wheat, but I had few other options. To my delight, it functioned perfectly. Ibrahim and I brought some grain to that kitchen and we ground it. Like every other part of the process, it was hard work. Rather than working my legs or my torso, it worked my arms. Around and around they went, pulling the crank and grinding the flour. After an hour – and after seeing the rough quality of the result – I understood why this was an industrial process.

But we needed to eat. So, Ibrahim slowly poured the grain into the hopper, and I ground the wheel.

As the grain flowed out the side of the small mill, a sudden euphoria came over me. My brother and I had accomplished something tremendous. We had taken grain – standing in the fields. We had harvested and threshed and winnowed it. And now, we were grinding it into flour. It was *our* flour. We had produced it.

I wanted to complete that process. So, I baked bread, with *our* flour. It was coarse, and there were a few rocks in it. But it was edible. And it was *ours*.

We kept on that way, for week after week under the hot sun, harvesting and threshing and, as we needed to, grinding and baking. My body grew strong. I hadn't been sedentary in Mosul, but short bursts of municipal repair were easy in comparison to weeks of manual harvesting. Now, I was far stronger than I ever had been before. And my endurance had also increased exponentially.

As the weeks progressed, I found yeast, and we learned to pick the rocks out from the grain before baking it. And, just as Ibrahim slowly got better at his tasks, I got better at baking the bread itself. We actually began to look forward to our evening meals. We would sit outside and eat, admiring our progress as more and more of the fields were harvested and processed.

We – just the two of us – were accomplishing something remarkably tangible.

I wasn't alone in my happiness. Ibrahim was delighted. He couldn't keep the history of what we'd done straight; he couldn't keep the whole process in his head. But when he saw the gathered stalks or the buckets of grain or small containers of flour – or even the bread emerging from the oven – he glowed with joy. He was accomplishing something – and, somehow, he knew it.

Every morning, Ibrahim would ask about our parents. And every day, I would give him the same answer, "Ibrahim, they aren't here." He always, somehow, seemed satisfied with it. One evening, as we sat there eating our evening meal, I found myself hoping that somehow, our parents could see us. And then I felt that they were. I can't explain it, but I could feel that they were proud.

I turned to my little brother. "Ibrahim," I said, "They're here."

Just that once, just like before the bomb, he knew what conversation I was continuing.

He smiled, joyfully. "Yes," he said, "They are."


Of course, the grain, and even my parents' pride, weren't the only development of those weeks in the village. All-h had answered my prayers as we'd run from Mosul. It was when my brother woke up, on the low hills overlooking Kalak, that the nature of those prayers changed. Before, I had prayed for help – out of desperation. I had prayed out of a kind of greed. I had prayed on *my* schedule and around *my* desires. But when he woke up, I began to pray to glorify All-h. I prayed on His schedule, and in the way He and His prophet commanded. I prayed to connect to Him and to bring Him into my life. And I prayed because I was overwhelmed by the responsibility of who I needed to be.

I needed His guidance and the reassurance of His path.

Ibrahim and I had grown up secular. Even after the Americans came, my father seemed to cling to a vestige of Baathist philosophy. But the world of Mosul was a religious one. I couldn't *not* know the call to prayer, the opening verses of the Koran, and the rituals connected to them. And I couldn't *not* know the times of prayer. For my entire life, the muezzins' loudspeakers had proclaimed the dominance of Islam in the city. At dawn, sunrise, midday, midafternoon, sunset and nightfall, their voices rang against the walls of every neighborhood – proclaiming the times of prayer and dominating those who were not Muslim. I had never paid much attention to those loudspeakers – like many of the less religious, I learned to sleep through them from a very young age. But now, I would rise at dawn each day and recite the Al-Fatiha, and I would close each night with my head bowed to the floor, and the words *"Glory be to my Lord, the most High Most Praiseworthy"* on my lips.

As we worked, Ibrahim and I lost track of the days of the week. I didn't know which day was Friday – a day for special prayers. But I knew that the next month was Ramadan. And I knew the new moon would herald that month. When the moon dwindled and finally disappeared, we began our holy month.

We would still work each day. And, despite the practice of Ramadan forbidding it, we would drink what we needed – our level of manual labor made that essential. But we would only eat and drink to satisfaction after sunset. The city of Mosul would be dormant during the day. But it would come to life at night with families and even neighborhoods sharing in daily feasts. The joy, in those days, was palpable.

Somehow, alone in the village, the cycle seemed even more beautiful to me. We would create the entire day. And then we would use our creations for our own little Ramadan feasts. Although I didn't say the prayers over food (because I didn't know them), the work we poured into those celebratory meals seemed to amplify our understanding of All-h's glory and His peace. Our labor seemed to be invested in something timeless, in something greater than our lives. All-h created for six days and rested on the seventh. In a way, we were imitating His path – the straight path – and we were drawing closer to Him as a result.

We didn't manage to harvest all the grain. By the middle of the month of Ramadan, some of the grain had started rotting after having been left on the stalk too long. We cut it anyway but left the stalks in the fields. I didn't know what I was supposed to do. I was worried the fallen stalks might block some natural processes, but I guessed that they were more likely to help the land fallow effectively. I never did find out which was correct.

And then, one afternoon, we were done. The work in the fields was complete, the collection of barrels in the storehouse were full of grain – and we had everything we needed to last us through the year. That evening, we both went down to the river and bathed and washed our clothes. They dried quickly in the sun. I felt strong and accomplished and deeply satisfied, and I could see Ibrahim felt the same. I was still Maryam Al-Mosuli – but I had also discovered something beyond *that* heritage.

The next morning felt luxurious. I woke up for my prayers. But then, I just wandered around the village. For the first time since we'd left Mosul, my brother didn't follow me. He was comfortable in the village, and we weren't working together – not that day. When we'd first come to this place, I'd found a left-behind book in one of the houses. I hadn't opened it before, but I did now. I had time to read. It was a children's book: the tales of Ali Baba. The fantastic old stories didn't fill me with as much excitement as they once had, but somehow, I could understand them more. In my own way, I had embarked on a dangerous journey, and All-h had rewarded me with great riches.

In the mid-afternoon, I laid out my prayer rug for the Zuhr prayer. I recited the opening verses. I touched my forehead to the prayer rug. And I breathed deeply. I thought of my brother and I thought of my parents and I thought of how much we had accomplished. I prayed for All-h's mercy and His forgiveness for my faults and shortcomings. And then I uttered the verse:

> *Glory be to my Lord, the most High Most*
> *Praiseworthy.*

I kept my head bowed to the ground, intent on my joy in the service of All-h.

And then, in the distance, I heard engines.

Fear ripped through me.

And then, in a sudden panic, I realized that I didn't know where Ibrahim had gone.

# Rabbi

*July 15, 2013: Jerusalem, Israel*

As Steven Gold entered the room, he was amazed by the transformation around him. He'd been to Israel before, of course. He'd seen the bright streets and the cacophony of architectural standards. He'd seen the high-end apartment buildings and the ramshackle slums. But he'd stayed in hotels and gone on sponsored tours of border fences and historic Jewish sites. The emphasis had been on establishing commonality, not accentuating differences. Unlike at the Embassy, those who had hosted him in Israel had always been trying to make him feel at home – despite being nowhere near home. Of course, he'd visited a few friends, but they had been from the United States, and their apartments reflected their backgrounds. They superimposed the thick couches and warm furniture of the United States with the sparse tile floors and concrete walls of Israel. He'd always consider their aesthetic qualities a little forced – like people trying to bring something alien to a new place. He imagined native-born Israelis, on the other hand, had a very clean, minimalist and modernist aesthetic. The billboards he'd seen for apartments certainly reinforced this.

That was what he'd expected when he'd entered the study of the Chief Sephardi Rabbi of Israel. Something clean and minimalist. Nothing he'd been exposed to prepared him for what he actually saw.

It had all started with an Internet search. Amy and Steven had been looking for Israeli political figures, on the right, who had spoken about the conflict in Syria. He'd been amazed when he'd found a potentially sympathetic voice in the Chief Sephardi Rabbi. The man had said, at a meeting with Palestinian religious leaders, that the war in Syria was like another Holocaust. He stated that it would be good to find a way to rescue people from the conflict, even though they were enemies of the Jewish people. It was an open-ended statement. As there was no particular policy being recommended, Steven saw an opportunity.

Because Steven was, despite his outsider status, still a Member of the Executive Committee of the JUC, securing a meeting with the Rabbi had required only a phone call. The Rabbi's secretary didn't even ask what the meeting was about – he just suggested a date, time and address. And Steven agreed to show up.

Three days later, he landed in Israel. Amy had stayed in DC, with their children Maggie and Brian. In their absence, Steven was realizing how abstract they were to him. They were his children, but he barely interacted with them. As he'd told himself many times, others needed him far more badly than his own children did.

Amy had stayed in DC, but they had continued working together, honing his approach to the upcoming conversation. She'd be expecting a phone call as soon as it was done.

After landing, Steven took a day to adjust to the time zone. And then he went, in the early afternoon, to the address given: HaRav Eliyahu Schick 43/12א Har Nof.

To his surprise, it wasn't a government building. There were no signs outside the doors proclaiming, "Chief Rabbinate of Israel." Instead, the address led to an apartment building in a neighborhood stuffed with other seemingly identical limestone apartment buildings. They were all stacked on the side of a steep hill. Number 43 was like all the rest. In this neighborhood, at least, there was none of the incongruity of other places he'd been to in Israel.

There was an elevator in the building, but no sign actually indicating where unit 12א might be. So, Steven used the stairs. He liked the exercise; he found it made him think more clearly. As he climbed, he worked out that the apartments were sequential. 1-4 were on the ground floor, 5-8 on the first floor and so on. His target was on the third floor. Unlike the other apartments, this one had two doors – parked next to each other. One was apartment 12. The other was 12א. There were no other markings.

Steven checked his watch; he was five minutes early. He knocked on the door, and it buzzed. He pushed it open. There was a small office stuffed into the space. The emphasis was on *small*. It couldn't have been bigger than 10 feet by 5. There was another door, directly opposite the one Steven had used. An efficient-looking brown-skinned man sat behind a chair squeezed between a desk and a file cabinet. He was positioned along the side of the room. He could see both doors without turning his head. As far as Steven could make out, he was a literal gatekeeper.

Steven looked at the man. His eyes and mouth and nose were all large, but his face wasn't. He resembled the office in a way – his features stuffed into a space not quite large enough for them. But the man stood out from his surroundings. Every surface in the office was a stark white, and the fluorescent lighting seemed to accentuate this. But the man was dark-skinned, and he wore a black suit and hat. It was almost like he was the only object in a featureless world.

In a very thick, Israeli-accent, the man welcomed Steven and supplied him with a cup of the same undrinkable coffee he'd been offered at the Embassy. Then, the man hit a button under the table, and the door opposite Steven opened.

"You can wait inside," he said.

Steven walked into the room; and entered what seemed like a parallel universe.

The first thing that grabbed his attention was the collection of sofas. They were more like well-padded benches with wooden backs set at harsh 90-degree angles. The fabric on the benches was dark and set with intricate patterns. The wooden backs were ornately carved – but they had no padding at all. Instead, pillows rested on the benches, promising an ad-hoc overlay for the hard wood and the right angles. The sofas looked both alien and comfortable – like the design had been arrived at through an entirely parallel but equally successful, process. In a way, Steven supposed, that was probably true.

The sofas were pushed against the walls and there were huge metal lamps hanging in the corners of the room. Lights shone from within them, casting diffuse patterns on the walls and the furniture. Steven could understand why they were in the corners; if they had been anywhere else, people might be injured by walking into them.

The floor was made of a dark wood, almost matching the backs of the sofas. Steven imagined that the standard concrete lay beneath the wood, but there was no sign of that. A number of oriental rugs, in dark blues and reds, were cast on top of the floor. A colored curtain hung over the only window. The sun was thus dragooned into casting yet more color into the space. The dark brown walls were only visible in small patches. Portraits of Rabbis decorated the empty spaces above the sofas, but every other part of the room was covered by bookshelves. On those shelves were leather-backed volumes in browns and blacks and occasional dark blues. They had alien-looking titles – suggesting tomes of ancient Middle Eastern wisdom. No wonder the man had been sympathetic, in a way he was a part of Arab culture.

Steven had noticed the couches first. But as he stood in the room a moment longer, he realized that it was the books which infused the room with its character. They seemed to be stuffed into every available space. They weren't only on the walls. There was a small table near the couches with more books stacked on it. And, to one side of the room, there was a small, angled desk with a reading lamp resting over it. It only had space for one large volume. Although that space was empty, it didn't take much to imagine a book there – with the Rabbi hunched over it. But the visual impact was only a part of the books' effect on the space. As the door closed, the room seemed to hug Steven. There was no echo – instead the closely-packed volumes absorbed the noises of both Steven's footsteps and of the street below. And the smell of the books – of leather and old paper mixing with the lush woods of the bookshelves themselves – overran every sensation. Despite not being able to read the words, or even the titles, Steven sensed that the room was infused with wisdom. He grasped for a word to describe the place. He shocked himself when he realized that the word he was seeking was "holy."

He sat, carefully setting his coffee on the table before him. He adjusted the cushions and sipped his strong coffee and closed his eyes. He just wanted to breathe in the feeling of this unexpected space.

It seemed like only a moment later when he heard a voice, "Mr. Gold?" Steven snapped open his eyes in surprise and saw the Chief Rabbi standing in front of him. He recognized him from photographs. The Rabbi was wearing a dark body-length garment decorated with intricate silver patterns near the neckline. His face emerged from a scruffy white beard – like a Middle Eastern Santa Clause. Somehow, the photographs of the man captured almost nothing of him. His eyes were surprisingly intense. They expressed power, warmth, and incredible confidence – all at once.

"Good afternoon," said Steven, rising from his seat, "It's a pleasure to meet you."

The Rabbi smiled warmly. But Steven detected an edge of mischievousness in the smile. "Good to meet you too, Mr. Gold." His English was excellent, but the words were delivered in an accent Steven was unfamiliar with. It wasn't Israeli, and somehow it was thick and smooth all at once.

At first impression, Steven liked the man. He was hopeful.

"I'm very curious why you're here," said the Rabbi, "Very few members of the JUC come to see me."

"Why do they come, normally?" asked Steven.

"Well," said the Rabbi, with a smile, "They don't normally come at all. They send messages, and they write editorials in the press – complaining about things I've said."

He was smiling, and so Steven did too. Unlike every member of the Executive Committee of the JUC, the Chief Rabbi was *not* a liberal man.

"I'm not here about that," Steven said, "I'm here about something else. An idea I have that I'd like to share with you."

The Rabbi smiled and gestured towards the couch. Steven sat again and the Rabbi followed.

"Go ahead," the Rabbi said.

"I read a quote of yours," Steven said, "You called the war in Syria something like a Holocaust. You said that we should do something. But you didn't say what. But I have an idea about what to do."

The Rabbi nodded for Steven to continue.

"In the 1600s, in Europe, there was an enormous religious war. By some estimates, a third of the population was killed. In many ways, the way out was led by a single city – Amsterdam. People could practice other faiths there, and the city boomed as a result. It became a model of Europe, and eventually other places even surpassed it. The important thing is that it reformed Christianity – making Christendom more accepting of other faiths. I think Israel should establish something similar: a small city, open to all faiths, to serve as an incubator for a better future. I think Israel can offer a place for people fleeing the Syrian Holocaust. And in the process, we can help develop the Middle East. But to do this, I need endorsements. I need support within Israel. I read what you said, and so I've come to ask you for your support."

Steven waited, holding his breath, desperately hoping for a positive response.

The Rabbi folded his hands in his lap and thought for a moment. Then he spoke again, "I can't support your proposal."

"Why not?" asked Steven, fighting the pit in his stomach.

"I don't think you want to know. In fact, I think you'll be more comfortable not knowing."

"What do you mean?" asked Steven.

"I've had conversations like this before. I've explained myself before. I've been doing this job long enough to recognize when the people I'm talking to won't understand but will just become angry. Anger helps nobody. Let's leave it at 'the Sephardi Chief Rabbi will stay silent on the matter of Steven Gold's proposal.'"

Steven sat there, almost stunned. Less than five minutes of conversation, and he'd already been dismissed.

"I'm sorry," Steven said. "But I would still like to know. A lot of people are suffering, like you said. Before I let you crush this idea, *I* need to understand what's wrong with it. I can promise, though, if somebody asks, I'll simply leave it at 'Steven Gold will stay silent on the matter of the Sephardi Chief Rabbi.' Okay?"

The Rabbi chuckled quietly. "Give me one last attempt not to explain," he said.

It was Steven's turn to nod.

"I have a 10-year term," said the Rabbi, "I have such a long term, so that I can act and speak according to the Torah, instead of popular will. You won't change my mind unless you have the Torah-based arguments to do so. And I doubt that you do."

Steven didn't really know what a Torah-based argument was. But he had come armed with one verse he'd heard delivered in a sermon in his Temple. He could deploy that when he needed to. He was confident enough to proceed.

"Just so we understand each other," said Steven, "I have a three-year tenure for the same reason – so I can act as I see fit." The Rabbi smiled softly at this, but Steven didn't understand why. There seemed to be some distinction that Steven didn't grasp.

Steven continued, "The result is that a lot of people aren't happy with me. But even though people are unhappy, I don't think they've given me any good reason to change my position. I'm doing what I think is right. Give me the courtesy of explaining your position and we can discuss it. I understand that we'll probably end up going our separate ways."

After a moment's pause the Rabbi responded, "Okay."

The Rabbi took a deep breath. "There's a joke," he said. "It's now an old joke. The question is asked, 'Why did the Oslo Peace Accords fail?'"

"Why?" asked Steven. He had a perspective: the Israeli government hadn't tried hard enough, and extremists in both camps had hijacked the unique opportunity for peace. But none of his explanations would make a good joke.

The Rabbi answered, "Because the Israelis sent Ashkenazim to negotiate with Arabs."

Steven didn't laugh; he didn't understand.

"Ashkenazim," said the Rabbi, "are Jews whose exile was in Europe. They have a certain culture. They don't understand Arabs. You are an Ashkenazi Jew, from America. But Sephardim and Mizrachim – their exile was in Arab and Muslim lands. They understand the Arabs and the Muslims. Ashkenazim negotiated, but didn't understand the negotiations. Because of this, the negotiations failed. Understand?"

"Yes," said Steven, unsteadily.

"But you don't," said the Rabbi. "And that is the problem. You think you understand what I'm saying. You think your 'reason' can work its way through it. But it can't. You can understand there might be a difference, but you can't understand what it might be."

"That's it?" said Steven, in exasperation, "I just can't understand?"

"Yes," said the Rabbi.

"Try to explain it to me," said Steven, "Give me the courtesy. I mean the Torah says we must resettle slaves who escape from our neighbors. So why shouldn't we rescue these people who are also escaping oppression." He'd deployed the verse he'd wanted to use.

"That is the problem," said the Rabbi. "You cherry pick from the Torah to find the bits that agree with what you already believe. But you can't read the Torah this way. It encompasses all of life. It is our job to conform to it, not to have it conform to us."

"If it isn't telling us to rescue the unfortunate, then what does it mean?" asked Steven, his voice full of challenge. He was beginning to find the Rabbi patronizing, instead of warm.

"The law you mentioned is about slaves – specifically people who had no will of their own – escaping from nearby lands. It isn't about oppressed peoples, but about individuals. The law serves two purposes. The first is to welcome a person to freedom. And not just any person, but a person with such initiative and drive that they've managed to escape the oldest and most successful form of human domination. The second is to weaken your enemies. In this region, your neighbors are your enemies. It has been that way forever. There are few natural defenses – so borders and power are always fluid. If somebody is not under your domain, then they threaten it. If you welcome your enemy's slaves into your lands, then you weaken your enemies. None of this has any relevance to the topic of bringing these warring Arabs into our territory."

"So, the problem is the Arabs?" asked Steven.

"Yes," said the Rabbi. "They are fundamentally interested in conflict. From the very beginning. Ishmael was the son of Avraham, and even before he was born, G-d said that he would be a wild donkey of a man, always fighting with the rest of mankind. G-d also said that Ishmael would dwell on the face of all his brothers. The Arabs want to fight, they want to challenge everybody around them. And they can't allow their brothers' reputation to shine. Instead, they have to dwell on top of it; they have to show their dominance. This is who they are. If somebody should dominate a place they consider theirs – if their brothers should rule over the small land of Israel, they will want to destroy them."

"Isn't it a bit too much to stereotype an entire people based on myths that originated two thousand years ago?" asked Steven. He was stunned by the Rabbi's racism. He realized he was getting angry, just as the Rabbi promised he would. "Aren't people today more responsible for who they choose to be than how some text defines them?"

"No," said the Rabbi, flatly. "This is who these people are. We know them. When Israel was founded, it was such an affront to Arab pride that they began to punish the Jews within their own borders. They had to defend their pride, even from a tiny territory 1/650th the size of the Arab lands. They wouldn't let the Jews leave, of course. They wanted to mock and persecute and hurt them. Like a weak man beating his wife. They denied us jobs. They took our property. They beat some of us to death and they threw rocks at our houses all through the night. They created a culture of constant fear and harassment. Eventually, almost everybody escaped. Before the founding of modern Israel, there were one million Jews in Arab lands. Now, there are fewer than four *thousand*. Today, Europe's population of Jews is 85 percent lower than it was before the Holocaust. But the Arab world's Jewish population has dropped by 99.5 percent. They conducted an almost totally successful campaign of ethnic cleansing. Why? Because Jewish control of this small land was too much of an affront for the children of Ishmael to bear. They are what they always were."

"Even if you believe all this," said Steven, exasperated, "You must believe that there are exceptions. There must be people who stand apart."

"Their society," countered the Rabbi, "isn't like yours. In America, people are searching for meaning. They have nothing real to hold on to.

But in this world, everybody knows their place, and nobody can escape it. If you try, you can find yourself dead. And the whole thing works. They remain Ishmaelites – even thousands of years after Ishmael. And, no, there aren't exceptions. The society is part of the people and the people are part of the society. And the character of that society is unchangeable."

"But if some of them can run to a new place," insisted Steven, "can't they break that pattern and make things better? Can't we create the conditions that can break down their reality?"

The Rabbi laughed, condescendingly. It grated on Steven. "We can risk land for peace – for real peace. But not for pipe dreams. You think you can reason your way through the problem? You think you can find a solution to these problems? It is very American of you. But the fact is that it is out of your hands. The only way we can bring a better outcome is through Torah study. Everything else is pure imagination. Accept that – accept that it is in the hands of the Holy One, Blessed be He – and you may begin to find solutions. But you'll find nothing the way you perceive things now."

"We can influence things," Steven insisted. "We can make smart decisions and we can impact the world. We aren't just helpless fatalists. We have an obligation to help."

"You do have an obligation to help, but you only *think* your efforts influence things," replied the Rabbi. "You know, the Torah records another story about Abraham. It describes a war. It was between a great King named Kedarlaomer and the cities of Sodom and Ammorah. Kedarlaomer got his name because he, Kedar, encircled the Omer – the grain. He was rich and powerful. Sodom and Ammorah, fertile and successful cities both, rebelled. Ammorah was also named after grain. They wanted to break the market. Kedarlaomer came and, on the way, he attacked many third parties. For example, he destroyed the fields of Amalek. He strengthened his hold on the grain market. And then, he attacked Sodom and Ammorah and took everything they had. He had complete control of the entire middle eastern grain market. He was unstoppable, right?"

It was a rhetorical question. Steven kept quiet.

"No," said the Rabbi, "He was not unstoppable. Abraham came and destroyed him. Not with a massive army, but with 318 men. And then, not much later, G-d himself destroyed Sodom. The fact is: G-d decides. If we keep G-d's laws and learn the Torah, then we will be blessed, and these animals will learn their place. And one of G-d's laws requires us not to risk the Jewish people for pipe dreams. Yes, we can help the world – but through Torah, not well-meaning but misguided efforts."

Steven had no idea how to respond. The man was relying on apocryphal stories from thousands of years earlier to argue in the modern age. He was defending racism and fatalism by using books from a time before modern science and reason had changed our understanding of things. It just seemed insane. The world had learned so much, how could this man ignore it? Real people were suffering and this Rabbi, this religious leader, was living in a fantasy. He just looked at the Rabbi, trying to get some sense of how to respond.

"I can see," said the Rabbi, "that you're confused. You think I live in some la-la land. You probably think your world – the enlightened world created by the Europeans – is somehow better. That you've discovered truth and stability and the value of tolerance. But it isn't true. The Europeans have better technology, but not better people. And that technology doesn't eliminate their failures. It just makes them bigger. As bad as the war is here, look at what happened in Europe – even after the supposedly wonderful impact of Amsterdam. Not even half a million people have died in Syria. As many as 80 million were killed in World War Two. Our reality isn't decided by our technology or our reasoning. It is decided by G-d."

"Modern communications," said Steven, "break down barriers and bring people together."

"Do they?" asked the Rabbi. "Or do they just empower the worst impulses of man? Your Facebook and Twitter and Skype have drawn recruits to both the Islamic State and to white supremacist groups. All they've done is super-power these human-driven movements by enabling global groups of these people to connect with one another. And these human-driven impulses almost always lead to death and war. There's a reason many Torah-observant communities don't use your social networking. It isn't to keep our people in darkness. Instead, it is to protect them from it."

Steven couldn't argue with the Rabbi. He knew the Rabbi was wrong, but he was arguing from territory that Steven simply couldn't relate to. He sat, dejected.

"Let me ask you," said the Rabbi, "Why does Modern Israel exist?"

Steven answered, "The U.N. voted it into existence. And when the five Arab armies attacked, the Israelis were successful at defending the land."

"No," said the Rabbi. "You think those are the reasons. But they make no sense. How could this tiny state resist five Arab armies? In reality, we are here because G-d redeemed us. The Jewish people were weak because G-d wanted us to be. It was by design. G-d exiled us and weakened us and punished us so that when He brought us back, we would recognize that *He* brought us home. We would finally recognize that our salvation comes from Him – not from ourselves. This is what he promised to Abraham. And this is what we have to learn if we hope to stay here. G-d will cast us out again unless we recognize that it is G-d who redeems us, not our armies or our science or our Facebook."

"But you said Syria was like another Holocaust?" Steven said, trying to bring the conversation back within more reasonable territory. "Don't we need to help?"

"I think we should help," said the Rabbi, "but not at the risk of Jewish lives. The IDF brings people from the conflict to Israel for medical care every day. That is helping. But it doesn't create risks for us. When Abraham was faced with Kedarlaomer, he didn't attack him right away. He only intervened when his own nephew was threatened. In the meantime, many innocents were killed. The decision troubled him. He was afraid he'd made the wrong choice. The Amalekites – who he didn't rescue – blamed him for failing to help them. They've kept that hateful grudge against us until this very day. But G-d said Abraham had made the right choice. And that's all that matters. We can't carry out our mission by force. We don't destroy evil just because it is evil. And we don't fight for good, just because it is good. If force was all that was needed, G-d would simply impose the reality He wants. We work another way. When we obey G-d, He will bless us so that we become an example to the world. But when we disobey Him, He punishes us – so that we become an example to the world. In either case, our treatment by G-d is an opportunity to improve the world around us by serving as an example. You talk about an example city, but we are an example nation. Like Abraham, we should fight only to save our kin. We cannot force the world into its own redemption."

Steven was frustrated. Even if the story of Abraham mattered as some example of human behavior, how could he argue about Abraham with the Chief Rabbi of Israel? He didn't know enough. He preferred to focus on reality, not mythology.

"I want to put it in the Golan," Steven suddenly burst out. "Except for our police, nobody will be armed. And we'll build a wall around it. It won't threaten the Jewish people!"

"How can you know that?" asked the Rabbi, calmly, "They can always build tunnels. They can shoot missiles. They can insist such a city is a concentration camp and embarrass the Jewish people and demand access to the rest of the land. Your idea will just give our enemies another opportunity to encroach on our safety."

"If we say the place will be Jewish-controlled," Steven countered, "then we'll only attract those people who are inherently more flexible. We'll only attract people who are willing to break with the past. Perhaps, we'll get other minorities like Yazidis or Christians. And we'll draw the strongest people – the people who want to live productive lives. We'll weaken our enemies in the process – just like we would by taking in our neighbor's slaves."

"The fact stands," countered the Rabbi, "that Abraham didn't save Amalek. He had the power. He could defeat Kedarlaomer. But he didn't. We don't learn Law from this, but it can help us understand."

"It isn't a fair comparison," said Steven. He was surprising himself. Now he was arguing about a two-thousand-year-old story like it actually mattered. "Abraham didn't know he had the power. The victory of his three hundred men was a miracle – you said so yourself. And he didn't have land. He certainly didn't have land which had been acquired to provide defensive depth. The Golan is there to provide defensive depth. With this sort of city, the Golan can also provide offensive opportunities. Not to conquer, but to undermine that which makes Israel's neighbors into enemies."

"Mr. Gold," answered the Rabbi, "These are the children of Ishmael. They are snakes who violate treaties and honor such actions.

132

Hamas talks about a truce with Israel – but only so they can grow strong enough to destroy us. Like the ancient residents of Canaan, they offer their own children to the fire. They are so dedicated to submitting to G-d, that they think G-d wants the destruction of all who do not submit. They think it will bring a world of complete harmony. Military jihad – successful war for the honor of G-d – is a fundamental part of their religion."

"And aren't you just like them?" asked Steven, "Don't you think that you alone can change the world because you alone know how to follow G-d?"

It was the Rabbi's turn to bridle. "We aren't like other religions," he said, "Our very existence is evidence of G-d's relationship to us. We have been around – as an identifiable people – for as long as any other nation. And we've spent much of that time in exile. Despite the exile, we have survived, just as the Torah promised. We have evidence."

"I'm sure they think so too," said Steven, "Perhaps their grand military victories count as such evidence."

"Of course they do," said the Rabbi. "But that conquest ended long ago. Our survival continues. But there is something else that is important. They believe they can change the world through force, just like many Christians believe they can change the world through conversion. But you know, with all your enlightenment, that neither is true. People resist force, and they resist uniformity. Even the Muslims, who maintain their religious identification and character, constantly fight with one another. The Islamic road to a messianic future is a mirage. But our road isn't. We don't want to conquer beyond our own little land. Like Abraham, we don't want or need to come into conflict – even religious conflict. Instead, we seek to lead by example. With a dot of territory in the middle of the world, we can follow G-d's laws, be blessed by G-d, and have our blessings demonstrate G-d's presence in the world. In the final book of the Torah, we are to build a rock wall and plaster the words of Torah on it. We are the rocks, imperfect but natural. The Torah is the plaster, enabling our people as a whole to rise above our human limitations. This is a recipe that can work. It isn't some conquest-hungry concept of world domination."

"Rabbi," said Steven, "You're acting as if Islamic State is the standard, not some outlier. If it were standard, your people couldn't have been in Iraq for thousands of years. Your condemnation of Islam as fundamentally violent simply isn't in line with the facts."

"I agree," said the Rabbi. "The Islamic State takes things to an extreme. But I think it is a natural extreme. It fits everything else."

Steven felt almost whiplashed. At the JUC, no criticism of Arab culture was valid. Here, no criticism of Arab culture was sufficient. "No," he thought, "that wasn't quite right." At the JUC no criticism *should* make the Arab nations adapt. Here, no criticism *could* make them adapt. It was, he realized, an important distinction.

Steven remembered something from Sunday school. Something about Abraham negotiating with G-d over the fate of Sodom. It could be an opening.

"Rabbi," Steven said. "Didn't Abraham negotiate with G-d over the fate of Sodom and Gemorrah?"

"Yes," said the Rabbi, "but I also think G-d was teaching Abraham about His own values. G-d basically told Abraham that he would not condemn a society if there was a nucleus of just ten righteous men to reform it. Abraham couldn't imagine any fewer having an impact. But G-d could. G-d sent angels to Sodom and created a pressure-cooker situation. He did it to check whether just one righteous man, Lot, would be a strong enough moral voice to rescue some part of the city. Only

134

when the entire city turned on Lot did G-d's angels decide to destroy it."

Steven thought about asking whether there might be ten righteous men in Iraq and Syria. But he realized that G-d was not condemning Iraq and Syria – they were condemning themselves. Thus, the Rabbi might dismiss his argument. On a hunch, he asked, "Rabbi, did G-d ever destroy another place like he did Sodom and Gemorrah?"

"No," said the Rabbi.

"Why not?" asked Steven.

"Because, almost immediately afterwards, Yitzchak was born. When Avraham had a son to carry on his legacy, the Jewish people were established."

"Why would that matter?" asked Steven. He suspected he knew the answer.

The Rabbi paused for a moment and then smiled, "Yitzchak and his descendants are to be the moral voice that can rescue the world. They are to be hated like Lot. But because we are a people, rather than individuals, we can be a more successful moral voice than Lot was."

Pressing his advantage, Steven spoke. "Rabbi, we don't have to pick sides. We just have to give people an opportunity to hear us. Their societies are locking out our voices. But we can bring them to this place – even just ten of them – and we can strengthen the moral voice that can improve their societies and prevent the destruction that is overwhelming them. It is our place, isn't it? Won't G-d bless our efforts?"

The Rabbi paused for a long moment. Then he got up and walked to a shelf. He pulled down a book, brought it to the small desk, and flicked on the light. He flipped through the tome quickly, found what he was looking for, read carefully, and then closed and replaced the book itself.

Finally, he turned to Steven.

"The Law isn't determined by arguments about Abraham. The Oral Torah, passed down from Moses himself and through the Talmud, is our guide. But I agree with you. It is the role of the Jewish people to serve as a moral voice. Sodom never occurred again because we exist. But we exist to prevent Sodom from ever occurring again. Their societies have locked us out. They are destroying themselves. But it might be happening precisely because they no longer have us among them, acting as a moral voice within their lands. If we can expose even a small number among them to a new path, then perhaps we can rescue them from the Holocaust of their own making."

"Okay?" said Steven, uncertain.

"So," said the Rabbi, "with all that in mind, I can support your project. You are right, we can use a tiny city to provide a moral voice for these societies. But there are two conditions, conditions necessary to keep the place from becoming dangerous to us."

"What are the conditions?" asked Steven.

"First," said the Rabbi, "the place must be governed by Jews. Handing it over to the Arabs and the Muslims will result in catastrophe. They will destroy each other and battle us. Second, the City must be made as strategically irrelevant as possible – from a military perspective."

"Okay," said Steven. The requirement for Jewish control bothered him, but he saw no way to push back on it. In time, he told himself, he'd be able to show the Rabbi his racism was unwarranted.

"I'm not endorsing the idea," said the Rabbi, "I'm not a politician. I run a state-sanctioned Rabbinic organization. I can't even begin to make these kinds of decisions. But I'll introduce you to other people: people with real political power. And if the military and economic ministers agree with your proposal, then I will endorse it as well – from a religious perspective."

Steven wanted to jump for joy. But he was also confused. The Rabbi seemed incapable of reason – but somehow, Steven had reasoned with him. Steven didn't understand how.

The two of them rose and shook hands.

"My secretary will be in touch," said the Rabbi.

And with that, Steven left the magical little room and emerged back into the harsh whiteness of the world outside. He was jubilant. He had found a way to help.

As he left the building, Steven thought about calling Amy. But he needed to think, just a bit more, first. Steven noticed the red and white stripes that lined the curb outside the building. Steven had always considered them unnecessarily obnoxious – like they had to scream about where you were, and where you weren't, allowed to park. But suddenly, in that moment, they made sense.

In Israel, so many people from so many cultures had come together in so short a time that there were no general rules or expectations for behavior. There was no common basis, even for reason itself.

The curb had to shout about where you could or could not park, because otherwise, people might not know how to listen.

He called a taxi on his phone. As he waited, he realized he could boil down his rule. In Israel, everybody knew what they wanted to do, but they had no idea how they were supposed to do it. Nonetheless, somehow, they worked it out.

It was a very flexible reality.

Steven realized, as he stepped into the taxi, that this was the only country in the world where an idea as strange as his own could actually become reality.

He didn't know any of the people he'd be helping, and they didn't know him. But already, he was on the road to transforming their lives.

With that happy thought, he picked up his phone and called his wife.

# Nikah

*December 5th, 2008: Abu Kamal, Syria*

"You understand that I'm not wealthy?" Mohammed asked, quietly.

The woman standing in front of him was named Aisha. She was clothed in an all-covering burqa, but Mohammed could not help but see that she had a shapely figure. Young men in his society could see a lot – despite the burqa. Mohammed's eyes were cast downwards, but his imagination was running away from him.

He closed his eyes for a moment and remembered the words of Mohammed: "Whenever a man is alone with a woman, Satan is the third among them." They weren't alone, of course, but he could feel the presence of Satan. He could feel Satan's presence threatening to undermine his dedication to All-h.

Somehow, Aisha unbalanced him more than even the man from the Mukhabarat had.

Perhaps it was because he wasn't used to talking to women.

Mohammed and Aisha were standing near one another in a courtyard. The courtyard was in the center of a grand home. It was probably the grandest home in Abu Kamal. The interior walls of the house surrounded them. Carved archways, intricately decorated windows and an impressive mosaic floor competed with slender trees and greenery that seemed to pop out of every available crevice. A fountain stood in the middle of all, seeming to compel the air of the courtyard to deliver on its own promise of refreshment.

Mohammed and Aisha weren't standing near the fountain. Its bubbling would have covered the content of their conversation. Of course, every word he and the woman said was being listened to by their extended families. Everything – their words and their movements – would be analyzed later. The families needed to determine that the two of them were suitable. "Chemistry" was unnecessary. After all, a marriage was really about joining families, not individuals. Through the web of marriage, an entire society could be knit together. Nonetheless, some basic level of compatibility was needed.

So, as they spoke, Aisha and Mohammed's only hope for privacy was brought by the giggling of the children who scampered around the protected space.

Mohammed glanced up at her, briefly, just to hear her answer. He was well aware that the Koran commanded Muslims to "lower their gaze and guard their modesty."

"I understand," she said. Her voice was demure, but her eyes flashed with excitement.

Mohammed knew that she didn't. She couldn't really understand the impact of poverty. She came from the wealthiest family in Abu Kamal.

It was remarkable that Mohammed could make such a match. It was remarkable he could make any match.

After all, when Muslims married, they gave their brides a *Mahr*, a gift. Should the marriage end, the bride would keep the *Mahr* – as an endowment to protect against the ravages of being a divorcee or a widow. The *Mahr* was required to be paid in two parts – the first upfront, and the second over time. As a 16-year-old impoverished orphan, a substantial *Mahr* was out of his reach. Thus, finding a willing bride was supposed to have been difficult.

But there was a greater problem. In Abu Kamal, like many places, a bride-price was also expected. Young men who hoped to marry were expected to give their fathers-in-law a substantial payment for their daughters' hands. After all, while a bride could technically refuse to marry a man, only her *wali* – or male guardian – could chose potential spouses. It took more than a little money to encourage the *wali* of a wealthy and possibly beautiful young woman to choose you.

Without money, Mohammed's choices were supposed to have been seriously limited.

Nonetheless, here he was, talking to the daughter of one of the most respected men in Abu Kamal.

He wondered whether she might have some secret disfigurement. Mohammed tried to tell himself it wouldn't matter. The bride was a means to an end – only through family could the relationship with All-h be continued. But despite his efforts, he couldn't entirely convince himself of the truth of that position.

Aisha spoke, "I want to live as a slave to All-h. I want to earn paradise. We do not need money to acquire the greatest of gifts."

Mohammed nodded; it was the answer he hoped for.

But he did not yet know whether he believed it.


After his parents died, Mohammed observed the prescribed three days of mourning. Countless people came to his sparse warehouse and offered their curt condolences. To make too big a show of death was seen as glorifying disaster. Mohammed told every visitor that he would revenge his parents and protect the glory and honor of G-d. He wasn't speaking in anger; he was broadcasting a message. With his mother gone, he didn't know who was running the Mujahidin in his region. He didn't know if *anybody* was. But whoever was in charge, or whoever was going to be in charge, needed to know that he was a ready fighter.

After those three days, Mohammed had left the warehouse. It was unbecoming of a 16-year-old boy to live alone. There were too many opportunities for sin. Instead, he moved in with his uncle and his aunt. They had a modest home – an apartment on a crowded street in the desert part of the town. Mohammed's presence was a major inconvenience. Before, his aunt and her daughters could walk in their own apartment without the niqab; only their immediate family was there. But with Mohammed present, all of them had to cover themselves anytime they were outside the women's quarters. It was uncomfortable.

Thus, within days of Mohammed arriving, they had begun to try to find him a wife. His aunt was desperate for him to leave. But everyone knew the search would not be easy. Mohammed had no money, and many young men wanted to be warriors for All-h. The fact that both his parents had been martyrs allowed him to stand out some, but the impact was limited. Wealthy men could take two wives, so there were few options left over for those like Mohammed.

Nobody was surprised when his family's inquiries yielded no response at all.

For his part, Mohammed wanted to be married. Simple *shahids*, martyrs, didn't need to be married. But Mohammed wanted to turn the tide of the war. In fact, he wanted to do more than that: he wanted to win the war. And for that to happen, he had to enter the ranks of leadership.

An unmarried man could never achieve such status.

But the weeks dragged on, without any response to his uncle's and his aunt's pleas.

Mohammed had been walking, heading to the market, when a van drove past him and a body was flung from the side of it. It was the mutilated, but living, body of Omar bin Abdullah. The young man was screaming in pain. Mohammed felt Omar's anguish pierce the core of his soul. Omar had suffered, terribly. He had been sacrificed. But, unmarried, Mohammed could not make Omar's sacrifice worthwhile. He could not rise in the ranks and betray their Shia and Alawite oppressors.

He was frightened, deeply frightened, that he would waste his own life, and Omar's, in pointlessness.

When the promised bullet pierced Omar's skull – and he fell dead onto the street – Mohammed was overwhelmed. He had a holy responsibility to make Omar's sacrifice worthwhile. But he had no way to deliver on it. He was unmarried, and without prospects. He had no path to achievement. With sickening fear, he realized he may have given another man's life away for nothing but his own vanity.

As Omar's blood was sucked into the sandy street, Mohammed grasped desperately for a shred of hope. He could be a martyr, he reasoned. But anybody could. Omar's death would serve no purpose. Perhaps he could join the Mujahidin in Iraq or Afghanistan, and thus earn the reputation necessary to find a wife and ascend the ranks and fulfill his promise. But that path was a long and desperate one, and his betrayal of Omar would have earned him nothing.

Omar's death hung over him, and so he hardly noticed the next day when a man bumped him on the street. When Mohammed returned to his uncle's home, he found a note in his jacket. It instructed him to carry a package – from one location to another. With relief, Mohammed realized that he had inherited Omar's job. The delivery was routine. It was a simple test of his interest, his reliability, and his discretion. He accomplished it, and more deliveries followed. And, aside from the first, each came with a small amount of payment.

Unlike Omar, Mohammed had no truck. He would simply put the packages, whatever they were, in his bag, and then walk from one location to the other. The deliveries were tedious. But like a shepherd herding sheep, Mohammed found that the monotony was an opportunity for thought.

Initially, those thoughts were hopeful. But as the days passed, he realized that being a courier brought no greater opportunities than he'd had before. After all, how can one distinguish oneself carrying packages from here to there? The thoughts that occupied his mind on his long walks shifted from hopes for great future success, to the pointlessness of the courier system itself. The courier system, long trusted and used by the Mujahidin, was fraught with risk and danger – even though the men within it were trusted implicitly. After all, with enough men and a bit of technology (and the Mukhabarat could muster both), the couriers and their drop-spots and pick-up points could be monitored. Even private locations could be surreptitiously watched. With this surveillance, a patient enemy could reconstruct the entire network of Mujahidin operatives. They could know more about the Sunni resistance than the Sunni resistance knew themselves.

Mohammed remembered that this is what the Americans had done in Iraq. His mother had talked about how the Americans, with their drones, had tried analyzing the movement of every car and person over an extended area and period of time. If there were a bombing, they would work backwards, assembling the chain of events and people that had led to the event. With just a few pieces of the puzzle, they believed their computers could assemble a framework of guerilla movements and unlock a network of targets. Their approach had been very costly at first – many fighters had been captured or killed. But Mohammed's mother, of all people, had solved the problem. She'd had the fighters park their vehicles in large, covered parking lots, and meet in very popular covered locations. The drones could only see who came and left. By dramatically increasing the number of possible suspects who had to be tracked, the puzzle was made infinitely more complex. Thus, the American program had been undermined. His mother had been clever.

But the Alawi were different. It would take them a few years to catch up technologically. But when they did, they wouldn't have to rely on drones for their surveillance.

All of this presented both a problem and the opportunity to design a solution. There were things that could be used to conceal patterns of movement – chalk markings, irregular timings, large groupings, and so on. But Mohammed had been trained in none of these – so other couriers hadn't either. And sneakiness was only as effective as one's enemies were careless or remote. The Alawites and their Shiite accomplices were neither careless nor remote.

There had to be a better way.

Of course, while very real, the problem was entirely theoretical. There was no way for him, a 16-year-old at the bottom of a vast pyramid, to shake what were the well-rooted foundations of how the Mujahidin operated.

But he had nothing better to do. He had many places to walk, and seemingly infinite time. So, as he walked, he thought and thought about solutions.

It was during one of these walks, just a few weeks into his new role, when a van pulled up alongside him. There was nobody else on the street, and so there was no point in shouting. A door opened, and two large men jumped out. Moments later they had thrown a bag over Mohammed's head and then bundled him into the van and sped away.

Mohammed's first thought was that he had been kidnapped by the Mukhabarat. He wasn't panicked. Whenever they got to where they were going, he would simply explain everything. These men's superiors would be informed, and Mohammed would be returned to the very street they had snatched him from. After all, administrative screw-ups happened. In fact, Mohammed realized, he didn't have to wait for them to get anywhere; he could start talking right away.

He was about to do just that when the van lurched to the side. As he recovered his balance, Mohammed paused just long enough for his blindfold to save his life. Mohammed realized that he couldn't see the men. But he *could* smell the van. As it bounced along the imperfectly paved road, he realized that it smelled of old food and old sweat. It smelled like it had been lived in for days. It smelled like travel.

With that, Mohammed knew that the men in the van must have been sent from somewhere else. But why? If they had been Mukhabarat, that would have been unnecessary. The Mukhabarat wouldn't send a group of men on a journey of several days to arrest a courier – administrative mistake or not. No, the men in the van weren't local, because it was important that Mohammed not recognize them. They were a part of some ruse that involved concealment of their true identities. The Mukhabarat had no reason to play such complicated games; not with a boy who was still just a courier.

But the Mujahidin, his own people, would have reasons to play such games. If the Mujahidin wanted to test his loyalty by pretending to be from the Mukhabarat, only men from far away would be able to pull it off. Mohammed might recognize locals. If Mohammed had opened his mouth – had shared his connection to the Mukhabarat – he never would have left the van alive. His nose had saved him.

As the van continued to bump along the road, Mohammed realized that he had to play this particular game very, very carefully. They couldn't suspect that he wasn't properly frightened.

Eventually, the van moved off the road. The jostling of the van did not have the sharp impacts of desert rocks, but the rolling character of tiny dirt hillocks. They were near the river, and they were close to their destination. It took far more effort than Mohammed imagined, possibly, but when the van drew to a stop, he managed to void his bowels. Mohammed wasn't a superb actor, and so he knew this sort of evidence would be needed to convince his captors that he was properly frightened.

The men lifted him roughly once again and wordlessly dragged him indoors. Then, they shoved him to the ground, shackled him and removed his hood.

Mohammed blinked in the sudden light. Standing in front of him was a slightly overweight man in a light jacket. It seemed to be the accepted uniform of Mukhabarat foot-soldiers. He was a remarkably light-skinned man with a particularly craggy face, considering he could not have been over 35. In fact, he looked almost Alawite. But Mohammed was *reasonably* sure that he was not.

Mohammed looked around. He was in a ramshackle hut in the middle of a field somewhere. Light burst from the corners of the tiny space where the walls did not come completely together. Ignoring his own stench, Mohammed realized the place smelled like irrigation, and life. He could see mosses and molds crawling their way up the metal siding that served as walls. It was, in its way, a hopeful place.

He didn't suppose that was the effect his interrogators were seeking.

He asked, in his best shaking voice, "What do you want?"

"We want to be your friends, Mohammed bin Hassan."

Mohammed tried to look confused.

"We would like to pay you," continued the man, by way of explanation, "in exchange for information."

"Who are you?" demanded Mohammed, his voice quickening. "What information?"

"You are a courier for the Mujahidin," said the man. "We can make such work quite lucrative."

"I'm not a courier," said Mohammed.

"We see you walking," said the man, "from here to there and everywhere. You're a courier."

"No," replied Mohammed, "My parents died recently. They were killed by the Americans. I just walk because it makes me feel better."

The man smiled, evilly. Unlike Mohammed, he was clearly a skilled actor. This kind of work demanded it.

"Mohammed, Mohammed," he said, slowly, "You and I know better than that. And you and I know the consequences of refusing our offer. You did watch Omar bin Abdullah die, didn't you? He was the courier before you."

Mohammed tried to open his eyes wider. In fear. But now he was completely certain the man was not from the Mukhabarat.

And then, suddenly, he realized *this* was his opportunity.

"You know I'm not a courier," said Mohammed, insistently.

"The package you were carrying," said the man, "It contained plastic explosives. Care to tell me the truth now?"

"That's ridiculous," said Mohammed. "You had to have made that up."

The man looked angry, as he should have. He hadn't made it up, of course. While Mohammed didn't know what was in the package, plastic explosives were not unlikely.

"Are you accusing me of lying?" asked the man, belligerently.

"Yes," said Mohammed. And then he braced himself, "You must be. You'd never pick a courier up on the street. You'd just follow them. With a little surveillance and leg work, both enabled by modern technology, you'd be able to piece together the entire Mujahidin network. Picking a courier up burns them. Thus, you know I'm not a courier."

The man was thrown off by the answer. This was supposed to be a one-dimensional tug of wills. Through inducement or fear, he was supposed to test Mohammed's commitment. He wasn't expecting another dimension to the conversation. Certainly, he *knew* Mohammed was a courier. But the response was so reasonable, he almost doubted himself.

"Why'd we kill Omar?" he asked. Perhaps he was hoping Mohammed would explain that mystery. But Mohammed only wanted to change the subject.

"I have no idea!" he said, "But Omar couldn't have been a courier either. There are no couriers!"

"What?" asked the man. He was too shocked by the obvious lie to be angry.

"I'm not part of the Mujahidin," Mohammed continued. "But my father was. And because of that, I know a little about how they work. They no longer use couriers. And you know it."

Now it was the man's turn to be confused – he had clearly not expected this line of defense. He tried not to show it, but Mohammed had wrestled some kind of advantage from him.

"What?" he asked, his confusion growing.

"It's too risky," said Mohammed, "That's why they stopped. The fight in Iraq, with the Americans, made them stop."

Mohammed could see the man trying to work things out. His subject, Mohammed, was seeming to be revealing the secrets of the Mujahidin. He was seeming to have been almost helpful to the Mukhabarat. But the man himself knew that Mohammed – and Omar before him – were couriers. Mohammed was lying, but the man couldn't let him know how he knew that. He clearly didn't know what to do next.

"Tell me more!" he demanded, almost out of desperation. It was the path Mohammed hoped he'd choose.

"I don't know much more," said Mohammed. "I mean, I know they've improved how they do things. If I had to guess, I'd say they send a flurry of messages now. Some are by email or text, some by mail. They even use Shia deliverymen. But the individual messages mean nothing. They are bits of a greater whole disguised in spam and routine communications. But the recipient knows how to put them together. Thus, the message is properly transmitted. Everybody between him the sender has no idea – can have no idea – of what's being said. That's the obvious way it has to work."

"What about packages?" asked the man. He was clearly curious.

"It depends on the material. Fertilizer can be shipped to Shia farmers and then stolen from them. Whole guns would never be shipped – just equipment that could make the parts. We'd use DHL and describe the parts as having other uses. Preferably, we'd break them up and make them components of other things. Barrels are, of course, hard to hide in this way. But they are reasonably cheap – and the Mujahidin have money. Thus, they would ship a bunch of them out – to a bunch of people, including those totally uninvolved in the Mujahidin. Some of them would even go to easily robbed houses where they could be collected by Sunni thieves. The recipients would know the addresses to pick things up from because they would be told using the messaging I described before. The whole idea would be to create so much noise that that the surveillance wouldn't be able to know what's actually happening or who is getting what. I mean, I don't know how they do it in reality. But I imagine that's their technique."

"Do they ship money that way too?" asked the man.

"You probably know better than I," said Mohammed. "I'm not in the Mujahidin or the Mukhabarat. But I'd imagine innocent family visits would be a cover for sending money. There would be couriers then, but not running a regular route. They'd have nothing to distinguish them from totally innocent travelers."

The man stood there, thinking. Mohammed knew he was trying to figure out what to do next. Should he report Mohammed as having been easily turned into a traitor – even though everything he said was a lie? What was the proper course when nothing added up? Mohammed let him think for a bit longer, and then he guided him along the final steps.

"You," said Mohammed, "aren't here to get information from me."

The man's face turned up quickly.

"If you were, you'd ask me to find out something more specific about the patterns used by the Mujahidin. But that question didn't occur to you because you are here on another job entirely."

"What are you talking about?" asked the man. It was his turn to be defensive.

"You aren't with the Mukhabarat," said Mohammed. "I knew it when I was still in the van. Of course, I couldn't let you know. You might have reacted badly if I hadn't appeared to be afraid."

The man looked at him, his head cocked at an angle.

"It smelled," said Mohammed, "The van smelled like men had been traveling in it for days. The Mukhabarat would use more readily available resources to question a simple courier."

"So, you are a courier!" said the man, almost triumphantly.

"Are you going to congratulate yourself for confirming what you knew before you even came to Abu Kamal?" Mohammed's voice was reproachful.

The man looked a little chagrined. And more than a bit confused. He still didn't understand what had happened.

"What I told you," said Mohammed, "about communicating. It makes sense. You know it. Assuring you that I'm trustworthy isn't enough to secure our communications. Our enemies can follow even the most trustworthy of men. So, tell your commanders that I am trustworthy. And tell them what I told you. We need to change how we do things."

The man nodded, as if he was suddenly ready to take orders from a sixteen-year-old.

Mohammed nodded back. Despite being shackled on the floor, he seemed comfortable in his role as commander.

"Get me some fresh clothes," said Mohammed, "And drive me home. When we're there, I'll need you to come out with me. To protect my own reputation, people have to see you aren't the ghosts of the Mukhabarat."

The man nodded again. He clicked his fingers, and two larger men entered the room. Mohammed figured this was about the time in the process when inducement changed to fear. They certainly looked like they were willing to torture him. But the man's voice stopped them. "Treat this one with respect," he said, "He has more than passed our test."

They, too, were confused. But they followed their orders.

Mohammed returned home, unhurt.

And the next day, his family's desperate search for a potential wife was finally rewarded. His uncle and aunt were told that Sheikh Abdul bin Hassan himself wished to have his daughter meet Mohammed.

The family was shocked, of course. Even Mohammed was shocked. There were two reasons such a woman might be ready to meet him. The first was that she had some horrible defect. Normally, Mohammed's mother would have confirmed that Aisha was not disfigured or otherwise damaged. But Mohammed had no mother. Instead, his extended family, his uncle and aunt, were handling the marriage negotiations on his behalf. If Aisha had a disfigurement – or was shockingly ugly – his aunt would say nothing. She wanted him out of her house. The second possibility, the one that Mohammed hoped for, was that her father saw Mohammed as a poor but promising young man.

There was a third possibility. It was possible that both were true.

"You know," said Mohammed, as they stood in the beautiful courtyard, "That I have no parents. Our children will only have one set of grandparents."

The young woman in front of him looked at him, directly. "The Prophet Mohammed, peace be upon him, was an orphan," she said, evenly. "Did his wives regret their marriages?"

"I'm not that Mohammed," Mohammed said. He could not be compared to the Prophet.

"And I," said Aisha, "am not that Aisha."

He nodded. She might be defective in body, he didn't know. But she was not defective in mind or in spirit. He could do no better.

He dipped his head modestly and lowered his eyes to the ground. "I will ask your father for marriage," he said, simply.

"And I," she said, her expression hidden by her burka, "will accept."

Eight sentences – that was all they had exchanged. But with that, they were engaged.

Her father, a graying man with a rugged and kindly face, negotiated the marriage contract on her behalf. Mohammed's *mahr*, his endowment to his wife, was the warehouse his parents had died in. While he owned it, legally, everybody knew that it belonged to the Mujahidin. Nonetheless, the fiction was allowed to stand. There was no bride price. Nothing Mohammed had could have impacted the wealth of Sheikh Abdul bin Hassan.

The engagement was only a few days long. There was no reason to wait. As befitted an impoverished groom, the *nikah*, or marriage ceremony was a simple affair. A small crowd of men assembled under the watchful eye of the *qadi*. Aisha was not present, of course. Instead, as was proper, Abdul signed the marriage contract on behalf of his daughter. Abdul dedicated his daughter to Mohammed.

And, with that, they were married.

The wedding feast, attended by the men of each family, was a modest affair. It was only after that feast that the couple actually met.

They entered her warehouse together. And then, between the exposed metal rafters and the concrete floor, Aisha finally removed her burqa. It was then that Mohammed knew she had not married him out of any form of desperation. She was beautiful, more beautiful than he had imagined possible. Somehow, by dint of a twisted interrogation, he had married far above his station.

Aisha was pregnant by the end of their first month together. She told him, joyfully, that she was expecting their first child. Mohammed found himself almost wishing that he could disappear into this domestic bliss. But she could have had children with any man. She had chosen him precisely because she wanted more from her life and more from her husband. He smiled deeply. He would do his best to raise his child. But should the risks of his life overwhelm him, he was confident that Aisha would raise the child in his footsteps.

With the expectation of a child, Mohammed had finally achieved the status necessary for leadership. He could finally see a route to repaying Omar's investment.

Mohammed was not surprised when, the same day in December 2008 that his wife learned she was pregnant, his wealthy and influential father-in-law summoned him for a meeting. There were five men at the meeting. They were the council that had replaced his mother. They were all trusted. They were all invested. And they were all, through the tender coils of family that wove through Abu Kamal, related. As he looked around the room, Mohammed realized that he would betray each and every one of them. But he would only betray them as mortal men; as slaves of All-h, they would ultimately rejoice at what their lives would purchase. They would be glad to sacrifice themselves for the cause of

Islam. They would be honored to serve as stepping stones for True Islam's great victories to come.

It was with a content smile that Mohammed watched them and listened to them and plotted his path to the very top of the Mujahidin.

# Silence

*July 20th, 2014: Northern Iraq*

When I heard the engines, the world just seemed to slow down. I knew, with incredible clarity, what I had to do.

I had to find my brother.

I had to find our emergency bag.

And we had to hide.

I couldn't tell how far away the engines were. I could find out. If I walked along the edges of the tiny village, I could spot the vehicles. But no matter how far they were, I had to move as quickly as I possibly could. Thus, I decided not to try and find out.

I knew what my priorities were. First was my brother, second was the bag and the third was hiding. Brother, Bag, Hide.

But that wasn't the order I'd follow. I didn't know where my brother was, but I knew where the bag was. I decided to go for it first, and look for him along the way.

I ran, as fast as I could, towards the house we'd stayed in when we first arrived in the village. As I ran, my eyes scanned for any signs of my brother, but I saw nothing.

I flung open the door and found the bag was where I expected it. I already knew it had water and food – ready to go. At least I hadn't neglected that.

I dashed back out of the house, but I didn't know where to go next. I couldn't possibly search the entire village – much less the fields and rivers – in the time I had. I had to pick likely spots. But, before, my brother had always been with me. I had no idea where he'd go by himself.

I saw a cloud of sand rising up between the houses. I knew then where the vehicles were. I wanted to look, to judge how much time I had, but I resisted the urge. I didn't *need* to know. I had to find Ibrahim, no matter how much time I had. And I couldn't afford to let the people in the vehicles see me.

I realized I could eliminate the fields quickly. We'd harvested them, they were shaved clean. Unless he was tucked behind one of the cast-up boulders, he would stick out – especially if you knew he was there. I ran to the edge of the village and scanned over the familiar crop land. But he was nowhere to be seen. Everything was as it had been the day before.

I glanced over my shoulder. The dust clouds were growing larger. The sounds of the engines were louder.

If he wasn't in the village, he had a chance of being safe. He might be among the boulders that jutted out of the ground. That was where I wanted to us to hide. But I wanted *us* to hide there, not just me.

I ran back into the center of the village. There were 12 houses. Only 12. And they were tiny. It was really 12 rooms in one very large house. I'd already searched one. I could search 11 rooms in a large house, couldn't I? I started with the nearest one. I threw open the door, glanced around the room, saw nothing – and ran out.

The cloud was growing larger. The sound of the engines was growing clearer.

I threw open a second door. Nothing.

I ran out.

I saw the nose of a truck between two houses. It was only a few hundred meters away.

In desperation, I threw open a third door. Once again, there was nothing.

I ran out. The trucks were close. I was running out of time. If they found me, scampering between buildings, I would have no hope.

I began to run towards the next house. If Ibrahim wasn't there, I'd hide and I'd pray. There was nothing else to do.

That was when I heard him scream. It was the engines; they had frightened him, and he was screaming.

For the second time, his fear was my joy. The noise was coming from the shed. I turned and rushed there. I found him, on the floor, covering his ears. His eyes looked like they had when he'd first woken from his coma. They looked like they had when I'd run the AMAR Industries threshing machine. He was overwhelmed with fear.

The trucks were getting closer. If he was screaming, they would be certain to find us.

I uttered a brief prayer for forgiveness and then I clamped his mouth with my hand – muffling his shout. I dragged him, kicking violently, behind the big threshing machine. "Hush, hush," I whispered, but to little effect. He was breathing frantically through his nose. If anybody came into this building, or even near it, I was worried that I'd have to hold his nose as well.

As we sat there, the trucks outside crunched to a stop. I closed my eyes in prayer and wrapped my legs around my brother's legs. I was much stronger. I was able to control him.

I heard doors open and calm voices talking to one another.

"This is not an impressive place," said one even voice. It was young, and male, but it carried the voice of command.

"We knew that before we came here," said another. This voice was also young and male, but it seemed a bit jumpier, a bit less certain and a bit less stable. "It is tiny. Only 93 hectares. There's a reason it's near the bottom of the list."

"Christian?" asked the commander.

"Of course," came the answer.

I could hear other men as well. They chatted amongst each other, but it was casual chatter – nothing serious was being said. I looked at my brother, willing him to be quiet. I couldn't understand what these men wanted, but I could tell they were dangerous.

"Who's the headman?" asked the commander.

"Ishaia Kaku," answered the voice. "I know very little about him."

"Okay," said the commander. "I can see the storehouse over there. Let's check it out."

I heard the crunching of feet, drawing even closer.

"It's full," came a surprised voice. "But it's small."

"Make the call," said the commander.

They were so close I could hear their phone vibrating as they entered a number into it. The phone was on speaker. I heard it ring.

A man picked up.

"Hello?" he asked.

"Ishaia?" asked the commander.

"Yes," said the man on the phone, nervously.

"My name is Fareed," said the commander.

"Okay," said Ishaia.

"I'm in your village," said Fareed. "And I can see you've done an excellent job tending your fields."

"I have?" said Ishaia, in some confusion.

"Before you left," said Fareed, not noticing, "You harvested and threshed all of your grain. We appreciate that."

Even over the phone and through the wall of the shed, Ishaia's confusion was palpable.

Fareed continued, "We need good farmers. We'd like you to come back and farm. It is one of the key industries of this region, and it will be a bedrock for the economic health of our state."

"What?" asked Ishaia, still sounding confused.

Fareed continued. "We need skilled farmers," he repeated, "and we'd like you to come back. The grain in your storehouses and in your fields will remain yours."

"Fareed," said Ishaia, "are you with Daesh?"

He used the name so many did when referring to the Islamic State. It was vaguely insulting.

"Yes," said Fareed.

"What would make you think I'd want to come back?" asked Ishaia.

"We won't kill you," said Fareed. "Instead, you will convert to Islam and you will live a proper life. And you will be honored among the slaves of All-h. And you will have your livelihood back – you won't need to be refugees anymore."

"I understand," said Ishaia.

"So, will you return?" asked Fareed.

"Fareed," said Ishaia, calmly, "I am Assyrian. My people have been there, in that land, for over three thousand years. We have been Christian for two millennia. We have lived under Muslim oppression for close to fifteen hundred years. But we remain Christian and Assyrian. We were before your people existed and we will remain so after your disgusting Daesh vanishes. I won't convert. My people, somehow, will outlast your sickness. And then, but only then, will we return."

"You understand," replied Fareed, "that we have now offered you your farm and your grain, but you have refused?"

"I understand," said Ishaia.

"It is wartime," said Fareed, "so we must requisition what you have to fight against the enemies of All-h. It is not theft – because we have given you the opportunity to retain your property as a Muslim. Do you understand?"

"I believe you are destroyers," Ishaia answered, a layer of anger in his voice, "and I believe you are the servants of Satan. I believe you twist and pervert your law and the will of G-d to suit your own sickness. I believe you will burn in the fires of hell. But I understand."

"Thank you," said Fareed. And then he ended the call.

In a louder voice, Fareed announced. "This village is like all the others. Take everything of value."

The engines had been off for a while, so Ibrahim had quieted down. Except for the sound of the men, it sounded like it had; it sounded peaceful. But then the engines started again, and Ibrahim's panic returned. I could hear a semi-truck rumble close to the shed. Then I heard the cranking of chains and the groan of metal. I knew what I was hearing. The men were lifting the barrels of grain onto the back of their truck. They were taking everything Ibrahim and I had created.

I sat there, in the shed, mournfully, as the village was stripped of everything even remotely valuable. The sounds of industry I had grown up with seemed evil. They were being used to destroy the other world I had discovered.

I was worried they would find the unlocked houses unusual. I was worried they would be suspicious of the doors I'd flung open. I was worried they would find us and kill us. They noticed everything, of course. But they explained it away. When a man told Fareed that the houses had been picked clean and the doors left open, Fareed was not bothered. He uttered just one word, "Thieves."

Eventually, the men made their way to the shed. They cast open the doors, shining the light of the sun everywhere but behind our AMAL Industries thresher.

"Fareed!" cried out a voice.

I bit my lip to stop from crying.

I heard Fareed walk over. "Yes?" he asked.

"Do we take the machine?"

Fareed didn't reply. Instead he walked up to the machine, less than a meter from me and Ibrahim. I could hear his breathing. He was examining it carefully. And then I heard him walk around the side of it, towards us.

I held still and closed my eyes, as if the monster would be unable to see us if we did not move – and did not look at him.

It was the only hope I had.

But then I knew that he had seen us. I opened my eyes and looked straight at him. He was wearing a three-quarter length tunic – favored by the radicals – and had a scraggly beard which seemed to sprout from random portions of his face. He was young, almost as young as I was.

He saw me. And he looked at me. I could see him thinking.

I silently mouthed a prayer to All-h.

He noticed. He seemed to smile at that.

And then he turned and walked back to the front of the shed.

"We have combines," he said, casually. "If farmland is any good, then this machine is useless. Let's leave it until we find farmers for this place."

"Okay," said the soldier. And with that, they closed the shed.

Ten minutes later, Fareed and his scavengers were gone.

Ibrahim and I stood and walked out of the small shed.

As I looked around the village, it seemed unchanged. But I knew that there was nothing more for us here.

All we had was the backpack of emergency supplies – and our lives.

Once again, we began to walk.

But I had no idea where we'd go.

And I had no idea how we'd survive.

# Favors

*September 4th, 2013: Jerusalem, Israel*

"People must have a thing for door buzzers here," thought Steven Gold as he walked into yet another office. He'd been to dozens of offices. With the exception of some belonging to low-ranking officials, every one of them seemed to have a secretary with a buzzer. There was no pattern to the secretaries themselves. But whether male or female, young or old, sleepy or engaged, their power and prestige seemed to be invested in the power of the button. It was a strange nod to consistency in a place that seemed to avoid anything systematic. This particular office was the most important he'd yet visited, so Steven had hoped for something distinct in the door buzzing department. But he'd been disappointed.

As he entered, Steven was surprised by how plain and small the office was. There was a faux wooden desk with a stack of faux wooden shelves lining one wall. But they looked cheap and old, like they had been purchased from IKEA knockoffs in the 1970s. The walls were a boring beige. And while the emblem of the State of Israel hung over the desk, even its splash of blue looked worn. There was no window. The place even smelled cheap. There was an underlying odor of decades-old cigarette smoke that seemed to be embedded in the carpets and the walls. The overloud whir of the air-conditioner testified to a long and losing struggle against the heat.

The low-budget feel of this particular office was so glaring that Steven couldn't help but think it was intentional.

Growing up, Steven had always been confused by the logic of real estate agents with their fancy cars. "People like success," his father had tried to explain. "If they see an agent with a nice car, they assume they're good at their job." For his part, when Steven saw an agent with a nice car, he assumed the agent was good at taking advantage of his customers. It took a long time for him to understand that the agents could only afford the flashy cars if they were good at getting business and closing it. The ones with the flashy cars made their customers happy. As he grew older, Steven realized that this rule applied in more and more situations. As a director of a charity, he was tempted to have a simple-looking workspace. But he didn't; even in the sphere of charity, people liked the feel of success.

As Steven looked at the man standing behind the faux-wooden desk, he realized he was face-to-face with an exception to this rule. The man was Shimon Bar-Lev, the Minister of Finance for the State of Israel.

But, somehow, this desk made sense. In a country famous for its history of corruption, it was more important for a Minister of Finance to look clean than it was for them to look successful. It often literally paid to have an office that looked like it belonged to a failed copier salesman. And, clearly, this Minister of Finance was not unusual in this respect. The place looked like it hadn't been redecorated in decades. Quite a few Ministers of Finance, financially clean and dirty alike, had embraced the drabness of this room.

Some offices, like the Oval Office, built up those who sat in them. They turned ordinary men into giants. But this sort of place ran the risk of doing just the opposite; of turning giants into ordinary men. In this light, the man in the chair was quite a surprise. Bar-Lev exuded success. Rather than bring him down, the low-key office seemed to accentuate his personal charisma. As a real estate agent, he could have ridden a broken bicycle and still represented any client he wanted to.

It worried Steven. The man was a politician. Steven knew, from long experience, that politicians exuded concern, but rarely felt it.

Mr. Bar-Lev extended his hand invitingly from behind his desk. "Mr. Gold, a pleasure to meet you." The Minister had a smooth, almost aristocratic American accent.

"Thank you," said Steven agreeably, as they shook hands. Steven had researched the Finance Minister before coming, but he hadn't expected the accent. After all, the Minister's mother was from Morocco and his father was from Poland. Steven was impressed that Bar-Lev had taught himself to speak like an American diplomat.

As Steven looked Bar-Lev over, he realized the man defied stereotypes. His skin color was a very light brown – neither European nor Middle Eastern. His features seemed entirely forgettable; somehow, his underlying charisma was divorced from them. And he wore a crocheted, short-rimmed fedora. In Israel, head-coverings (or the lack thereof) are almost like gang signs; they mark the religious sector you belong to. Very few people stepped out from one of the established conventions. But Bar-Lev was one of them. While it wasn't particularly flattering, his hat carried faint echoes from every sector. It too was the product of his practiced ambiguity. In elections, the man and his party were nobody's first choice. In a direct democracy, people voted for those who represented them most closely. Arabs voted for Arabs, religious for religious and so on. Generally unstable coalitions of these narrow factions were then formed in Parliament. Bar-Lev stood outside of all of this. He was, he'd said in an interview, "Everybody's second choice." Nobody really identified strongly with him, but they preferred him to everybody but their own narrow representative. This had been enough to get his party a few seats in Parliament. And, when the coalition talks came, it was enough to make him a consensus candidate for Minister of Finance. He'd need a lot more popular backing to become Prime Minister, but perhaps, with a solid track record in office, he'd be able to pull even that off.

Beyond his physical and political affectations, the man had a reputation as a straight-shooter and a history of supporting dynamic markets. Steven had no way of knowing if the reputation was well deserved. Bar-Lev acted outside both the "business" and "labor" factions of society. With a doctorate in economics from Stanford, he was one of the few Israeli ministers (the Minister of Defense being the other) who actually had education and experience in the area they managed. Most other Ministers did their jobs the way Steven had begun to think of as the Israeli way: they knew what they wanted to accomplish, and they figured out how to accomplish it along the way.

Bar-Lev made his way from behind his desk. Then they both sat down, on the visitor's side of the table. It was surprisingly friendly and informal.

"You've certainly knocked on a lot of doors to get this far," Bar-Lev said.

"I have," said Steven, smiling. "But I think what I'm doing is well worth the effort."

"Well, as you probably know," said Bar-Lev, "Israelis are very straight talkers."

"I am used to that," said Steven.

"Okay. Then I'll tell you up front that I don't think your plan has legs."

At one time, a sentence like this would have come like a gut punch. But Steven was used to it now. He'd overcome it many times. In his briefcase, he had a detailed report covering all aspects of the model city – from sewage to taxes. He and Amy had worked with experts in every field to put together the proposal, and he was confident he hadn't made any glaring errors.

"Can you show me what's wrong?" he asked.

"Don't get the wrong impression," said the Minister. "Your project is very inventive. I just think it has some fundamental flaws. Do you have your pro-forma with you?"

The pro-forma, in this case a forecast of cash flows, was the mother-sheet of all things financial when it came to the model city. It showed forecasts of population, welfare, tax and infrastructure spending on an annual basis. Steven pulled it from his bag. He had it on computer of course, but he found pens and paper a far more effective way to communicate in person.

"Great," said Bar-Lev, "This pro-forma is annual. You need this quarterly or even monthly. Short-term cash flows can kill you."

"Okay," said Steven. He pulled out a notebook and began taking notes.

"Secondly," said the Minister, "You underestimate security costs." He pointed at a line item. "If you look here, you have 44 police per 10,000 people. I think you'll need more."

"I used the same ratio that Afghanistan has," said Steven, defensively.

"Yes, but Afghanistan has quite a few other security forces. In reality, your ratio is going to be quite close to the one in New York."

"But the place will be small," Steven protested. "I'm forecasting capping population at 100,000. Smaller places tend to have about 30 percent fewer police per capita than large ones. Plus, it will be very dense. Dense urban areas tend to have lower density of policing."

Steven had stopped being surprised at his familiarity with these statistics.

"But it won't be a normal city," said Bar-Lev. "You'll have a bunch of different groups of people, lots of whom hate each other. And you'll be in Israeli territory. And, as I'm sure you're aware, Israelis will be very nervous about what you're doing. Some police will need to be protecting the population from itself, but some security forces will be needed to protect Israel from the population. You can put up a wall, which you have in your plans. But you'll need people to man it. I'd suggest raising your ratio to 50 per 10,000."

"Okay," said Steven. He knew the real ratio would probably be set when the city was actually built.

"That'll add a few million to your annual costs. Not a huge deal, but you want to be aware of this."

"Understood," said Steven, taking notes furiously.

"Next," said Bar-Lev, "You've suggested a site within the border fence. But the border actually lies outside the fence. There's a no-man's zone which is used for monitoring. If you shift your city partially into that zone, you'll raise some risks for the residents. But you'll also be cutting the amount of productively used land which the State would have to purchase to support your initiative. I'd shift it over. And I think the security forces will support that so long as they have eyes on the ground within your city."

"Okay," said Steven.

"This is all the little stuff," said the Minister. "You understand?"

"I understand," said Steven. He was impressed with the work the Minister had put into the review.

"Okay, let's continue," said Bar-Lev. "You are starting without paved roads or pipe-based water distribution. You're using camp-style sewage. All of these things will cut your upfront costs. Building out the infrastructure over time is smart, in my opinion. But be aware that building these things underneath people who already live someplace can be hard and expensive. You also might reduce the appeal of the place."

"I understand," said Steven. "I want the place to be appealing for ideological reasons. I want people who want to be involved in building the city itself. People who just want welfare and material handouts are going to have a hard time transitioning to a productive economy."

"You're right," said Bar-Lev. "And that is the heart of your problem."

"What is?" asked Steven.

"How," asked Bar-Lev, "will you transition these people to a productive economy?"

"If they come, they aren't going to want to or be willing to live on welfare forever – so they'll start working. It is an issue of pride."

"You know that it isn't true," said Bar-Lev. "Look at your JUC programs in the United States. Some people take the aid and manage to build their way out of a temporary poverty trap. But many others just bounce along from this handout to the next one. They never escape. It's an article of faith that redistribution is justice and makes everything work better – but the track record is mixed."

"So, what's the solution?" asked Steven.

"I don't think there is one. But it's a risk. You need to transition people to productivity, and there's no formula for doing so."

"But these people are coming from a place that had a functioning economy just a few years ago. They are in a temporary poverty trap. They'll want out of that trap, and they'll have the skills to get out."

"I'm not sure they will," said Bar-Lev. "I know Israel. Israel has the highest poverty rate among rich nations. Some of it is due to structural issues we have – for example, we have tremendous concentrations of financial power. But some of it is cultural. Many people, so long as they don't feel they are actually going to starve to death, are willing to withstand substantial hardship in order to dedicate their lives to something they perceive as bigger than themselves. You might be bringing in a fair number of these people. And they won't get you to a functioning economy. Trust me. Second, the people you're bringing in *weren't* in a functioning economy. They were part of a barely functioning *oil* economy. If they were farmers, oil subsidized what they received for grain. If they were small manufacturers, oil effectively paid for the tariffs that enabled them to keep their prices high. In your city, they won't have oil behind them. It won't be easy to adjust."

"But they managed to build functioning economies in Hong Kong and Amsterdam."

"Hong Kong and Amsterdam were port cities. They were trading cities. They had a natural business, and one that benefited from bringing in people from various cultures. But your city won't be on the ocean. It'll need something else. A better comparison than Hong Kong or Amsterdam might be West Berlin. It survived only because of massive subsidies. In 1982, the German government subsidized West Berlin to the tune of $9 billion a year. This is over $11,000 per person in today's dollars. And this was the normal annual spend. For your town of 100,000 people, that's over a billion dollars a year. That kind of outcome, for this particular ideological war, is out of the question. Your city will need to actually function. It can't afford just to be a poster child."

"It could still be a port city. It could be an inland port, between the Arab and Israeli worlds."

"Maybe. But you'd need the Arab world to accept that. And if they accepted that, why not accept imports directly from Israel? And if they do that, your economic reason for existence vanishes."

Bar-Lev paused and then said in a softer tone, "Steven, I'm not saying economies can't be created. The key thing about creative business is that it is actually very hard to predict. If it wasn't, it wouldn't be creative. But I am saying that it is very hard to actually get a sustainable reality started up."

"I'll start small and low-cost," said Steven, "like I have it in the plan. And then we'll grow bit by bit. We'll limit the risk until we see success."

"It might work. But there's still a fair amount of upfront cost involved. And the risk is substantial. Remember, we still haven't worked out the secret sauce that makes cities happen. North America is littered with cities people tried to imagine as the next great trading hub or Utopia. Churchill, Longview, Soul City. But they didn't work. We don't know what makes cities work."

Steven had done his homework. He was familiar with each of those places. Churchill was to be *the* trading port of the North. Longview was to accomplish the same thing, but in the West. And Soul City was to be a city entirely managed and populated by African Americans. Of course, there was also Salt Lake City, the most successful of these projects. But it had been brought together by a unified religious zeal and that wasn't the model Steven was pursuing.

"But each of those cities," Steven said, referring to Longview, Churchill and Soul City, "was founded and laid out before almost anybody came to them. There were lots of black cities in America established by freed slaves. They survived because they had a

173

population first and infrastructure second. That's exactly what I'm proposing here. We'll bring the people in. And then we'll transition them to an independent reality. We'll start small and low-budget so we can prove the concept."

"I can see building after the population. But your population will be coming simply because they're running from something else. Not because there is some opportunity drawing them in to your place."

"A place like Sugarland, in the U.S., was populated by people running."

"Sugarland?" Bar-Lev asked with a smile. "I did my research, but even I didn't expect *that* to come up. It's a tiny example. And I'm not so sure you'll be able to start so small. There is a tremendous need for refuge. Not just from the Arab world, but from Africa. Are you going to leave 100,000 or 500,000 people camped outside your boundaries, waiting for entry? There would have to be a whole other refugee infrastructure just to support them."

"I don't know what I'd do if the numbers were much larger than I forecast," admitted Steven, "But at least we'll have the population to drive growth – rather than trying to attract it with infrastructure that never gets used."

"You have a point there, but a potentially pricey one. You might very well get the population you need. But you could find yourself with a huge obligation. And you'd either need to meet it, somehow, or you'd risk creating a horror story."

Steven thought for a minute, "We can make our quotas very, very public," he said.

"People will imagine they'll fit under the quota and show up in greater numbers anyway," countered Bar-Lev.

"Yes," said Steven. "But we can solve that too. We can actually enforce the quotas from a distance. We can make an app so people can register for the city. They can get provisional rights to enter the city, from the app. We can even use their phone data to see their range of activities and verify that they are real people. They're doing this in Kenya for small-business loans. When they show up, we can give them an entrance interview and verify everything is legit. The invite will remain open for a set period of time so they can travel to the city. Anybody who shows up without an invitation will be rejected. If an informal settlement starts up outside, that is not a problem for us. We might actually establish businesses to service them. But it will be clear from the outset that we won't be helping the people who show up without invitations."

Bar-Lev looked impressed. "That's not a bad solution. I'd actually suggest adding a phone-based deposit that's required to hold one's place."

"But you'd lock out the people who need the city the most!" objected Steven.

"It can be waived, but people would have to explain why. This will prevent you from having lots of 'just shopping' reservations that keep out people who really want and need a place."

"Okay," admitted Steven, after a moment, "I can see that."

"Of course," said Bar-Lev, "you could go further and use people's phone data to estimate whether they are capable or desirous of economic contribution. It could help solve the problem of a non-productive city."

"We could do that," admitted Steven. "But we wouldn't want to go too far. A city is not just economics."

"But the economics are important," insisted Bar-Lev. "Especially if you want to borrow the money you need to get the place going."

Steven tipped his head in acknowledgement.

He was hoping Bar-Lev could supply a large amount of those funds.

"Okay. We've got four steps so far," summarized Bar-Lev. "One, raise your costs some. Two, shift the site outside the border fence to reduce usage of land which is already accounted for. Three, spend slowly at first to prove the place can be economically viable before throwing in huge funds. Four, choose applicants and regulate their arrival using phone-based screening. If the magic sauce works, you'll succeed. If not, you'll be able to cut your losses. Does that cover it?"

"Yes," said Steven, surprised by the summary.

"Let's assume this is viable," said Bar-Lev, "Where are you going to get the money? You're talking about spending $253 million dollars over two years before your tax revenues begin to turn positive. Jump that up to $300 million to be realistic and you've got a serious expense on your hands. This is about 1.2 billion shekels or 0.75 percent of our total state budget. It might seem small to you, but it represents about 150 shekels per person in Israel – taken without their agreement and spent on people who generally want us to violently disappear. And, despite all the measures you take, that commitment might be open-ended. You –"

Steven cut him off, "We've just reviewed why it wouldn't be open ended. And we've discussed how we'll minimize the risk."

Bar-Lev continued, "Steven, you can sit in this room and explain it all to me and I can agree, face-to-face. But although it is my responsibility, it isn't actually my money. I need to be able to say, in a way that the public can understand, that I was careful and wise with their funds. The story has to be simpler, and you need to find other sources for money – not just the State of Israel."

"Like matching donations?" asked Steven.

"Exactly. Israel should provide land and security. But you need other money to come from private places and even from other governments. That will not only save Israelis money, it will reassure them that other people think the idea is a good one."

"Okay," said Steven. He was beginning to realize that Bar-Lev *liked* the idea, even though he wasn't convinced it was realistic.

"I have to be careful with the government money," continued Bar-Lev. "Of course, so do you. You're doing something new, and government money often comes with strings that restrict you to doing what is already being done. So only use funds when you know the money will fit perfectly with what you're doing, and where it won't stop you from being flexible."

Steven kept writing in his notebook.

"Finally, in order to make the sale here in Israel – you'll need the financial story to be a lot clearer than it is. All the complexity we've described here won't sell. It will get distorted and create real issues politically."

"I was planning on issuing bonds," said Steven, "just like a normal city. The State of Israel would hold those, and it'd be clear then that we'd be responsible for making our payments. It would be a simple story everybody could understand."

"But it wouldn't allay their fears of your city collapsing," said Bar-Lev, "You need something more positive. Think about it. You aren't selling this as a haven to protect people from death; you're selling this as a model city to provide hope to an entire region. That is a positive sale, and it can work. Somehow you need to do the same thing on the financial side."

"We can have a higher interest rate on the bonds?" suggested Steven, hopefully.

"All that will do is make people more worried about you not paying your bills," said Bar-Lev, definitively.

Steven sat, thinking for a long while. And then he spoke. "A lot of the people who would come here – Muslims and Christians alike – are opposed to interest. The bond idea would be somewhat incompatible for them."

"They all issue bonds though," said Bar-Lev. "Islamic countries issue debt just like Israel does. They each just structure it a bit differently to get around their own religious issues."

"But what if we didn't issue debt at all? What if we issue shares in the city?"

"What do you mean?" asked Bar-Lev.

"As part of our city management," said Steven, "we'll track its economic product. It would be its GDP or equivalent. Instead of saying we'll pay x dollars in debt service, which can choke the city in bad times, and fail to truly reward people who took a gamble on it in good times; we'd pay x percent of that gross product. If the city is successful, the investors would receive more. It would get everybody invested in the city's success. Israel and others would want population growth and economic growth, because that would provide a greater return for their investment. It would reward them for their trust."

Bar-Lev smiled. "I hadn't thought of that. I believe it was Alexander Hamilton who said that a country's debt was a way of insuring that others had a stake in its survival. To put it another way, if the country doesn't survive, then it can't pay its debt. Because of this, debt makes others care about a country's survival. But I hadn't thought about a country's equity. That could make others care not just about its survival, but about its success. The impact could be huge. I like this idea..." he trailed off. He was clearly mid-thought, so Steven just waited.

Then he continued, "We'd have to work out how to track and audit the GDP in a mutually acceptable way. But that's a detail. And, of course, both of us would have to personally invest in the city."

"Both of us?" thought Steven. It was the first indication Bar-Lev was seriously thinking about going forward.

"What do you mean, 'invest'?" asked Steven – he wasn't feeling rich, even with his three-year contract.

"You wouldn't invest in a start-up," said Bar-Lev, "if the CEO didn't have shares. Right? If we believe in this financial model, we'd have to put our money where our mouths are. It's too unusual a model for us to commit others' tax dollars to otherwise."

Steven smiled ruefully, "My wife will certainly appreciate borrowing from our retirements."

"Mine too," said Bar-Lev, with a smile. Then he continued. "We'll set the investments up so that investors get a set percentage based on how much they invest. The money is just meant to cover the first three months. Then, based on how the city is going, we'll negotiate the rate for the next three months and pick the investors – state or otherwise – who offer the best deal. Once the city is more stable, you won't need as much money, and you'll be able to offer lower rates of return to a wider group of investors. Make sense?"

"Every three months?" asked Steven, "Won't we be in constant negotiations?"

"Look at it from the investors' perspective," said Bar-Lev. "You put your city on the market, so to speak. If it totally fails, we won't want a lot invested. But if it is completely successful, you won't want to have paid too high a rate on the initial funds. It wouldn't be fair to your citizens. That's why a short timeline helps, whether we succeed or fail."

"I understand," said Steven.

"We'll start off slow. You'd publish a few basic metrics – number of people, growth in internal GDP, etc., and then have a regular auction for additional equity. That way people know what they're buying, and you always get the best price."

"Okay," said Steven, nodding. It felt like it was coming together.

"I'm surprised," said Bar-Lev. "But I think this can actually work. We're taking a leap of faith, but we're not making it too big a leap."

"Okay," said Steven, "So let me summarize. We'll start small. We'll bring in smaller amounts of investment. We'll get money from a variety of sources. And then we'll grow over time as we show the place is viable. We'll sell it all as an opportunity, not just as charity. I'm sure you know; I have a history of selling community investment as an opportunity for personal growth. It'll be new for me to sell it as both an opportunity for personal *and financial* growth. But I think I manage it. Finally, we'll screen the candidates by mobile app."

"That sounds like a good package," said Bar-Lev, with a broad smile. "Update it and get it back to me for review."

"Great," said Steven. It felt like the meeting was over. It had been tremendously successful.

He was about to stand when Bar-Lev interrupted him.

"One more thing," Bar-Lev said, cheerfully. "You're going to be spending a lot of money. You'll need somebody on your team who really knows the local landscape and who is familiar with my office."

"I'll interview for a controller," said Steven, confused about why this was suddenly coming up. "It's in my plan."

"I have somebody specific in mind," said Bar-Lev. "His name is Itzchak Ben-Chaim. He has excellent connections here and he'll make a tremendous controller."

"I'd certainly be willing to interview him," said Steven, cheerfully.

"I'm not sure you understand," said Bar-Lev. "He's required. You must employ him to get my support and that of my office."

Steven settled back down on his chair, confused. Bar-Lev had a reputation as a straight-shooter. But here, he seemed to be demanding that a friend get a job in return for his political favors.

"Tell me about him," said Steven, stalling for time to think.

"It isn't relevant. He comes with my recommendation, and he'll be excellent for the job. I'm investing, not only my money, but the government's. So, I care. From your perspective, what's important is that he's required."

"I can interview him," said Steven, repeating himself. "But he will need to compete with other candidates."

"Commit to hiring him," said Bar-Lev. "Commit now, or I'll actively oppose your project."

"Is he really that important?" asked Steven.

"I need to know," said Bar-Lev, "that the two of us can have an understanding and a reliable conduit for communications and coordination. He won't cost much, maybe 20,000 shekels a month. And it can cement the entire deal."

"I'm sorry," said Steven, rising from his chair reluctantly. He felt dizzy. Suddenly everything seemed to be on such shaky ground. "We've just had a very productive meeting. We've really strengthened the financial model for the city. I'll use what we've done to shop this model around to others. But I can't hire your friend. I'll just have to try and do it without you."

"You know it will be impossible without me, right?" said Bar-Lev.

There was silence. Bar-Lev was right, Steven realized. He couldn't do it without the Finance Minister's support. If he didn't hire the man's friend, he'd be killing everything. None of the people he was trying to help would be helped. And all because of 20,000 shekel a month. He'd be condemning people he'd never met.

Finally, Steven made up his mind. "It might be impossible to go forward without you," he said, looking down at Bar-Lev. "But I can't play these games."

He stepped towards the door, turning his back on the crooked Minister with the straight reputation.

He heard Bar-Lev rise quickly behind him. Then he felt Bar-Lev put his hand on Steven's shoulder. Steven wanted to shake it off. It revolted and angered him.

He'd been so impressed by the Minister, but now he was just disgusted.

"Good," he heard Bar-Lev say, quietly.

"What?" asked Steven.

"You're going to get these pitches a lot," said Bar-Lev, as Steven turned to face him. "And if you go for them, you'll discover half of Israel and three-quarters of your own population will find themselves on your payroll distributing favors to one another. Those favors could be jobs, overpriced contracts, or straight embezzlement. It's a common problem around here, but it would destroy you. I needed you to turn me down. Understand?"

Steven suddenly realized how tense Bar-Lev's request had made him. He didn't feel relief. He felt demolished. He didn't really understand.

Them, surprisingly, Bar-Lev embraced him in a hug. Steven was shocked. A few moments later, the Minister stood back with his arms still on Steven's shoulders.

"Steven," he said, "You're doing good work. Excellent work. From the get-go, I've wanted to invest personally and politically in your model. I believe it is a fantastic thing. But you and I know that it probably won't work. For us, personally, the risk is worth it. But I have to represent not just myself, but my citizens. I have a responsibility to them, and they will make me responsible. I have to do my best to minimize their risks. I had to test you and know that you'd be clean."

"Okay," said Steven, quietly.

"You surprised me," said the Minister, "by passing the test. Most people don't. I don't let them know they've failed, I just let their programs and careers fizzle away. But you passed."

"Okay," said Steven. He still felt angry at the Minister.

"There's a Biblical saying," said the Minister: "*chazak v'ematz*. Do you know it?"

"*Be strong and of good courage*," said Steven. He was surprised his voice was shaking.

"Yes," said Bar-Lev, "*be strong and of good courage*. It isn't about physical battle; it is about moral strength. It isn't easy, and it isn't common. But you just demonstrated it. Do you know the rest of it?"

"No," said Steven.

"It continues," said the Minister, "'Do not be afraid, and do not dread your enemies.' With what you're doing, you'll need all of this. 'Be strong and of good courage, do not be afraid, and do not dread your enemies.' You can make it happen, but you have to continue *not* to let your fear bend you."

Steven nodded. Despite being 46 – close to the same age as Bar-Lev – he felt almost like a child being supported by his mother.

"Good," said Bar-Lev, with a satisfied smile. "You'll get me your updated report as soon as you can."

Steven nodded, quietly. And then left the office and building and reemerged into the bright sunlight of Jerusalem.

It was odd, but he felt like a new man.

Now, all he needed to do was raise a few tens of millions of dollars.

# Regret

*May 1, 2014: Raqqa, Syria*

"Hassan," Mohammed said, "I love you with all my heart, you understand?"

Hassan, the five-year-old child of Mohammed and Aisha, was screaming. Mohammed and Hassan were in his upstairs bedroom. Outside, the sun burned against the roofs of al Raqqa. But this room was covered in shadow. Only a hint of sunlight cut through the gaps in metal shutters on the room's only window.

"What happened to Mama?!" Hassan shouted. His face was contorted. Mohammed was holding him tight as he struggled. Mohammed put his hand over the child's mouth to quiet him.

"Hassan," Mohammed said. "Look at me."

Hassan did. Fear and confusion were in his eyes.

"I love you, Hassan," Mohammed repeated. "You understand?"

Hassan started crying. But there was no relief in the tears.

"Your mother," Mohammed said, in as even a voice as he could muster, "is in Paradise."

Hassan looked at his father, his eyes were asking, "Really?"

"She is," Mohammed said, reassuring his son. "She was a wonderful woman. She was smart and obedient and dedicated and a good mother."

Hassan nodded. He was calming down, just a touch.

"Hassan," Mohammed asked, gently. "What happened here?"

With that question, Mohammed moved his hand from his son's mouth.

In a shaking voice, the child answered, "You killed her."

And then he added, "Because she said something about the desert."

Mohammed nodded, solemnly. The boy was a good listener. He was bright.

But Mohammed realized there was no way he could explain his actions to a five-year-old.

With tears in his own eyes, he drew Hassan close into his shoulder.

"In'shall-h," he whispered into the ear of the young boy, "I will soon see you in Paradise."

The little boy's eyes couldn't see his father's. But they darted with sudden desperate confusion.

And then, in one swift motion, Mohammed pushed his only child away and snapped his neck.

As he looked at the bodies of his wife and child, a simple thought crossed his mind. "This," he said to himself, "was supposed to have been the happiest of days."

---

Mohammed's rise through the ranks of the Mujahidin had been swift. As he rose, he'd transformed the floundering movement. Of course, his communications protocols were adopted almost immediately. But his greater goal was making sure that the lives his people dedicated were used meaningfully. Bringing the return of the Caliphate required more than just killing the enemy and sacrificing one's own people. Thus, the wasteful and often counterproductive suicide attacks that his mother facilitated were brought to an end.

Instead, he turned the focus of his people's lives towards building, not destroying.

They had, for the first time in generations, the hope of establishing a new and better Islamic future. Not just tearing down their enemies but establishing a true state to replace them.

It was, of course, easier to set this goal than it was to realize it.

Mohammed's understanding of how the faithful should move forward had started with the assassination of his own parents. The enemy had come in helicopters. The helicopters didn't simply fly; they enabled the enemy's infantry to move from place to place quickly and without needing to overcome ground-based obstacles. In fact, the enemies – all of the enemies – had air power. The best of them tightly integrated it into their ground operations.

They used it to frighten, kill, and outmaneuver enemies. Helicopters and fighter aircraft and drones were not just a tactic in their own right but were integrated into a greater philosophy. The enemies called that philosophy "Combined Arms."

This idea inspired Mohammed. After all, while the Mujahidin could not match or even counter American or Syrian air power, they had their own unique weapon. They had the ultimate dedication of Jihad.

They had martyrdom.

Mohammed realized that young martyrs no longer had to waste their lives on symbolic mass casualty attacks, revenge strikes, or counterproductive attempts to undermine their enemy's peace of mind. They didn't have to go to Paradise simply for the sake of making an impression.

Instead, they could have their actions intimately folded into conventional military assaults. Suicide attacks, in trucks, in cars and even on foot, could pave the way for conventional assaults. They could be tightly integrated and coordinated. They could be the Mujahidin's "Combined Arms." The goal would no longer be to kill dozens in a market; instead, it would be to undermine the key points of an enemy's infrastructure. Truck bombs could crack open strategic choke points. Bomb-laden Humvees painted with Iraqi insignia could infiltrate to the core of enemy camps. And the fear of each could cause even the most resolute of enemies to doubt their own strength and to flee before the relatively tiny forces of the Mujahidin.

It was Mohammed who developed this. And with it, the Islamic State flourished militarily.

Of course, Mohammed's efforts went beyond warfare. His goal wasn't simply to conquer and to kill, but to build. Cities under Islamic State control had to be well run. Essential industries – oil, manufacturing, farming and milling – had to continue. Justice had to be fairly administered. And even the highest of officials were to be required to answer to All-h's law.

Mohammed learned not only from his mother, but from the Mukhabarat as well. He learned that resistance was not eliminated by the slow weight of oppression. Instead, shocking and overwhelming fear had to be deployed to compel peace and harmony within the borders of the State itself. The purpose of video-taped executions was not murder or sadism. The purpose was to take the heart out of the opposition – and thus bring about true peace.

But for all of the impact that he had, Mohammed's leadership was indirect.

Although he was a strategic mastermind, he was neither a religious leader nor a great scholar – he could never deliver sermons on the Koran or inspire men to great sacrifice. Abu Bakr al Baghdadi filled that role.

And while he was a planner, Mohammed was no engineer. He worked with another man, Youssef Al-Falluji, to test his more physical ideas.

And despite enabling the Islamic State to accomplish tremendous victories, Mohammed could not afford to be known as an enabler. The Mukhabarat thought he was working to undermine the Mujahidin. It was likely the Mukhabarat had other informants within the Mujahidin. If those informants knew that he was the great enabler of the Islamic State, then his privileged place within the Mukhabarat would vanish. He occupied that place so that, at some point, he could exploit it to utterly betray his greatest enemies. For all the successes of the Islamic State, he knew his own defying of the pattern was their greatest weapon. If he were discovered as a great force behind the Islamic State – and not simply a well-positioned source – then Omar and those who came after him would have sacrificed their lives for nothing.

Mohammed did not present his thoughts to others in the senior leadership. Instead, his innovations were passed on to his father-in-law – Abdul bin Hassan. It was Abdul who took credit and rose publicly within the ranks. It was Abdul who doted on his wife's gifted husband, seeming to practice pure nepotism. And it was Abdul who ensured that Mohammed always came with him – sharing in whatever official position Abdul himself secured. It was through Abdul that Mohammed realized his greatest successes. Only Abdul and Youssef al-Falluji knew the true scale of Mohammed's contributions.

When Abdul asked about Mohammed's reticence to take direct command, Mohammed's answer was always the same. "The great men of the Mujahidin respect your maturity. If the ideas were seen as mine, they would not be adopted. But they must be adopted, for the glory of All-h and His faith. That is why you must present them."

To the Sheikh, the answer was satisfactory.

The morning of his wife's death, Mohammed set out on one of his regular desert walks. Everybody knew that he walked. He had walked in Abu Kamal, and when he and Abdul had joined the leadership of the Mujahidin, he had walked in Raqqa. Everyone assumed that Mohammed simply loved the desert. On two occasions, they had tried to verify that this was true. Of course, in the desert it is easy to tell if you are being followed. On those occasions, Mohammed had simply detoured from his rendezvous with the Mukhabarat and wandered until the men who had been following him had grown bored.

In Abu Kamal, you could enter the desert in a few steps. But Raqqa was far larger than Abu Kamal had been. Raqqa had, after all, once been the capital of the great Caliph Harun al-Rashid. Because of its size, Mohammed's long walks to the desert took more time than they once had. But he didn't mind. As when he had been a lowly courier, he found that the opportunity to think was deeply productive.

That morning, as always, he inhaled the mad hustle of the capital as he stepped out of his home. A short distance away, he found himself at the river. As he crossed, he admired the lazy progress of the life-giving waters. And then, as he passed through three kilometers of farmland, he breathed in the sounds of the birds and the smells of harvests in their prime. Finally, he reached Highway 4 – a two-lane road that shadowed the Euphrates. He crossed it and came to a small rise – the spot where the topography of the land limited the reach of man's irrigation. There, in a sharp line, the green fields that bordered the Euphrates were replaced by the grey death of the desert. Mohammed stopped for a moment, admiring the rapidity of the change, admiring the lines All-h had drawn around man's ambition. And then he walked up the gentle slope and left the world of men.

The meeting in the desert had been like any other. Mohammed had passed on tidbits of information to his contact. He took great pleasure in the increasingly unkempt and nervous appearance of his handlers. Their old cockiness had been erased. Recently, his handler had been a woman. The change had shocked him at first. But then he realized, with joy, that she had come because all the men had been pulled into combat.

That morning, both he and his handler had known that the fall of Mosul was imminent. Mohammed wanted to rejoice – to hiss and spit in the face of his enemy. But he could not let himself do so. Instead he mourned with her and commiserated about the costs all Syrians shared in the wars imposed upon them by the Western powers. He found the logic harder and harder to maintain – but he maintained it nonetheless. They needed to believe he was their ally.

They parted, as usual, and then Mohammed made his way home.

When he returned to the city, there was jubilation in the streets. Men were handing out candies. Car horns were honking. And the regular staccato of celebratory gunfire rang through the air. Mohammed realized Mosul had fallen.

He came to his house, glowing with happiness. He opened the door and greeted Aisha with a kiss and little Hassan with a hug.

Everything, for that moment, seemed perfect. It was the happiest of days.

He had been upstairs, changing out of his sweat-stained clothes, when Aisha came into his room. She was holding her phone.

"Who is she?" she asked. Her voice was quiet but edged with anger.

"What?" asked Mohammed.

"Who is the woman you met with?"

"I don't know what you're talking about," Mohammed said.

"On your walk," Aisha continued, "in the desert. Who was the woman?"

Perhaps Aisha was jealous, he thought. Perhaps she had made up some story for herself about why he went walking in the desert. Of course, she had no right to be jealous. Mohammed could take another wife if he wanted to. So, he ignored her.

"You're obligated to tell me," said Aisha, "before you take another wife."

She was right, thought Mohammed. It was a part of their agreement. Nonetheless, he stayed silent.

"Is she married?" asked Aisha, a tone of fear in her voice.

Even a man as senior as Mohammed could be executed for sleeping with a married woman.

"Aisha," he finally replied, reasonably. "Why are you suddenly so jealous? I go for walks. I'm not seeing another woman. We have a tremendous marriage – ours is a credit to our people's timeless relationship to All-h. Why are you making up accusations?"

It was then that Aisha raised the phone. "I'm not making anything up," she said, with a hint of sadness, "I hid my phone in your bag. And I tracked and recorded you."

Mohammed's heart felt like it would stop.

"It was muffled," Aisha continued, not realizing what she was really saying, "So tell me what happened, honestly, or I'll forward the recording to my father."

Mohammed just stood there, considering his options.

His true allegiance was to the Mujahidin. It was to his Sunni people – long tortured by the Alawi Mukhabarat and their Shia allies. But he had given a tremendous amount of information to the Mukhabarat. Many had died. And he had told nobody – because the Mukhabarat had eyes and ears everywhere. If they knew he was crossing them, his ability to make the big play – to manipulate them into a grave mistake – would vanish. He would have wasted everything and everybody he committed to his plan.

But now, somebody knew. Specifically, his wife.

But he had not told her, she had caught him. His protestations of innocence, his claim to the playing the Mukhabarat, would count for nothing. His own people would never believe him. After all, his passing of information had accomplished nothing on behalf of the Mujahidin; all he had done was give information to their enemies.

If his wife forwarded the recording, his own people would almost certainly kill him as a traitor. And, if they didn't, word would get around. More people would know what he was doing. And the Mukhabarat would know he was double-crossing them. The people he'd betrayed would have lost their lives for nothing.

It was a cost they shouldn't have to bear.

His secret had to stay a secret – and none could be entrusted with it. Not even his father-in-law.

His face dropped in sudden and overwhelming sadness. And then, in three short steps, he closed the distance to his loving and beautiful Aisha. With a single movement, he snapped her neck.

And then, as she fell to the floor, he looked up and saw little Hassan.

The boy had been watching the whole thing.

---

Moments after he gently lay Hassan bin Mohammed next to his mother, Mohammed bin Hassan walked swiftly and calmly from his home.

In the street, the celebration was continuing. Mohammed forced himself to smile and cheer, like all the rest. But he was shaking inside.

He walked, slowly but purposefully, to the house of the only man who could help him – Youssef Al-Falluji. He arrived at the gate and pushed it open. Quickly crossing the untidy front yard, he reached the front door and knocked on it.

Moments later, it was opened by Youssef himself.

Mohammed was surprised and delighted to see him. Despite Youssef's value as an engineer, the man enjoyed walking the checkpoints of the city and seeing what he could of battle itself. He claimed it was only to enhance his own work, but Mohammed and he both knew that Youssef craved the excitement of combat.

Mohammed nodded to him and stepped in from the raucous and celebrating street. Youssef closed the door, and Mohammed found himself encased in a tremendous silence.

Like many of the leaders of the Islamic State, Youssef worked from home. But he was an engineer and a bomb-maker. While the bombs of Islamic State looked entirely improvised, the designs were actually perfected here, in this house, so that units in the field could deploy them using readily available materials. The house had primers, explosives and irreplaceable engineering. Because of this, it was critical to insulate it from the surrounding world. In the midst of the most sensitive work, a tremor, caused by a distant bomb or even an earthquake, could both kill everyone inside the home and threaten the viability of military units across the Islamic State.

Because of this, the house had been custom-built for Youssef. While it looked entirely conventional, especially from the air, it had a series of protective measures to keep the noise and disruption of the street at bay. They started with the unusually thick walls and windows. But they didn't stop there. The house itself was separated from the surrounding earth by rubber dampers meant to limit external shocks. Even the foundation's footings were of a thick rubber.

The result was a house that was silent and still, but not the least bit peaceful.

Mohammed found the sudden change from the noise of the street to the silence of the home unnerving. Somehow, the very absence of sound seemed oppressive.

"Are you alone?" Mohammed asked. His voice was an undertone, almost a concession to the building he was in.

"Yes," said Youssef. "Everybody is out celebrating."

He looked more closely at Mohammed.

"Are you okay?" Youssef asked, concern creeping into his voice.

"I killed Aisha," said Mohammed.

Youssef reeled back, "What?"

"I killed her," said Mohammed, breaking down. He wanted to maintain his composure, but he couldn't. He fell to his knees, suddenly overwhelmed by grief.

He wanted to wail, but he knew it was wrong to make a show of mourning.

"What happened?" asked Youssef.

"She found secrets," Mohammed said, choking up. "Secrets even she was not allowed to know."

Youssef stood there, watching.

"And where is Hassan?" Youssef asked, in a quiet undertone.

"He saw me do it," said Mohammed.

"And..." said Youssef, his voice trailing off.

"He heard her talking – about the secrets – and then he saw me kill her."

"You killed Hassan too?"

"I did," murmured Mohammed in a quavering voice.

Youssef whispered in disbelief, "Surely, All-h takes what is His, and what he gives is His, and to all things He has appointed a time...so have patience and be rewarded."

From the floor, his body shaking with his grief, Mohammed answered, "All-hu Akbar."

They stayed there, for a long moment. And then, finally, Mohammed sat back on his heels.

He looked up and Youssef finally asked, "Why are you here?"

"Because I need you to make it look like an accident," said Mohammed.

"An accident?" asked Youssef.

"I need it to look like a work accident. Like she was building a bomb and it went off."

"But why would she build a bomb?" asked Youssef.

"Obviously, to be a *shahid*," said Mohammed.

"No," said Youssef, "Why would she build a bomb when I could build it for her?"

"We can say I forbade her from being a *shahid*; and so, you wouldn't help her."

"And then she did it herself…" started Youssef.

"…but made a mistake," concluded Mohammed.

Reluctantly, Youssef nodded his head, and they began to work.


Three hours later, they sat together in the basement of Youssef's home. There was a trigger in front of them. Together, Youssef and Mohammed had moved Aisha and Hassan to the floor of Mohammed's basement. It wouldn't have been credible for his wife to have been secretly working with explosives in the bedroom. Youssef had placed the bomb next to the bodies of his dear Aisha and his beautiful son, Hassan.

As Mohammed sat there, Youssef at his side, he remembered the words of his first handler.

"I need you filled with regret," the man had said. "It is a part of any commitment to a greater cause."

As Mohammed pushed the trigger, he imagined that he could feel the shockwaves from the explosion. But, of course, he couldn't. At least, not physically.

In resignation, he lowered his head to the workbench. His dear Aisha and his beautiful Hassan had joined Omar and the others – all of them investments in the deception, and ultimate destruction, of their oppressors.

But, so far, Mohammed had no opportunity to use the Mukhabarat against itself. He had paid and paid and earned nothing in return. Not even an opportunity.

As he imagined the remains of his wife and child being gathered up and wrapped in shrouds, he closed his eyes and lifted his heart to heaven.

"All Merciful All-h," he begged, silently, "may their sacrifice be for the glory of Your Name."

# Hunger

*July 25ᵗʰ, 2014: Northern Iraq*

I knew the hunger was going to win.

Ibrahim and I were standing in front of a small house with a smaller domed structure attached to its side. Five days had passed since we'd left the village. What we'd seen was an Armageddon. Fields were scraped clean of their crops, while the villages that dotted the landscape – with Muslim exceptions – were not only vacant but ransacked. It was like Islamic State meant to control the movement of people by simply eliminating all the food that refugee travelers might find.

We'd set out with only a few days' worth of food; our emergency backpack had been stuffed with everything I could carry. But we'd found nothing more along the way. When that food was spent – on our third night of travel – we began to grow hungry. We had water – we refilled at the occasional small rivers – always cleansing our water with chlorine tablets. But water wasn't enough.

At first, the hunger just made us weak; I had trouble concentrating, but my muscles still worked. We were able to push on. I experienced an odd, light euphoria as the early stages of hunger set in. It was in this almost mindless state that we walked past Mosul, giving our old home a very wide berth. And then, we continued. I had decided we would try to go to Aleppo. When the traffic was clear, we crossed Highway 1. And then we paralleled the road from a distance. It could guide us, but we had to avoid the checkpoints that almost certainly dotted its route.

As we traveled, we grew ever more hungry. Before long, the euphoria passed and the need for food came to dominate everything. Ibrahim incessantly asked for something to eat – as if he'd forgotten that he'd asked just moments before. But, short of going down to the highway and stopping a passing car – there was nothing I could provide. And I knew that going down to the highway would almost certainly be a fatal mistake.

The Islamic State wanted us dead. I didn't know why, but I knew enough to stay clear of them.

The second night without food was overcast. We weren't under cloud cover; that was almost unheard of in the summer. Instead, we were under the red haze of a sandstorm. The storm wasn't some wild and violent sweeping of the landscape, as might occur in the heart of Arabia. It was simply a thick sandy haze. It didn't tear at our skin, but I could taste the grit on my lips. And, just like a thick fog, it obscured the moon and the stars and erased our vision of anything distant.

It was on that second night, when I was saying the evening prayer, that I decided to go to down to the highway. The hunger was unbearable. I needed to eat; we needed to eat. The Islamic State might kill us, but starvation could do that job just as easily.

But one of the side effects of my near delirium was that I lost track of things easily. It was tremendously hard to focus. Thinking about my own hunger, I had forgotten to keep track of the highway. By the time I decided to go to it, I no longer knew where it was. It was with horror that I realized that I didn't know where we were or even what direction we were heading in. Lacking any other guidance, I stood up, picked a direction, and tried to walk in a straight line. We might have been heading to the highway, or not. I couldn't know.

We'd walked the entire night. And as the first light of dawn came, the sandstorm began to clear. The area around us was desolate. At nightfall, we'd been surrounded by a patchwork of marginal farms. Now, only a few distant fields were even visible. Most of what surrounded us was the lifelessness of the desert.

And then, in the distance, I thought I saw a light.

I walked towards it, bringing Ibrahim with me.

As we drew closer, it became apparent that it was a house, standing alone in the desert. It had electric power. It almost certainly had food. As we grew nearer, it seemed to physically pull at us. Food. It was a simple repetitive thought. There was food. There was tremendous risk. But it didn't matter. There was food.

Our father had shared the story of Hansel and Gretel with us. I understood now why they could not resist the witch, despite the obvious trap she represented.

I did manage to will myself to stop well short of the home. I wasn't going to simply walk into this house. I would think first. I would try to find some alternative to it. But when I stopped, I realized I couldn't think of alternatives. There might have been alternatives, but I couldn't piece anything complex together. All I could think was, 'there is food here – I must get it.'

I kept standing there, desperately trying to reason my way through the challenge the home presented. And then, surrendering myself to All-h, I decided to pray.

It was as I touched my head to the ground for the second time that All-h chose my path.

The door opened. Like a portal, light streamed out of it. There was a man standing there. With the distance and the light streaming out from behind him, I couldn't make out his features.

"Come in!" he shouted. The shout seemed friendly; he just needed to cover the distance between us.

Like a commanded robot, I rose and started walking forward. Ibrahim followed.

And the man led us into the home.

Long before we crossed the threshold, I smelt the tea. It had a powerful aroma of deeply layered mint infused with an almost caramel-like sweetness.

"Tea?" the man asked.

I got a good look at him then. He was an older man, and his face was weathered from years in the sun. It seemed kindly, but I resolved to keep my guard up. I had no idea why he was here, and in my confused state I imagined that it might be to entrap refugee children.

"Yes," I said, "Yes, please. We haven't eaten in days."

"I can give you food as well," he said, "But tea first. You can hurt yourself by eating too much too quickly."

The floor of the house was stuffed with cushions and thickly embroidered carpets.

The man gestured towards a basin in the corner of his one-room house. "Wash," he said.

We went there and washed our hands thoroughly.

"And now," he said, indicating a set of cushions, "come and sit."

We sat, and he placed clear glass cups in front of us and poured some of the aromatic tea into them. It was somehow bitter and sweet at the same time. It crossed my mind that the tea itself might be drugged. I drank slowly, trying to be careful. But as I drank, I became more – not less – alert.

The man was sitting by a small propane stove. A pipe led from it and out the roof of the one-room house. There was a frying pan on the stove, and he was mixing eggs and various spices into a richly populated omelet.

"Who are you?" I asked.

"I was going to ask the same of you," he said, not turning from the frying pan. I imagined he was smiling.

I'd forgotten the names I'd told the Islamic State soldiers in Mosul. But I could give this man something.

"I'm Fatima," I said. "And this is my brother Ibrahim." I wanted to make up names for both of us, but I wasn't thinking clearly enough. And Ibrahim might not have been able to keep his straight.

"I am Akil," he answered. "And I don't get many visitors."

"What do you do here?" I asked.

"I am an astronomer, of sorts," Akil said, turning to look at me. "I have a doctorate from Saddam Hussain University."

I kept drinking.

"It was called that," Akil said, "when I got my doctorate. Now it is called Nahrain University – because it is located at the merging of the two rivers." *Nahr* means "river".

"My father went there," I blurted out.

"He did?" said Akil, obviously impressed. "Outside of Islamic Studies, it is by far the best university in Iraq – maybe the entire Arab world. It used to be very, very hard to get in."

"Did you have a thesis?" I asked, pushing the conversation back to him.

"I studied the history of astronomy," said Akil. "In the birthplace of astronomy. My doctorate was about how astronomy impacted culture – and how culture impacted astronomy."

I was confused, but knew that once I'd eaten, I'd be less so.

"I'm sorry," I said, "I can't follow. Not yet anyway. I think we need food."

"Almost ready," Akil said.

"You're Ibrahim, right?" Akil said to my brother.

"Yes," Ibrahim said.

"It is a wonderful name," said Akil, as he began to dish out small portions of his omelet onto a plate.

"Do you know," he asked Ibrahim, "what Ibrahim was famous for?"

Amazingly, my brother remembered, "He was famous for helping travelers," he said.

"Correct!" said Akil. "Travelers would show up, and he would offer them the best foods and drinks."

Ibrahim smiled proudly.

Akil continued with an almost conspiratorial smile, "But do you know why?"

"Why what?" asked Ibrahim.

Gently, Akil repeated himself, "Do you know why Ibrahim helped travelers?"

Akil placed the plate in front of us. There was a portion of the food in front of Ibrahim and a portion in front of me.

"Eat slowly," he said, in a serious voice.

In an undertone of thanks, I said, "In the name of God, the Beneficent, the Merciful."

"Amen," said Akil. He then smiled more broadly.

There was no silverware, and so we ate the small portions with our hands.

"More tea?" he asked.

"Yes, please," I said, gratefully.

"I'll give you more to eat, soon," he promised, "But you can hurt yourself by eating too much too fast."

Turning back to Ibrahim, Akil said, "The original Ibrahim could have just given money to the people around him. He could have opened a soup kitchen. He could have given startup money to small businesses. There are many ways to help. But he chose to help travelers. Can you imagine why?"

Ibrahim seemed stumped, but that didn't bother Akil.

"He helped them," Akil said with a laugh, "because travelers leave afterwards."

My brain was clearing some.

"So, he wasn't very helpful after all?" I asked.

"Not at all," insisted Akil. "He couldn't possibly have been more helpful!"

"What do you mean?" I asked.

"If you give normal people money in their normal lives, they can become dependent. They can lose their drive to work and produce and earn their own living. They can lose their purpose and pride. But if you shower travelers with blessings and hospitality and kindness, you spoil nothing. Instead, like Ibrahim himself, your hospitality can be an example for them. When they leave, they will have a gained a great deal, but lost nothing."

"And then, they'll need to produce and work and earn their living, despite what you've given them."

"Exactly!" said Akil, "You can help them and teach them and bless them, but not corrupt them."

He dished out another small portion of egg and refilled our tea. And then he sat with us.

I looked around his kitchen. There was almost nothing here. He had no vehicle outside. I was suddenly worried that he wouldn't be able to survive if he fed us too much.

"Do you have enough," I asked, "to feed us like this?"

"And now," Akil answered proudly, "you've seen how it works. For the cost of a meal, you've become grateful to me. So grateful that you care for me and want my good fortune. That is how people are brought together."

He was smiling.

"Seriously," I repeated, "do you have enough?"

"I have plenty," he said, "Inshallah, I have plenty."

We ate this morsel of food more slowly. And then our situation began to feel like one of my father's puzzles.

"Why are you here?" I said. "Is it just to help travelers?"

"No," said Akil, cheerfully, "I am here to watch the stars. That little dome next to my house is a telescope. I live here and I watch the stars."

"Aren't there better observatories in other places?"

"Of course, there are," said Akil. "But I'm not a scientist trying to discover new physical principles. I just love the poetry of the stars. Think about it: astronomy is as old as humankind itself. You've been walking at night. How can a person see those stars and not want to understand them?"

It wasn't a real question, so I just nodded.

"So, they studied them," continued Akil. "And for generation after generation, people passed down what they learned. But they didn't only learn the way Westerners try to – with the scientific method and their rules of reasoning and their emphasis on the physically practical. Instead, they found associations between the movement of the lights in the sky and occurrences here on earth. They learned poetry and lore, and they carried it and embedded it in the story of human civilization. They didn't care about gravity or black holes. They cared about the tangible effect of the stars on their lives. From generation to generation, over millennia, the stars became part of the tapestry of humanity. And, of course, the way they understood the stars became influenced by how their understood their more terrestrial existence. Even as the Sumerians and Babylonians and others began to make systems to describe the movement of the stars, the stars became gods. And those gods, through their movements, actually influenced events here on Earth. You might think it is silly, but these weren't stupid people. Thousands of years before Copernicus, there was a man named Seleucus of Selucia who lived just south of what is now Baghdad. Seleucus recognized that the sun was the center of the solar system, that the tides were caused by the moon, and that the universe was infinite. But even Seleucus himself was discarded, that wasn't what people wanted from the stars. Thus, the deeper human bond to the night sky was preserved. And that is what I study. I guess I'm trying to unlearn the science and see the human poetry in the stars themselves. And this place is perfect for that."

I just stared at him. It all made sense. But it didn't make perfect sense.

"You're a smuggler," I said, finally.

"What?" asked the man, clearly surprised.

"You're a smuggler," I repeated.

"If I was," said Akil, "why would you say so? Clearly, I'd have been trying to hide it with all the astronomy talk. Wouldn't it be dangerous for *you* to admit you knew the truth?"

He was right, I shouldn't have said anything. But I guess I wasn't thinking as clearly as I imagined I was. I had to explain myself.

"It's a game my father used to play," I said. "We'd do things, but he wouldn't tell me what we were doing or why. I'd have to work it out. Like a puzzle. I'd have to figure out not only the answer, but even the question. It was how I was educated. This house seems to be a puzzle – to be solved. You have almost no food, but you aren't worried about starving. This means you have a hidden cache. This wouldn't be unusual, not living by yourself in this place. However, you study ancient gods, but you aren't worried about the Islamic State. This suggests you fill a critical role even for them. You're Bedouin. The tea, the food, the carpeting – all of it is Bedouin. Bedouin are often smugglers. It all points in the direction of smuggling."

"Perhaps, my doctorate is more recent" said Akil. "And perhaps Bedouin can be something other than smugglers." He had a bit of harshness in his voice.

"You went to Saddam Hussein University," I said. "I believe that. You seem generally disappointed about its decline and genuinely impressed by my father's degree. But you went to Saddam Hussein University, not Al Nahrain. Your degree wouldn't be recent. But your face is weathered by the sun – like you've spent decades beneath it. Astronomers work at night. You aren't an astronomer – at least not full time. Instead, you're covering something up. But out here, there aren't many things to cover up. I'd imagine this house is a waystation for smuggling."

Akil's face clouded some. He thought for a long few seconds. And then his smile returned.

"I'm impressed," he said. "But I'm also worried. If you know who and where I am, you could be a threat to me and my people. And my people can't accept such threats. So now, we can drop the polite lies, and you can tell me who you are and where you're going."

I hesitated. If I lied, he might kill us. And if I told the truth, he might turn us in. But he was a smuggler – and the men who truly believed in the work of Islamic State didn't pay the homage he had paid to even the shadows of the ancient gods.

"My name is Maryam, Maryam al-Mosuli," I said. "My brother is actually Ibrahim. Our parents were killed, and my brother was injured in a bombing in Mosul. We were targeted in our home, but I don't know why. Our father was a civil engineer. He went to Saddam Hussein University, just like I said. We're running to Aleppo."

"Why Aleppo?" asked the man.

"I know it sounds strange," I answered. "But I don't know what tribe or sect we truly belong to. We are al-Mosuli – we belong to the city itself. We don't have friends or relatives or a tribe which can take us in. I've heard the Sunni dominate the refugee camps – expelling or killing others. And I know that Baghdad is entirely divided by sect – so, without connections, there is nothing for us there. Because of this Aleppo, a more mixed city, makes sense."

"Have you tried Erbil?" Akil asked, "It is much closer."

"We tried," I said, "But we couldn't cross the river."

The man nodded.

"I believe you," he said. "But I can't imagine how you'd thought you'd make it with just the food in your pack."

"We didn't have a choice," I said. "We'd managed to settle in an empty village and actually harvest the crops there. But then those crops were taken. The bag was all we had."

Akil paused for a long moment. "Aleppo is not safe," he said, carefully. "But it does seem like your best option."

"You'll let us go then?" I asked.

"I could ask you to promise not to talk about this place," he said. "But you'd say anything to get away alive. Then again, if you were planning to betray me – you wouldn't have admitted to knowing what this place actually was. You would have stayed quiet."

I nodded hopefully. He didn't respond.

But then I realized that I hadn't solved the whole puzzle. And my curiosity got the best of me. "This can't just be a rest stop," I said, "You went to University. That's unusual for a Bedouin. But not only that, you went to Saddam Hussein University. I'd guess you're a very driven and independent individual. This place must be something really special. I know this sounds ridiculous, but I love to learn how things work. I'd love to see what you're actually doing?" I phrased it as a question.

Akil looked at me in something close to astonishment. "I just threatened your life for knowing too much, and you want to know more?"

"It's like your stars," I said. "You don't just study something to learn about it. You study it because it can change you. You can pass stories and poetry from one moment of your life to the next. But if you don't study, then there is only darkness."

"You want to see what I've built?" the man said, "Because you want to know the poetry of it?"

I nodded.

"Your brother," he said, after a pause, "he can't see. He might remember and share. Okay?"

"Okay," I answered.

"You're tired?" he asked.

I nodded.

"He'll sleep soon. When he does, I'll show you."

So, we waited. We sat there, drinking tea and eating additional morsels of food. And then Ibrahim fell asleep on the cushions.

Akil silently rose and gestured for me to follow him.

We went into the room with the telescope. Surprisingly, it was a computer-controlled instrument. Akil typed a code into the keyboard and a hatchway slid open in the floor. There was a ladder there. Akil asked me to go first, and so I did.

The ladder seemed to go down about 30 feet. And then it ended. I stepped forward into total darkness and heard Akil come down behind me. I heard him flick a switch. With a clonk, floodlights came to life all around us.

In front of me was a warehouse. It was huge. It must have been 20 feet tall, 400 feet long, and 400 feet wide, and it was punctuated by raw stone columns. There were bags of goods everywhere, separated by lines on the floor, but no pallets.

"Sometimes," said Akil, "it is easy to move from the north or west to here. And other times it is easy to move from here to points south and east. This is the middle of those zones. Some smugglers specialize in crossing the Syrian and Turkish borders. Others in penetrating Iran or the South. Everybody knows their own business and their territory, and everybody has their own timing. They've studied the poetry of these places for generations. This place lies between those zones. We are between the zones of enforcement, and we are between the zones of expertise. That is why cargo is placed here, to move from zone and zone. This warehouse exists to supply a vast territory with all sorts of goods."

"They move it all through your telescope?" I asked, "I can't imagine it fitting."

"There are tunnels," said Akil, proudly, "They lead to here from places miles in various other directions. Caravans – of trucks, jeeps or even camels – can stop near cliff sides or wadis and discretely unload their cargo. Others can pass by and pick up those same cargos for onward transport. I monitor the area. I saw you coming from miles away. When a cargo is deposited, I account for it. When others pick it up, I note that. In addition to moving cargos, I also act as a sort of bank. I make sure everybody gets paid or gets paid the appropriate amounts. I do take a small fee, of course."

I just stood there, admiring the scale of the place.

"What kinds of goods are these?" I asked.

"It changes," he said. "But the nature of smuggling is that you only move things that people want and that the government makes unusually expensive or difficult to get. Without the added "tax" of government controls, this sort of subterfuge wouldn't be worth pursuing."

"Drugs?" I asked.

"Drugs have a very, very high value-density," he said. "In other words, you can move a lot more value in a much smaller package, and it can be too easy to steal too much too quickly. It makes smugglers paranoid and jumpy, and would make warehousing far too dangerous. So, no, we don't handle drugs. We do bring in hard alcohol. But most of our business is more mundane. We move rugs and stereos and cameras and watches and heat exchangers. We move canned food, some art, and quite a few stereos. We move guns. We move silly things like feather dusters. And we move large things like motorcycles. But probably the biggest part of the business is small electrical appliances – like you'd find in a kitchen."

"Appliances?" I asked.

"Yes," said Akil. "One of the Prime Minister's cousins owns a small appliance manufacturer. That's why the tariffs are so high. And that's why they're worth smuggling."

I had a million other questions, but I didn't want Ibrahim to wake up without me there. So, we went back up to the house that existed precisely because it was in the middle of nowhere. We talked for a little while longer and then, reluctantly, I fell asleep.

Ibrahim and I both woke up, safe and sound, hours later.

Akil was watching us.

"It is almost night," he said.

I nodded.

"You are only guests," he said. "After your prayers, it is time for you to go."

"Thank you for your help," I said. In the back of my mind, I was worried again about food.

"Praise be to All-h," he answered.

"I've repacked your bag," he continued, "But with higher density foods, like halawa. You've got another 20 days or so of walking until you reach Aleppo. Even with the halawa, you can't carry nearly enough food, so I've also put a small GPS in there. It is only a receiver – nobody can track you. But it can be charged from the sun, and it is preloaded with the locations of food caches we use to travel light. You won't go hungry. If others get too interested in you, there's a button on the top that you can hold down to erase the memory. Don't let anybody know about these caches – their location is critical to our business. You understand?"

"I understand," I said.

He nodded. And then, in a quiet voice, he intoned: "In the name of All-h, and Praise be to All-h. Glory unto Him."

"Amen," I answered.

I prayed.

And then I stood, lifted the backpack and turned away from Akil the smuggler, and the human poetry of his odd little house in the desert.

Ibrahim followed me as we began the slow walk to Aleppo.

It was a journey that we never completed.

# Speech

*Jan 5th, 2014: New York City*

Steven Gold always felt uncomfortable in front of a spotlight. It wasn't stage fright; it was more fundamental than that. Steven liked to work with other people. He liked to highlight their contributions to a project. He enjoyed the effects a successful project had on other contributors more than he enjoyed the success itself. And yet here he was, standing in front of the spotlight with all the attention on him.

With Steven's success in Israel, the JUC had lent its full support to him. The room was packed with 250 extremely wealthy and influential people – people the JUC had invited. It was Steven's job to move them to action. He was used to working with such people. But he was used to a conversation. He was used to hearing and seeing their feelings and their reactions. But here the spotlight was in his face and those in the darkened and unseen room were quietly waiting for his words. He felt blind. And he was frightened that when he spoke, he would be unable to tell what was drawing them in and what was pushing them away.

He was frightened that he would fail.

He looked to Amy nervously. She was seated at the closest table, just barely visible at the edges of the lit area. She tried to smile encouragingly, but it didn't help.

Steven stood there, for a moment, and then he closed his eyes and tried something more direct. He tried to *feel* the room. And just like that, he could sense the people seated at their tables. He could sense anticipation. He could sense boredom. He could sense curiosity. As he stood there, the curiosity grew.

It grew until he realized, with a start, that it was focused on him and his closed eyes.

It was with that realization that he opened his eyes and began to speak.

"After the Protestant Reformation in Europe, the continent was wracked by a series of religious wars. By some accounts, 30 percent of the population was killed. There seemed to be no end in sight. There were basic and universally accepted religious principles at play. First, there was the belief that only the right practice of the faith would lead to salvation. And second, there was a belief that a country must be drawn into total religious conformance in order to achieve success. These beliefs, when combined, led to terrible conflicts and crushing wars. These principles impacted the Jewish community even before the Reformation. But with the Reformation, society as a whole crumpled."

Steven wanted to look out at the crowd, but he couldn't see them. Were they listening?

"As many as eight million people died," he continued. "If we'd lived in those days, we would have been tempted to write off European society. After all, what hope could there be in such chaos and destruction? But even as the Continent crumbled, one city rose. It became one of the most influential cities in the world. The city was Amsterdam. How did it escape the chaos? Through a simple act of convenience that eventually transformed Europe itself."

Steven pretended to look around the room before continuing. He couldn't actually meet the eyes of his audience, but that didn't stop them from imagining he had done so.

"It was convenient for Amsterdam to be tolerant of multiple religions. Like every other European state, there was an official Church – the Calvinist Church. And like every other state, only the official faith was allowed to be practiced publicly. But there was also a willful blind eye turned towards non-conformance. Roman Catholics, Lutherans, and Mennonites, all officially banned, had private house churches. Jews established synagogues. Why? Because successful trade demanded successful people – even if they were Catholics or Jews.

"There was some religious justification, of course. There was an idea that people had to come to their faith through their own hearts. This religious justification led to a unique reality. In the midst of war, there was a European city that was stable and at peace while the world around it collapsed. The example of Amsterdam changed European Christianity and enabled the religious toleration we see today."

Steven stopped again, taking a sip from his water, girding himself for the more controversial part of his speech. He inhaled deeply and then continued.

"Today, another part of the world is embroiled in religious war. It is a very old conflict, but in recent years – fueled by oil, social media, and perhaps even climate change – it has taken on new proportions. We in the West, who went through our own religious wars, are all very eager to provide our solutions to the problem. We claim Islam is this, or Islam is that, and our prescriptions follow those declarations. Some claim we must leave the region. Some claim we must squeeze the violence out of the faith. Others claim that we must welcome refugees and bring them into our world. But all of these claims are based on blanket – and thus necessarily false – definitions of Islam. After all, I am a Jew, but I have learned that *I* can barely define what Judaism is. None of us have any effective ability to define Islam."

Steven saw his wife looking at him from the corner of his eye. She was watching him carefully. But were his words actually impacting her. If she were to be a donor, would she lend her support to what he was doing?

"But Islam, like Christianity and Judaism, *can* define itself. It can define itself as conservative and spiritual, in opposition to the progressive and materialistic values many see in the West. It can define itself as promoting peace, in opposition to the violence of those like the Islamic State. Or it can define itself as fighting a physical Jihad for the glory of All-h, against those who deny His place. It *can* define itself. But it cannot be defined by us.

"When we take in refugees, some will be killers. On the other hand, when we distance ourselves, many innocents will die. There seems to be no solution to the problems plaguing their world. There seems to be no way to stop those problems from impacting us. The region is undergoing a constant war with itself.

"With this constant war, the worst and most destructive of all possible definitions will become reality. If the other side in the conflict killed your family, you will respond in kind. Even if they haven't, you might act preemptively – knowing that they would, if given the chance. As a result, your positions will harden, your ideology will narrow, and the narrow bridge to peace will become ever narrower." "But there is a solution," Steven announced with a sudden smile. "We can create a place of peace and opportunity for the region's fearful and oppressed. We can welcome refugees from the region to that place – whether they be Christian, Muslim, or Yazidi. We can, as Amsterdam did, select the most productive and accepting of the people fleeing the region's wars. And then we can allow the people of that region to build something better. We can provide peace and opportunity. And in so doing, we can create a city state in which the religious peoples of the region can find new definitions of themselves and, ultimately, new definitions of the world they come from. We can't define them. But we can give them the opportunity to redefine themselves."

Steven looked around the room again, meeting unseen eyes. He realized, in a brief moment of panic, that the fate of helpless and forgotten people depended on his words. He wished there was a spotlight on at least one member of the audience, somebody he could look at and judge his performance by.

"Many people have joined hands behind this venture. The JUC – which has asked you all to come here today – endorses this project. They understand that the Model City, as I've taken to calling it, is not an act of cultural or physical imperialism; it is only providing the conditions by which a better reality can emerge. It is only lifting people out from under the threat of their current oppressors. But the JUC is not alone. In Israel, which will be providing the land for the city, there is widespread political support for this effort. The Sephardi Chief Rabbi has endorsed the project as an opportunity to play our role in repairing the world. The Minister of Finance has said that the State of Israel will invest in the project. The Minister of Defense has said it is viable and defensible. There are plans in place to provide water, connections for trade, and new immigrant screening. There is even a bill in front of the Knesset, to approve the entire project."

Steven breathed deeply. Now was the time for his request.

"That is why I am here today. There is a great deal to do. The rough beginnings of infrastructure must be laid out, a support network for new immigrants must be brought into being, a screening program and health program must be established. And more. We are not building a refugee camp, but a City of Refuge. And the expense required to bring such a city into existence will be substantial." "As you all know, the State of Israel is a small country. The metropolitan area of New York City has more land, and twice the population of the State of Israel. The GDP of the New York metropolitan area is five times the GDP of Israel.

"Because of its small size and limited resources, the members of the Knesset who are voting on this project must see that others will support it. They must see that the cost will not be borne by the citizens of Israel alone. Whatever resources we can secure here, tonight and in coming days, will increase the chances of this project going forward. Every dollar invested here will help one more member of Knesset switch his vote to support what we're doing."

Steven felt himself reacting. This next part he was used to.

"The Torah speaks of the life of Noah. According to the Torah, he lived 950 years. But of all that time, only one year and ten days were actually recorded in the book itself. The story of Noah is not unusual. We live our lives, often long ones. But in the end, a few decisions and a brief span of time define us. Before Christmas 1938, a 29-year-old British stockbroker named Nicholas Winton planned to fly to Switzerland for a ski vacation. But instead, he went to Prague, where he led an effort to find homes for refugee children. He rescued 669 Jewish children – many of whom went on to live their own lives of significance. He rescued them. And with one act, in one moment, he lived a life of significance.

"We only have a few opportunities to truly influence and change the reality around us. If we miss them, we vanish from time itself. But if we act, we can transform our world and be woven into its fabric. Forever. This City is just such an opportunity. Investing in it – whether it be in pledges to support its programs as it grows, or whether it be your unique expertise – is an opportunity to change the world for the better. Even if the City is not a petri dish for renewed Middle Eastern culture, those who support it will still have provided hope and escape to those who need it most. You will have rescued women and children and men seeking a better reality."

Steven paused.

"Of course, the City is not meant to be a charity case. If it were a charity case, no real and sustainable culture would emerge. No, the city is meant to be a living and dynamic place with a functioning economy. Thus, I am asking you not for charity, but for investment. In tune with the religious values of the region, the City will not be issuing bonds. Fixed debt creates risk and drives poor decisions. Instead, the City will pay out a percentage of its future Gross Domestic Product to those who invest in it. As with shares in a company, the rights to those revenues will be tradable. In this way, we will all be literally invested in the success of this project."

Steven picked a bound document from his table, lifting it for the room to see.

"At each of your tables, you have a prospectus. You have pro formas and plans. You have financial and demographic projections. Read all of it. Discuss it. Ask me questions as I walk from table to table. But in the end, recognize that you are not only investing in the City. In the end, recognize that you are investing in yourselves. Like Nicholas Winton and Noah long before him, the decisions you make tonight and in the coming days will define you. They will give you the opportunity to live a life of meaning and impact. Opportunities like this do not frequently arise.

"Thank you in advance for the wonderful things we will all accomplish together."

Steven looked around the room once more and then stepped back from the microphone.

The spotlight receded and the lights in the room came back up.

The crowd was visible once again.

As Steven looked around, he realized that every eye was on him.

He looked to Amy for the second time and saw, to his surprise, that she was crying.

And then, a moment later, he realized that he was as well.

# Redemption

*June 1st, 2014: Raqqa, Syria*

"Because I'm done," said Mohammed bin Hassan, in a quiet voice. He was looking at his phone. He wasn't surprised by the tears that were rolling from his eyes.

Mohammed was in his basement. The wall behind him was scarred with the damage caused by the bombing he'd carried out to cover up the murders of Aisha and Hassan. He'd hoped that destroying their bodies in the basement would somehow contain the impact of their deaths. Somehow, the rest of the house would be bearable.

But it hadn't worked. He'd known it wouldn't.

While the bodies themselves had been removed and buried, the blood of his wife and child had seemingly been implanted in the concrete walls. He had tried to bleach those walls, but it had been unsuccessful. The physical stain seemed impossible to remove.

He tried to avoid the basement, to avoid the constant reminders. But the cold air of the basement circulated through the house and brought with it the scent of their deaths. Day after day, that scent came over him with a chill.

Mohammed imagined that Aisha and Hassan had become *djin*, torturing him and following him everywhere in this house.

Mohammed himself was a ragged mess. He hadn't bathed in weeks, he'd eaten nothing more than what was absolutely required, and his house had fallen into a terrible state of decay.

And yet, here he was, in the basement haunted by the *djin* of his wife and child. And all for the purpose of a phone call.

It had started two weeks earlier when Mohammed had read a headline in the Arabic edition of the *Jerusalem Herald*. Even in mourning, Mohammed had kept reading the *Jerusalem Herald*. He read it because it was important to keep track of the larger strategic picture. It was the only way he could achieve redemption. As his original Mukhabarat handler had pointed out, the Western powers tended to follow a policy of backing the weak horse. The Israelis were the same, but they were less idealistic about it. Where the Americans ostensibly stood up for the little guy, the Israelis were just making sure the big guy didn't get too big. The strong horse in Lebanon – and increasingly Syria – was Hezbollah. Hezbollah, a stateless Shia military force under Iranian sponsorship, represented both Israel's and the Islamic State's most dedicated enemy.

Their strength created a confluence of interests.

But finding those interests, and exploiting them, required knowing something of the Jewish State. And that required reading the *Jerusalem Herald*.

Even as a shell of a man, overcome by grief, Mohammed recognized that the headline in front of him represented his redemption. It read, simply: "Knesset Approves City of Refuge."

Even in his broken state, he knew a City of Refuge offered him hope. It was the kind of thing he could manipulate. It was the kind of thing he could use to manipulate and destroy the Mukhabarat. With a City of Refuge, sponsored by the Israelis and populated by a microcosm of Syria and Iraq, he'd finally be able to turn all of the enemies of the Mujahidin against each other.

Mohammed read the article, carefully. And then, in a flurry of online research, he studied everything he could find about the City. He read everything Steven Gold had proposed and he read the rationales behind those propositions. When Voice of Israel in Arabic and the *Jerusalem Herald* published an address on SilentVoice, Mohammed responded almost immediately.

Using SilentVoice was clever. It was the same app the Islamic State used for international recruiting. The Islamic State used SilentVoice because it was very hard to trace; the same lack of traceability could enable others to contact the City without triggering alarms on the Islamic-State-controlled data network. The Israelis were using the Islamic State's own tools against it.

In an automated chat, Mohammed shared his basic information. His name, photograph, birthdate, home city and current occupation. He didn't suppose many others with the job title: "Member of the Islamic State Central Coordinating Committee" would be applying.

Not surprisingly, a response didn't take long. He was texted a range of open interview slots and selected one. At 2 p.m., the following day, he'd have his chance to be admitted to the City of Refuge. In preparation, Mohammed had set up his phone in his bomb-scarred basement. Despite all the hope the City offered, it had been hard to reenter that terrible subterranean space. But the gashes in the walls and their traces of dried blood were too effective a backdrop for him not to use. His wife and child had sacrificed their lives. He could accept some discomfort in order to maximize the benefits of their sacrifice.

When everything was positioned correctly, he sat, unsteadily, and waited for the call.

It came in at exactly 2:00pm.

Mohammed answered and was surprised to see Steven Gold himself on the other end of the line. Mohammed had been largely impressed with what he'd read about the man. But on video, another truth emerged. Steven Gold was utterly plain. His dark brown hair framed a slightly pudgy face with no features of note. His eyes betrayed neither hardship nor great success. He had lost no one and gained nothing. He seemed like a child in a grown man's body. Mohammed realized, in amazement, that Steven Gold was a fool.

"Why do you want to come to the City of Refuge?" asked Mr. Gold, as soon as they were connected.

The question was in English. Mohammed caught a word or two. But before he could assemble something cogent in his head, the translator delivered the question in a mellifluous Arabic. Mohammed was taken aback. As much as Steven Gold seemed unimpressive, the translator was something else again. Arabic is not a unified language. There are variations from region to region. And, even within a single country, there are regional differences in language or, at least, accent. But this man's language and accent were a perfect match. Not for Damascus or Aleppo or some other major Syrian city. They were a perfect match for Abu Kamal. Getting that right either required recruiting somebody from Abu Kamal or using an incredibly gifted and well-trained interlocutor. If the Israelis were trying to convince him of their power and effectiveness, they had started on the right foot.

"Because I'm done," said Mohammed. It was then that the tears had stated flowing.

"Done?" asked Gold, after a brief pause for translation.

"I'm done with the fighting," said Mohammed, "I want out. No, I need out. I can't take this anymore."

Steven suddenly shifted topics. "You're Mohammed bin Hassan, correct?"

"Yes," said Mohammed, "That's me."

"Do you know where you were born?"

"Abu Kamal," said Mohammed. But, of course, they knew this; the translator wasn't an accident.

"And what did your parents do?"

"They were involved in the Mujahidin."

"How?"

"My father ran suicide bombers into Iraq. To fight the Americans."

"Mohammed," said Gold, "you and I both know your father did nothing of the sort. It was your mother who ran that effort, correct?"

Mohammed was stunned. Nobody had known this. How had the Israelis, of all people, figured this out? He'd never seen an Israeli agent in his life.

"Yes," said Mohammed, the surprise heavy in his voice. "That's correct."

"It's important," said Gold, "for you to tell us the truth. We know a great deal about you. But if you engage in lying, we won't be able to come to trust – or admit – you. This City is important to me and many others. You are, as you must know, a risk. You have to convince me, and the people with me, that the opportunities of admitting you exceed the risks. Understand?"

Mohammed nodded. He would be more careful.

"Good," said Mr. Gold.

"Your parents were killed in the Abu Kamal raid, correct?"

"Yes," said Mohammed.

"Is that when you got your start in the Mujahidin?"

"I joined shortly afterwards," said Mohammed, "As soon as the opportunity presented itself."

"Why?" asked Mr. Gold.

"Why did I join?" asked Mohammed.

"Yes," said Mr. Gold. "We need to know why you joined so we can understand whether you actually want to leave."

"Okay," said Mohammed, wondering just how much they knew, "I joined because I wanted revenge."

"Against whom? The Americans who killed your parents?"

"No," said Mohammed, "against the Shia and their Alawite puppet masters who put them up to it."

Mr. Gold nodded.

"Did you get your revenge?"

"I did not," said Mohammed.

"So why are you stopping now?"

Mohammed paused, and then he answered. "Do you know how your Holocaust survivors say their greatest revenge is either children or success?"

"Yes," said Gold.

"I realized that would be my greatest revenge. Not killing my enemies but building something. The greatest revenge would be achieving peace and self-determination for my people. That is what my parents really wanted and that is what they were killed for. They wanted to build a religious Sunni state in the heartland of Islam. Thus, I sought that rather than just the death of my enemies."

"And did you achieve it?"

"In a way," said Mohammed, "Yes. With the Islamic State, we achieved self-determination. But it all went terribly wrong, which is why I want to leave."

"What do you mean?"

"You've seen the news," said Mohammed. "You've seen what we've become. I think it started with the brutality of our battles. The war consumed us, as people. It made us into something terrible. We've become killers. We've been willing to do horrible things for our cause. And it, I don't know, the horror of it all is tearing me apart."

He knew this was something Gold wanted to hear.

"So, you don't support the use of suicide bombers?" asked Gold.

If Gold knew his mother had run things in Abu Kamal, he wouldn't be able to lie here.

"No," said Mohammed, "I did support them. In fact, I still do. On the battlefield. Against soldiers. The way I see it, you can send 100 men against an objective and lose 40 of them and maybe accomplish your goal. Or you can send 2 bombers and 98 men and end up losing fewer than 10 while having a greater chance of success. Yes, with suicide bombers, you know who's going to die. It isn't random like it might be without them. But it is the bombers' choice to sacrifice themselves. And, as a result, lives are saved. It is like a soldier choosing to fall on a grenade to save his comrades. This sort of attack is heroism, not terrorism."

"And what about bombing marketplaces or mosques or European cities?" asked Gold.

"Those attacks achieve nothing, they just waste lives. They are simple terrorism."

"Your parents were terrorists?" asked Gold.

"Yes," said Mohammed, without pausing. "They were. They killed just to frighten their enemies, not to build anything. It achieved nothing. As far as I was concerned, getting away from those attacks is one of the core reasons I joined the Islamic State. But they too have turned to these pointless acts of terror."

Gold sat and thought for a moment. Then he asked: "This is why you want to leave?"

"Do you see the room behind me?" asked Mohammed.

"Yes," said Gold.

"It is the basement of my house. My wife, Aisha, and my only son, Hassan, were killed here."

"How?" asked Gold.

"Two weeks ago," said Mohammed, the tears reentering his eyes, "my wife was making a bomb. I don't know who or what she thought she'd attack; she wasn't in any military unit. But the bomb she was making went off while she was working on it. It killed her, and it killed my son."

This was a lie he needed the Israelis to believe.

"I'm sorry," said Gold. His regret seemed genuine.

"So am I," said Mohammed, with a heave in his voice. His statement carried more meaning than Gold could possibly understand. "It was a terrible waste. I know what you might think about Islamic marriage, but my wife was my partner in life. I loved her. And my son was my future. He was so bright and so promising. And I lost them both in one moment. Just like that, I'd never see them again... I can't possibly explain what it has done to me. And all for what? She failed; but if she had succeeded... it would have been worse."

"You decided to leave, then, after her death?" asked Gold, softly.

"I didn't decide anything," said Mohammed. "Not then. I was just going to keep going like, like I had before. I had no other path. It was hard though, to keep going. You can ask any of your informants – I've been devastated. But then I read about the City. And it seemed like a gift from All-h. It seemed like the answer to the horror my world had become."

"You said you wanted self-determination," said Gold, ignoring the effort to question Mohammed's informants, "But the City will be run by me, a Jew, and by Israelis."

"I know," said Mohammed. "But because you are a third-party, you can bring us together in a way we can't do ourselves. I understand that the City has to be run by you in order to spawn a positive revolution throughout the region. It will enable others to copy what we learn there. It will drain the poison that the worst impulses of Islamic State have created. I don't want to live under your rule. But maybe, by living under your government, we can learn to live under our own. We'll be able to do more and better."

Mohammed could see the man's pride through the video. It lasted only a moment, but it didn't escape Mohammed's attention. It was a clear sign of progress.

Mohammed continued, "The war here has consumed us, making us worse. Maybe your peace can have the opposite effect."

Steven Gold cleared his throat and said, "You're a senior commander in the Islamic State. We'd be safer not to accept you."

"Just to be clear," said Mohammed, "whether or not you accept me, I'm abandoning this war. I'm done with it. I'm not a threat to anybody."

"Given your reputation," said Gold, "that could be hard to believe."

"You feel there are risks, Mr. Gold," said Mohammed. "But you know there are rewards too. That is why you, and not some underling, are interviewing me. You recognize why I'm important. You know what I can do for you. I sit on the Central Governing Board of the Islamic State. If I come to you, I can endorse something better; and even the most dedicated of jihadis will trust me. I have a track record of dedication to the cause of Sunni freedom; I can strengthen your project tremendously. I can show, even for the most dedicated of our men, that there's a better way than the Islamic State. But I can't do it without your City to hold up as an example. I'd be crushed by those who stand against my people; or by those dedicated to the terror of the Islamic State. But together, we can do far more than either of us could do alone."

"Or you could undermine our project," said Gold.

"How?" asked Mohammed, defiantly.

"We don't want to give you ideas. But maybe you'd bomb the City."

"Mr. Gold," replied Mohammed, "if I wanted to bomb your city, *I* wouldn't apply for admission. I'd send some of my men, or even women, instead. We have plenty who love death and who would gladly launch such attacks."

"You could denounce us."

"Would I be in a more powerful position if I denounced you from within your city? What benefit would being there offer me?"

Gold sat there for a minute, contemplating. He couldn't think of what else Mohammed could do.

Finally, he said, "We'll get back to you."

"I pray," said Mohammed, "that I can join with you in your blessed work."

"So do I," said Steven Gold. "So do I."

And then the call ended.

Mohammed turned off his phone and put it down.

He looked across to his father-in-law, Sheikh Abdul bin Hassan.

"I think," said the older man, "that they fell for it."

"Praise be to All-h," said Mohammed. "I think that they did."


And then, silently, he thanked All-h for answering his most fervent prayers.

It was the first time he had felt truly happy since the moment of Aisha's death.

Perhaps her influence could still live on.

Two weeks later, on July 15<sup>th</sup>, 2014, he left Raqqa for Steven Gold's City of Refuge.

--

Steven Gold sat back from his computer. He knew what he wanted to do. He wanted to accept Mohammed bin Hassan. The man was a risk, certainly. And the Israelis would watch him carefully, at least at first. But in his heart, Steven needed to believe you could unlock the goodness in anybody. And he knew nobody could demonstrate that truth more effectively than Mohammed could.

# Sludge
*July 28th, 2014: Northern Iraq*

"You're a pretty one," said the man with a lewd stare.

He then glanced at Ibrahim. "And he'll make an excellent *shahid*."

I just stood there, transfixed. We had been so close to freedom, and now we were here. I was about to be auctioned off as a sex slave, and my brother was about to be deployed as a bomb.

At least I finally knew why we were here.

And why the Kurds had shot at us.

After leaving Akil, we'd continued through the desert. With the GPS in hand, I was confident we could ignore the roads completely. So, we did. We cut straight across the landscape. I expected to find boulders and rocks routinely and randomly impeding our progress. But there was nothing of the sort. The land was smooth, but vacant. Rocks and boulders did appear, but their location seemed controlled. They could be found on the sides of the small hills that rippled out of the earth or in occasional lines that cut across the terrain. But for the most part, the land was boulder-free. But I couldn't figure out why the boulders weren't there. And then, with horror, I realized what I was seeing. We weren't traveling through a patchwork of occasional farms on a flat desert landscape. Instead, we were traveling through vast tracts of vanished farmland. The land had been cleared and the boulders arranged between the fields that had been created. But now the fields themselves had almost disappeared. The loamy smell of living earth had been replaced with a dry echo of life that had been.

There had been drought in Iraq, but never this scale of abandonment. I wondered what had happened, and where all the farmers had gone.

My wonder didn't slow us down. It had no impact on our slow and seemingly endless progress west.

At the break of dawn, we came to a thin straight line cut into the land. I looked at the GPS and realized it was the Iraqi-Syrian border. It had no impact on us. We simply stepped across it and kept walking.

It was on the third night of walking that I saw the explosion. A good fifteen seconds later, I heard the shockwave.

Ibrahim, almost on cue, started screaming in fear. That was when I finally understood his fear of loud noises. He must have remembered something about the bombing, on some level. Every loud noise – whether it was a piece of farm equipment or a bomb – viscerally reminded him of what had happened.

We stopped and I worked to calm him down. But I kept my eye on the distant area where the explosion had been. Was it a single bomb, perhaps something dropped from an airplane? Or was it a battlefront – a border between the Islamic State and something else?

My question was answered by a burst of tracer fire. It wasn't aimed skyward, like it was meant to bring down a plane. Instead, it was aimed at another point on the horizon and it cut across the sky. I was watching a battle. And there were two sides here.

My hopes soared. I looked at the GPS and saw we weren't close to Turkish territory. Somebody else was fighting the Islamic State here. And, unlike at Kalak, there were no narrow bridges filled with combatants. There was open land. I realized we could escape. And that was when I decided to turn north.

Within an hour, we were walking over a softly sloped ridge, perhaps 50 feet high, when the ground around us started to make a distinct "thup thup" sound. Moments later, I heard the distant report of automatic weapons and I realized we were being shot at. I dove to the ground and pulled Ibrahim with me. The sound hadn't been loud enough to unnerve him. Those firing were too far away. But he was confused.

Of course, so was I.

I raised my eyes to look over the edge of our little ridge and saw a tiny outline of a familiar flag. It was red, white and green, with a sunburst in the middle. It was the flag of Kurdistan. It was freedom.

I raised my arm to wave in greeting. But the response was a hail of gunfire. The Kurdish forces were shooting at *us*. Or at least near us. I couldn't understand why. We were a woman and a child. I tried to wave again, and they fired again. I tried shouting, but I knew they couldn't hear us. I thought about trying yet again. But at some point, they were going to stop missing.

That's why, our bellies on the ground, we slid back down the hillside. We'd failed to escape, and our very attempt had probably sealed our fates. After all, those trapped between armies tend to draw attention to themselves.

I tried to sneak us away from the scene, but I knew what was coming. We offered no resistance when a small company of Islamic State fighters caught up with us. I erased the Bedouin cache locations from our GPS, and I covered my face. And then, moments later, we were bundled into the back of a small pickup truck and handcuffed to its roll bar. We weren't blindfolded.

A fighter jumped up into the bed of the truck. He was eyeing us greedily as he played with his gun.

We'd been avoiding capture for what seemed like years. And yet, here we were.

Moments after our greatest opportunity to escape, all of our choices had vanished. But I didn't understand why it had happened. Why had the Kurds fired at us? We were a woman and a child. What threat could we have been?

I expected we'd to be taken to a local command post. I expected somebody there would decide what to do with us. They might investigate and figure out who we were. That would be the end of us. I expected a short ride and then a long detention. And then... fate.

The truck's motor was quiet enough that Ibrahim was calm. It started moving and picked up speed. The territory whirred by – at least it seemed that way from the perspective of someone who hadn't driven in what seemed like years. Every time we slowed, just a little bit, I imagined we were drawing near to some hidden fortification. But then the truck would accelerate again. We'd simply been navigating rough territory. For the first twenty minutes or so, we crossed open terrain in this way. Eventually, we reached a road. It was dawn and we stopped for prayers.

It was then when I realized we weren't yet close to our destination.

We headed south. I kept expecting us to stop at any time. But we drove for hours and I began to wonder how two prisoners could justify pulling two men and a truck from an active battle for so long. Perhaps they knew who we were. But how could they have known so quickly? And how could we have been this important?

The questions floated through my mind. We'd lost our chance at freedom, but I gave no thought to resistance. Whatever was to happen was well outside our hands.

I just wanted to understand what was happening before it all ended.

Eventually, we came to the edges of a city. The sign read: "Welcome to Deir ez-Zor." I'd heard of it before.

As we entered the river district, I realized that the city had once been a beautiful city. It was not only green with the life of the Euphrates, it had its own – human-built – beauty. Some of the bridges and the buildings had an art to them that I had never seen before. Mosul's beauty lay in its distant past. For almost a thousand years, nobody had tried to build humanity into the city itself. Even the design of the Grand Mosque seemed to emphasize the distance of All-h from lowly man. It was meant to be shocking. It was meant to awe the observer. But it was cold and clinical. It had no beauty that could touch the heart. But this city was different – or at least parts of it were. The churches and mosques were more than simply functional; there was a softness in their designs.

They had human love poured into their creation.

But the city was no longer beautiful. The love had been driven away by war. As we drove, I saw buildings torn apart by cannon fire, mosques and churches collapsed by bombs, and abandoned apartment blocks crawling with molds rising from the river.

I found myself mourning for a city I had never seen before that day.

The truck turned with the highway, slanting to the northwest and running parallel to the river. Soon, we were out of Deir Ez-Zor. We'd spent no more than 20 minutes there. I looked back longingly. Especially since I now knew where we were going. We were headed to Raqqa, the capital city of the Islamic State.

I smelled Raqqa long before we got there. The river reeked with the scent of raw sewage. We passed close to it occasionally, and I caught glimpses of it. There was no sewage visible. But the smell was strong, and as we got closer to Raqqa it only grew stronger. The fighter in the truck covered his face with a cloth, like some Jihadi in a video. But I knew, hidden behind my own burqa, that a strip of cloth was little protection from what was enveloping us.

As we arrived at the outskirts of Raqqa, I still couldn't understand how an active military operation could justify spending five hours, two men, and a truck to transport two civilian prisoners.

Then the truck pulled up to a small building with a lot and a wooden stage-like structure outside of it. We were uncuffed, ushered out of the bed of the truck, and guided towards a doorway.

As we passed through, I noticed a sign. It read: "Office of Prisoner Disposition."

It was there that I met the man with the lewd stare.

"You're a pretty one," he'd said, seemingly seeing through my *nikab*.

I said nothing.

It was when he'd glanced at Ibrahim and said, "And he'll make an excellent *shahid*," that everything came together.

This man saw a brain-damaged child and thought of him as a useful munition. The Kurds had shot at us because they thought we were suicide bombers. And they had good cause to think so.

The Islamic State had brought us here because we were valuable. I could be sold as a bride, raising revenue for the cause while rewarding some loyal fighter. And my brother could be trained to be a bomb – extending the borders of All-h's true faith.

The Office of Prisoner Disposition, this man, was about to seal our fates.

And there was nothing I could do.

And then I remembered how my father and his truck could drive through every checkpoint in Mosul. And I found myself opening my mouth and saying four words that could rescue Ibrahim and I from a terrible fate.

"I can fix it," I said.

"Fix what?" asked the man behind the counter, aggressively.

"The smell," I answered.

He cocked his head, confused.

"It is the sewage plant," I said. "I didn't see any clumps in the river, so my guess is you've got a failure in the Sequencing Batch Reactor."

He looked even more confused.

"Do you want the smell to go away?" I asked, simply.

"I do, I do," he said, as he finally found his voice. "I don't believe you can do anything about it, but I'll make a call."

I had, at least, bought some time.

Ibrahim and I stood there, shifting occasionally, for thirty minutes.

Ibrahim was much better at standing still than he had been before his injury.

Eventually, a short and slightly overweight man walked through the door. He moved deliberately, almost carefully. Like all the others, he sported a full and unkempt beard. But unlike the others, he didn't look like a fighter. Small, but thick, glasses were perched above his beard. And while his eyes were excited, they didn't have the cold dedication of a killer. Even given all of that, what truly set him apart were his hands. They were small and soft, almost delicate.

The man brushed right by Ibrahim and I, as if we didn't exist.

"Salim," said the new arrival, greeting the man behind the desk. "Where's the woman who knows about sewage?"

"Youssef," said Salim, with almost groveling respect, "I didn't say she knew about sewage. Just that she might. She's right there." He pointed at me.

Youssef turned.

"What's wrong with the plant?" he asked me, dismissively, as if he had better places to be.

"Something is wrong with the Sequencing Batch Reactor. The SBR," I said.

"What's the SBR?" he asked. He didn't ask it like an actual question. I had the distinct idea that he knew the answer. It was a test. And I could pass it.

"Typically," I said, "there is a pair of pools, maybe three. Over a few hours, they each go through a cycle of filling, aeration, and drainage. The pools have bacteria that process the sewage and clean it up. Something is wrong with them."

"What?" he asked.

"I'd need to see it," I said. "It could be all sorts of things. The bacteria could be dead. The cycle could be running too fast. The return rates of the underlying sludge might be too high or too low. I'd have to get a look to figure out which it is."

"And how do you know it's the SBR and not something else?"

"Like I told Salim," I answered, "the sewage in the river is not in obvious chunks. This suggests the filtering and grinding process are working well enough. There might be processing steps after the SBR, but their failure would leave a much less noticeable odor. That leaves the SBR."

Youssef looked somewhat more impressed.

"We could have another kind of plant," he said.

"You have an SBR," I said. "It was a big thing, in the regional news. A few years ago, the Syrian government bought new water treatment plants in the region. Everyplace around here has SBRs."

"I didn't read about it," he said.

"Your father," I answered, "didn't think sewage was as important as my father did."

It was then that Youssef chuckled.

"Let's have a look at the plant," he said, with a smile, and he gestured for me to follow.

"Only with my brother," I answered, seriously.

Agreeably, he responded, "Bring him along."


We drove to the sewage processing plant in Youssef's Toyota Land Cruiser. It took us across the polluted river. The smell was everywhere; and it was overwhelming.

"How long as it been going on?" I asked.

"A few weeks," said Youssef. "It is making people sick."

As we got nearer to the plant, the smell only got worse. When we parked, Salim dropped out of our small expedition. He didn't want to go any nearer. Ibrahim wanted to stay with him, but I insisted otherwise. As near as I could tell, Salim was an officially recognized slave trader. I would rather Ibrahim go to a malfunctioning sewage plant than be alone with a man like him.

As we approached the front gates of the plant, a worker came towards us.

"Youssef," he said. "Welcome." The man was tall and lanky. He looked a little weak, like he couldn't hold his food down. His face was flat, and he had almost no nose. Considering his job, that was probably fortunate.

"Achmed," replied Youssef, "this young lady knows a thing or two about sewage. Can you show us around?"

"Yes, yes," said Achmed. Unlike Salim, he was polite, but not obsequious.

We walked through the gate of the plant and I asked Achmed, "Who's in charge of the SBR?"

"Nobody," he answered.

"What do you mean, nobody?"

"The Syrian State pays our salaries, not the Islamic one. Every month or two, we travel to Hama to collect our paychecks. The manager of the SBR was traveling to Hama when the government accidentally attacked his car. Nobody else will come to replace him; this is an undesirable work environment." Achmed chuckled to himself.

"That said," he continued, "the people who worked for him are still here. Unfortunately, they can only handle routine problems, and the problem we have isn't routine."

Achmed guided us to a platform overlooking the reactor itself. There were four pools here. Two were full, the others were filling. Human waste, along with some industrial, waste, was floating through them. As the waste moved through the ponds, it should have been gathering in clumps formed by the bacteria binding themselves to the waste. Those clumps, called flocs, should have been settling to the bottom of the pools and forming a solid mass where other bacteria would process them further, allowing the clean-looking effluent to flow off the top of the pool. Instead, only a few clumps were forming, showing the bacteria were present. But the clumps were few and far between. Thus, when the pools were draining into the adjacent Euphrates, the waste was going with the water. This was what was producing the stench.

I was surprised I hadn't seen people in downstream Deir Ez-Zur falling over in the streets.

The problem was obvious: the pools were supposed to be bubbling. Bubbling diffusion systems should have been running oxygen through them, feeding the bacteria. But there was no bubbling, and so the bacteria were barely surviving.

"What kind of filters do the bubble diffusers have?" I asked Achmed. He looked a bit confused.

"When these pools are running normally," I tried a second time, "are there big bubbles in them, or just tiny ones?"

"Tiny," he said, confidently.

I had my diagnosis.

"Take me to the air compressor," I said to Achmed. He led us to the largest building on the site.

We opened the door and entered a space that was both better smelling and considerably worse sounding. The air compressor was emitting an unhealthy whine.

"The problem," I said to Achmed, "is that the filters on the bubble diffusors are clogged. They need to be cleaned."

"I don't understand," said Achmed. "They are membrane filters. They don't need to be cleaned."

Youssef looked at me, doubtfully. He suddenly thought I was on far shakier ground.

"They aren't supposed to need cleaning," I said. "That's why they use them instead of ceramic filters. But they do."

"Explain," said Youssef, simply. His challenge had some danger to it.

"Ceramic filters used to be the standard," I said. "But among other problems, if the power went down, then the air compressors would die, and the bubblers would stop producing bubbles. When that happened, the water would backflow, the sludge would get sucked into them, and you'd need to drain and clean the tank to repair the issue. But in a place like this, where power goes out regularly, they switched to flexible membranes. When there is no air pressure behind them, they close off, protecting themselves from the sludge. But these have, nonetheless, become blocked."

"How?" challenged Achmed. He and his crew were at risk of looking incompetent next to a 16-year-old girl.

"The water here is very hard," I answered. "There are lots of minerals in it. Calcium carbonate, that gray scaly stuff that sticks to dishes and hot water kettles, can accumulate on the membranes and can lock them open. Then, when the power dies, they can get blocked by sucked-in sludge."

Youssef nodded. He was following well, which suggested he was at least somewhat technical.

"What's the solution?" asked Achmed.

"Hydrochloric acid," I said.

"Wouldn't pouring it in the pools kill the bacteria?" asked Youssef.

"We don't pour it in," I said. I turned to Achmed. "Can you show me where it is?"

Achmed guided us to the far end of the room. He opened a large double door, revealing a chemical storage area. As expected, there was a lot of hydrochloric acid. It was stored in five-gallon buckets.

There were gloves, goggles and chemical suits hanging on a wall of the storage area. I dressed myself and Ibrahim in them. Youssef and Achmed followed suit. Then I easily picked up a five-gallon bucket of the acid, surprising myself with the strength the farming had given me. I carried it towards the moaning air compressor. The system was huge. A small output ran out of the top of it, and a massive intake stretched to the side, reaching the side of the building. There was a door next to the intake. I opened it and we stepped outside. The huge screens that protected the air compressor from sucked-in debris towered over us. Today though, they weren't protecting much. The intake was weak.

"Is there a hot water urn in the office?" I asked Achmed. He nodded and trotted off to get it.

I positioned myself upwind from the acid and untwisted the top of the large bucket. Achmed returned with the urn and a very long extension cord. Then he plugged it in.

"The acid will dissolve the tiny amounts of sludge blocking the membranes," I explained. "And then it will react with the calcium carbonate, pushing open the tubes and restoring their function. We won't need much acid, and we won't need it in a hurry, so it won't kill too much of the bacteria."

Youssef and Achmed nodded.

Their permission granted, I positioned the urn below the air intake, poured the acid into it and turned it on. In a moment, a fine mist of boiling hydrochloric acid was making its way into the air compressor.

"How long will it take?" asked Youssef.

"It depends," I answered, "on how bad the blockages are."

We waited for a half an hour before we began to hear a difference in the moaning noises of the air compressor. It was beginning to function more effectively. The mist accelerated. We went to look at the pools and saw some aeration already occurring. Plant workers started to accumulate around the pools. Within another hour, the compressor was sounding normal and the clumps in the pools were forming properly and dropping to the bottom. The reactor was back in shape.

I turned off the urn and poured the remaining acid back into its bucket.

It was then that the plant workers began to clap.

I nodded politely towards them. Youssef was smiling as he guided me back out of the plant.

As we left, I had only one question in my mind. I knew I'd been useful, but had I been useful enough?

Salim was waiting for us outside the gates.

"So?" he asked Youssef, ignoring Ibrahim and me.

"She fixed it," said Youssef, clearly impressed. "I think the smell will clear up in a couple of days."

He paused for a moment, and then asked Salim, "Can we talk?"

The two of them shuffled away, heads close in conversation. I considered making a run for it, but I knew we'd never get far.

Then, as I watched, Salim pulled a paper from his pocket, and Youssef signed it. Moments later, Youssef was back.

"Let's go home," he said.

"What?" I asked, totally confused.

"I need your help with something, so let's go home."

"I'm a single woman," I said, protesting. "I can't go home with an unrelated man."

"You're not unrelated," said Youssef. He pressed a coin into my hand. "This is the first part of your *mahr*. You'll get the same amount each month to come. Salim acted as your *wali*. I signed the contract. We're married now."

I was stunned. I considered being angry. But then I considered the alternatives. I could have been sold as a sex slave. Instead, I'd been unwillingly married to a man who would value my knowledge and my talents. I might even do, in Raqqa, what my father had done in Mosul.

In context, the marriage was a rare opportunity.

"And Ibrahim?" I asked, a bit of worry remaining in my voice.

"Is that your brother?" Youssef asked.

"Yes," I said.

"He is in your custody," said Youssef. "He comes along."

I smiled broadly. The education my father had given me had bought me something akin to freedom. Ibrahim and I would have a home. I would have a job. And we wouldn't need to run.

My heart was full of hope.


It didn't last long.

# Opening Day

*14 August 2014, Israeli-controlled Qunietra*

Steven Gold woke up earlier than usual. He was excited, after all. As he lay there in bed, the first thing he noticed was the quiet. The wind had been howling around his trailer every night for the better part of a week. The square edges and thin walls of the portable structure just seemed to accentuate the sound. The howling had bothered him. As he'd lain there in bed, it had seemed like nature itself was constantly reminding him of just how unformed his project was. But not today. Today, there was silence. Today, he felt peace.

Steven got up from the thin mattress, trying hard not to disturb his wife, Amy – or their two children. He got dressed quickly and quietly, grabbed his phone, and padded out the door of the trailer. He put his shoes on outside. He wanted to cherish this day from beginning to end. It would start by watching the sunrise.

The trailer sat, with a group of other trailers, on a bluff overlooking a dip in the terrain. The City would start in the dip. But the security forces had insisted that the city management, including Steven and his team, live on the bluff. It had long been an Israeli army position, and they recognized its defensibility. Steven had objected at first, believing that the administration should live among the citizens. But the army hadn't been accommodating, and so he'd eventually accepted the arrangement.

Now, every morning, he relished their insistence. He could sit on the edge of the bluff, in a lawn chair outside his trailer, and watch the sun rise. Sitting on a lawn chair outside a trailer was not the kind of thing he would ever have done in the States. But he felt freer here, and less constrained by class and convention.

As he looked into the dip, he could see the streets and the buildings rising in their places – at least in his mind's eye. In reality, there was almost nothing there. The space was covered with tall, dried-out, grasses and tiny wind-swept trees. It looked like a no-man's land, abandoned and inhospitable. From his lawn chair, Steven could see farmland, green farmland, only a few miles away. But not here. Here, the stacked pallets of refugee tents and scattered camp toilets seemed to offer only temporary and hopeless resistance to the emptiness around them. The solitary playground was the only thing that looked permanent.

On the bluff, there had been more construction. In addition to the water tank and step-down transformers necessary to provide basic infrastructure to the site, there were 31 single trailers where the administrators and soldiers were barracked. There were no trailers for the construction workers, they had been bussed in from nearby towns and were going to be replaced very soon. There were also two larger trailers. Both could be classed as triple-wide. One housed security and surveillance equipment, while the other was the home of the municipal government. The municipal government trailer contained a collection of workstations around a central table. Every station had noise-cancelling headsets. If you were working independently, you'd put them on. If you wanted or needed to talk to others, you'd take them off. It was cheaper than office space. That one trailer, plus a few others set up for private meetings and interviews, was where all the civilian work got done.

The thing Steven liked least about the city was the solid concrete wall that surrounded the Syrian side of the site. The wall wasn't high, perhaps 8 feet tall, but it was studded with sensors and had raised guard posts at regular intervals. Between it and the bluff, the city had an imposing, almost claustrophobic, feel. Opposite the wall, at the top of the bluff, there was a tall observation tower which complemented the wall. Together, they made the place resemble an open-air prison. Steven had objected to both structures, of course. But he'd been informed that shooting, bombing or other attacks were quite likely, and that the wall and the tower would keep the residents themselves safe. He had reluctantly agreed to their inclusion.

Looking at the wall reminded Steven that he wasn't entirely happy that Amy and the kids were here. This life wasn't comfortable, or safe. In their way, they were wading into a war. There was no reason his wife and kids had to be here. They could have stayed in DC, or even Phoenix. But they were here. Amy had insisted. She'd said the children would learn from the experience; that watching their father would show them just how much a person can do to make the world a better place.

He hoped her trust was warranted.

Just then, Steven heard the cry of a muezzin in the morning air. It wasn't the amplified voice he'd heard in Israeli cities. It was an actual, unamplified, muezzin's voice. It was the first time Steven had ever heard it. Steven couldn't see over the concrete wall – but he imagined there were people there now. They had collected together in order to gain entry into his City. Tomorrow, the dip in front of him would be filled with families.

Steven felt a hand on his shoulder and looked up to see Amy.

"It's beautiful, isn't it," she said.

"It is," he answered, simply.

She sat next to him and they stayed there. They listened to the muezzin and watched the sun creep up over the horizon. It was only 60 degrees now, but both of them knew the sun promised an extraordinarily hot day.

The muezzin's prayer stopped and the subdued activity of the trailers on the bluff began. Lights turned on. Toilets flushed. Some soldiers awoke while others went to sleep. And, one-by-one, Steven's administrative team made their way to the room where they all worked. Steven checked his phone to read the news. And then he stood up to go.

"Steven?" said Amy.

"Yes?" he said.

"I am so very proud of you."

Steven smiled, deeply, and kissed his wife on the forehead. And then he walked the 200 feet to work.


There were six departments Steven had established: IT, Finance, Diplomacy, Infrastructure, Absorption, and Cultural Relations. Each of the department heads had a permanent seat at the literal table in the administrative trailer. When there was a focus on a particular area, others could join the central conversation. But for the most part, they worked in the trailers set up for private meetings, or even in their own quarters.

However, today was special: everybody was in the room.

When Steven got to the administrative trailer, he opened the flimsy door and then mapped out a path through the crowded room to his own workstation. Eventually, with all eyes on him, he made it there.

"Hello, everybody," he said jovially.

There were smiles all around.

Steven had run the project using an Agile project management philosophy. The goal of an Agile process was to have small tasks with easily measurable progress. The City would reach some kind of steady state every two weeks. Then, over the next two-week cycle, new functions and capabilities would be added to the place. It might be streets, it might be water, or it might be debit card systems. The key was that development took place in spurts. And at the beginning of each day, Steven met with his department heads, who summarized what they had achieved in the last day, what they intended to achieve in the coming day, and what impediments they were facing. In a project as complex and multi-faceted as this one, the daily meetings had helped him, and the others, keep their eyes on the larger picture.

"Information Technology?" Steven asked. He turned to a tall, blond, American woman by the name of Elizabeth. She had made billions on Internet payment systems and was ready for a new challenge. She was donating her time.

"Everything is ready. We have the records up and running with interfaces that enable us to review resident status, history, and other details. We'll have smooth processes for bringing people in, assigning them permanent IDs, collecting biometrics, and all the rest. We are ready for our first citizens! That's what we intend to support in the coming day. And I'm happy to report, we have no impediments."

The group clapped. All of this had been done in two and a half months – they had been working superhuman hours.

"Infrastructure?" asked Steven.

A brawny-looking man with close-set eyes spoke up. His name was Benny.

"The water and power systems are up and running. Both are reliable. As per your plan, we'll only have water from the pipe available initially. Hookups on a building-by-building or family-by-family basis will only come later. The soldiers have been trying out the camp toilets, and they appear to be functioning exactly as intended. We'll be showing new arrivals how to use the water, power and sewage facilities. We are also ready for our first citizens. We have no impediments."

The group clapped. Building the pipe up to the City site had been difficult. Not only had it been long, but it had had to maneuver around numerous archeological sites along the way.

"Finance?" It was Elizabeth's turn again. Her background was well-suited to this.

"We have sixty million shekels in our accounts right now. Our burn rate to date has been admirably low. We have worked with IT to set up our debit card system. This will enable immigrants to collect their own benefits as well as load their own money onto our e-money system. At this point, we have committed 0.75 percent of our future GDP to secure this cash, and the land we're on. We expect this number to rise, but I want to commend everybody on their caution so far. I believe we can get this City up and running and in stable financial shape in only a few months. Today's work will be focused on distributing the cash cards. No impediments!"

Again, the group clapped. They had been very careful with their spending. Steven wanted the City to preserve as much of its GDP for its residents as possible.

"Diplomacy?" A clean-cut man with sharp features spoke up. His name was Daoud, and he was a Druze from the nearby city of Majdal Shams.

"We have import and export permits ready. The Israeli government will allow us to ship through Haifa, although inspections will be heavy at first. A Cypriot airline will provide passenger service to Nicosia from the Afik airfield. However, we'll need to get the EU to set up a visa program before we can set up flights to Cyprus. So far, only Israel will recognize our travel documents, and even then, only on a case-by-case basis. It will take a while for things to settle in, but once we have a track-record, I think we'll be good on these fronts. Today, we'll be informing new residents of their status. We have no impediments."

Steven nodded. The clapping was more muted, but Daoud's capabilities were blunted by the interest and trust of people outside this room.

"Absorption?"

A woman named Yael answered. She'd worked in new immigrant absorption in Israel for decades.

"We have some information on the immigrants, so we've been able to plan ahead. The interview system has been set up to do secondary processing on those who already have their entry approved. In addition, we have volunteers from the Arabic-speaking Israeli communities who will serve as counselors. The basic rules and expectations of the City will be spelled out clearly to new arrivals. Finally, our small business coordinators have already scheduled work sessions to help develop the business ideas of the immigrants and then help connect them to overseas funding sources. All of this work will start today. We have no impediments."

Another round of clapping followed.

"Security?"

A retired Israeli general named Itai spoke up, "Everything is in place. We have excellent perimeter security and full access to Israeli government vetting resources. We have set up the access points so we can search people for weapons and explosives and clear people for entry. We'll be bringing people through the perimeter and supporting interviews today. There are no impediments."

There was sporadic clapping. People were nodding in acknowledgement of his important work.

"And finally," Steven said, "Cultural relations."

The group turned its head nervously in the direction of Mohammed bin Hassan. Everybody knew his history, and as much admiration as they had for his decision to join them, their apprehension was palpable. Steven realized, given Mohammed's history, that he'd been an odd choice to run Cultural Relations. But he'd argued – to himself and others – that accepting Mohammed, despite his history, would show the openness and dedication of the City. He wanted Mohammed in that role.

"Nobody is here yet," said Mohammed, with an open smile, and in his rapidly improving but still broken English, "When they come, I talk with them. I learn who the leaders are, and we work together to make everything peaceful. No impediments."

Again, the clapping was muted. Mohammed hadn't done much of anything yet – and so judgment was being withheld.

Steven looked around the room. Every face was turned towards him, waiting.

"Folks," said Steven, "Have you read the news this morning?"

Most of the people in the room nodded in confirmation.

"If you did, and most of you did, you saw that the Islamic State banished all Christians from Mosul – on threat of death. Not many were left, anyway, but there were 60,000 Christians in the city just two years ago. They have all been banished."

Steven continued. "In my past life, I would have read the news and felt both sad and helpless. But not today. Today, I feel empowered.

Why? Because we, the people here in this room, can change the reality. We are no longer just observers. We are participants now. We will be providing a place for those who are fleeing, and we will be providing an opportunity for them to renew their societies and reject the intolerance and violence that has overtaken them."

Steven paused briefly. Looked around the room, he continued.

"There is a story about Mother Theresa. A woman came to her in New York and said she wanted to join the Sisters of Charity in India. She wanted to do important work. Mother Theresa took one look at her and said, 'You can't do what I do if you want to do it for yourself.' Mother Theresa rejected the young lady. Why? Because she understood that a true leader is successful not because they want to be a great leader, but because they care about the people they lead. In this way, all of you are true leaders. You are all here to enable others. It is your dedication to others that will make this place work.

"You've done an enormous amount of work so far. But we are only getting started. Now is the time when we stop laying the groundwork for what could be and actually begin to rebuild lives and empower the best elements in a society. Now is when the rubber hits the road."

He paused again and looked around the room.

"The Islamic State expelled all Christians today. I want to be clear to everybody here: this kind of action repels us. I've had people come to me and say that Sunni Muslims should not be admitted. I've had them tell me that they are incompatible with tolerance and peace. But I reject this. Before the Christians were expelled from Mosul, they had lived there and in the surrounding plains for close to two thousand years. Before Jews were expelled from Iraq, they lived there for more than two and a half thousand years. Zoroastrians have been there even longer. It is possible for this region to have multi-ethnic and multi-religious societies. Despite many historical imperfections, we know it is possible for a better reality to exist. So, don't come to me suggesting we expel this or that group. We are the opposite of the Islamic State. We will not only accept all these groups, we will embrace them."

Daoud the Druze looked doubtful. Mohammed the Sunni looked grateful. Elizabeth looked inspired.

"We have a long day today," said Steven. "Right now, we have a patch of dirt. Beyond that gray wall there is a hellish world. But tomorrow, there will be thousands of families – who will have escaped that world and entered this one. Among them we have shopkeepers, builders, engineers, road builders, and even merchants. We have the makings of a better society waiting to come in.

"Today, we aren't working from this office. Today, we will be welcoming and interviewing our newest citizens. Today, we will be helping them get started on their new lives and on the building of their new society. I don't want to see anybody in here, all day. I don't want us working on ideas. I want all of us, myself included, out there working with people."

Steven looked around the room and then concluded, "Let's get to it."

Nobody clapped this time.

They just filed out of the room, ready to get to work.

Mohammed couldn't help smiling as he walked.

Everything was going perfectly.

# Basement

*July 28th, 2014: Outside Qunietra*

It had all started when I reacted the wrong way to a question.

We'd driven to Youssef's house together. He parked the car in a carport. It was an unusual feature for a home in the region, but perhaps he was worried about satellite surveillance. We got out of the car and then entered his house through a side door.

It was then that the most amazing thing happened. When he closed that side door, the world outside seemed to shut behind it. The house was silent – like a tomb. It was a bit frightening. Ibrahim started crying as soon as we walked in, but Youssef ignored him.

"Incredible, isn't it?" he said.

"Yes," I said, hopefully. "It is." I wrapped my arm around Ibrahim.

"This house," he said, as he began to lead us through it, "was built to my own specifications. It is a specialized place, separated from the surrounding terrain with advanced vibration-dampening technology."

"Do you have problems sleeping?" I asked.

He chuckled again; I found myself liking his chuckle.

"No, no," he said. "I sleep fine. This house is not only where I live, it is my laboratory. I do sensitive work here, and there are unwelcome vibrations in the area, and so it is dampened."

I nodded, not really knowing what he was talking about. The only vibrations I could think of would come from aerial bombing.

He guided us to a staircase, and we went downstairs. There was a large room in the basement; its footprint somehow seemed larger than the house itself. There was a rubber floor and multiple gleaming workbenches. All were fitted with grounding straps. Along one wall was a set of tall steel cupboards. There was a set of steel shutters concealing something else along one of the walls. A thick-looking steel door stood next to the shutters. I guessed there was a room there. The place was extraordinarily well-lit – it was almost like being inside a fluorescent bulb. It was also incredibly sterile.

"This," Youssef said, "Is my laboratory." He was grinning broadly. He had reason to be impressed.

"Do you have your own generator?" I asked. Power was spotty in the region, at best.

"As a matter of fact," he said, "I do. It could be very unpleasant were I to suffer an outage during my work."

I looked around to try to figure out what he worked on, but the benches were clean.

"What do you study?" I asked.

Youssef smiled broadly. "I am the Senior Engineer," he said, "for the Islamic State."

I didn't really know what that meant.

"So," I asked, "what do you study?"

He laughed this time.

"Weapons," he said. "I study weapons!"

I felt a chill come over me. It appeared I wasn't going to be doing municipal engineering.

"Weapons?" I asked.

"Well," he said, "primarily explosives. I try to construct simple bombs our forces in the field can implement by themselves. I design and build trigger mechanisms. We often ship those out to our units. I look at adhesives, catalysts, shrapnel, whatever. There is a huge difference in quality between a completely ad-hoc bomb and one built using ready supplies, but well-tested methods. Oh, and I test small explosives out in the chamber." He pointed to the steel shutters.

"Ok," I said. This man had probably designed the bomb that had ripped my parents apart – and injured my little brother.

Youssef said, more seriously, "And, I work on more experimental projects."

I didn't want to ask, but I knew I was expected to. "Like what?" I said.

He was smiling broadly.

"Chemical and biological weapons."

I suddenly felt ill, but I held myself steady.

"You want my help with those?" I asked, shakily. I already knew the answer.

"Well," said Youssef, "you demonstrated a very hands-on knowledge of chemicals, so I thought you might be able to help."

"I doubt it," I said. I wanted the conversation to end. I was the man's wife, so I would submit to him in everything. Well, almost everything: he couldn't ask me to help him with this.

"Did you know," said Youssef, "that chemical weapons generally aren't very useful?"

"No," I said.

"It's true," said Youssef. "It is very hard to control them. And it is very hard to create large enough concentrations to kill. Only 7 percent of people exposed to chemical weapons in World War One were killed."

"I didn't know that." I said, quietly.

"They were banned," said Youssef. "Not because they killed, but because they caused pain and created fear."

I just looked at him.

"The Germans needed fear," said Youssef, "Because their backs were against the wall. They used gas, and they used submarines to create fear. It was their ultimate weapon."

"It didn't work, though," I said.

"No," said Youssef, "it didn't. Even with their resources, they couldn't solve the problem of concentration. But that was because they didn't have All-h behind them. It *will* work for us."

"So why do you need me?" I asked.

"Chemical weapons need to be concentrated. But we can't do that. We can't drop barrel bombs or inundate an area with artillery canisters. We have small mortars. We need to modify them so that the chemicals can be more effective, even in limited quantities."

I wanted to argue the morality of it. But I knew it was pointless. The Syrian government used such weapons – so why shouldn't the Islamic State?

"Youssef," I said, "I assume the Americans and Russians and Iraqis and even the Syrians have poured billions of dollars into this. And they may have solved it. I know Sarin and VX are far more potent than chlorine and mustard gas. But you can't make those, not here. And that's the same reason I can't solve your problem. You just have this lab here. You can't work miracles."

"But I think maybe *you* can," said Youssef. "Your arrival, timed as it was, is clearly a gift from All-h. I believe you can help, even if you don't realize it."

"I can't make a gas stay concentrated on a battlefield," I insisted.

"There's another problem," said Youssef, as if I hadn't spoken. "Often, our enemies occupy our cities. We don't want to kill our people. We want to discriminate. We want to kill their soldiers, but not our own."

"That's one thing I know," I said. "Gas doesn't discriminate."

Unfortunately, in the back of my mind, I was already solving the problem. *Poison gas* may not discriminate, but *poison* does. A moment later, I had a complete solution to his problem. The flash of achievement reached my face before I managed to suppress it.

Youssef smiled.

"You have an answer," he said. "You are All-h's gift."

"No," I lied.

"No," said Youssef, insistently. "You have an answer, and you won't tell me."

His voice had taken on a vaguely threatening tone.

"I have no answer," I said, flatly.

"What is your name?" he asked.

I was shocked. We were married. We'd been married, but he hadn't learned my name. Of course, even I'd forgotten the name I'd used before, in Mosul.

"What did you put in the contract?" I was asking, just to get time to think.

"I described you," said Youssef, "and where you were found."

"My name is Hasna," I said. It meant "powerful."


"Okay," he said, "my dear wife, Hasna. You are a wife. My wife. Under the tenets of Islam, it is your responsibility to serve me. I support you and the house, outside the house. And you support me from within it. It is your obligation."

I nodded. He was right of course. I was a Muslim wife, and I had obligations. But did they extend to murder? I didn't know. I'm sure there was a law about it somewhere.

"I don't have an answer," I insisted.

"Hasna," he said, "we are the true lovers of peace. Our enemies demand war. They war on All-h. We must establish All-h's glory and All-h's peace, because only that peace will be everlasting. For the sake of the True Umma, you must tell me what you know."

I said nothing.

And then, in a burst of movement, he swung his fat fist at my brother. The 5-year-old boy dropped to the floor with a thud. Then he lunged towards me. I tried to fight him off, hoping my body, strengthened by the farming, could resist. But I was no match for his weight. He dragged me, kicking and screaming, towards the thick metal door next to the shutters. With one hand, he opened the door. And with the other, he shoved me in. I bounced against the far wall.

Then, he slammed the door behind me.

In a moment, I had gone from the bright and sterile lights of the lab to the complete darkness of this new and tiny space.

And for the first time since the killing of my parents, I was overwhelmed. Ibrahim was still out there.

If he'd asked me to kill for him then, at that moment, I would have agreed. Anything to get Ibrahim back.

But he didn't.

Instead, he let me think.

---

I dropped to the ground, in that confined space. And I prayed, desperately, for All-h's help. I don't know how long I prayed for. But despite my desperation, nobody came to the room. Nobody told me that Ibrahim was okay. After pouring my heart out, I still felt not only powerless, but disoriented.

I knew nothing and I had no power over anything.

Eventually, I realized that in order to change my reality, I had to learn *something*.

I began to reach out in each direction. The first thing I learned was that the room was tiny. I could stand in it, barely. But I couldn't lie down. The length from the door to the far wall was less than the length of my arm. And the room was only as wide as the doorway and the steel shutters next to them. My two elbows could simultaneously touch the two walls. I could bow in prayer, but I could not lie down.

I felt my way along the walls, trying to figure out what they were made of. The answer was some sort of heavy-feeling steel. It was cold to the touch. I rapped it with my knuckles but felt no echo or reverberation. It was thick.

Next to the door, where the shutters were, there was something other than steel. It was warmer. It was some sort of smooth plastic surface. I pounded on it. It felt like the sort of thick acrylic they use to bomb-proof windows. That was probably why it was there. This was a test chamber, after all. The shutters probably covered a viewing area. They were probably lowered for particularly dangerous tests.

Beneath the plexiglass, there was a small bin with gloves. They were thick and connected to the wall. I couldn't find their openings. I imagined they were on the other side of the plexiglass. A technician would put their hands into the gloves on one side of the wall and manipulate materials on the other. It enabled the technician to experiment with dangerous substances from the safety of the main room.

I expected, and found, what I thought was the frame for a tray that could slide forward, transferring items from outside the room to inside it. But it was tiny. It was also latched closed from outside the chamber.

I felt around the rest of the tiny room's walls and found nothing but a small vent. It was only large enough for my hand. But there was a small amount of air coming through it, which meant I probably wouldn't asphyxiate.

I felt for the ceiling, which was almost touching my head. It too was cold steel. But there was what felt like a small plexiglass panel there. It probably covered an observation light. The plexiglass felt a little loose, like it wasn't perfectly maintained. But that wouldn't help much. I couldn't escape through a light fixture.

It was clear within five minutes of my prayer that I was in a steel cage. And it was far better built than any prison cell.

I slumped down and sat against one of the walls. I had learned, but I had no answers, and I had no hope of finding them.

The brief solace of my explorations retreated, and I returned to my mad panic. I was responsible for Ibrahim, and I had let him down. My mind became chaotic with regret and confusion. At some point, I realized I had to go to the bathroom. I used the bin below the plexiglass. Perhaps, it would be cleaned.

And then I sat again. It was odd, but the stench of my own excrement made the situation more bearable. The room was lifeless and sterile before. At least now, it stank.

It seemed like forever before there was any light at all. I must have slept, but I don't remember. And then, without any warning, the observation light in the ceiling burst on. It was a harsh white light. I slammed my eyes shut and covered my face with my hands. It was incredibly violent. But perhaps I was to be saved. Perhaps I could be released. The shutters slid open. I tried to look out, but the light within the chamber made it impossible to see.

I shouted, "Is Ibrahim okay?" I shouted it again and again; but there was no response. Instead, the gloves moved and collected my excrement into the bin. It withdrew, like the tray at a bank teller. And then the bin opened again and there was some food and water. The food was, thankfully, in a wrapper. And the drink was in a cup. I scarfed it down, desperately. I hadn't realized how hungry I'd become.

But then the light turned off and I was thrown back into darkness.

I sat, silent. The question I cared most about in the world hadn't been answered.

But at least Youssef wanted to keep me alive.

It gave me something akin to leverage.


The darkness went on, perhaps for hours, or even days. And then, seemingly out of nowhere, I saw somebody with me. It was my father. He was sitting there, opposite me. He was looking at me. And I realized there was a question here, and there was an answer.

But I couldn't think of where to start.


The next time the light came on, a voice accompanied it. It was Youssef, my husband. I wanted to ask if Ibrahim was okay, but I knew I couldn't let him see how easily he could control me.

"Do you hear that rumbling?" he asked, through the hidden speakers in the room. His voice sounded tinny. I strained to listen. And, indeed, I could just detect something far off.

"That," said Youssef, "is why you'll never be rescued."

I was weak and dehydrated. I just wanted the food and the drink.

"Those are bombings," said Youssef. "The Western powers are bombing Raqqa."

How did that predict the survival of the Islamic State? I was curious, but I didn't ask.

"They aren't bombing *us*," said Youssef, expecting my question. "They are bombing Raqqa. We pretend to have the functions of our state in another part of the city. It is all very convincing. And they bomb it, again and again. It is like a goose attacking a stick. It doesn't hurt the man holding the stick. Why? Because nobody important actually works there. You see, we live in the modern age. We have the Cloud and the Internet and encryption. Our government is conducted from our homes. They think they bomb workshops, but they don't know that my house is the most important workshop there is."

I tried to look through the glass, but I saw nothing. I imagined him smiling pleasantly.

"Do you know who set this all up?" he asked.

I didn't answer.

"The Cloud, the structure, everything?" said Youssef, as if explaining the question would make it clearer.

"Of course not," said Youssef. "It's a big secret. Only two people know. I know, and his father-in-law knows. Well, I guess if we include him, then three people know,"

He chuckled. Now, it was less endearing.

"The man who set this up is a friend of mine. He is only 21. But he made all of this possible. He is a gift from All-h. Like you. It is because of him that the Western Goose attacks the Islamic State's stick."

I couldn't imagine why I would have cared.

"He is on another mission," said Youssef, mysteriously. "A very secret mission. Nobody but us three know what he's doing. But with this mission, he'll shape the world for us. It will make the tricks here in Raqqa seem like child's play. But he can't work alone. He can make the world dance, but we still need to take advantage of what he does in order to achieve victory for All-h. With your help, our victory will happen far more easily. Fewer people will have to die. Fear will prevent a wider and more dangerous war. You'll come around to believing this. After all, you've really got no other choice."

I wanted to ask about Ibrahim. But I knew that would weaken my position.

Before he closed the shutter, Youssef added one last word. "Ibrahim is alive. Perhaps you'll keep him that way."

And then the light turned off. And there was total darkness. The tray was cleaned, and food was provided.

I began to eat.

I looked around, curious if I could still see my father.

Thankfully, he was there. He was still watching me.

I asked myself, what was the question? That's where my father's lessons always started. Was the question whether I would be able to sacrifice my life to slow down the Islamic State? The answer was yes. But that wasn't the hard question. The hard question was: would I be willing to sacrifice Ibrahim's life? Perhaps, more critically, *should* I sacrifice his life? Was it my place?

Wouldn't doing so make me like the Islamic State?

My father just watched. It didn't seem like I was asking the right questions.

My father had been nobody's enemy. But the Islamic State had killed him. Whatever they said, they were murderers.

But my father didn't care about that question. He just watched me, and I realized that I was getting nowhere.

The food came again and again. I never saw or heard anybody. I never knew what schedule the deliveries adhered to. And I never spoke to those who brought it.

As time passed, I realized I was getting weaker.

I was getting more desperate.

Then, without warning, the lights came on and I heard Youssef's voice again.

"I've decided," said Youssef. "I've decided that you're useless as an assistant. We have important work to do, and you're impeding it. You've run out of time."

I sat there.

"But I don't like wasting lives," said Youssef. "That's why I need to figure out what to do with you. Your brother is useful. He'll be a *shahid*. People are reluctant to shoot five-year-old kids with obvious brain injuries. Ibrahim will die for a worthy purpose. In fact, he will achieve great things, especially considering his limitations. But you, you're a harder case. You should be worth good money on the slave market. If I sold you, they would probably rape you until you died. Our fighters will enjoy that, and we'd raise some money. But there are other options. I could use you to experiment with. I do need subjects. Of course, I wouldn't kill you all at once. I'd experiment with different compounds, in low concentrations. Just to see what they would do. That might even be more useful than the money I could get selling you. I could ask you which fate you prefer, but I don't care."

I wanted to cry. I knew he was serious.

"On the other hand," said Youssef, "if you volunteer now, I can give you your brother. He screams a lot. We've chained him up in the courtyard. But he annoys us. But if you help me, maybe it will be worth keeping him alive."

The food came. There was a small piece of meat.

I looked at it, scared. It seemed to be harbinger of my own future.

I needed to agree to do whatever Youssef wanted. But, somehow, I couldn't.

Then the lights went off and the shutters closed, and I was left to imagine my fate. I had no idea how long Ibrahim had.

Just then, I knew the right question. It was a simple one, "How can I get out of this?"

I looked at the meat in my hands, and an answer came to me.

My father smiled, and then he disappeared.

I stood up and yanked at the cover for the observation light. I pulled and tugged until I finally had it off. I felt around with my hands and found the bulb. I pulled it towards me. The fixture came with it. I unscrewed the bulb and put it on the tray. Carefully, I pulled the wires from the fixture. They had 220V of power. I took my meat and wrapped it around one of the leads. And then I grabbed the plastic encased parts of the wire and pushed the other lead towards the meat. There was a massive spark and the smell of burning flesh filled the room.

I stuck my hand in my mouth and forced myself to vomit. And then I dropped to the floor, falling in an uncomfortable lump and placing my face in my own vomit. I had to make my "electrocution" believable. Youssef had to believe I'd seen my fate and killed myself. Helpfully, I left my feet near the door.

It must have been no more than a few minutes before the shutter came up. A flashlight shone through the glass. It passed over my body.

And then the heavy steel door opened. I heard Youssef sniff the air. He smelled the burned flesh and the vomit. "Shit," I heard him mutter.

I kept myself limp as he grabbed my feet and pulled me from the room. It was dark in the lab; I must have blown out the main fuse. Youssef stepped back towards the test chamber, to inspect the mess I'd left. It was then that I stood up behind him, quickly and quietly and launched myself towards him. He wasn't expecting me. He bounced, just as I had, off the far wall. And then I scrambled back, as quickly as I could, and slammed the heavy door on him. Now, he was the one in the room, and I was the one who was free.

I locked the door.

There was light coming from the stairwell, and my eyes were sufficiently accustomed to the dark that I could see. I found the tool cupboard and felt around until I grasped a small hammer. It would do. Next, I maneuvered to the stairs and then up them. It was impossibly bright on the floor above. I listened but heard nobody. I ran towards the courtyard and found Ibrahim there. He was chained to a post, just as Youssef had said. He was gaunt, and his eyes were red from crying. At least he was asleep. I used the hammer's prybar to pull the chains off of him. And then, I woke him up. He opened his eyes, ready to cry, but then he saw me and broke out into a huge smile.

"Quiet," I said.

He nodded.

Next, I found the house's fuse box. The master had blown. I reset it. And then Ibrahim and I went back downstairs to the now brightly lit lab. I ran to the shutters. Youssef was still inside the chamber, and though I couldn't see him – because it was dark in the room –I saw the shadows of light playing off the glass.

We needed to escape. But a woman and a child would never make it. I needed another solution.

I needed a beard.

I looked around the lab for supplies. I went through all the cupboards. There was latex. I could layer my face with it to look something like Youssef's. But there was nothing I could use that would pass as hair.

I needed a beard.

And then, with a sick feeling, I realized that *Youssef* had one.

I grabbed a pair of scissors and went to the plexiglass. There was a control panel, which had been hidden by the shutters. There was a microphone symbol on a button. I pressed it.

"Youssef," I said, "I need your beard."

"No," he answered, flatly. He was angry. But he was confident. His people, maybe even his family, would be back soon. And then my time would be up.

"Youssef," I said, "I'm going to have your beard. I have scissors here; you can use them to cut it off and put it in the bin."

"No," he answered.

I went back to the cupboard and I found out a canister of chlorine gas. It was small. I came back to the cupboard and waved it in front of the glass.

I pressed the button.

"Give me your beard," I said. "Or else, I'll take it."

I just wanted to scare him. If I'd been threatened with chlorine gas, I thought I might have done anything. But then I realized that wasn't true. I wouldn't have helped Youssef.

There was more hesitation this time. But then Youssef said, "No."

Perhaps he thought I was bluffing. Or, perhaps, helping me escape was beyond what *he* could accept.

Either way, I needed his beard. And he had called my bluff.

I looked at the chlorine, studying the canister. I had to figure out how it worked. It seemed simple enough. I'd just have to open the canister to release the gas.

I put the chlorine in the tray while holding the microphone button down. I wanted to give him a chance to change his mind.

I intended to use the gloves that went from my side of the room to his in order to open the canister. But they looked thick, and his dexterity in the room would probably exceed mine. I realized, I'd have to open it outside the room and then shove it in as quickly as I could.

"Please, Youssef," I said. "Please don't make me do this."

I meant it.

This time, he said nothing.

I told Ibrahim to sit someplace where he couldn't see. And then I went to the lights and turned them off.

Now, because of Youssef's flashlight, I could see inside the test chamber. Youssef was staring at me. His hatred was complete.

"Last chance," I declared.

He just glared at me.

I twisted the top off the canister. And then I shoved the transfer tray into the tiny room. I saw the horror on Youssef's face. His hands went for the tray, to try and push it back out. But I locked it from my side of the wall. Next, he tried to stop the gas – with his hands. But the canister was already rapidly emitting a sickly yellow-green fog. It was probably too late for him. But I needed to be sure. I stuck my own hands in the gloves, letting go of the microphone. He tried to grasp the canister and close the lid, but I fought him off, just a little. More of the deadly gas escaped. Most of it crept downwards, towards the floor. But not all.

The test chamber was slowly taking on a dangerous hue.

I saw his hands and eyes turn red. He started screaming, but I didn't want Ibrahim to know, and so I left the speaker off. I would see him screaming and coughing. But I couldn't hear him. I just watched as he screamed less than a foot away from me. I watched as he started having trouble breathing. I watched as he fell to the floor, no longer trying to stop me. I watched as he started tearing at his face. I let the canister remain open. I expected it would kill him faster. I thought it would kill him more humanely. I watched as his dark beard turned white. And I watched as he died.

I was a killer. I hadn't wanted to be. But I didn't feel like I had had a choice.

I closed the canister and pulled my hands from the thick gloves. I looked at the area near the transfer tray. There was a button for a fan. I pressed it and watched the deadly fog retreat from the chamber.

Then I turned the lights back on and opened the steel door to the test chamber. Only the faint odor of bleach remained. I pulled Youssef's scarred body from the chamber. I took toner from his printer and sprinkled his beard, restoring something resembling its original color. And then I used scissors to cut his beard off. It was horrifying, but it was why I had killed him.

What I had done may or may not have been justified. But I did it. And as I did it, I knew I never wanted to make that kind of decision again.

Using the Plexiglass as a mirror, I scrubbed my face and then applied latex to it. The goal was both to fatten it and to create a layer to apply the beard to. And then, piece by piece, I put Youssef's beard on my own face. In only a few minutes, I was no longer a young woman with a child. Now, I was something approximating Youssef himself. I grabbed his eyeglasses and put them on to complete the look. I could see through them; he hadn't been too blind.

Ibrahim and I went back upstairs. I prayed nobody else would have returned home, and nobody had. I found Youssef's bedroom and I changed into his clothes. I had never worn a man's clothes before.

Finally, we made our way outside, to the car port. The Land Cruiser was there. For a moment, I paused. I thought about destroying his lab before we left. There were ample explosives there. There were triggers everywhere. And a detonation there might have covered our tracks. But it would have raised immediate alarms. Instead, Ibrahim and I got into the truck.

I imagined a man like Youssef didn't have to worry about theft, so I wasn't surprised to find the keys in the ignition. Ibrahim was next to me. I asked him to put a seatbelt on and then I turned the key. The engine started, and we slowly and calmly drove away from Youssef's house. The gas tank was full.

We drove across the river, and I took the first road out of Raqqa. Immediately south of the city, the road entered the desert. Not long afterwards, there was an Islamic State checkpoint. Men had once waved my father through, when they saw his truck. Thankfully, Youssef was accorded the same treatment. They took one cursory glance at the truck and then at me and they let us through. We weren't stopped or slowed. If we had been, my disguise would have failed completely. But the beard had worked.

At least Youssef's death had served a purpose.

I turned on the radio. It was then that I learned that I'd been in captivity for three weeks. I wasn't surprised, but I was disoriented.

We kept driving. Soon, all we could see was the desert. And then, in the distance, I saw another checkpoint under a Syrian flag.

I pulled the latex from my face as I drove. It was clear, once again, that I was a woman.

As we drew near, the soldiers waved us to a stop.

Most of them kept a very healthy distance, but one of them stepped forward. He looked at me and my brother.

"Who are you?" he asked.

"I was forced into a marriage," I said. "We've just escaped."

The soldier nodded cautiously. I imagined he was cautious, for the same reason the Kurds had been. And then he said, "I'll need you to step out of the car — so I can check you, and it, for explosives."

We did as we were told. We held our arms to the sides and let the soldiers see that we had nothing on us. And then, as the first soldier watched us, another entered the truck and searched it as well.

"All clear," said the second man.

"I suppose you're headed for the City on the Heights," said the first soldier, before we could begin to make our way back to the truck.

"That's right," I answered. I had never heard of such a place.

"Well," said the man. "To get there, keep driving on this road. You'll pass Palmyra. Look for signs to Qunietra. You'll have to go through more terrorist-controlled territory. But they're letting people through — at least those who want to get to the City."

"Thank you," I said.

The soldier nodded, seriously.

"Take care," he said.

"We will."

And then the soldier stepped back and waved us through the checkpoint.

Six hours later, we arrived at a low, sensor-studded wall.

A small sign proclaimed what it protected, "The City of Refuge."

# Entrance

*August 8th, 2014: Outside Qunietra*

I was sitting in a trailer, alone, on one side of a table. The small room we were in seemed worn out and depressing. Across from me were two men: Mohammed bin Hassan, and an Assyrian named Tadeo. All three of us were lying with every word we spoke.

Ibrahim and I had arrived at the wall the day before. A small town had sprung up outside of it – reoccupying parts of the once abandoned town of Qunietra. It didn't take long to realize that there were two classes of people in that place. The first were those, like us, wanting to get in. The second were small-time merchants, selling things to the refugees. It didn't take long before both sets of people told us about the City and the application process. Those who wanted to get in were almost wistful. The others just wanted to make a deal.

From what we heard, the City seemed like exactly what we needed – a safe haven from the chaos.

Ibrahim and I had arrived in a very nice truck. It stuck out. Because we didn't need the attention, I sold the truck at a bargain price to a man who offered me cash and promised not to ask any questions. As I figured it, we didn't need the truck. The City didn't look large, and we were used to walking. I bought food from a family that had set up a little shop. And then I picked from one of the many children renting phones so people could apply for admission to the city. The kid wanted a ridiculous amount of money. I haggled a bit and paid him a lower, but still ridiculous, sum. Then we used the phone to apply for admission.

Then, like every refugee around us, we prepared to wait. People had been there for weeks with nary a response, so I wasn't holding my breath. But, somehow, the very next day, we were invited for an interview. Not an interview on the phone, mind you, but an interview in person. As Ibrahim and I made our way towards the city, jealous eyes followed our every step.

As we drew near the wall, signs and fences warning about mines funneled us towards a small gate. Next to it was a protruding booth. It looked like an armored porta potty with a window. It seemed well protected. From behind seemingly foot-thick glass, the guard inside the tiny fortification waved us forward and a small door opened next to his post. We entered and found ourselves in a small empty space surrounded by walls. The floor had some kind of rubbery substance punctuated with small holes. I was suddenly worried that the whole city was some kind of elaborate trap.

Then a voice asked, in Syrian Arabic with an Israeli accent, "Do you have any belongings?"

"Nothing," I said, "except some cash."

There was a puff of air from beneath us. I leapt in surprise. But nothing else happened. A few moments passed. And then the door opposite us opened. A soldier wearing a uniform with Hebrew lettering on it greeted us and beckoned us forward.

At first glance, the City looked almost like I imagined a refugee camp would. It was packed with dirty-white tents. They weren't in straight lines but scattered around randomly. There were patches of dead-looking grass on a hillside, and other shoots of it pushing up between the backs of the closely packed tents. For the most part, the ground seemed to consist of sand and dirt, crushed by continual and overwhelming foot traffic. There were spare-looking trailers sprinkled around. I imagined some were bathrooms, while others were for security or administration. But I couldn't tell from a distance. Everything seemed indistinct and temporary – like a camp formed by a poorly disciplined army stationed in a desert.

I looked up and saw another complex at the peak of the hill which loomed over the area. The grasses had survived there, so obviously there was less foot traffic in that area. But the trailers perched on the side of the hill seemed to lord over the tent city. That feeling was reinforced by an observation tower that stood high above those trailers. My initial impression – of an army camp – seemed to have been optimistic. Now, the place seemed more like prison than anything else.

But then something else caught my eye. In the middle of the camp, in contrast to the dirty white tents and the churned-up brown of the terrain, was a massive structure festooned with pastel colors. It rose up above everything else – towering over the tents and the dirt and the people. It was a playground. In all my life, I'd never seen anything like it. Of course, I'd always lived in the midst of war; playgrounds didn't tend to spring up in those situations.

Confronted with this incongruous vision of happiness, Ibrahim and I both stopped and stared.

"This way," said the soldier, beckoning us forward. His Arabic was poor.

We followed him, but our eyes stayed on the structure. It was covered with children screaming in delight. I'd never seen so many happy children. We were still looking, in amazement, when we came to a trailer. I almost walked into it. On the door was a label in Hebrew, Arabic and English. It read: "Admission Interview Office A."

The soldier opened the door and ushered us in. We were immediately engulfed in a dark and shallow hallway. At the soldier's direction, we took a right and then a left through another door. And there, sitting at a desk, were two men. They both rose – but, as modesty dictated, neither extended his hand. The door was shut behind us.

I was surprised that I knew one of the men. He was an Assyrian, from Mosul. He was a friend of my father. He had been an accountant with the city government. Before I could say anything, he looked at his notes and, in a deliberate voice, said "Hasna?"

"That's me," I answered, uncertain why my false name was being used by a man who knew me well.

"And Ibrahim?" He glanced at Ibrahim and then jerked back reflexively, seeing the head injury.

"Hello," said Ibrahim.

"I am Tadeo," said the man, as if we'd just met for the first time.

"A pleasure to meet you," I answered, politely. Something was wrong, but Ibrahim might not realize it. I needed to get him away from the conversation.

"Can my brother play outside, in the playground?" I asked.

Ibrahim looked hopeful.

"Yes," said Tadeo, almost grateful. "Absolutely."

"That isn't normal," said the other man. "We have to do the interview first."

"As you can see," I said, "he's brain-damaged. He was hurt in a bombing. His memory isn't any good. And he won't run or anything, he hasn't got the capability."

The man I didn't recognize looked doubtful.

"I'm afraid," I lied, "that this interview will trigger one of his attacks."

Tadeo looked at the other man, and the other man reluctantly nodded.

"Sergeant!" said Tadeo, in a somewhat louder voice.

The door popped open, and the soldier stuck his head in.

"Bring this kid to the playground."

The Sergeant smiled.

"And keep an eye on him," Tadeo concluded.

The smile only grew larger. This soldier loved kids.

"You can go with him," I said, gently, to Ibrahim.

"To the playground?" asked Ibrahim, hopefully. He hadn't really been following the conversation.

"To the playground," I said. Ibrahim smiled and walked peacefully out of the door. And then the door shut behind him.

"Thank you," I said, to Tadeo.

He just smiled.

The other man looked at me, coldly.

"I am Mohammed bin Hassan," he announced.

"Nice to meet you," I said, cheerfully; pretending I had no idea anything was wrong.

"I am a former commander in the Islamic State," he said.

"Okay?" I said, with uncertainty.

"I left," he said, "to be a part of something better. To be a part of this City."

"That's good," I said. On the edge of my mind, I was suddenly curious whether he might have been Youssef's brilliant friend. I was curious whether he was here for less than straightforward reasons.

"I left that life," said Mohammed, unbidden. "But I still have many friends there. And a very dear one, Youssef Al-Falluji, was killed yesterday. You'll forgive me if I'm a bit upset."

"I'm sorry to hear that," I said, forcing sadness into my voice. "Was he killed in battle?"

"No," said Mohammed, as he scrutinized my face, "he was killed by his wife."

I said nothing. I was posing as an escaped wife – which I really was – and so I shouldn't have seemed too unhappy about the man's fate.

"She killed him with chlorine gas," said Mohammed, flatly.

"That's horrifying," I said, with a shudder. I didn't have to fake my reaction. I remembered how Youssef had died.

"It is," Mohammed said, staring at me. "I have abandoned the ideals Youssef served, but he didn't deserve what happened to him."

"Why are you telling me this?" I asked, trying to look confused.

"I just want to explain," said Mohammed, "that and, in a very interesting coincidence, his new bride was also named Hasna."

I tried to look confused. But I was almost totally certain that Mohammed knew who I was. I was also almost totally certain that I knew who he was. He was Youssef's friend. The genius with the plan.

As promising as the playground had been, I realized I was suddenly surrounded by even more danger than before. And I was a nobody. If Tadeo couldn't expose this man, then I couldn't.

"Hasna," said Tadeo, breaking the tension, "you've been invited to interview so quickly, because our founder puts a special emphasis on rescuing women who were forced into marriages by the Islamic State. Can you tell us your story?"

"Yes," I answered, calmly. I then told them of a marriage, but not quite mine. I told them of being picked up trying to cross Kurdish lines. I told them I was taken to Deir ez-Zor. I told them I was forced into a marriage with a man named Mohammed; I figured the common name would make my story harder to verify. I told them I escaped when he was out of the house. And I told them I crossed to the government side of the city and then just kept on going – until I finally came here.

They asked questions and I gave answers. Nobody believed a word I said. But I gave Mohammed no reason to reject me.

At the end of it all, they had me step into the hallway.

After a brief discussion, Tadeo walked out of the room and in an undertone whispered, "Maryam, you're in, but be careful; that man *might* be dangerous."

I smiled back.

"Thank you for the warning," I said quietly. "But these days, *everyone* is dangerous."

He tipped his head in agreement and guided me back outside.


We retrieved Ibrahim from the playground and then headed for the absorption trailer. The process was straightforward. They scanned our fingerprints, and then took photos of our faces and samples of our blood.

They issued us electronic payment cards. The cards were easy to use. All I had to do was scan my fingerprint on the card and then touch it to another card. I could then enter how much money I wanted to transfer to the card I'd selected. I put 100 shekels on the card, just for show. I kept the rest of the money from the truck in cash. In this part of the world, people don't willingly report their transactions.

It was explained to me that, as I was 16, I'd be expected to work and report my income – after we'd had a few months to acclimate. I thought it was a naïve expectation. That wasn't how this part of the world worked; people here didn't report their incomes. For the first few months, the City would pay us a small amount of money, via the cards. It was meant to support us in our transition.

Finally, we were assigned a tent in the "new immigrant" part of the city. We could stay there for as long as a year. We'd also been allocated a tiny plot of land in another part of the city. It was enough to build a truly tiny house – smaller even than the tent. However, we'd have the right to sell that land or even pool it with others to build vertically and thus establish apartments that made better use of the space. Of course, that process would take time and money.

Within 30 minutes, we were done with our absorption.

Ibrahim wanted to go back to the playground, and so we did. Tadeo came with us.

As we sat on a bench and watched Ibrahim play, Tadeo asked, "Were you actually a victim of forced marriage?"

He looked concerned.

"I was," I said.

He looked truly saddened.

"With a man named Mohammed, in Deir ez-Zor?"

"No," I said, leaning close and speaking in an undertone, "I was married in Raqqa."

"How did you escape?" asked Tadeo.

"My husband's name was Youssef. Youssef Al-Falluji."

I saw the gears move in Tadeo's brain as he realized that Youssef was Mohammed's friend – the one who'd been gassed by his wife.

Tadeo's eyes widened.

I repeated what I'd said before.

"These days," I said, "everyone is dangerous."

Tadeo shook his head. His sadness was replaced by respect.

"You might," he said, "grow to be greater than your father ever was."

I didn't know what he meant. I didn't ask. Tadeo sat there for another few minutes and then he said his goodbyes and wished me well and went on his way.

I just sat there, watching Ibrahim until it was too dark to play.

Only then, as the temperatures dropped and night fell, did Ibrahim and I finally abandon the playground for the tent we were to call home.

# Gambit

*August 30th, 2014: Outside Qunietra*

Mohammed had debated not using the trailer. It was risky, after all. His plot might be discovered if his men were found there. But the effect of using an official trailer – rather than a tent – was too powerful for him to pass up.

As Mohammed sat in his tent, earbuds pressed firmly against his head, he pictured the trailer in his mind. He could see the thin steel walls, and he could feel the night air creeping through them. He could imagine the cheap tables and chairs, prematurely aged by long workdays and spilled coffee. And he could smell the dry rot that somehow managed to encroach on even the metal itself.

He could see it all, at least in his mind.

But in reality, he could see nothing. The meeting that was about to take place was the most important in his life, but he couldn't be there. His presence would have undermined the whole operation. He'd thought about using a camera to watch the proceedings, but there was a chance that that would have raised uncomfortable questions.

So, all he could do was listen.

One of Steven Gold's deputies – he thought it was Elizabeth, the Internet billionaire – had put potted plants in the middle of almost every conference table in the City. They were something called Chinese Evergreen. She'd said something about adding a little bit of life to the room. The effect was just the opposite; the lonely little evergreens just emphasized how dead the rooms really were.

Mohammed had taken advantage of this particular evergreen; he'd literally planted a bug in the soil. And because of that, he could hear everything that happened in the room.

Mohammed had thought about putting earbuds on his men – the type the secret service uses. That way, he would have been able to direct the conversation. But even that could have raised suspicions. Thus, despite his misgivings, he decided to trust in his men and let them do what he had recruited them for. If things went in the wrong direction, his men could clean up their own mess.

Now, as he sat on his cot, all Mohammed could do was pray that they wouldn't need to do so.

Mohammed heard the one man in the room take a sip of his coffee. It was Hamid. He had proven to be a very quick learner. Moments later, Mohammed heard the door swing open on its poorly lubricated hinges. He heard footsteps. A few men had come in. Judging by Hamid's silence, Mohammed realized that they were the men he was expecting. He heard the door close.

"Please, take a seat," Hamid said, in his Israeli-sounding Arabic. He'd worked hard at that accent. He'd lost his native gutturals and replaced them with the shallower and, at least in Mohammed's opinion, far more grating Israeli *ch*.

There were only two of Mohammed's operatives in the room. The men he'd chosen had not only done well with their accents, they had demonstrated their intelligence and decision-making.

Mohammed heard chairs in the room scratch their ways backwards as the invited guests took their seats. He heard more footsteps, all part of the pre-choreographed dance he'd worked out with his men. He knew that the second man, Rashid, was now walking around to talk to Hamid. A moment later, they did what they practiced. Rashid leaned close to

Hamid and whispered in an undertone. Mohammed listened as Rashid sprinkled a few Hebrew words in the stream of fast gibberish. Of course, it was all so quiet that it could seem like Rashid was informing Hamid about something, in rapid-fire Hebrew.

The short burst complete, Hamid spoke again.

"Welcome," he said.

"What are we doing here?" asked one of the invited men, in a somewhat defensive voice.

"Easo?" asked Hamid. The name was a derivation of Joshua, Moses's general and successor.

"Yes," said the man.

Silently, Mohammed thanked Hamid. Now, he knew what Easo sounded like. Mohammed had reviewed both men's official files carefully, and he'd known who they were long before they had come to the City – but he'd never heard them speak. Nonetheless, he'd expected Easo to be the one who'd do most of the talking.

"Easo Pothen Olikara, correct."

"Yes," said the man again.

"It says here that you are 19, is that correct?"

"Yes," said Easo.

"Easo," said Hamid, "you lied to us when you applied to live here."

"How?" challenged Easo.

"You claimed," said Hamid, "that you had never been involved in acts of violence."

"I haven't been," said Easo.

"In fact," said Hamid, "both of you have been. In Damascus."

There was silence.

"I need you," said Hamid, "to tell me about it."

There was more silence.

Then Easo said, quietly, "All we did was defend our neighborhood. We were part of a neighborhood watch, like all other able-bodied men."

"Ah, yes," said Hamid. "Your neighborhood, in the Northeast of Damascus, came under Islamic State attack on a number of occasions. And your so-called 'Neighborhood Watch' repelled it, correct?"

"For a while, yes," said Easo.

"Until, eventually, you were overrun and you became refugees."

"Yes," said Easo, "that's right."

"So, you were involved in acts of violence?"

"They were all in self-defense," insisted Easo. "We didn't attack anybody. They attacked us."

"Easo," said Hamid, "you became somewhat famous. Daesh even had a special bounty on your head. Something like $40,000. Correct?"

Hamid had called the Islamic State Daesh. It burnished his Israeli credentials.

"I didn't know that." said Easo, with a bit of pride.

"Mathu," said Hamid, turning to the other man. "You were apparently worth $15,000. Somewhat less, but still an unusual sign of respect."

"What do you mean?" asked an unsteady voice. Mohammed knew that was Mathu.

"Daesh doesn't like putting bounties on their enemies," said Hamid. "It risks making them look weak. Like the Americans. This is particularly when dealing with 'neighborhood watchmen' from minority communities like the Syriac Orthodox Church."

"So why put one on us?" said Easo.

"You know why," said Hamid. "It was because you were more than just watchmen. In fact, when we looked into it, we learned that you – Easo – were a first-rate sniper and you – Mathu – were his spotter."

"No," said Easo. "Not true. I was in the watch. And I fired a few shots. But I don't think I ever killed anybody."

"Easo," said Hamid, almost chuckling, "We are not here to criticize you. You know that we Israelis respect a minority that stands up for itself. We think it is quite noble."

"You might respect it," said Easo. "But I'm still no sniper, and Mathu here is just my friend. He's not a spotter."

"Easo," said Hamid, "you have to understand that we've managed to attribute the deaths of 112 Daesh fighters to just the two of you. Of course, you didn't shoot them all. One time, you got near a Daesh camp and blew up a truck bomb that was still being assembled. That claimed over 60 lives, all by itself. It also cost the Islamic State some territory, temporarily."

Easo said nothing.

Mohammed listened from his tent, impressed by Hamid's even voice in the face of the accomplished militiaman.

"Easo," said Hamid, "there's no reason to be worried. We're here to make a deal."

"A deal?" said Easo.

"Yes," said Hamid. "A deal. We have a confluence of interests. We Israelis – we Jews – have enemies in this so-called City. And while Mr. Steven Gold talks about peace between communities, we know – just like you do – that that isn't going to happen in reality."

Mohammed imagined Easo nodding.

"In this region, every country is controlled by Muslims: Lebanon, Syria, Iran, Iraq, Saudi Arabia, Jordan, Turkey, Egypt, Sudan, the UAE, Yemen – etc... etc..."

"Except Israel" said Easo.

"Except Israel," agreed Hamid. "Israel is an exception. And we think this City should be too."

"What do you mean?" asked Easo.

"We think *you* should be safe here. You, Christians, should be safe here."

"We are," said Easo. "Nobody's been hurt."

"You are, *for now*," said Hamid, with emphasis, "But how long will that remain true? When Gold begins to hand over control to the people who live here, when the world demands that we go along with ceding control of this place to the locals, who will take power?"

He let the question hang there. Everybody knew it wouldn't be the Christians.

"No," said Hamid. "For you to be truly safe, this has to be a *Christian* city. You have to control it, and you have to dominate its population. Like you learned in Damascus, you have to take matters into your own hands."

"We have no guns here," said Easo, tacitly admitting his past.

"We can remedy that," said Hamid.

"You brought us here to give us guns?"

"Well," said Hamid, "it isn't quite that simple. We have a confluence of interests."

Easo said nothing.

"Hezbollah has a senior commander here, a man named Ali al-Arzusi."

"I've heard of him," said Easo. "He's some kind of politician."

"That is his cover. In fact, he works for Hezbollah. He is an infiltrator for them – he's trying to undermine Israel."

"And what do you want from me?"

"We want you to kill him," said Hamid.

"Why can't you do it?" asked Easo, almost immediately. He wasn't stupid.

"Because we can't be seen determining what happens in this place. It needs to happen 'organically' for the world to accept it. We need you to do it."

"And in return?"

"In return," said Hamid, "we'll give you guns and information. We'll help you make this place uncomfortable for your people's enemies."

There was silence. Mohammed could almost imagine the gears turning in Easo's head. The silence stretched on.

"We could," said Hamid, "ask your Assyrian brethren. Perhaps they'd like to take the lead?" His voice trailed off.

A moment later, Easo said, "Okay, okay, we'll do it."

In his tent, hundreds of feet away, Mohammed wanted to whoop with joy. But he stayed silent and listened. He heard the rasp of a pistol sliding across the conference table. He heard it being picked up. And he thought he heard the rustling of clothes as it was swiftly and expertly pocketed.

"Thank you," said Hamid.

And then he heard the chairs slide back, and he heard the men rise and the door squeal on its hinges as the men left the room

Mohammed allowed himself to smile. It was done.


When Mohammed was younger, the Shiites had helped the Sunnis fight the Americans. And then, in turn, they had driven the Americans to fight the Sunnis. The war that resulted drove both the Americans and the Sunnis from their positions of dominance. Neither understood what had happened. But the Shiites did. Because of this manipulation, Iran and their proxies controlled everything from Western Afghanistan to the Lebanese Mediterranean. This incredible manipulation had taught Mohammed a critical lesson: He'd learned that you don't need to defeat those who oppose you; you just need to drive them to fight amongst themselves.

In this City, the region's ethnicities were living on top of each other. In this City, there was a massive media presence. This City was justly seen as a petri dish for the entire region. And because of this, one death here could have the impact of a thousand just a few miles further east.

That was why Mohammed had come here.

From this place, he could drive his enemies to war with one another.

And now, he'd started the process.

There had been rumors that the Russians – whose Orthodox Church occupied a place of prominence in their society – would bring their Air Force to bombard the Sunnis in Syria.

But with a single pistol and a clever conversation, Mohammed might have just undone all of that.

The young man, Easo, would kill the Shia politician. He was a kind and respected man who probably had nothing to do with Hezbollah or Iranian-style religious government. The Shiites would ask Mohammed, their trusted source in the City of Refuge, who was at fault. Mohammed would pretend to investigate, and then he'd tell them the parts of the story he wanted them to know. He'd even tell them about the Christian plot to dominate the City. And if his Syrian handlers checked it, Mohammed's story would be confirmed.

As a result, the Iranian-backed Shiites would respond to the assassination of one of their own by killing Orthodox Christians, at least in this City. Soon after, once the whole community was inflamed,

Mohammed would supply those Christians with guns. And then the two ethnicities who had been allies in Syria – the Christians and the Shiites – would be driven apart from one another. Their coalition would be shattered and replaced with distrust and violence.

Most importantly, the only foreign powers who mattered – the Russians and Americans – would see the Shiites joining in the slaughter of minorities. The Russians, in particular, would see Orthodox Christians being massacred by their potential allies. Even in a world of realpolitik, they would hesitate to come to the rescue of those slaughtering those who shared so much with the Kremlin-backed Russian Orthodox. They might even turn on the Shiites themselves.

It was possible that, because of a single pistol and a clever conversation, all of Mohammed's enemies would be driven to destroy each other.

Of course, Mohammed wouldn't leave it at that. This was only the first step in his greater plan.

Mohammed pulled the earbuds from his ears and lay back on his cot.

He closed his eyes and imagined the sound of Easo's pistol.

It wasn't hard to imagine that that single shot would begin to justify the many sacrifices that he had made.

As he slept, he dreamt of paradise.

# Quicksand

*September 22ⁿᵈ, 2014: Outside Qunietra*

Steven Gold hit the red button at the bottom of his screen. The face that had been in front of him, the face of Shimon Bar-Lev, the Israeli Finance Minister, disappeared.

Their conversation hadn't been a good one.

It had been seventy days since the City had opened. It seemed like so much had been accomplished. They had grown a little faster than expected: 20,000 people had been admitted. Although there were a few Kurds and Yazidis, the vast majority were Muslim Arabs and Christians. The City government had raised 90 million shekels from a wide variety of donors. But only a few hundred thousand had been invested in local businesses by overseas benefactors. Most were little groceries. In Phoenix, they would have been called *bodegas*. The Israelis called them *markolet*.

Keeping to his original plan, Steven Gold had raised only what he needed initially. His high hopes pointed to being able to raise the money without giving up as much of the City's future GDP – once the enterprise got off the ground. Basically, once jumpstarted, the City would create its own economy, and that economy would be able to draw investment more cheaply than had been possible on Day One.

But it wasn't working.

His plans had called for the City's own economic production to meet almost 10 percent of its own needs. For every 100 shekels the population needed, 10 were supposed to come from the population itself.

But the Finance Minister had been right. Transitioning people to a productive economy, especially when they had come from the farce of an oil economy, was difficult. Perhaps it was even impossible. The population was producing next to nothing. Bodegas weren't enough to support it.

Even with the bodegas, there was no tax revenue, and ration cards were being completely spent. The businesses people were spending at had almost no margins. There was some suspicion that people were hiding their real incomes. But for Steven, a quick walk through the City was enough to convince him that there wasn't a sudden outpouring of economic activity. It was obvious that people here weren't secretly becoming able to feed themselves.

His City wasn't working.

He had set up the City, he had given people a chance, and they weren't grasping it. Slowly, that reality was squeezing the life out of both Steven and the City.

All the major investors had full access to his books. They knew just how poorly things were going. The City had opened with 65 million shekels in the bank – about 16 million dollars. And while they had spent only 18 million so far, they would burn through close to 55 million shekels in just another 10 weeks. And then, the jig would be up. They would be forced to evacuate the people and close the site. The numbers didn't lie.

Steven tried to save his project. He'd been willing to give up more of the City's equity. But because of the apparent failure of his plan, Bar Lev had gently pointed out that Israel would need to demand so much of the City's future GDP that its economy would be forever crippled.

Steven had tried other investors. If the State of Israel wouldn't invest more, perhaps his donors in America would. But, one by one, they refused. None would give him more money. None would buy him more time. Even Elizabeth – who had given so much of her time, and even some of her fortune, had realized the City was at a dead-end. She continued to work, but she invested no more of her money.

She, like everybody else, had seen the writing on the wall.

His last conversation had been another attempt to persuade Bar Lev. But it had been another failure. He closed the laptop reluctantly, like he was closing the door on Hope itself.

It was dawning on him that everything he'd tried to create was going to vanish. The region would resume its hopeless cycles of war, oppression and death. And nobody would ever find a better path. The failure of the City would only reinforce how hopeless things really were.

In every conversation, the Minister's last words to him had been the same: *Chazak v'ematz, be strong and of good courage.* But those words had come to anger Steven. How could Bar-Lev have the audacity to tell him to be strong, even as he denied him the resources that were so desperately needed? But the words also confused him. What was the point of being strong in the face of the inevitable?

Steven stood up and tucked the laptop under his arm. He walked out of the trailer he'd been working in and began his slow journey home. It was still light out; he was home in only a few minutes.

Amy opened the door for him and stood aside as he shuffled in. The kids shied away. His mood hadn't been good. He'd been under such pressure. He regretted that. But hadn't done anything about it. Maybe he would, soon.

Amy had gotten used to his exhaustion. She'd gotten used to his increased desperation. But she saw something new this time: resignation. But it didn't make her more sympathetic.

"Would you like some dinner?" she asked, annoyance in her voice. Steven felt her frustration with him. He understood it. It was right. He had to be a father, even if everything else wasn't working. Especially if everything else wasn't working. But even knowing all of that didn't help.

He nodded. His mind was elsewhere; but, at the same time, it was nowhere at all.

The kids had already eaten, and he ignored them as they played.

Instead, Steven consumed his dinner, robotically.

But even as his mind seemed to be sleeping, various vague ideas nibbled at the corners of his consciousness. He could make a speech, exhorting people to work, because otherwise the City would fall. He could cut back on benefits, but people were barely getting by now, and he'd just be starving them. He could audit the little bodegas. But he didn't want to crush, prematurely, what little enterprise there was. How had Hong Kong done it? They had provided nothing. But the situation there was different. The people who'd been fleeing had come from a real economy, one that had just collapsed under Communism. And Hong Kong had been a true port city. It had a natural industry. His people were different – they didn't have the skills necessary to make something out of this useless piece of land. Perhaps nobody did. Maybe the people of the City were doing what they could, and Steven just hadn't given them enough of what they needed? Strangely, the thought comforted him.

When he finished his dinner, Steven grabbed a beer from the fridge. Then he picked up a light sweater and headed out the door. He didn't even look at Amy and the kids. He felt like he'd let them all down.

He was embarrassed. He'd put everything on this bet, and none of it was working out, and now he couldn't even hold himself together.

Beer in hand, Steven settled into his new favorite spot: the lawn chair overlooking the City. The sun was going down. Steven realized a shadow, cast by the very bluff he was sitting on, was overcoming the hopes of helpless people. It seemed strangely symbolic.

And then, there was darkness.

Steven just sat there, nursing his beer. And then, eventually, he fell asleep.

Steven's sleep was fitful. He dreamt he was one of the people stuck in the City below. He dreamt of looking up at the man in the lawn chair. And he dreamt of hating that man. When the City collapsed, the man in the chair would go home to America. But the families who'd placed their hopes in him would be expelled into a world that had a fresh reason to hate them. He dreamt of killing the man in the chair. He dreamt that he'd climbed the bluff and then stood over the sleeping man – a gun in his hand. He was about to pull the trigger, he was about to kill himself, when he awoke with a start.

His body was covered in sweat. He could hear the cry of the Fajr prayer from the City below. He looked at his phone. It was 4:48 a.m. on Sept 9th.

The phone had a notification, from ESPN. In only 30 minutes, the Arizona Cardinals were playing their first game of the season. Steven had forgotten that he'd been tracking their games. He wasn't a big football fan, but when he'd been in Phoenix, he'd always watched the first game of the season. It had become a kind of ritual.

Maybe he could watch it here?

He could use the escape.

Steven snuck into his trailer and grabbed his laptop, his headphones and some snacks from the kitchen. Within a few minutes, he was back outside. Steven popped open the laptop, found his WiFi router and connected. The WiFi made it look like he was in New York. He smiled at that, a little. In one way, at least, he wasn't trapped on a lawn chair in the Golan Heights.

Steven hunted around for a website that could stream the game. Eventually, he found it. He registered, paid with his credit card, and began watching moments before the game began.

But then, just after the kickoff, he heard something. And it wasn't from the broadcast.

Steven pulled his headphones off and looked around. Everything seemed normal.

But then he looked behind him and saw a soldier running towards him at full speed.

Before the man got there, Steven looked around again.

This time, he noticed that the City was awakening – but not gradually. Instead, all around and in every direction, people were calling out. He saw the glow of innumerable cellphone screens below him. Something was wrong. But it all seemed so surreal.

And then the soldier reached him.

"What's going on?" Steven demanded, as the man bent over with his hands on his knees, breathing heavily.

"Sir," said the soldier, in broken English. "Somebody shoot!"

In that moment, Steven was wrenched back from the very brief escape the football game had provided him: there had been a shooting.

"You need to get inside!" shouted the soldier, quickly recovering his breath.

But Steven just sat there. He should have been worried about his own security, but there was really only one question on his mind: "How much is this going to cost?"

He hated the question.

Soon, he learned that that was the least of the problems.

# Kindling

*September 26th, 2014: Outside Qunietra*

It seemed like it took forever, but Ibrahim finally fell asleep.

We were hunkered down, our faces near the sandy bottom of our small tent. We'd been there for hours. And, the entire time, he'd been screaming in abject terror.

The first murder in the City, of the Shiite politician, had acted as a kind of kindling to a bonfire. It took only days before the first reprisals occurred. Before the murders, there had been huge divisions within the various communities. Outsiders saw blocs, but things are never as simple as they seem from a distance. But with the feud, the various groups pulled together into larger and more ominous masses. They were defending themselves and seeking revenge. Smaller disputes could be set aside.

In less than a week, the entire City had erupted. There was gunfire. There were even the occasional explosions. Somehow, weapons were being smuggled in, and every group seemed to have formed its own camps. The playground had been abandoned.

Every group seemed to have been involved. Every group, that is, but one. The Sunnis, whose most dangerous elements answered to the Islamic State itself, had not fired a single shot. Somehow, they had excluded themselves from the circle of reprisals. And when one them was killed, there was no response.

The Israelis tried to intercede, of course. On the first day of major violence, Friday the 12th of September, the Israelis seemed ready. Arrests occurred minutes, or even seconds, after shots were fired. The dominant theory was that the Israelis could determine exactly where every shot had been fired from.

So, on Saturday, the shooters tried to disguise themselves, and then disappear immediately after attacks. They would fire from cover and then run into crowded temporary mosques, discarding their clothes in favor for other garments they wore underneath. And then, they would emerge on the other side, looking completely different. The only evidence of what they were doing were the castoffs on the mosque floors. These were familiar tactics to many.

But it didn't work. Saturday night, in the middle of the night, Israeli soldiers raided the tents of the combatants, and took them from the field of battle. The only explanation that made sense was that, through their monitoring systems, the Israelis could rewind to what had happened *before* the attacks. It was like what the Americans had done in Iraq.

So, by Sunday, the attackers had learned to disguise their locations *before* they fired their guns. They would cover their faces and walk through the covered sanctuaries of our temporary mosques or churches – and then they would launch their deadly assaults. That seemed to work.

For the most part, the assassins targeted the prominent. But that was hardly a rule. Some victims were at prayer. Some were hunted down in their tents. And some were murdered purely by accident; bullets fired at a tent can easily tear through it and hit another, unintended, target.

Within a week, the original system of allocated plots fell apart. Instead, people moved to be with those they could ally with. Miniature settlements formed within the City as a whole. There were Christian, Shia, and Sunni sub-settlements, as well as a tiny Kurdish enclave. Their borders were defined by piles of inorganic trash. The idea was simple, metal and wood and nails and plastic sheeting would channel people coming into the area through chokepoints that could be monitored. At the same time, potential infiltrators would be slowed by the barriers. It might even be harder to aim at people in other areas if you had to avoid hitting the obstacle courses that lay between the communities.

The small grocery markets that had been in one area or another, serving a variety of people, suddenly found themselves frequented only by those within their newly defined communities. Prices rose.

But not everything lay within these new borders. Between the communities, there was common space. People rarely traveled through it. Almost nobody lived in it.

But we did.

Ibrahim and I had no community. We were Muslim, but we had no ethnic group, no allies, and no tribe. There was no "Mosul" section of the City; the people from that troubled place had disbursed along other lines. Our only friend was Tadeo – my father's friend. He visited when he could.

We were living by ourselves, in a sort of no-man's land. Around us were the irregular piles of garbage that defined the sub-settlements. We were literally outsiders. We'd been in a community; we'd been hearing the filtered news of the street. But now, we were aware of almost nothing.

But the violence stayed with us. In the twelve days since the first shooting, two bullets had torn through the fabric that protected us from the weather. The fabric did nothing to hold back the war. We snuck out, as rarely as we could, to buy food and to fill our bottles of water in the Sunni part of town. But otherwise, we stayed in our tent. We rarely stood up. It was safer close to the ground.

We had a propane tank for cooking, and I was worried it might be blown up. But I wasn't the only one with that idea. One day, when we were shopping, I saw one such tank being shot at, intentionally. It expelled its fuel but, thank All-h, did not explode.

While the bullets didn't physically hit us, they still struck at Ibrahim. With every loud noise, he screamed. With every attempted killing, he fell into abject fear. He was shaking and crying and distraught from dawn until well beyond nightfall. Eventually, he would start whimpering. And then, exhausted, he would fall asleep. He would rest, fitfully, until morning came, and he could start the cycle once again.

In a way, his troubles distracted me from my own.

That night, when he'd finally fallen asleep, I noticed the whistling was coming from not four, but six holes in the fabric that surrounded us. I needed to know, beyond the reports of guns and the screams of victims, what was happening around me.

I pulled out my phone and looked for the news.

It was dire.

Our little battlefield had shot fissures into the territory beyond our walls. There were reprisals not only here, but in the heart of Syrian government territory. Russia was condemning Shiite and Alawite attacks on Christians. Without an ally for foreign powers to embrace, everybody seemed to be giving up on the region. Everybody was giving up on the City.

The City of Hope seemed to have become a coffin nail for entire peoples.

And then I saw the face of Mohammed bin-Hassan on my phone.

I clicked on it and a video started.

I watched as he spoke, from within one of the many trailers in the City.

"The Festival of Eid al Ada," he said, "is fast approaching. It is the holiest day in the Muslim calendar. I have counseled my own people to remain peaceful, despite the violence and the threats. But, make no mistake, this City of Refuge is being overrun by hatred and despair. When I was with the Islamic State, the Shiites, the Alawites, and the Christians were our enemies. Even the Sunnis – those who did not pledge allegiance to us – were attacked. When I was with the Islamic State, we would have delighted in this violence. But these people are my enemies no more. We've come here to establish a new peace. I've pleaded with the Sunnis who live here to remain peaceful, and they have. Now, I plead with every other group – stop the fighting! Islam means peace and the Christians preach love. No matter which faith you follow, G-d's way is not war. Let us celebrate Eid al-Ada, the celebration of Abraham's complete submission to G-d. Let us celebrate it properly, with submission to the values of All-h. Let us celebrate in peace."

When the video ended, I almost found myself believing what he'd said. But he was the friend of Youssef the Engineer. He had to be, right? He had to be the friend who Youssef had said would "make the world dance," didn't he?

Somehow, he was the cause of this violence.

I turned to look at my sleeping brother. Even in his slumber, his face was contorted with his fear. But what could I do? We couldn't leave, we knew what was waiting for us outside these walls. And we couldn't stay; it was becoming unbearable for the only living person I loved.

I looked back at my phone. There was a special weather bulletin. I clicked on it. A huge sandstorm was coming. It was expected to contain high levels of pollutants – agricultural blow-off from the abandoned fields of Syria and Iraq.

"Great," I thought, sarcastically. "Something else to look forward to."

And then, like a message from All-h Himself, the solution came to me.

I needed to build a bomb.

# Slaughter

*September 28th, 2014: Outside Qunietra*

Mohammed bin-Hassan cried as he stood among the shredded bodies of women and children. The attack had come so recently that the area had barely begun to smell – aside from the odor of freshly charred flesh. Emergency lights flashed around Mohammed as he looked at the victims. They had been innocent people, people who had simply come together for a rare evening out. Clowns and circus performers had been invited from Israel, to perform for the City. The goal had been a simple one: to provide the community with a break from the stresses of the war around them. But its purpose had been perverted.

The event had been slapped together in a hurry. With violence in almost every district, only the newly defined Sunni section of town was peaceful enough to host it. It was the only place the performers were willing to visit.

Of course, a large swath of the community disapproved of the public mixing of genders. So, all the attendees had been women and children. Men, even Mohammed himself, were unwelcome. In a sign of the City's official blessing, even Elizabeth, the City's IT and Finance genius, had shown up.

And now, within 30 minutes of the clown's first acts, almost everybody was dead.

Mohammed turned and found himself staring at a bank of television reporters. They had seemingly materialized from nowhere. But they knew he was the one to talk to.

As he began to speak, tears streaming down his face, he realized with a hidden joy that he had finally succeeded.

The whole thing had started with a few words from Mohammed. He'd suggested some sort of break – specifically for the women and children. Steven Gold, desperate for something to counteract the rapidly declining mood of the City, had latched onto the concept with vigor. Before long, everything had been organized: a location had been chosen, performers had been found, a big top tent had been rented and soldiers had been selected as guards.

And on the evening of the great event, Mohammed had watched it unfold from outside the Administrative trailers on the bluff.

The sun went down, but it was still warm when the people started to emerge from their tents. Small groups of women, their frightened children crowded close to them, gathered together and formed up into columns that were then fed into the tent itself. There was security there, of course. Both the women and children were searched, by female Israeli soldiers, for weapons. Nothing suspicious was found.

Mohammed waited for the first laughter from the big top before he pulled out a phone. It was a temporary phone. He would use it for only this call. He'd left his real one in his tent.

When Mohammed had left Syria, he'd maintained contact with his newest handler in the Syrian Mukhabarat. He didn't know her name, but she'd reached out to him a few times. One time had been after the killing of the Shiite politician. It had been dangerous to communicate, and so even though he was using SilentVoice, they had always communicated in code. He'd assumed the Israelis could intercept the messages. Of course, this not only slowed his correspondence, it limited it. He could only use the vocabulary he and he his handler had already established. He was limited in what he could say, but he always told her the truth. The reason was the same it has always been. For years, he'd been building up the trust of the Mukhabarat.

Today, he was going to make it all worthwhile.

Mohammed opened a voice-modulator app and then opened SilentVoice. For the first time, he sent a voice chat request through it. He was calling his handler.

He heard an uncertain voice on the other end. This wasn't the protocol.

"Hello?" said Mohammed.

"Hello?" said the voice of his handler. She was confused.

"I'm using a voice modulator," said Mohammed, "So I don't sound like I usually do."

"Okay?" said the woman on the line.

"They're all here," said Mohammed.

"Who?" asked the woman.

"All the commanders."

"What do you mean?"

"All of them," said Mohammed. "The Commanders of the Islamic State and of the Free Syrian Army and of Al-Nusra. Even the leaders of Rojava!" He was referring to the Kurdish controlled territory in Northern Syria.

"What?!" said the bewildered voice on the other end of the line.

"I've met quite a few of them, one at a time. But never all together. The Israelis must have invited them. It makes sense. This is neutral territory, it's well-protected. That's why they've all come here. It must be for some sort of conference."

There was a pause on the line. The woman was digesting what he'd told her.

"I'll call back," she said.

Two minutes later, his phone vibrated in his hand.

"Yes?" he said, answering the call.

"I have our senior leadership here," said the woman, "They are aware of who you are, and where you are."

"Okay," said Mohammed, "did you tell them what I've seen?"

"Yes," said the woman. "They want to take action."

"I don't think they can," said Mohammed. "Soldiers are guarding the site."

"What site?" asked the woman.

"It's a big top," said Mohammed, "The cover is a circus. But they're meeting in there, I saw them walk in before the event."

"Hold on," said the woman. She muted the call.

Mohammed waited.

The woman came back on the line. "We'll take it from here," she said.

"What are you going to do?" said Mohammed, trying to sound a bit desperate.

"We'll handle it," she said.

"Maybe," said Mohammed, "I can try to get close and listen to what they're saying?"

"We'll take it from here," said the woman, firmly. "Stay away from the site."

Mohammed paused.

"Thank you," said the woman, firmly. And then she terminated the call.

It had all gone perfectly.

Mohammed had expected to see gunmen come from other parts of the camp. He expected to see them converge in a coordinated attack. The Syrian government and their Shiite allies would be utterly condemned.

But, seven minutes later, something beyond his imagining had occurred.

With the exception of the sounds from the big top, the night was quiet. The circus was having its intended effect. But all of that was shattered when rockets suddenly shot out from an anti-missile battery on the bluff next to Mohammed. He watched them scream skyward. He was confused by what he saw.

Were the Syrians firing rockets at the City? That wouldn't work – the Israelis could stop rockets.

Moments later, automated cannons on the edge of the City began to spit a hail of fire into the air. They were close-quarters anti-rocket systems. But they didn't succeed. Milliseconds later, as if conducted by clockwork, the big top itself exploded.

And then Mohammed knew his victory was complete. The Syrian army itself had fired a cruise missile at a gathering of women and children. And it hadn't been some easily defeated Saddam-era Scud; it had to have been the sort of modern missile only the Iranian military could have provided. The condemnation would be final. His enemies would be driven against one another.

As Mohammed faced the TV cameras, he was genuinely mourning the dead. He did not have to ask the tears to come. Hundreds of women and children had been in the tent. The vast majority had been killed by the missile. They were innocents, like Aisha had been. He mourned their deaths.

But he also knew that they were necessary losses in a far greater war.

Iran, and its proxy Syria, had undeniably sent one of their missiles into a gathering of innocents under Israeli protection. The press was here, in vast numbers. All Mohammed had to do was give the situation a nudge. With a few words, the world's fears would shift from the Islamic State to Iran. With a few words, his enemies – the Shiites, the Syrian government and the apostate Iranian regime – would be isolated.

It had cost hundreds of lives. It had taken years of his own life. And it had probably cost any credibility he had with his handlers.

But it was worth it.

He had finally, and forcefully, outmaneuvered his enemies.

He would drive his enemies apart.

And his people would be triumphant.

He had played his cards well.

What he didn't expect was Maryam and her bomb.

# Evaporation

*September 30th, 2014: Outside Qunietra*

Elizabeth checked the account balances a second time. She'd known they had dropped quickly, but the speed still surprised her. Seven days earlier, they had had 10 weeks of reserves – close to $14 million dollars. Now, almost everything was gone. There was no tax revenue replenishing the accounts. All she had left was enough for one more transfer. She'd move close to $1 million dollars to the electronic cards held by the City's residents; and that would be it. They would stay until after the Eid al-Adha festival, using the last of the money to fund their celebrations. Then the army would move in and forcibly push them out of Israeli territory. They had no choice. Even Israel couldn't contain the cancerous bubble the City had become.

Considering the violence, it was both surprising and frightening how few people had already left. The army had already retreated to guarding the residences on the hill. Israel had lost 23 soldiers and 11 performers in the attack on the big top. It was a horrifying price in a country so small and so tightly knit. The army was no longer making any attempts to secure the peace within the City. Even things as mundane as garbage collection had stopped; nobody trusted that the trash wouldn't be used to conceal explosives. The place was violent and smelled horribly. But despite all of that, the reality across the border – in Syria – was so bad that almost nobody had fled back to it.

In this light, moving the last of the money over seemed like a waste. The City was dead. It had become worse than a failure. And yet they were spending another million dollars of their donors' money preserving it for another week. Just so people could celebrate a festival before they were expelled.

How did that make sense?

Elizabeth had first heard about the City only nine months earlier. She had just left an oncologist's office when a text had shown up on her phone. She'd ignored it, at first. Her sister had just heard the most devastating news of her life. They had discovered cancer, again. Her sister had already survived breast cancer twice. The two of them weren't close, but Elizabeth had still done what she could to help out. Both times, early and aggressive intervention had saved her. But this time, it was too late. It had spread beyond her breasts and beyond her lymph nodes and had begun to invade the tissue in her stomach and other organs. One day, she had gone to a routine screening, and the next thing, she had been informed that she almost certainly had less than a year to live. Strangely, Elizabeth's sister had been calm. In the fifteen years she'd been wrestling with cancer, she'd come to grips with the reality that it might eventually claim her. But Elizabeth had never learned such acceptance. In those same fifteen years, she'd gone from being a brainy college kid to being one of the wealthiest women in the world. The business she'd built, focused on enabling seamless online payment transactions, had become an empire. An enormous amount of money flowed through it, every day. The tiny fraction Elizabeth and her company collected was enough to make her a billionaire several times over.

Elizabeth had become used to encountering problems and finding her way over – or through – them. Her bullheadedness seemed to live in a symbiotic relationship with her success. Each fed off the other.

Her mind flashed back to the opening of a movie she'd seen once. She couldn't recall the title. But she knew the scene. A man was dying in bed. He was in agony; his body was frail and gaunt. He was sweating profusely and cursing heedlessly. He was fighting, but he was weak. And he was ordinary; so completely ordinary. But when he died, at the beginning of this movie, the scene shifted outwards, and it was suddenly clear he was no ordinary man. He was one of the most powerful and successful Kings Europe had ever known. All of his resources were nothing in the face of disease.

Elizabeth felt like that King. She knew that her billions could not buy her sister's life.

She'd brought her sister home that day. After Elizabeth and her mother helped Emma's family with dinner, Elizabeth had decided to stay the night at her mother's house. Her mother and sister still lived in the same neighborhood. When she stepped into the old house, the scent of the old wallpaper and carpeting brought her back to a simpler time. But just as she was about to disappear into that happy oblivion, she felt the pallor of oncoming death invade her reality – poisoning everything.

Seeking a distraction, she'd finally checked her phone.

It was a message from the Development Director at the JUC. It was an invitation to a speech, that night, by somebody the Development Director claimed was remarkable. Elizabeth doubted it; the man was on the Executive Committee of the JUC itself. Members of the Executive Committee of the JUC were rarely remarkable people. Most Development Directors, a fancy name for top fundraisers, would have called. But this woman had wisely learned Elizabeth's preferences; Elizabeth hated the interruption of phone calls.

Elizabeth checked on her mother and then, without changing or providing any sort of RSVP, left. She could, and would, show up to an invite like this in jeans and an old shirt.

There were benefits to being a billionaire.

She went to the speech seeking simple distraction. But she came from it feeling empowered. Her life could mean something. And this man had showed her how. She invested some money in the City. But then she did something more important. She decided to dedicate her expertise.

Her familiarity with the intersection of finance and software – and the IP she owned – gave her something truly unique to offer. She could make the backend of the City work in a way few others could. But beyond that, she could build a financial system from the ground up – not just graft something onto an already extant reality. It was a tremendous opportunity. And she'd enjoyed the work. She'd been excited on opening day. But then, slowly, she'd seen the financial aspects of the City begin to fail. Soon after, the first killing came. And then, in a few short weeks, everything seemed to get exponentially worse. And the entire time, her sister's condition had been inexorably deteriorating.

And then the circus had presented itself. Like Steven's speech, it was a chance for a distraction. But more than that, it was a chance to experience a bit more of the magic of the place; some of the hope and opportunity that had drawn her in the first place. Maybe some of it could be restored. She hadn't really thought of the violence. Yes, the self-defined Sunni part of the City had been largely violence free; and, yes, Israel's own soldiers would be guarding the entrances. And yes, nobody had had the temerity to attack them, yet. But none of that mattered, because she was running away from a far more certain death, her mother's.

She'd come, on time, to the performance. She'd joined the streams of women and children making their way past the soldiers. In line, she felt remarkably self-conscious; her face and hair were uncovered. Her clothes, while hardly tight by Western standards, were far more revealing than those of the other guests. But nobody gave her evil looks – she was not Muslim, so she could dress differently than they did. At the entrance to the tent was a small sign in Arabic, Hebrew, and English. It read, "Women and Children Only."

Elizabeth's apprehensions flipped when she got inside. Inside the tent, away from men, the women had removed their baggy overgarments and head coverings. Every chair seemed to be piled with black niqabs, chadors and hijabs. Not only were hair and faces uncovered, but almost every face appeared to have been enhanced through the use of artfully applied mascara, lipstick and even rouge. Finally, to Elizabeth's surprise, most of the younger women seemed to be wearing not just tight clothes, but outright *sexy* clothes. The excitement in the air seemed to be enhanced by the almost clandestine nature of the shift. Elizabeth found herself whiplashed by the difference between the reality outside the tent and the reality within it.

As Elizabeth settled into the crowd, she realized that the women around her were happy, tremendously happy. This circus, Elizabeth thought, had been a fantastic idea.

Before long, the circus itself had started. People weren't silent, they called out and talked even as the performers carried out their stunts. It seemed expected, by everybody in attendance and by the performers. The show was only a part of the show. And then, not long into the performance, Elizabeth's phone had buzzed. It was a call. Elizabeth hated calls. But then she looked at the screen and realized it was her mother. Her heart fluttered as she answered it and then rushed out of the tent. As soon as she was outside, and clear of the laughter of the crowd, she spoke urgently into the handset. "What's going on?"

"It's Emma," said her mother.

"What?" asked Elizabeth.

"She just ate her last meal," said her mother, "It was tiny. The cancer has completely overcome her digestive system. They're using IVs to sustain her, but she's already pretty beat up. She's got maybe a week left."

Elizabeth felt the tears streaming down her face. She said nothing.

Then her mother said, "I think it's time you came back."

Elizabeth nodded, and was about to answer, when the world around her seemed to disappear.

When she awoke, she thought she'd passed out. But when she opened her eyes and smelled the burning of flesh and saw the smoke – and didn't hear the laughter of the women – she realized something else had happened. She stood up, on shaky legs. Her face and hair and body were covered with soot and debris. She was bleeding from somewhere, but the pain wasn't too bad. She started to wander back to where the tent had been. Maybe she could help somebody. She found a body and she urgently lurched towards it – feeling for a pulse – seeking signs of life. She found none. It felt like she had been stumbling from body to body for hours before there was a sudden rush of rescue personnel. In reality, it had only been a few minutes. With the rescuers had come phones and TV cameras. Thus, dozens of videos and pictures of her – tears and blood streaming down her face – were captured. She was one of the richest and most influential women in the world, yet she was captured staggering helplessly through a field of death.

The horrifying poetry of it made it the iconic image of the attack.

It threatened to become the iconic image of the City itself.

She felt even more like that dying King.

Despite all the blood, she didn't appear to be seriously injured. A helicopter had ferried her and a few other survivors to the hospital in the not-so-far-away city of Safed. The doctors there gave her a tentative bill of good health, although they prohibited her from flying for three days. They just wanted to make sure nothing was wrong. It seemed a little pointless to her, given that a helicopter had brought her to the hospital in the first place. But she didn't argue. Yes, she needed to get back to New York, she needed to be with her sister.

But she secretly welcomed the excuse to avoid that reality.

So, she'd gone back to the City. She'd gone back to her trailer. She called her mother and talked to her. She told her she'd come soon enough. She even Skyped with her sister. The woman was dying, but she'd minimized her pain medications. She was remarkably clear-headed. She'd seen the photos, everybody had, and so she was worried. But as Elizabeth looked on the darkness of her mother's far away hospital bed, Elizabeth assured her sister that she didn't need to be worried. She wasn't going into the City anymore. She'd stay where she was – and once the doctor's ban was lifted – she'd come straight back to New York.

On the second day, the day when the next transfer had to be made, she opened her computer and was made to come face-to-face with the fiscal truth of the situation. It was then that she'd realized she'd been wrong to try and change the world. It was far more important to be with her family, even in times of pain and helplessness. Those joys and those pains were the core of human existence. Life wasn't about grand sweeps of policy. It wasn't about moonshots to create new realities for millions. It was about the daily reality of life and death and joy and sorrow.

She realized, suddenly, that the last million dollars weren't a waste.

They would buy another week; another week of life and another week of respite for 20,000 condemned souls. With sadness, but not reluctance, she clicked the button and watched the money vanish from the City's account.

That was it, the last transfer.

She sat back in her chair. And then she realized she was shaking. Moments later, she started crying. She tried to stop but couldn't. And then she tried to understand why. She couldn't put her finger on it, not at first.

And then the sickening thought that was overwhelming her came into perfect focus: in every aspect of her life, time itself seemed to be evaporating. She was dissolving, fading away helplessly, like the great King himself.

It was Maryam's bomb that saved her.

# Boom

*October 1st, 2014: Outside Qunietra*

I scramble up the side of the boulder strewn hill, dragging an increasingly heavy weight behind me. I am trying, desperately, to clear my mind. But I can't. Everything feels so incredibly uncertain. Risks are shouting at me from every direction. They aren't the risks of failure; they're the risks of something far worse. I'm worried that I might die. But I'm more worried that Ibrahim will have nobody to watch over him.

I look up, briefly. In theory, there is a half-moon high above me. But it, like everything else, is obscured by the sandstorm that seems to have wrapped the world in a thick fog. I am enveloped by darkness and uncertainty. I'm reminded of a famous Christian psalm my father once read to me. I only remember one line though: *Though I walk through the shadow of death, I fear no evil.*

My father had been asking one of his puzzle questions when he'd read it, but I couldn't grasp what it was. Not at the time, anyways. But now, I understand. He was asking me how you can walk through such a place and fear no evil. Maybe the rest of the psalm has an answer, but I can't remember it.

The shadow is enveloping me, and so is my fear.

I push myself forward. It is not only a mental exercise. The effort is physically staggering. I'm dragging 80 pounds up a hillside covered in tall grasses, grasses concealing the uneven terrain beneath them. It was the one thing I'd been certain of. I'd been certain I could manage the weight. When I'd first lifted it, it seemed like a task no harder than those

I'd done in that faraway field in Iraq. But now, pulling myself, foot-by-foot, up the side of the bluff, I realize that my assumptions had been fundamentally flawed.

I hope I've done a better job with the rest of the plan. But I'm not reassured. In a place like this, cell phone traffic had to be monitored. The necessary keywords, the keywords that would tell me what I needed to know, would have set off alarm bells. If somebody knew what I was doing, that would have created even greater risks. So, I'd had to work entirely from memory.

Every path came with risks.

Under my breath I begin to utter the opening lines of the Koran:

> *In the name of All-h, the Entirely Merciful, the*
> *Especially Merciful.*
> *All praise is to All-h, Lord of the worlds –*
> *The Entirely Merciful, the Especially Merciful,*
> *Sovereign of the Day of Recompense.*
> *It is You we worship and You we ask for help.*
> *Guide us to the straight path –*
> *The path of those upon whom You have bestowed*
> *favor, not of those who have evoked Your anger or of*
> *those who are astray.*

I repeat one line: *Guide us to the straight path. The path of those upon whom You have bestowed favor.*

Maybe All-h will grant me success.

One of my gloved hands finds a small tree – more of a bush, really – and I grab it. I want to rest, but I know I'm going too slowly. I have a rough window of opportunity. That window might be poorly defined, but there was no need to introduce even more uncertainty by missing it.

I keep pushing. My legs and arms and torso are all hurting now. The effort is burning through me.

I have a small bag strapped to my back. It has my basic supplies. There is thick rubber tubing which I've cut from a cooking stove in the Sunni neighborhood; the valve from that hose still dangles from one end of it. There is the core of a lithium battery. I shredded it into smaller pieces, which have been individually wrapped in newspapers. Tadeo, at my request, had managed to find me a small amount of potassium powder. This is mixed with the lithium. The whole mess – newspaper, lithium and potassium – has been soaked in oil and surrounded by two plastic sandwich bags. I also have Teflon tape and zip ties, as well as a screwdriver with various magnetically attachable heads. And, finally, behind me, being dragged up the hill, there is the propane canister I stole from yet another family. I had nonchalantly walked it past the community's guards. It is forty liters. In all, it weighs 80 pounds; 40 pounds of tank, and 40 of fuel. At least I hope it does. I saw it being filled, but I didn't have a chance to measure it. It seems to weigh a ton, now, but I can't leave it behind. It is the cornerstone of everything.

The sandstorm had come with an advisory. Outdoor exercise was being heavily discouraged. There are the usual problems with breathing sand – particulates in the lungs and all that. But there is something else, as well. The sand isn't coming from the desert, it is coming from the desiccated fields of Syria and Iraq. It isn't "clean." Instead, it is laden with it all the pollutants of those failing fields – the fertilizers, the fecal matter, the filthy residue of modern agricultural runoff. What I'm doing isn't healthy, at least in the long term. On the other hand, that very pollution is what makes it worthwhile.

I decide to focus on that: the unhealthiness of it all. Maybe, someday, I'll be seventy years old and suffering from some kind of horrible respiratory illness. It is strangely reassuring to think of the distant future; even if it needs to be terrifying in order to distract me from my present reality.

And then I hear something. Voices.

I stop, immediately. It must be soldiers, nobody else would be out here at this time of night. The question is: are they sentries just watching things, or are they specifically looking for me? I know the Israelis have infrared systems. I can only hope the sand has obscured their computer vision as much as it has obscured my own eyes. But even without infrared, there are other ways they could detect me. For one thing, vibration or sound-based alarms could have heard me as I scrabbled for footing, as I dragged my propane canister behind me, or even as I breathed. By stopping, I've brought two of those sources to a halt. But I can't seem to slow my breathing. I lower myself to the terrain – lying against the incredibly steep slope. I place my face close the ground. Maybe, somehow, the sand and the sparse grasses will mute my breathing somewhat. And then I listen, hoping against hope that whoever is nearby can't hear me.

The voices are speaking, one to the other. I can't speak Hebrew, but the soldiers' voices are calm. In fact, they almost sound bored. That tells me what I need to know. Not only am I safe, but I'm close to my target.

The invisible footsteps move away from me. Slowly, I get up. My breathing has slowed, and some of my strength has returned. I lift the canister and I keep going. With only a few more steps, I've reached the top of the hill.

I turn left and start walking. I think, but am not sure, that I'm walking away from the voices I'd heard. In under a minute, I come to a large pipe. I turn to the right and there, looming like a shadow in the darkness, is the massive shape that is my target: the municipal water tank.

Nobody's detected me. Probably, nobody is going to shoot me; at least not yet.

There's a valve a few feet in front of me. I step towards it and then stare towards the tank itself. I can see nothing other than smooth pipe from this point onwards. I'm where I need to be. I look over the valve, finding the features I need. There's a large round shut-off valve – twisting it around will stop the flow of water into the City. There's a small tap for testing water quality. And there's a pressure-relief valve – which enables excess air or gasses to be vented from the system.

I start with the pressure relief valve. When there is too much pressure in the pipe, the end pops up, allowing the excess to escape. The pressure limit is set by a screw at the top of the valve. I use my screwdriver, hunt for the right head, and tighten it.

I don't want what I'm putting into the pipe to escape too easily.

Next, I turn to the sampling valve. It is a small opening, like a household hose would have. A small wheel next to it opens and closes it, just like a household hose. I stuff the small lithium-potassium-oil and newspaper balls into the end of it. I don't have many of them and so they fit.

Next, I fit the rubber tubing over the end of the sampling valve. I tighten the tubing on with a zip tie. I hope it can hold the pressures.

I turn the propane canister upside down, so liquid propane (and not gas) will be expelled from it. This will prevent the canister from freezing while ensuring it expels its contents at high pressures. That done, I screw the valve end of the rubber tube onto the tank.

Next, I stand and close the large pipe's shut-off valve. This cuts off water downstream from where I'm working. The cut-off won't be immediate. There is still water in the pipe, and venting valves further downstream will prevent a vacuum from building up and prematurely turning off the water. But it is the beginning of some sort of clock. I need to start working quickly.

Thankfully, I don't have much to do.

The theory is simple. When I open the sampling valve and the propane valve, the pressure from the propane tank will push propane into the sampling valve, rather than letting water come out of it. It will push into the water main and expand as it is relieved of the pressure in the tank. As the downstream has been shut off, the expanding gas will flow upwards. The tightened the pressure relief valve will prevent it from escaping. The propane, with the potassium-lithium-oil and paper balls being pushed ahead of it will emerge into the open area at the top of the water tank, where it will expand fully. The 40 liters of liquid propane will expand to roughly 10,000 liters of propane gas. The potassium powder will be exposed to water as the oil and paper fall away. It will bob to the surface of the water and begin to burn. Potassium ignites in water. But it won't burn for long. Instead, it will ignite the shredded lithium, which also floats, and burns for longer. The lithium will then ignite the propane, hopefully causing a massive explosion.

It is time to begin. I open the sampling valve and see my rubber tube expand a bit with the flow of water. The paper and oil around the lithium and potassium will keep them dry, but not for long. I open the gas valve on the propane tank, releasing the propane into the pipe and thus into the water tank itself. I hope the lithium has shot out of my tube and into the sampling valve. I really have no way of knowing. I have no way of knowing whether every step in the process will actually function as designed.

Whatever is done, is done.

I turn, and as quickly as I can, I run back down the hill. It is faster going than the climb had been.

I find the closest set of bathrooms within a minute, and I step inside. The place is completely empty. I go to the sinks, but I don't turn them on. Instead, I look in the mirror and I wait.

I hate waiting.

I envision the next day coming without incident. Somebody will discover the propane tank. Maybe they'll investigate and figure out that I'm behind it.

On the other hand, just maybe, they'll be too busy for that sort of exercise.

I run through the calculations again; even though it is far too late to change anything.

I hope I haven't made any serious mistakes. Even if I hadn't, the next steps had risks I couldn't even begin to calculate.

I look at the mirror.

Any second now, I tell myself.

I'm gripping the counter.

But nothing is happening.

I want to pray to All-h, but I can't, in the bathroom. It would be disrespectful.

I turn around and leave. Stepping outside, I utter a short, discrete and heartfelt prayer. There's no way the propane could take this long to explode, could it?

Reluctantly, I begin to walk back to my tent. Perhaps it is time to run, again. Perhaps we can find a new place to hide.

And then I glance up towards the water tank, almost regretfully. I can't actually see it through the sand. But in that instant, there is a massive burst of light that pierces even the dirty fog that surrounds me. Moments later, the sound wave hits me with a thud. I step back in shock and surprise.

It worked!

I'm about to run back to Ibrahim, to reassure him that everything is okay, when I hear something else. It is something almost like a massive hammer cracking through a metal wall.

In that instant, I realize that I might have been too successful.

In a complete panic, I begin to run back up the hill.

# Aftershock

*October 1st, 2014: Outside Qunietra*

Elizabeth is sleeping when she hears her phone ring. It is sometime in the middle of the night. Groggily, she pulls it off the utilitarian bedside table and looks at the number of the screen. It is her mother. Instantly, she's awake.

"What is it?" she asks, urgently.

"It's Emma," her mother says, in a shaky voice.

Elizabeth waits. She knows what's coming, but she doesn't want to make it come any faster.

"She's gone," her mother says. Elizabeth just sits there, the phone to her ear. She can hear her mother sobbing softly. She can imagine her tears. But she just sits there. She's been so selfish, not spending more time with her sister. She's been selfish, running off to this project half a world away. She hadn't been there, in the end. She might have said "I love you" to her sister, but she hadn't shown it through her actions.

So, she sits there. And then as the finality of it all sinks in, she too begins to cry. She doesn't sob, not like her mother. Tears just begin to flow down her face. She doesn't have to say, "I should have been there." Her mother knows that. There is no anger, and no apologies are uttered. There is just a feeling of silent remorse.

A question should come next, shouldn't it? Elizabeth should ask, "What can I do?" But she doesn't. In reality, Elizabeth's question should be for herself. What should she do now? Where should she go? What should come next?

There is silence now. Almost like they are sharing a very distant hug.

Elizabeth and her sister haven't been close in a very long time. Their lives have gone in very different directions. But they both loved their mother.

The silence grows uncomfortable. Finally, Elizabeth's mother says, "I should go, Michael just came in."

Michael was Emma's husband.

"Okay," Elizabeth says. "I love you."

Without another word, she hangs up.

Elizabeth sits there, in bed, sinking into her own emotions.

"What now?" she asks herself, aloud.

As if in response to her question, her room suddenly lights up with the fury of a massive explosion. A piece of metal shrapnel flies through her window and embeds itself in the far wall of her trailer.

Elizabeth looks up, as if in a dream. Another noise comes soon after. This one like a massive metallic "CLANK!" Elizabeth wraps herself in her robe and rises calmly from her bed. She walks out her door to see what is happening. There is sand everywhere. Sand and darkness. But she hears somebody running up the hill. Are they going to attack? She hears shouting. It isn't an aggressive shout – it is a plea. And it isn't a crowd. But one person.

Somebody is running up the hill, asking the people at the top to do something.

What is going on?

Elizabeth keeps walking – towards the voice.

Whoever is shouting sounds like a girl. Not a little girl, but a teenager. The voice grows louder. And now she hears other voices. It's the soldiers, shouting to one another in Hebrew. And they are also running. They are running towards the girl. Elizabeth is between the soldiers and the girl. Elizabeth quickens her pace. In a moment, out of the fog of sand, comes the running form of a teenager. She is shouting something in Arabic, but she has no weapons.

"What is it?" Elizabeth asks, in an oddly calm voice. She is speaking English.

The girl answers, in English. "Close the valve!" she says. "You must close the valve."

Then, the soldiers arrive. They surround Elizabeth and the girl but keep their distance. The girl raises her arms and opens her palms. She is wearing jeans, a shirt, a face-revealing, but hair-covering hijab, and – oddly – gloves. She turns slowly, showing all sides of her torso and her open hands to the soldiers.

"No weapon!" she says, in Hebrew. "No weapon!"

Elizabeth knows that phrase. You learned it quickly here. She still thinks it's funny that the word for "weapon" and "kiss" are basically the same.

One of the soldiers spits something back at her, in rapid Hebrew.

"No Hebrew," she answers. "I don't speak Hebrew." It is another phrase Elizabeth knows.

Another soldier asks her a question in Arabic.

She answers back, pointing urgently towards the huge water tank with her outstretched hands. He turns to one of his cohorts and gesticulates with his rifle while issuing a quick command in Hebrew. The man runs off.

"What's going on?" Elizabeth asks.

"The pipes," the girl says, her arms still partially raised. "One of them must have burst. We're wasting water."

"How do you know?" Elizabeth asks.

"I heard it," the girl says. "Like a hammer crashing through a metal wall."

"I heard that too," Elizabeth says. "A metallic noise. But how did you know what it was?"

"My father," says the girl, "worked in a water treatment plant."

It doesn't really explain anything. But Elizabeth lets the answer stand. They all wait. Two minutes later, the soldier comes back at a run. He says something unintelligible. The Arabic-speaking soldier turns to the girl and says something else that Elizabeth doesn't understand. She lowers her hands.

The soldier gestures towards the girl, and two soldiers come forward.

"They're going to arrest me," the girl says.

"Why?" Elizabeth asks, still in a daze.

"Wouldn't you?" comes the girl's curt reply.

Elizabeth decides to walk with the girl, and the soldiers. Before long, they come to one of the trailers. They bring the girl into one of the interview rooms, and Elizabeth sort of just wanders in afterwards. They close the door, and the girl sits down.

"What's going on?" asks Elizabeth.

"You're going to need my help," the teenager says, confidently. She doesn't answer Elizabeth's question.

"Why?" Elizabeth asks.

"Somebody blew up the water tank," the girl says. And then, as if anticipating Elizabeth's next question, she adds, "I saw it."

"But why would somebody do that?" asks Elizabeth.

"Terrorists," says the girl, with a shrug. "Who can understand why they do anything?" Somehow, the answer seems both depressing and disingenuous.

Elizabeth sits there for a minute. And then she asks, "Why is your English so good?"

"My father taught me," the teenager says.

"Ah," says Elizabeth. Another non-answer. Then she asks, "Why will we need you?"

"To fix the water," the girl says.

"But the tank's blown up," says Elizabeth. "You said so yourself."

"Just the top," says the girl, "All sorts of sand and grit is getting into it now. It needs to be cleaned. There's a lot of toxic pollution in this sand."

"Your father taught you how to clean the water?"

"Yes," the girl says, with a nod. Then a moment later, she seems to panic for no reason at all.

"What's wrong?" Elizabeth asks, surprising herself with her concern.

"My brother," the teenager says. "He's totally by himself."

Elizabeth looks confused.

"He's five," the girl says. "And his brain was damaged. By a bomb. I just went to the bathroom. And then I heard the bomb and rushed up here. But now he's all by himself, and he's terrified of explosions."

It is the first real explanation Elizabeth has heard.

"I don't think they're going to let you out," Elizabeth says. "Can't you just call someone."

"I didn't bring my phone to the bathroom," the girl says. "Can I use yours?"

Elizabeth realizes her phone is in the pocket of her robe. She fishes it out and hands it to the girl. Immediately, the young woman dials a number. Somebody picks up on the other end. She speaks to him in a language Elizabeth can't quite place. It isn't Arabic, Hebrew, or English. There are a few bursts of speech. And then there is a long pause. Elizabeth watches the young girl's face as it seems to soften and

341

transform. And then, she utters a few simple words. Finally, the young girl hangs up and hands the phone back to Elizabeth.

"Thanks," she says. "He'll check up on my brother."

Elizabeth can't shake the feeling the little boy hadn't been the only subject of the conversation.

"What's your name?" Elizabeth asks.

The girl takes a moment, as if considering. Elizabeth realizes she's going to lie.

"Here," she says, "my name is Hasna."

"And before you were here?" Elizabeth asks.

"Before," the girl says, after a moment's pause, "I was Maryam."

Elizabeth wants to know why she's using a false name, but she expects she'd get another non-answer. The girl isn't volunteering to explain. She probably wouldn't explain, even if asked. Elizabeth looks sideways at the young woman. She suspects, for some reason, that the incredibly bright-looking young lady is responsible for whatever had just happened. At the same time, Maryam betrays absolutely no sense of malice. Elizabeth can't figure it out.

And then there is a knock at the door.

"Come in," Elizabeth says.

She isn't surprised when Steven Gold tips his head into the room, gestures with his hand and says, "We have a problem."

Elizabeth stands up and walks out after him.

In the hallway, Steven speaks quickly. "Somebody blew up the water tank. This sand is dangerous and it's blowing into the tank in huge quantities. I suspect the water isn't drinkable. Plus, the pipeline leading here from Israel got blown out by the hammer effect of the explosion."

"What's that mean?" Elizabeth asks, even though she knows.

342

"It means everybody who lives in the City is suddenly in mortal danger. They don't have any water."

"So, order trucks; water trucks," Elizabeth says.

"We don't have the money," Steven says.

"I can pay for it," Elizabeth says.

"It won't be enough," Steven says. "Nobody is willing to drive them here. It's too dangerous. And we'll need a lot of them. And the Israelis want to wrap this up soon anyway. They don't want to repair anything – they just want to move up the evacuation by a few days."

"What about the girl? The one in there?" Elizabeth says, gesturing with her thumb.

"What about her?" Steven asks.

"She said she can fix it."

Steven just looks at her, thrown off. Finally, he asks, "What?"

"She said she came up the hill because she knew the pipe burst. I saw her warn the soldiers and they closed the valve."

"How did she know?" Steven asks.

"She says she heard it. She said her father was some kind of water engineer."

"Huh," Steven says, flatly.

"Do we have any other way of fixing it?" Elizabeth says, in a challenging voice. She is finding herself quite curious about what the young woman has up her sleeve.

"Not right now," says Steven, shrugging his shoulders.

After a moment, they both turn and walk back into the room. They pull out chairs and sit. It is Steven who speaks first.

"What do you need?" he asks, simply.

The girl almost smiles; Elizabeth can see it. Then she speaks, "The problem here isn't typical water-borne pathogens. We don't need heat or other highly advanced filters. What we need is to clear out particulate pollutants, which is quite a bit easier. I need a water testing kit. If you can't get everything, I need at least a pH monitor. And I need a supply of alum – that's potassium aluminum sulfate – and I need chlorinated lime. And we'll need a compressed air pump and a clear water pump; both the largest you can get quickly. We'll also need people, and tools."

"Is this stuff dangerous? The alum and chlorinated lime?"

"I don't know," the girl says, innocently. "I suppose it could be. But you'll be watching us carefully."

"Us?" Steven says.

"Me and the people who will be helping me," the girl says.

"And how much of alum and chlorinated lime will you need?" Steven asks, levelly. He seems a little amused, like he couldn't quite take the girl seriously. But in the back of his mind, he is also worried. This all seemed too convenient.

"I don't know exactly. It's one of these things you figure out as you go along. Let's say half a van each of the alum and chlorinated lime. And all the men we can muster. Give me access to the City's speaker system, and I can ask for the men."

"Do you want tractors?" Steven asks, "We can probably get some of those."

"No," the girl says, with unexpected force. "I want men."

Steven wants to ask why, but he doesn't.

Instead, he turns to Elizabeth. "Should we do it?"

Elizabeth smiles at the ridiculousness of it. A teenage girl is going to rescue them all?

"I think we need to," she answers.

"I can drive the van," Steven says.

"And I can write a check," Elizabeth says.

They both turn back to the girl.

"Okay," Steven says. "I'll make the calls."

Within a few minutes, they've worked out the girl's provisional release from the interview room. Nobody really sees her as a threat. She gets on the P.A. system, explains the situation, and calls for volunteers in Arabic. The Israelis move their cordon back, so the men who answer her call can assemble and access the water tank, but not the trailers or the wall.

In the meantime, Steven has made his calls. The alum is remarkably easy to source. It has apparently been used for water purification since Roman times. It clumps unwanted particles together, making them large and easy to filter.

The chlorine, otherwise called chlorine powder, is a little harder to get. It isn't that it is terribly dangerous; it comes in a pill form when used for water purification and it has to be collected in a large mass and burned to cause serious problems. The soldiers can keep it from being misused by doling it out in small doses. The real issue with it is that the only large reserves in the country come from the army. In advanced countries, people don't need water purification on that sort of scale. But Steven sorts it out and, within three hours, a van with the required substances, along with another with an industrial grade air compressor, are parked ten minutes from the City. Elizabeth and Steven both go to retrieve them. By the time they get back, the dawn prayer is complete. The sand is even clearing up.

They get back in time to see the girl, standing on the bluff, next to the big pipe leading down the City. There's a little boy placidly standing next to her. He's wearing a hat.

There's a bullhorn in the girl's hand. Over a thousand men and a few hundred women have assembled at the bottom of the hill. As Elizabeth watches, the people below break up into teams. A subset seems to move first, followed by a larger, reluctant mass. Elizabeth isn't sure what is going on. But, in the end, they seem oddly willing to listen to the young girl. It is probably for the same reason Elizabeth and Steven were willing to listen: they need water.

As Elizabeth watches, she realizes that the girl is assembling teams that liberally mix Christians and Sunnis and Shiites. Elizabeth knows, because even she can distinguish some of the people by how they're dressed. She can also see how, within each team, the different groups are eyeing each other distrustfully.

The teams haven't been formed along ethnic lines, but along physical ones. There is a team of wiry young men, there are two others of more burly men and there is a team of women. Finally, there is a small group of older men. But not everybody is chosen, a large mass just watches the proceedings. Elizabeth's curiosity keeps growing.

The young girl demonstrates something with a valve on the pipe. And then, with a command, everybody seems to begin moving at once. The wiry team goes to the stock of tents, which had been intended for the next wave of immigrants. Immigrants who will never come. One of the burly teams goes to the stash of tools and then to the bottom of the hill, following the path of the pipes. The other burly team goes to retrieve the pump and compressor. And the older men disburse, seemingly to monitor the other men's work. Finally, hundreds of women, some in hijabs, others in chadors, and some with no hair-covering at all, begin climbing the hill.

For her part, the girl has started climbing the access ladder on the side of the water tank.

An hour later, the entire water system has been reconfigured.

The air compressor has been attached to the bottom of the water tank while the clean water pump has been installed at the bottom of the hill. Pipes lead from the water pump back up the hill and to the hole on the side of the water tank. And at the bottom of the large pipe leading down the hill, there's been a major change. A twenty-foot section of pipe has been filled with fine sand and less-fine gravel, covered with screens at both ends, and then bolted on to the existing system pipe network. The end of that pipe has been connected to a curved pipe and then to the pump. A circuit has been created. The water will flow down from the water tank and through the sand and gravel filled pipe, and then to the pump and back up into the water tank. It is a cyclical purification system.

At the same time, the team of wiry young men has brought a number of the remaining tents up the hill. The women have sewn the fabric together, layering it for strength. The team of wiry men then scaled the water tank and laid the fabric over it – covering the hole and preventing even more external pollution from reaching.

The girl herself has reviewed the entire assembly, checking joints, verifying valve positions and ensuring the fabric can withstand the sharp edges of the shredded tank. As she went, she nodded here and there and corrected what had been done in other places.

Her expertise is obvious, and baffling. Finally, she climbs the water tank, bullhorn in hand. Everybody else just waits. She pulls up an edge of the fabric and looks down into the water and then up again, her bullhorn carrying her words over the crowd. Whatever she's saying is long-winded. But it is clear she is delivering another set of instructions to each team. As she speaks, the wiry team forms a human chain up the ladder to the tank. At the bottom is the supply of alum. One of the teams of burly men has moved to the sand and gravel-filled pipe. The other team is stationed near the curved pipe that leads to the pump. And the older men disburse between the sand and gravel filled pipe and the air compressor. Finally, the women disburse along the pipe, each placing one of their hands on it.

And then the girl says something through the bullhorn, and everything comes to life. The air compressor fires up, shooting air into the water tank. The alum is passed up the ladder and thrown into the tank as the girl watches. Elizabeth is beginning to understand, now. A few minutes pass. The air compressor is turned off. And then the valve for the pipe down the hill is opened.

Using her phone as a reference, Elizabeth begins to put together what the girl is doing.

The alum will gather the pollutants together, its chemical reaction enhanced by the air compressor's agitation of the water. Because of gravity, the water that flows down the hill is pressurized. That pressure will force the water through the sand and gravel filter. The filter will capture the pollutants, and the water will continue through the curved pipe and then the pump. It will end up back up the hill, in the water tank itself. With the water forced through it, the sand filter itself will sort its grains by size, the smallest grains will stay at the top, capturing the pollutants, while the larger grains are captured at the bottom and keep the rest of the mass in place.

There is only one thing Elizabeth can't understand. She knows the huge pipe-based filter will fill with pollutants quickly. When it does, the water flow will basically stop, and the whole process will shut down. What then?

One of the women, at the curved pipe below the sand and gravel filled pipe, shouts something. Like clockwork, one of the older men

348

closes the valve directly above the sand and gravel filter. One of the burly groups moves forward and disconnects the curved pipe at the bottom, while another disconnects the huge filtering pipe from the pipes above it.

One of the teams lifts the massive filter, in unison, and then turns it around. Now the fine sand is at the bottom. The other team lifts the curved pipe away and pours whatever debris had made it through the filter onto the ground.

Then, the filter pipe is reconnected to the pipes above it. And then the valve connecting them is opened. And then Elizabeth understands. The filter has been reversed. It is being backwashed by the water pressurized by the hill. As she watches, a flood of dirty water shoots out the pipe. One of the older men watches intently. And then he raises his hand and the valve is closed and the water stops flowing. The men pack some new sand into the pipe and then reverse it again and place it back in its original position. Everything is reattached and the circuit is back in place.

It has required enormous effort, but the filter has been cleaned. When the valve opens again, Elizabeth realizes that the woman who shouted (and kicked the whole thing off) must have been feeling for the water flow. Realizing it was getting slow, she knew they had to clean the filter.

The whole operation repeats again and again. The girl keeps pulling up the edge of the fabric and looking over the water. Occasionally, more alum is added. And, slowly, the time between filter cleanings gets longer and longer. Until, finally, it seems like it is no longer needed. Then, and only then, the girl raises her bullhorn to the soldiers. She asks, in Arabic, for chlorine. They, like almost everybody else, had been watching her performance with wonder. They come forward, and in the doses she requests, they chlorinate the tank of water.

The girl clambers down the side of the tank. She asks for, and receives, a cup. Going to a small valve, she opens it and collects a sample of the water. She holds it up to the sun. She tests it with the small kit Steven had provided. And then, satisfied, she drinks.

With a smile, she raises her thumb in triumph.

Not surprisingly, a cheer goes through the crowd.

The water isn't enough to last long. But the girl isn't done. Her teams disassemble the pipe that leads from the pump back up the hill. They then busily reconfigure everything.

In the end, one of the pipes that had been leading down the hill has been moved to replace the burst supply pipe from Israel. One of the bathroom facilities loses its water. Its pipe has been using to fill in the missing section of pipe leading down the hill.

By the end of the day, with the exception of the one bathroom, clean water has been restored to the City.


Elizabeth is blown away. She asks Steven for permission to have the girl and her brother stay with her. Steven asks around and Elizabeth's request is approved.

The tired girl and her peaceful brother come to the small trailer. Before long the boy, Ibrahim, has gone to sleep.

Elizabeth and the girl sit at Elizabeth's small table slowly drinking their cups of tea.

Eventually, Elizabeth asks the question that has been growing in her mind.

"Why?" she says, "Did you blow up the tank."

The girl – Hasna or Maryam, or whatever her real name is – seems to realize Elizabeth isn't to be lied to.

"What sounds did you hear today?" the girl asks.

"What do you mean?" asks Elizabeth.

"What sounds?" asks the girl, repeating herself.

"I heard the explosion," Elizabeth says.

"Okay," the girl says. "What else? Afterwards?"

"I heard the air compressor. I heard people working. I heard you. I heard the pumps. I heard the cheering."

"And what didn't you hear?" the girl asks.

It is then that Elizabeth understands.

She heard no shooting. No death. No cries of mourning. Aside from the eventually harmless bombing of the water tank, she heard no violence. But it went deeper than even that. She heard no shouting, no fighting, and no argument.

With a start, she realizes that even she had not been mourning.

"I heard peace," she says, in wonder. "And I heard purpose."

The girl smiles. Elizabeth doesn't know it, but the girl is smiling like her father once did: when his daughter understood the answer to one of his questions. And Elizabeth doesn't know it, but Maryam has done what her father once did, momentarily bringing people together so they can survive.

In a way, she has gone further, giving them a taste of the joy she felt harvesting the fields in Iraq.

"Will it last?" Elizabeth asks.

"No," says the girl. Her voice is tinged with sadness. But then, she adds, "At least... not without help."

Elizabeth looks at the child. She's young enough to be Elizabeth's daughter. Suddenly awed, Elizabeth realizes the girl is not just intelligent, but wise.

The wind blows in through the shattered window. It is then that Elizabeth remembers the question that had weighed on her that morning.

The question had been simple: "What now?"

It is with a smile, that Elizabeth realizes that the answer is sitting right in front of her.

--

Mohammed sits in his tent in the dark. His laptop is open in front of him, and it casts a bright glow over his face as he reads the news.

He finds article after article discussing the remarkable cooperation the girl he knew as "Hasna" had wrought. Their pieces are capped by majestic shots of her standing on the water tank – directing people this way and that.

"Hasna," he realizes, "represents the hero they are all so desperately seeking."

The day before, the coverage had still been focused on the missile attack. The death toll had been calculated: 173. The vast majority had been women and children. The Syrian government and the Iranians had insisted that the target had been Islamic State commanders. They had insisted they had superb intelligence before they had acted. But with every denial, their place as paragons of evil had been reinforced.

Ever since the death of Omar, the dead have tortured Mohammed. When he slept, he could see their faces. They haunted his dreams. He could see Aisha, his wife. He could see his son. He could see their eyes condemning him for his failures and the price they had paid.

As their ranks grew, he had tried to reassure them that they had died for a greater cause. He had insisted that he would make it right.

And with the missile attack, he had finally succeeded. With the missile attack, he could finally justify what he'd done. He could tell them that they had given their lives for a reason: they had given their lives to liberate their people from the worshippers of Ali and the cult of the Alawite.

With the missile attack, he could tell them they were martyrs of the true Islam, and that All-h would embrace them.


There were 173 new martyrs, but Mohammed slept well the night after the circus attack. It was the first time he had slept well in years.


Now, though, in an instant, his greatest triumph has faded from view. Now the accusations of the dead are returning. And the 173 martyrs of the circus attack have joined their ranks.

And it is all because of "Hasna."

The articles all talked about "Hasna," but none had actually interviewed her. Instead, they all shared the remarkable story of her life under the Islamic State and her escape from persecution. They all shared the lies she had told.

None of them knew the truth.


Mohammed turned from his computer and opened a small folder.

Slowly, almost reverently, he removed its contents. He fingered each item, almost in disbelief at the story they told.

The first time he'd met "Hasna", he'd asked his contacts in the Islamic State to find out who she really was. Earlier this same day, they had delivered. The folder contained her reality. It contained everything he'd need to destroy her and the work she was doing.

But, of course, destroying "Hasna" wouldn't be enough. He had to, somehow, find a way to keep the accusations of the dead at bay.

He had to find a way to rescue his people.

Reluctantly, Mohammed closed his computer, casting his tent into darkness.

And then he lay down on his small mat, preparing once again to defend his soul against those he had condemned.


Mohammed knew that, somehow, he would rescue his people. Somehow, he would destroy their enemies. Somehow, the truth of Maryam Al-Mosuli's story would help him justify his life.

He just didn't know how.

He closed his eyes and allowed the souls of the martyrs to tear through his very being.

# Retribution

*Maryam's Story, October 5ᵗʰ, 2014: Outside Qunietra*

Only four days have passed since I'd welded a temporary truce in the city. I'd meant for that day to change the City for the better, or at least to give my brother some short respite from the noise and violence. But that day had changed me as well. It hadn't been the bombing or the repair that had done that. It had been the phone call I'd made while waiting in the trailer with Elizabeth.

I needed somebody to look after Ibrahim. That's why I'd called Tadeo. He'd known us in Mosul, but we'd also seen him regularly in the City itself. I'd asked him for the potassium, and he delivered. Of course, I didn't just need somebody to look after Ibrahim. I needed something more, something the American woman with me couldn't know about. That's why I spoke to Tadeo in Aramaic, ensuring that whatever words of Arabic she might have would be useless.

Very few people spoke Aramaic, but my father had insisted I learn.

I remember the conversation perfectly.

"Elizabeth?" Tadeo had asked when he picked up the phone. He recognized the phone number. It made sense, he worked closely with the City government.

"No," I said, "This is Maryam. There's been a bombing. Of the water tank."

"I've heard," he answered.

"I ran up here to help, and they've arrested me. I need you to check in on Ibrahim. He might be quite upset."

355

"Okay," answered Tadeo, calmly. But his voice left something hanging, like he expected something more. I didn't disappoint.

"And another thing," I'd said, "I'm going to fix the water tank. When I ask, I need you to bring men and I need to have volunteers quickly. Just to set the tone. I want everybody working together on the repair. I think it might help the City."

I heard Tadeo chuckle lightly.

"You know," he'd said, after a moment, "you're just like your father."

"What?" I'd asked, confused.

"He used to call me, and others. He wanted us to show up with men. He thought, by having us repair Mosul, that we could somehow repair the people who lived there."

I was stunned by what he'd said. I had imagined my father worked by magic. I imagined people spontaneously gathered to support his work. But now that vision had disintegrated in a puff of smoke. I'd believed that my father had had some strange power over others. But now, suddenly, I knew better.

My father had *engineered* every one of those projects. It had all been a part of his attempt to rescue the city he loved.

My father needed to ask for help.

And if he needed to ask, then he couldn't have believed he was invincible. If he needed to ask for their help, it wasn't simply granted. Instead, he'd gone out into Mosul, day after day, trying to create a reality that wasn't there. Through sheer bluster, he wanted to make the imaginary into the truth. He risked his life to impose a vision nobody else saw.

His illusion worked on me. I believed he was impervious. I believe he magically brought people together. But now I knew his illusion was only an illusion. I knew he was risking his life to create a reality that wasn't there. And I knew why.

I remembered my own words that day at the dam: "We exist to sustain the city of Mosul." That was what I had said. My father had been so proud when I'd realized that. I'd thought he was talking about infrastructure. I had realized he was talking about the social fabric of Mosul itself.

With a sentence, Tadeo had changed my life.

In a suddenly solemn voice, I said, "Thank you, Tadeo."

"Hasna," he'd said, his voice taking on a strange tone, "You'll be the salvation of us all."

I hung up.

When I'd first tested the water the day of the bombing, I'd realized it was drinkable. The water was dirty, but not deadly. Nobody had to know, though and I didn't tell them. Instead, we set to work. The drinkable water was made pure. And in the process, I bought a few days of peace.

As I worked, a thought chewed at the back of my mind: had my father had ever committed his own sabotage?

There was no way to know.

The holiday of Eid Al-Adha started two days later. Seemingly out of nowhere, thousands of sheep appeared in the City — only to be sacrificed and butchered. Meat was distributed liberally, and huge communal meals were arranged. But the people were not rich. While it was a tradition to wear new clothes, few could afford them. Thus, many people simply exchanged with others, patching up and cleaning their own damaged garments before passing them on.

For the first time in a long time, people felt safe. As I walked through the spaces between the tents, that feeling was palpable. But there was another undercurrent: people were looking at me in a new way. I couldn't understand it at first. But eventually I did. They were looking at me the same way they had looked at my father: with gratitude and with respect. I was creating my own illusion.

This place was becoming my home.

I found myself giddy with the possibilities.


Then that night, the first night of the holiday, Elizabeth explained the financial reality of the City. She explained that, the day after the four-day festival of Eid Al-Adha, the City would be shut down. Soldiers would move in and the people would be pushed out. My home would be destroyed.

I protested, claiming that we had tamped down the violence. But the violence wasn't the real problem. It was only the most obvious problem. The problem was that the place was completely bankrupt: no real commerce had emerged, and that reality couldn't be sustained indefinitely. I watched, like I was in a dream, as she explained that my brother and I would be exempt. This fabulously wealthy and powerful woman would take care of us. She wanted to take Ibrahim and I wherever we wanted. She even suggested a university in America.

A day earlier, this would have been the answer to all my dreams. But now, because of what Tadeo had told me, it was no longer enough. I wanted more. I had an opportunity to walk in the footsteps of my father. I could engineer like he had engineered. And, perhaps, I could succeed where he had failed.

My dream of a new home had only lasted hours. And now, it was being taken away from me.

I asked her if she could support the City. I knew she was rich. But she seemed almost angry at the request – like the City was guilty of some great crime against her.

We fell into an uncomfortable silence.

And then, from the City below, I heard the all-too-familiar *tat-tat-tat-tat* of gunfire.

The violence had returned. I had expected it. But it seemed like the death knell to my newborn dreams.

I was crushed.

I went to sleep, crushed.


I'm woken up by a hand on my shoulder. For a moment, I think I'm back home. But it is not my father. It is Elizabeth. And, standing next to her, is a boy I did not recognize.

"Hasna?" asks the boy, hopefully.

"Yes," I answer, groggily. I don't want to wake up. I don't want to be pulled back into my nightmare.

"There's been a killing," says the boy.

"I know," I say. "We heard it."

"It wasn't just anyone," says the boy, as he begins choking up.

I wake up a bit more then. Who has died? Ibrahim is with me.

"Who was it?" I ask, suddenly awake.

"Tadeo," says the boy.

And with that, I know my nightmare has returned.

Minutes later, Ibrahim, Elizabeth, and I are being guided to a large tent by the small boy. It has been assembled from a number of other tents, all reconfigured to make something grander than usual. At one end, a heavy-looking cross has been mounted beneath a rounded arch. I realize the tent is a church.

As we walk in, I notice that the edges of the dark tent are encircled by older men. Many are priests. They look reserved and careful and greatly saddened. Some are dressed differently than the others, representing other Christian faiths. We are guided to the center. And then an old man, one of the oldest, stands up from in front of the cross. He walks slowly to us, smiling sadly.

He stops in front of us and then looks down at little Ibrahim. Ibrahim smiles back at him.

The man places his hand on Ibrahim's head and utters, "May the Lord lift his countenance on you and give you Peace."

He then leans over and gives Ibrahim a kiss. The boy's smile broadens with the kindness.

The old man straightens up to face me. "Maryam," he says, in an undertone. Despite the whisper, his voice seems almost regal – like it carries thousands of years of authority behind it. I suddenly find myself appreciating that *he'd* said my name. I don't even ask how he knew it.

"I am Maryam?" I answer, quietly, in Aramaic. Elizabeth just looks on.

"You knew Tadeo," the man says. It isn't a question.

"Yes," I say, surprising myself with my tears. He lifts a hand and brushes one of my tears to the side. He is smiling sadly, like he is both comforting me and mourning within himself.

"I knew him in Mosul," I say. "And he was one of the few who spoke to my brother and I over the last weeks."

The man nods.

He turns to Elizabeth. "And you?" he says, in heavily accented English, "you knew Tadeo?"

Elizabeth looks surprised and honored by the question.

"Yes," she answers, "I worked with him."

"Yes," says the man, with a sad smile. "He believed in this City."

"I Bishop Thoma," the man continues, the broken nature of his English becoming clear, "From the Ancient Church of the East. Elders are here from my church, and other churches, because we decide what to do."

I nod, as did Elizabeth.

"Can I speak," he asks Elizabeth, "in Aramaic? It easier for me to say what I mean. And our people do not speak English."

"Yes, yes," says Elizabeth, almost urgently eager to please.

"Thank you," says the Bishop. Elizabeth glows with the appreciation. Then, to me, he adds, "You will translate as necessary."

Again, it is not a question. I just nod my agreement.

"Good," says Thoma. And then he walks slowly back to the front of the tent and sits down in front of the cross.

He continues in Aramaic.

"Tadeo bet Sargis was loved in our community. His name meant 'heart', and in his way, he was the heart of this place. He believed in it. Because his English was good, he worked with the government here. But he was not a prominent man. And he was not a young hothead either. We cannot understand why anyone would murder him."

There are nods around the room.

Thoma himself nods with the others, acknowledging their agreement.

Like a child, I had never known that Tadeo's full name had been Tadeo bet Sargis.

The Bishop continues. "We have brought Hasna, a Muslim woman, into this church because of Tadeo."

The assembled men watch. The Bishop continues, speaking to me. "Tadeo spoke about you many times. He said you could rescue this place. And we need this place to be rescued. Beyond this City's walls, this community will be exterminated."

The Bishop pauses and then adds, "Tell Elizabeth what I said."

I translate into English.

She seems confused. "Exterminated?" she asks, in an undertone.

I just nod and she sits back, surprised.

"Tadeo insisted," says the Bishop, "that you could heal this place. He said it was in your blood."

I just look at him. I have no idea what I could do. I want to ask Elizabeth if it even mattered, or if any efforts to deal the violence were condemned to failure. But I can't, not in front of these people.

"We feel trapped," says the Bishop. "If we are weak, our enemies will not only dominate us, as in times past. No, this time they will kill us. And if we try to be strong, well... we cannot be as strong as they are. We will not survive strength. Assur was founded in the 25th century before Christ. But now, we are on the verge of extinction in our own lands."

"G-d will protect us," he says with conviction. "But I cannot understand how."

He sits silently. And I hear the unasked question. "What should we do now?"

I sit there, thinking, for a long while. The men around me watch me, carefully. Waiting. They clearly have no answers. This community

362

must be like a porcupine. Those who attack it have to feel the pain of their actions. I know that. Their enemies have to be discouraged. But porcupines are not invulnerable.

Somehow, the pain they cause has to bring an end to this war.

It is then that I have my idea.

An hour later, I am watching the scene carefully through the binoculars Elizabeth has loaned me. It is the early morning, the preferred time for attacks on Muslim targets. Even if they are aware of the dangers of their trips to or from the mosque, people can't help but be groggy at this hour. This man's guards are doing a good imitation of responsiveness. They scan the area with alert eyes. They know that when the enemy is waiting, dropping a tiny fraction of a second, driven by sleepiness, can cost them their lives. They crowd close to their man, serving as human shields. The man they are defending is the Hujjatu I-Islam. The man is a Shiite cleric. He isn't an Ayatollah or Grand Ayatollah, but he is the highest-ranking Shiite cleric in the City.

That's why he is the target.

"They deserved this," I think to myself, "they deserve far more than this."

This attack is to be a retaliation. But even it won't truly repay the murder of Tadeo.

I watch as the man moves slowly, surrounded by his bodyguards. They know there is danger.

As I watch, I pray for a successful hit.

Only a target this great has the hope of changing the course of the Assyrians in this place.

And then I hear a *pft-pft* as two rounds hit the man in the chest. Somehow, a gifted Christian sniper has found a way through the men protecting the Hujjatu I-Islam. The Hujjatu I-Islam falls back in shock. And then he looks down in surprise and sees that giant blue splotches have appeared on his garment.

They are paint balls, fired from paint ball guns purchased by Elizabeth. She'd had the binoculars before. The paint ball guns were a special rush order.

The man looks confused. His bodyguards are shocked.

And then his phone rings. He fishes it from his pocket, hands shaking, eyes shooting around – mind overcome by fear.

I know what the voice on the other end is going to say; I'd scripted it myself.

"We could kill you if we wanted to. But we want to talk."


I see the man nod, and then utter the word that will unlock the future, "Hasenaanan."

It means, 'okay'.


I smile and put down the binoculars. The Assyrians have maintained their honor. They have stung their enemies, warning them. But they have not stung them so badly that outright war must follow.

Of course, outright war *can* still follow. But at least, for now, there is hope

# Justice

*October 5th, 2014, Outside Qunietra*

We arrange a time and place for the meeting.

It is to take place in a tent assembled for just this purpose in the newly defined Christian quarter of the City. The space has to be larger than one of the normal tents. Nonetheless, asking the Shiite leader to meet in the Church would have been too much. As far as the time is concerned, the meeting is to take place in only one hour. I don't want to leave much time for scheming or backing out.

But I do want enough time to pray.

The new tent doesn't exist, not yet. The young men of the Assyrian community are still scrambling to assemble it when I come back from the bathrooms, having washed my hands and feet. The frame is already up, but the workers are still attaching the walls. The sun is casting its light on the camp. But it is not yet warm.

Elizabeth is sitting in the embryonic tent. She seems to follow me now, although I'm not sure why. She is watching Ibrahim, who seems happy around her. She gives me a freedom I haven't known since Mosul.

I find myself nervous about the prayer I'm about to perform. It is not a *salah,* or obligatory prayer; it is a *dua*, or personal supplication. I've certainly made personal supplications. But as I've learned more from those around me, I've realized there is a proper way in which such prayers are to be offered.

There is a proper way, but I don't yet know enough to say what it is.

I have seen men perform a *dua,* facing Mecca with their palms raised towards the heavens. But I don't know what verses they recite, or if there are particular things one is supposed to ask for. I have only fleeting knowledge of the Koran; I can't quote from it or find verses that express my own thoughts. I feel that lack – that absence – now. I wonder why my father didn't teach me. Perhaps he truly believed in Baathism?

As people work around me, I place my prayer rug on the ground. Is that a part of the *dua?* And then I kneel, facing Mecca, with my hands on my knees.

I don't know how to begin, so I start as I always do, reciting the opening to the Koran.

I feel the curious eyes of the Assyrian men watching me. They all know who I am. But I wonder, as they watch me, what they think about me. Are they looking at me with fear, my prayer recalling the violence of the Islamic State? Or perhaps, they watch with hope, imagining that having me among them promises a more peaceful future? Or, perhaps, they simply dismiss me as a silly little girl who is good with plumbing?

I try to stop thinking of them. It isn't *their* guidance that I need.

I close my eyes. And then I force myself to leave my surroundings.

"*All-hu Akbar... All-hu Akbar... All-hu Akbar,*" I recite slowly, in an undertone. Is this the ritual?

I raise my palms to heaven, and I recite the verses from the *salah,* the obligatory prayer. *Guide us to the straight path...* I chant quietly. I repeat the mantra again and again. It is what I desire. I want to follow the right path. I want to know what it is.

I am about to meet with Bishop Thoma and the Hujjatu I-Islam, a man named Hassan Zaidi. These are two men who, in the space of weeks, have grown to hate one another. They are now not only steadfast, but justified, enemies. And yet I imagine I, a teenaged girl, can bring them together. Is this pride? Unacceptable hubris? Am I insane?

I know the natural path of things. It is conflict – deadly conflict, until the honor of one party is broken, and the honor of the other is redeemed.

Do I actually think I can find a better way?

*Guide us to the straight path…* I intone, desperately.

I beg. But I hear no answer. I experience no flash of insight. I need All-h's guidance, but I am not finding it. Reluctantly, I put my hands on my legs, sitting straight-backed. And then I breathe deeply. I sit there for what seems like hours, trying to collect myself, trying to be ready. But the challenge seems insurmountable.

Eventually, I give up, wiping my face with my hands, as I've seen others do. And then I open my eyes.

The tent is brighter now. The sides and top glow with the soft light of the sun. It is growing warmer as well. I look towards Ibrahim. He is undisturbed, happy in Elizabeth's company. In a way, he is a blessed contrast to the situation that surrounds me. His memory is too short to maintain a feud.

And then I rise from my knees. The walls have been completed and chairs have been set up. There are about fifteen in all. They have been laid out in two groups of seven, facing each other. The final chair is in between the groups, perpendicular to them, and off to one side. It is meant to be mine.

My father made me read about the layout of chairs. He made me read about round tables and square tables and rectangular ones. I thought it was silly. And then he started rearranging how we sat for dinner. And, eventually, I began to understand. Who you see and how close you are to them directly affects the dynamics of how you communicate. It can impact the outcome of conversations. I don't know why he taught me this. But he did, and now I appreciate it.

I am to be an arbitrator. I can rearrange the chairs, if it would help.

I try to imagine the conversation. The reality of the situation is that the leaders of each group will want to bark at each other across the narrow aisle. Their attendants will sit behind them, glowering with shared hatred. Would a circle be better? Should I force the groups apart, interspersing them with one another? Would the change actually help?

I leave the chairs as they are. The men will shout, but maybe they need to.

Perhaps, I think to myself, I should just take Elizabeth's offer and leave. What benefit could I possibly provide? At best, I could create a week of peace. After that, the City itself would cease to exist due to its financial collapse.

And then I think of Tadeo. Perhaps, with this meeting, I can save a single life, a life like his. Even if the City is crushed, that would be worth it. But I will need All-h's own guidance to make it happen.

I think about sitting and waiting, in that lonely chair. Maybe it would be better to stand near the entrance to the tent, greeting people as they arrive. Maybe I should try to make everybody feel welcome. Of course, that won't work. This is the kind of meeting that is for men, not girls. It would be better if I came afterwards, forcing the Christians to greet their enemies, but leaving nobody with a chance to be put off by me.

That makes sense.

I go to the corner of the tent to talk with Elizabeth and be with Ibrahim. I want to make myself unobtrusive. Elizabeth is intensely curious about what is happening, but she does not speak Arabic. I promise a full report afterwards. She seems fascinated by me. But she fascinates me as well. She has been to so many places I have barely heard of. And she is friends with those who everybody knows. I could learn from her. She could make me so much more than I already am. I could learn from her and then, afterwards, I could come back to Syria or Iraq, empowered by her. I could do more then.

I don't have to be here. Maybe I shouldn't be.

It is then that I realize I *have* a choice. Ever since that first bombing, I've been driven by necessity – by a need to survive and to protect my brother. But now, I have a chance to leave. I have a chance to disengage. It would be an honorable choice. It would be far less risky than the road I'm on.

But I don't choose it. For the first time, I freely accept responsibility.

My father would be proud.

As we talk, in English, the Assyrian attendees begin to shuffle in. They are senior men: Bishop Thoma, a clerk, and five of the elders. Most of them take seats, but the elderly Bishop remains, standing near the entrance. He will greet the Shiites when they come. It is an intelligent thing to do.

The Shiites come as a group. We hear them before they enter, arguing with the guards at the entrance to the tent. They would be armed, I imagine. And that can't be allowed. After repeated protestations, one of the men – a burly and rough-looking man – comes into the tent alone. He glances at Elizabeth, Ibrahim, and I, confused.

But he pays us no more attention. And then he pats down the Bishop, the clerk, and each of the elders. With a grunt, he turns and heads back to the entrance of the tent. He's satisfied that there is no ambush here.

It seems funny to me that he'd care. There had already been an ambush. If we'd wanted to kill his man, we would have done so an hour before.

A few more words are spoken, and then the group enters. There are six guards, and then there is the Hujjatu I-Islam, Hassan Zaidi. He alone will represent his people. These Shiites are more hierarchical than many other Muslims.

As Hassan Zaidi walks towards the chairs, he is clearly angry. We've compelled him to come, but we cannot compel him to be happy. As he draws closer to the chairs, I rise and walk towards the last, unoccupied, seat. The one between the groups. The two of us sit almost simultaneously.

The Hujjatu I-Islam turns to the Bishop and asks, with a glare, "Why is *a girl* here?"

"We need an arbitrator," says Bishop Thoma, calmly.

"A girl?" asks Hassan.

"Better somebody with respect, but no hope of power, correct?" says Thoma. He does not bother pointing out that I was neither Shiite nor Christian. They both know it.

Hassan nods, with some resignation. For my part, I wonder how long "powerless, but respected" can be a stable reality. I feel like one or the other will need to go, soon enough.

"So why am I here?" glowers Hassan.

Quietly, Thoma says, "Because we want justice."

"Justice?!" Hassan says, "For what?"

"One of the cherished members of our community, Tadeo bet Sargis, was killed. We want the killers brought to justice."

"And you think the killers are Shiites?"

"Yes."

"Well," says Hassan, "I know nothing about it. I don't think my people killed your Tadeo. But I'm sure he deserved to die; *we also seek justice.*"

I see Thoma grit his teeth.

"What?" says Hassan, challenge in this voice, "You kill our people, and you expect my sympathy, love, and support? This didn't start with a Christian man being killed. It started with the murder of a Shiite man, Ali al-Arzusi. I admit I didn't like him much. But justice had to follow. And it has."

Bishop Thoma sits there, silent. Then, after a time, he says, in an undertone, "We just want peace."

I groan inside. It is a statement of weakness.

"Peace?" says the Hujjatu I-Islam. "You murder my people, seeking Christian control of this place. And when the stakes get too high, when you realize you can't and won't be allowed to dominate this patch of earth, then you sue for peace and pretend to be friendly. Your mask as a kind old man has fallen. You've laid your cards on the table. You've lost. It is too late to hide your true self behind an image of peace."

"We could have killed you," says Thoma, quietly.

"Yes," says the Hujjatu I-Islam. "Like the great martyr Ali ibn Abi Talib, I could have been assassinated. It would have been a high honor, to be like the first Imam. But it would have been pointless for you. You would have killed me but strengthened my people. They killed Ali but strengthened his people. But *your* people, they would not have been strengthened by such a murder."

Ali ibn Abi Talib was the son-in-law of the Prophet and the first Shiite Imam. He had been assassinated with a poisoned sword while praying the Fajr prayer.

I haven't said a word. I've just watched the two of them. And then Hassan stands up to leave.

"Wait," I say.

"What for?" he barks, angrily.

"You said your death would strengthen *your* community, right?"

"What of it?" he answers. "Are you offering to try to kill me, little girl?"

Images of Youssef dying in a cloud of acid fill my brain. I did kill, once – but I can't do it again.

Hassan sees something in my face. His eyes furrow slightly.

"I want to know," I say. "Were you just talking about the community in the City, or outside of it as well?"

"Who cares?" he mutters, moving towards the door. His guards encircle him.

"Who would benefit?" I ask, more loudly.

"From what?" he calls back, not breaking his stride.

"From the Christians and the Shiites fighting, like this?"

He stops.

Hassan Zaidi, the Hujjatu I-Islam, looks back at me, quizzically.

I know the answer. My dead husband Youssef told me about his friend. I remembered what he'd said. He'd said his friend in the City would shape the world for the Islamic State. He'd make the tricks in Raqqa seem like child's play. Perhaps that is what he's done here.

I continue. "How far does this little battle with the Christians extend? Does it just affect the Assyrians and Chaldeans here? Or does it affect the Europeans, the Americans, or even the Russians?"

"So what if it does?" the Hujjatu I-Islam says. "We don't need them."

"But they can hurt you," I answer. "They can narrow your choices. A war with the Christians here can make things harder in other places. Your people often fight from weakness. But since the death of Hussain ibn Ali, you've always done so intelligently. You don't just push into martyrdom. You're too smart to make things unnecessarily hard."

Hussain ibn Ali was the grandson of Mohammed and the son of Ali. He had been killed when his tiny group of fewer than 150, including women and children, had marched hopelessly against an army of thousands. It is one of the most famous tragedies in Islamic history.

"We're used to hardship," he answers. "It is how we were forged."

"Yes," I say. "But you've also grown to understand that you must work with the world. You can't simply try to march against adversity and hope to succeed. You lack the firepower."

"So how should we work with the world?" he asks, with a chuckle in his voice. He is mocking me.

"I suggest," I say, "that we find out who killed your politician, Ali al-Arzusi. And I suggest that we find out why. And then we punish them and unravel this entire mess. Then you can have peace. And everybody will be stronger for it."

"And you'd support this little girl's proposal?" Hassan asks Bishop Thoma.

The old man nods. "There was no justification for Ali's murder."

I admire the phrasing. He could have been referring only to Ali al-Arzusi, the Shia politician. Or he could have been referring to Ali ibn Abi Talib, the first Imam of Shia Islam.

"So, who investigates?" asked Hassan, slowly moving back towards his chair. He still hasn't sat.

"Ali's widow," I answer, quickly. "She is the aggrieved party."

"You'll let the widow ask questions, here in your community?" asks Hassan of the Bishop.

"I will," says Bishop Thoma.

Hassan sits.

"And then, whose justice will the killers face?" asks Hassan, "If you try them here, your people will simply protect the killers after they are found."

"Would they prefer they face trial among your people?" challenges the Bishop, "That would not be fair. You'd gladly execute whomever the widow accuses – so long as they are Christian."

"We have laws!" says Hassan, insulted.

"As do we," says the Bishop.

I raise my hands to silence them. Miraculously, they look to me. I almost panic when I realize I don't know what to say.

But then, for some reason, a strange memory of my father pops into my head.

He'd brought me to Mosul's water treatment plant, and he'd asked how I'd go about recombining the waste and the water – short of aggressively stirring them together or killing the organisms in the waste itself.

I protested at the question. What possible reason would there be to reverse the process of purification?

"Perhaps," he'd answered, "you *want* a vibrant and smelly pool of organic life?"

I'd thought about the question for weeks. But I couldn't work it out. Short of brute force, I couldn't figure it out. The bacteria in the pools glommed the waste together into large particles called flocs, and then that flocs grew heavier and heavier. Eventually, the flocs sank –

separating the waste from the water. The flocs had grown stronger, and more separate, by being pulled together into the growing groups. The key to breaking those groupings up was to shatter the bonds the bacteria had formed, but I didn't know how to do that.

Eventually, I'd almost forgotten the question. I'd never realized my father hadn't been talking about waste.

Until now.

Now, I realized my father wanted to reverse the binding that pulled one group from another in the city of Mosul. He wanted them to mix again. He wanted to recreate Mosul, the vibrant and smelly pool of organic life.

But, just like me, he'd never been able to work out how.


"The laws are pulling us apart," I say. "We need new courts, ones that don't have ethnic alliances."

Hassan and Thoma look at me like I'm an idiot.

"How?" asks Hassan, almost smirking.

"I don't know," I admit.

"Then it is back to war," says Hassan, conclusively.

"Wait," I say, raising one hand.

"What for?" asks Hassan, growing angry.

"Just give me a minute," I beg. "We might be able to work this out. Isn't it worth just thinking about it for a few minutes?"

Surprisingly, both he and Bishop stop. They just wait. It gives me a small burst of hope.

I close my eyes, blocking them out.

The key to the sewage had been undermining the alignment of forces that separated the flocs from the water. The floc falls not just because it binds together, but also because it weighs more when it does so. Neither bonding nor gravity work by themselves.

Maybe the Shiites and the Christians are the same? The problem isn't that they're separated, it is that the forms of that separation combine to create conflict and permanent division. Here, the groups may have gathered together, like the flocs; but their separation is not yet total. They can still be mixed in some respects.

"I have an idea," I announce, opening my eyes.

The two leaders are still looking at me.

"Let's take every person in this city and let's form them into tribes. Not preexisting tribes like Shiites or Arab or Kurdish, but random, made-up tribes. They'll vote for judges, but just within their own artificial tribes. But because those judges don't represent preexisting groups, the courts won't be biased for one side or another. Perhaps we can separate justice from ethnicity and religion."

Hassan thinks, but just for a second.

"You want to make a court this way?" he asks, somewhat incredulously. "It doesn't matter what made-up tribes you create, if you elect a council like that, whichever group is most numerous will dominate it. They will decide every question and every case. There won't be any justice."

Thoma speaks up. "There can be justice."

"How?" Hassan asks.

"The story is from the Old Testament," he says. "Moses created groups, layered groups. And he chose judges from each group. Judges of ten, and judges of forty, and judges of a hundred, and so on. We could mix all the people together into groups of 10, 100, and 1000. And they could choose judges for their own groups. Then, if judgments are challenged, they could move up the levels."

"It has the same problem," I said. "You'd end up with judges representing whoever is most numerous."

"We could choose the judges randomly," says Thoma, "but let them be replaced if 2/3rds vote for a new judge. That way, we'll be sure to have many minority judges, and it won't be possible to replace them unless a large majority rejects their judgment."

"And how would we choose a judge in this case?" Hassan asks, "Would we use the plaintiff's group, or the defendant's?"

"Why not one of each and then a third, random judge?" Thoma says. "You might get an unfair court, but the chances are lowered."

Hassan is sitting quietly.

"Let's take this case," I say. "We find a suspect. The widow's judge and the suspect's judge and a third, random, judge, sit on a court. They give judgment."

"Whose law do they follow?" asks Hassan, insistently.

The Bishop and I sit, silently.

Then Bishop Thoma speaks, "That was a question about Moses's judges. There was no law when they were given their positions. Perhaps they did what was right in their own eyes."

"So, the law would form itself?" I said, "As the cases were decided?"

"Yes," says the Bishop. "Although G-d brought His law soon after."

"No," says Hassan, firmly. "We must live by the laws of All-h, not man. Man's law is not enough."

"All of us here are informed by G-d's law," says the Bishop. "We are not making it up for ourselves. We will be living by the laws of G-d."

"You will live by the laws of Mohammed and the Imams?" asks Hassan.

"No," says the Bishop. "Something else will emerge, from the courts and from customary ideas about fairness. Just like what happened with common law."

"Then you are not living by All-h's laws. But by a perversion of them."

The Bishop says nothing, a lifetime of religious weakness has taught him well.

But I am not as old as the Bishop.

"Are your courts just?" I ask Hassan.

"No human court is perfectly just," he answers.

"They might be just as imperfect as courts formed by just men," I say.

"No. Courts that try to follow the laws of Mohammed are inherently better. Those laws have been brought by the true Prophet, peace be upon him, and carried forward by All-h's chosen Imams and maintained by His scholars. It is better than the random and often evil choices of unguided men. At least Muslim Judges have the will of All-h in their hearts."

"These courts will be influenced by your laws. There will be Shiite judges." I say.

"Even you," says Hassan, "are not silly enough to think that will be enough."

"And you will die, all of you, rather than accept these courts?" I ask.

"Is that really your threat?" asks Hassan, "Your Christian friends might kill me, but they won't kill all of us. A few of us might be martyrs, but you can threaten nothing more than that."

He begins to stand, once again.

"The City is almost bankrupt," I say. "If the people who pay for it don't see any improvement, soon, they will destroy this place.

Everybody will be kicked out. How will your people fare outside these walls, in the territory controlled by Al Qaeda, Al Nusra, and the Islamic State?"

Hassan stops.

"We can work it out," I say, pushing my advantage. "Or else, your people and the Christians here can both die at the hands of your common enemies."

"We are used to being martyrs," Hassan states, flatly.

"But you accept others' laws," I insist. "You do it in Europe and in the United States. I know they don't accept Shiite law there. So why don't you fight to the death in those places?"

"Those places don't have the same status," he insists. "They are not Muslim lands."

"You do it in Saudi Arabia, under Sunni law, and in Israel, under secular laws? At least here, *your understanding* will influence what happens."

"It is not our understanding!" says Hassan, sharply. "It is All-h's law."

My father had talked enough about the conflicts of Iraq for me to know there is nothing so simple.

"You are enough of a scholar to admit that even within the Shiites, there are disputes. Even your Grand Ayatollahs argue about whether Shia religious rule is a good thing. It is not as simple as being All-h's law."

"And there are ways of reconciling those differences," says Hassan.

"Even between Grand Ayatollahs?" I ask.

Hassan is silent. There are, of course, ways of adjudicating such disputes. But they aren't simple.

I press on. "Like almost everybody else here, you and your people *came to this place to compromise.* So, let's compromise and find justice along the way."

Hassan sits, slowly, and then he asks, "What will happen in this case?"

Thoma answers him: "We'll form the groups, of randomly chosen adults. Everybody will be a member of a group of 10, of 100, and of 1,000. We'll assign the judges randomly but allow 2/3rds voting to change them in case they are truly unacceptable. In this particular case, the widow will pursue the case, gather her evidence, and accuse those she thinks are guilty. The court of 10, one judge from the plaintiff's court, one from the defendants', and a third chosen randomly, will decide what they think is just. Both parties will be able to appeal. Over time, the courts will establish rules of appeal, but we'll start with none. All the early cases will make their way up to the courts of 100 and then 1,000. And then, that court will make the final decisions."

The Bishop and the Hujjatu I-Islam both sit thoughtfully.

"Why not a court of 10,000?" asks the Bishop.

"We don't have enough people," I say. "The judges would always be the same, and the majority would have too much power."

Hassan thinks, for a long minute. And then he says, "Okay."

The Bishop bows his head and states, "We will accept it as well."

There is no love between these men.

But peace might just be possible.

I can't help but wonder if Mohammed bin Hassan, the apparent leader of the Sunnis in the City, and the man I believe to be Youssef's scheming friend, will accept what the Bishop and the Hujjatu I-Islam have agreed to.

# Prosecution

*October 5th, 2014, Outside Qunietra*

Elizabeth, Ibrahim, and I leave the meeting with the Bishop and the Hujjatu l-Islam. As we walk, Elizabeth picks my brain, curious about what has happened. She tells me she could program the system to assign people to groups and pick judges randomly – that same afternoon. We keep talking about the idea as we walk, covering different possible scenarios.

And then, I look towards the hill where her trailer was. And I notice small groups of people heading up the makeshift tracks in tiny groups. I've never seen that happen before.

I ask Elizabeth about it, but she also has no idea what is happening.

As we draw closer to the hill, one of the people heading up it happens to turn his head in our direction. He is a young man, maybe 25 years old. A flash of recognition crosses his face and he changes his trajectory, heading straight towards us. And then another person, a woman, notices what he's done. She looks at us, and then she too changes direction. Before long, the effect has rippled through the entire group of scattered individuals; one by one, like magnets, they suddenly shift and begin to move towards us.

"What's going on?" Elizabeth asks, nervously.

"I have no idea," I answer.

As those nearest to us draw closer, they accelerate. The first man calls out, but I can't understand what he is saying. And then the woman shouts something, also unintelligible.

Ibrahim looks up at me, nervously. Elizabeth seems suddenly concerned.

And then moments later, we are surrounded by people – all shouting and screaming and pleading. I hear fragments of words and snippets of sentences, but not enough to understand. I pull Ibrahim close as the crowd pressed forward.

"QUIET!" I shout in Arabic.

But nobody listens. The crowd presses closer. I can't see beyond the initial line of faces.

"QUIET!" I shout in Arabic, a second time.

But the volume only grows. Elizabeth is standing next to me; her face is white with terror.

Nobody seems to want to hurt us. They are asking for something. Begging for something. But it doesn't matter. The effect is the same. The force of the crowd is beginning to crush us. Ibrahim is near my feet; I'm worried he won't be able to breathe.

But I can't get down to him. I can't pull him up.

He's trapped, and I'm scared he can't breathe.

The crowd surges forward again, and my worry only grows.

I look in every direction for some sort of salvation, but I see nothing.

After all we've been through, will an overeager crowd kill him? Can it be that simple? That fast? That random?

And then, I hear Ibrahim scream. The sound is primal. He hasn't done it since before the bombing of the water tank. But today, it seems far more frightening and visceral than any time I've heard it before.

The men and women closest to me fall into silence. They whisper to those around them. And then, like spreading of a brush fire, the message is carried back through the crowd. The press of the mob diminishes. The crowd is silent. Soon, all that can be heard is Ibrahim's piercing cry.

I see shame on the faces close to me. But I feel relief. I lean down and scoop Ibrahim up. His face is terrified. He seems lost and confused and out of place. I hold him close, and then we walk – Elizabeth and I – up the slope of the hill.

The crowd watches silently. They make way for us, eyes downcast at the harm they've caused my brother. Elizabeth is shaking, and Ibrahim is screaming.

But I still don't understand why they're here.

We come to a perimeter of soldiers and they let us through. In a moment, we pass from the shameful desperation of the mob to the peace that had existed only minutes before. Except, Ibrahim is still screaming.

I look back and see the people. I still don't know what they are demanding.

I see Mohammed ahead of us. I need him for the courts to work. But I want to steer around him, I don't trust him. Elizabeth, though, walks straight towards him. He smiles warmly as we approach.

"What was that?" Elizabeth asks him.

"This is a small place," says Mohammed. "People heard about the courts."

"And what do they want?" I ask.

"They want the honor of avenging the crime against their families."

I nod. But Elizabeth seems confused.

"In our laws," Mohammed says, "the family of a murder victim is the prosecutor. These are the family members. They want to deliver justice."

"Okay. We'll make a list," says Elizabeth. "We'll mark down each crime and its prosecutor."

"It won't be that easy," says Mohammed. "173 people were killed by the Circus attack. We can't have 173 prosecutors."

"There's a mob," I explain, "because they all want the honor of prosecution. They are fighting to be the ones who can deliver vengeance."

Elizabeth looks from one to the other of us and back again. Finally, she asks, "What do we do?"

I want to answer, but Mohammed beats me to it.

"I've been thinking about that," he says. "And I have an idea. We can make a list of potential prosecutors for each crime. And then we can form a little board, with Bishop Thoma, Hassan Zaidi, and myself. And we can choose who will lead each prosecution."

Elizabeth nods. I look at him carefully, suspiciously. I know he must have some other plan. This must be part of a plot. But his idea seems entirely reasonable and not the least bit threatening. I also nod my agreement.

As Ibrahim slowly calms down, Thoma and Zaidi are located and brought up the hill. They are seated side by side at a single folded table resting precariously on the uneven landscape. As the three men start talking with one another, the scene grows steadily quieter. They decide to start with the easy crimes, those with a single victim.

Mohammed calls out the names of victims – collected from the City rolls. And then men and women step forward. They present their petitions, argue their qualifications, and emphasize the strength of their losses. And, one by one, the board establishes new rules. They agree on whether a wife, a child, or a father takes precedence. They weigh what makes a prosecutor qualified. And they watch as, in a few cases, one

384

potential prosecutor defers to another, in recognition of the other's superior capabilities. But even as the initial crimes are assigned their prosecutors, the bulk of the crowd jostles behind them. There are well over a hundred potential prosecutors for the Circus attack. And they are waiting less and less patiently for the chance to avenge their dead. They are building up pressure, like a boiling pot.

Finally, Mohammed reads the names of the Circus victims. As he reads, his voice falters and his eyes tear up. He has to stop, at least for a while, broken down by the deaths in his community. There is silence as he reads; respect is being paid to the dead. And then, finally, he stops. He's read 173 names, but everybody knows there could be more. Quite a few people were seriously injured.

He lifts his head and crowd surges forward. They are almost all men, husbands and fathers of the dead. The wives and the children were the victims. One by one, they present their cases. They talk about their qualifications. They claim degrees from universities that cannot be verified. They claim past experience that cannot be cross-referenced. And they show pictures of their dead children, demanding the pity of the makeshift board.

And then the very last of the men steps aside.

And, behind him, a woman steps forward.

Elizabeth.


Mohammed looks surprised to see her. The assembled men look confused.

"Why are you here?" asks Mohammed, in English. Translations whisper through the crowd.

"I am a victim," says Elizabeth. "I was injured by the attack."

"But you are far less of a victim," says Mohammed, "than these others."

It is then that Elizabeth turns away from the board. And she turns towards the others.

"I'm not appealing to the board," she says. "I'm appealing to you."

She speaks slowly, allowing translations to make their way through the crowd.

"This was not a crime committed *here*. It was committed beyond our walls. It was committed with radios and phones and hidden messages."

Heads nod in agreement.

"You know who I am. I am a computer expert. I have access to people you do not have access to. I have a better chance of being trusted by the Israelis."

Heads continue to nod.

"I don't want to prosecute to claim an honor or to deprive you of yours. I want to prosecute because I think *I have the best chance of finding out who committed this crime.* I have the best chance of ensuring we all get our vengeance."

"So," she says, wrapping up, "I ask you to choose me."

A burst of conversation runs through the group. Mohammed raises his hands to silence the crowd. The gesture is mostly futile.

"You're not a victim," he protests, loudly, "Not like these people."

"I CHOOSE HER," says one man in the crowd, shouting in defiance – and to be heard over the din. He is the first man who'd seen us on the way up the hill.

The crowd grows suddenly quieter.

"I DO AS WELL," another calls out.

And then, like dominoes, the crowd falls into agreement. Elizabeth turns back to the board. And, one by one, they vote to select her.

Even Mohammed agrees.

Perhaps he is not Youssef's devious friend.

# Plan

*October 5th, 2014, Outside Qunietra*

Mohammed was surprised by how much time he spent on Twitter. While it wasn't possible to express useful or complex thoughts in such a format, it was a tremendous tool for keeping track of the sentiments that flowed through the City. It fascinated him how quickly ideas and attitudes could spread, so long as those ideas reinforced what people already believed. And it disturbed him how simplistic those ideas needed to be to fit in 127 characters. He had hoped his own community would be above that. He had hoped they would be more complex and more erudite. But they weren't. They expressed their own simple thoughts in the medium, and Mohammed watched as they did so.

He wondered, sometimes, whether Twitter made people simple or whether it simply enabled the simple to express themselves. He knew it was a powerful tool. The Islamic State had used it to recruit. They could reach out globally and interact with people. But oftentimes, they were recruiting the simple; great scholarship is not necessary in a simple shahid. All that is necessary is commitment.

Mohammed knew that many people posted things on Twitter or Facebook or Instagram, and then watched and waited to see how popular their presentations were. How many likes did a particular photo receive? It seemed to him the ultimate vanity, an expression of humankind in opposition to the glory of G-d. But, in a way, Mohammed figured that he was no different. He'd had Maryam's friend, Tadeo bet Sargis, killed the night before. He hadn't done it because he'd disliked

389

Tadeo. He'd done it because Maryam's stunt with the water tower had been far too successful. He wanted to stir things up again. It wasn't a long-term or complex plot. He'd chosen Tadeo simply because Maryam needed to lose an ally. The killing did nothing to relieve the accusations of the dead.

Nonetheless, although he felt like a common Twit, Mohammed was watching his feed. He was watching to see whether his kindling would turn into a fire. Some were curious why he was in the trailer all night. He had a simple answer: he'd heard about the killings and was simply watching to ensure the reactions didn't spin out of control.

As expected, in the hours that followed the murder, accusations flew. Angry Christians condemned the death of an apparently beloved man. As their tone sharpened, Mohammed knew a reprisal was coming. And then, early in the morning, it seemed to have happened. A shooting was reported. The target was no less than the Hujjatu I-Islam. Mohammed smiled at the success of his action. But then, moments later, another report claimed the so-called "assassination" had not been an assassination after all.

Somebody had risked their life to shoot the Hujjatu I-Islam *with a paint-ball gun.*

Confusion reigned. Mohammed watched his feed frantically, trying to figure out what had happened, and what was happening. And then it became clear that the Hujjatu I-Islam was traveling to the Christian part of town. He was there to meet the Bishop.

Mohammed was stunned, but still confident that nothing could be resolved.

Then, less than an hour later, news of the court system emerged.

Mohammed hadn't believed it at first. It seemed so unlikely. But, slowly, he'd realized it was real. He felt a pit in his stomach; it seemed that everything was falling apart. And then, he felt anger.

He had thought of the City as an opportunity to manipulate the world. But now he knew that the City was, in itself, an evil thing. It denied the honor of the Muslims, of Mohammed, and of All-h Himself. Jews, of all people, had decided the Muslim people needed guidance. And now they had established *courts* to supersede the judgment of rightfully chosen religious judges? And they had done it in Muslim lands? The affronts to the glory of All-h piled up. Maryam, the instigator of this new movement and the killer of his only friend, needed to be destroyed. But the destruction needed to go further. The City itself needed to be destroyed. And the ideas that lay behind it needed to be obliterated.

These people, the Jews who had built this place, could never be allowed to present themselves as morally superior.


Mohammed stood outside to wait for Maryam and Elizabeth to come back up the hill. As he waited, he tried desperately to come up with a plan to destroy them, to drive his enemies apart, and to bury the City and the ideas behind it.

Then, as Mohammed watched the mob form around Maryam, Elizabeth, and Ibrahim, he realized what he needed to do. Twitter was the real world now. In moments, an idea could seize people's minds and overcome them. In moments, they could be turned into a powerfully destructive force.

All that was needed was an idea that reinforced what everybody already believed.

Given the right ingredients, the world could be made to grasp certain ideas, and never let them go.

All that was needed was an idea that reinforced what everybody already believed.

And he had just the idea.

The first trials would focus on the first killing: the killing of the Shia politician, Ali. Of course, while Mohammed himself had arranged the killing, there was no way it could be traced back to him. More importantly, his Christian assassins had thought they had been working for the Israeli government. If Mohammed sent Hamid and Rashid away, nobody would ever believe the Israelis had not been involved. The young Christian snipers were good killers, but they weren't terribly smart. When they were prosecuted, the City would be undermined. The hypocrisy and hubris behind it would be laid bare. The Christian leadership would be condemned for their actions, and the duplicity of the Jews would be laid bare. The population would turn on the City itself, as the manipulative tool it was.

The whole world would turn on the City, and on the motivations of the Jews who had established it.

As Maryam and Elizabeth and Ibrahim began to finally make their way up the hill, Mohammed realized he could do still more. He could stage an attack by the Shiites. It could be cast as a reprisal against the Christians, a final act of anger and revenge. He could stage an attack so brutal the world would condemn the Shiites and their allies.

It would be an attack so brutal that the world would never forgive or forget.

And just like that, the pieces locked into place. And, best of all, it was the courts that would enable his plan. And the courts would start with the prosecutions.

When Maryam and Elizabeth and the screaming Ibrahim finally made it through the cordon of soldiers at the top of the hill, Mohammed was ready. He was smiling and cheerful and supportive. He would embrace their arrogant courts and use them as a weapon against Maryam and against the City itself.

Everything else proceeded according to plan. The only setback was the choice of Elizabeth as the prosecutor for the circus attack. Perhaps, somehow, she could find something on which to act. But he doubted that. He had been very careful. In a way, her choice as prosecutor had been a gift from All-h Himself. If she was invested in the prosecution, her money would ensure the City lasted long enough for him to crush the arrogance that had created it.

For the first time since the circus attacks, Mohammed was pleased.

Once again, he could hold the accusations of the martyrs at bay.

Once again, he could justify the sacrifices those closest to him had made.

And his enemies suspected nothing.

# Programming

For the first time in months, Elizabeth is feeling some of the drive that built her empire and that brought her to the City. She's feeling the opportunity, once again, to make a difference. She senses the chance to justify being *here* while her sister was dying halfway around the world.

As she boots her system, she eagerly waits for the release her work will give her. She will be distracted. She will be satisfied. Even knowing that, she didn't get to work right away. Instead, her feeling only strengthened as she made sure Maryam and Ibrahim were fed and were comfortable. She knows taking the time to feed Maryam and Ibrahim might have been a bit silly. After all, they had managed to trek across Iraq and Syria without somebody mothering them. But just thinking about their voyage has made her even more conscious of the care and support she somehow feels they need. She's taken the time to take care of them. Even though she is bursting with desire to get to work, she doesn't regret it.

The login screen comes up, and with a rapid-fire burst of keys, Elizabeth is into her system.

Elizabeth is far from her office, but she still has a computer setup appropriate for a billionaire software mogul. In front of her are six screens, in two stacks of three each. Her actual computer is only a laptop, albeit a particularly powerful one. The real power lies on the other side of her network connections. The laptop is used to access databases and services on other, far more capable, rack-based systems.

As she begins to work, Elizabeth consciously puts aside the prosecution of the circus attack. There can be no prosecution without courts.

In some ways, the job will be a simple one. Elizabeth can set up the computer code to choose the judges in just a few minutes. She just has to randomly select names of adults from the database to make groups of 10 and then randomly select groups of 10 to make groups of 100 and so on. Maybe she will make some boundary rules, so no groups are too imbalanced in favor of one ethnicity over others and so close relatives aren't on the same courts. But whatever little rules she adds, that part won't be hard.

That part is easy; it is the other parts that are more challenging.

First, there are human elements that are beyond Elizabeth's toolkit. For example, if the judges decide something, who will really enforce it? Elizabeth supposes the buy-in of the community leaders like Hassan and Thoma would make that happen. And she supposes that, as that happens repeatedly, the judicial system will acquire real power of its own. Maybe some sort of cross-ethnic law enforcement will be established.

But there are also technical questions Elizabeth can tackle. The most important is letting people know which cohort they are a part of and who their judges are and whether they themselves are judges. There are 20,000 people, about 15,000 of whom are adults, and they aren't already organized in any way that relates to the judicial groupings. Posting a book or broadcasting names by speaker will be incredibly impractical. There is just too much data. Text-messaging won't work, because Elizabeth doesn't know which phones are connected to which people. And while making a database people could use to look up their own records is feasible; it won't help those people get to know each other.

As Elizabeth understands it, that is a critical part of the task.

It was while making dinner for the children that Elizabeth came up with the bones of her solution. She realized that almost every person in the City has a payment account. They access them through the E-ink payment cards Elizabeth designed for her business. A person can pick up any card, scan their thumbprint, and access their account. The cards can display a small amount of information and allow a small amount of data entry. They can even communicate with each other through a central server and a 3G cell-phone signal. Elizabeth plans to broadcast information on the cohorts to each card. The next time people open their accounts with their thumbprints, they will see the groups they belong to and who their judges are. She can probably even modify the cards so that groups of 10 are automatically placed on shared, card-based, messaging platforms. That way, they can get to know one another.

It will be an incredible system. And it might even help with the enforcement of judgments. Elizabeth is as excited as she's ever been since she'd set up her first online payment system.

As she searches for the firmware that manages the payment cards on one screen and for the server-based software that manages their communication on the other, she turns briefly to Maryam.

"This is going to work, isn't it," she says, trying to contain the excitement in her voice.

"What?" Maryam asks, confused.

"The courts," Elizabeth says. "They'll bring peace, won't they?"

She sees Maryam think for a moment.

"I don't know," Maryam says. "I was born in 1998. I was five when Saddam fell. I don't know what brings peace."

Elizabeth looks at Maryam sadly.

But the girl isn't wallowing in self-pity, she is still thinking.

Maryam continues, "But, I don't think the courts will be enough."

"Why not?" Elizabeth asks, with a touch of unexpected self-pity.

"Well," Maryam says, "doesn't the U.S. have stable courts?"

Elizabeth nods.

"I've never been to America," Maryam says. "But I've seen movies. It's violent, isn't it? Do the courts stop that?"

Elizabeth thinks about that for a moment.

"I suppose they don't," Elizabeth says. "But there are differences in degree."

"So," says Maryam, "I guess this could *reduce* the amount of violence. But the problem remains, people want to fight. The one difference is they will hopefully use the courts to do it."

Elizabeth turns from her computer. Pausing in her work.

"What do people fight for?" she asks, in a general sort of way.

Maryam answers immediately. "Honor," she says.

"Not money or resources or power?" Elizabeth asks.

"I guess," Maryam says, "when they have no choice, they'll fight for those things. But most of the time, those things are just the tools use to acquire honor. People respect you if you're rich or powerful. And you feel dishonored if you are powerless. Victory is how honor is acquired."

"Honor?" Elizabeth states. It isn't really a question. The concept, as Maryam explains it, seems a little foreign to her. She liked to think about the world as more than a zero-sum game for respect. But then again, she was near the top of the pyramid. But she hadn't always been. Had she done what she'd done for honor?

She doesn't think so.

After a long pause, Elizabeth continues. "But honor doesn't have to involve victory, does it? After all, you can behave honorably and respond only when others violate your honor. You don't *have* to fight others in order to have honor? Right?"

"I suppose," Maryam says. "But often, it is communities that fight, not individuals."

"Same thing," Elizabeth says, warming up to the topic. "Communities can behave honorably and respond only when others violate their honor. It doesn't have to lead to communal war, even if that war is fought only in the courts."

"I suppose," Maryam says, her voice uncertain.

Elizabeth turns back to her computer. Elizabeth has to reacquaint herself with the system she designed. It wasn't simple to build and, once built, most of the thoughts behind the design migrated solely to the comments in the code. She begins to scan those comments, taking notes on paper as she considers the ways in which she can tackle the technical task she's set for herself.

A few minutes later, Maryam says, "They don't just fight for their own honor. They fight for the honor of G-d."

"The honor of G-d?" Elizabeth asks, not turning away from her computer.

"It's the most important honor there is," Maryam says. "As we bow in prayer, we say: *Glory be to my Lord, the most High Most Praiseworthy*. We sacrifice our lives for All-h's honor."

Elizabeth turns back to Maryam. "So, behave honorably and respond only when others violate your honor. That will honor G-d too, won't it?"

"No," Maryam says, "it won't. When others misrepresent All-h or His wishes, they violate His honor. You have to fight."

Elizabeth just sits there, thinking.

"It is actually a beautiful thing," Maryam says. "You dedicate your life to something greater than yourself, and you acquire meaning for your life. A nobody can give their all and be deserving of the highest praise."

Elizabeth had never thought of it that way. She closes her eyes, thinking, and trying to get her head around the concept. She'd never thought of suicide attacks as a beautiful thing, but that seems to be what Maryam is suggesting.

Eventually, Elizabeth asks, "Can we get past honor?"

Her question is almost a plea.

Maryam looks like she's about to answer. But she stops herself. Then she takes a breath and begins to speak more slowly.

"The obvious answer," Maryam says, "is 'no'. But I'm not sure I believe it. My father stayed in Mosul because he thought he could do something to improve the situation. He tried, again and again, to bring people together. And he succeeded. But they never stayed together."

Maryam pauses, thinking. Elizabeth just waits.

"Maybe," Maryam finally continues, "all he hoped to do was to start peace by stringing together brief bursts of it until it broke out on its own. But he wasn't a naïve man. I have to believe he had other reasons to think it was possible. After all, what he was doing clearly wasn't working."

There's a silence, and then Elizabeth says, in a hopeful whisper, "Maybe it was helping?"

"Maybe," said Maryam.

They just sit there, and then Elizabeth asks, "Is there any way, other than victory, to honor All-h? Is there some greater path?"

Maryam hesitates. And then a tiny, deeply satisfied, smile appears on her face. "Ibrahim and I," Maryam says, "harvested crops in Iraq. We cut them and gathered them and even milled some of them to feed ourselves."

"And?" Elizabeth asks, unsure of the connection.

"It was the most rewarding thing I've ever experienced."

"Enough to displace the honor of All-h?" says Elizabeth, doubtfully.

Maryam allows her smile to grow just a touch. "The odd thing," she says, "Is that it was honoring All-h. At the end of each day, we ate a little meal. Our simple flour and water wasn't really a feast. But it was Ramadan. And it was of food *we* had harvested. And every night I felt the greatest connection to All-h I've ever experienced. It was like our *creation* was being dedicated to something beyond us – to All-h Himself. I believe it honored All-h, deeply."

Elizabeth manages a wry smile. "You know," she says, "I was hoping to find that same feeling here."

"What do you mean?" Maryam asks.

"I wanted to invest some of what I've created into something beyond me. My sister was dying, and I wanted to reach for something bigger. Something to get beyond death. That's why I invested in the City. It was my chance to make a real difference. It might still be." Her voice is tinged with a hint of regret.

"You wanted to invest in something bigger?" Maryam asks. "But not in G-d?"

"I wouldn't have thought I was investing in G-d," says Elizabeth. "But maybe I am."

There's silence for a moment.

"What happened to your sister?" Maryam asks.

"She died," Elizabeth says, slowly. "Four days ago. Of cancer."

It's the first time she's said the words. Maryam sees the expression on her face and rises from her chair. She walks over to Elizabeth. Silently, she leans over and wraps her arms around the sitting woman. Elizabeth finds herself crying as she pulls herself against the body of this strange teenager.

She finds herself mourning for the first time.

The sobs come in deep waves.

Eventually, Maryam stands. The younger woman's own face is overrun by her own sorrow.

Elizabeth wipes at her eyes and then asks, a long moment after they separate, "Is there hope?"

Maryam just stands there. And then she answers, "I think there is. We just have to find a way for the people here to experience the joy I felt in those fields. Or the joy you're seeking. We have to find a way for them to experience the joy of investing in something greater – other than military jihad."

"I don't see how we can do that," Elizabeth says, pulling herself back into the present, "They have to have something to invest. But there's no business here."

"There is business here," Maryam counters. "Just not much."

"Yeah," says Elizabeth, with a dismissive huff. "There are markolets that don't make any money."

Maryam looks at her with an odd expression.

"What?" asks Elizabeth.

"They make money," says Maryam, matter-of-factly.

"I've seen the numbers," says Elizabeth. "I know they don't."

"Which numbers?" asks Maryam.

"The transactions on the payment cards," says Elizabeth. "We track them all. They buy milk for four shekels a liter, and they sell it for virtually the same price. Sometimes they sell it for less."

Maryam almost laughed. "That's what they charge on the cards," she said. "But they get more than that. People set up credits with the businesses. Milk costs four shekels from the cards, and then another two shekels that has to be paid another way."

"What other way?" asks Elizabeth, suddenly very curious.

"For some, it is cash. Dollars or Euro, nothing else is trusted. But for the most part, it is in gold."

"Where do they get the gold?" Elizabeth asks.

"They buy it using the cards."

"But I haven't seen people buying gold."

"It shows up as other things," says Maryam. "Like canned tuna or other non-perishable goods. You pretend to buy the tuna, but you actually get gold. And then the seller stores up those other commodities and sells them later, under the counter, or to people with cash. Of course, they could also be eating a lot of tuna."

Elizabeth hadn't thought of that.

"But you're right," says Maryam. "There isn't much business. The only money that's coming in is coming from the cards."

After a pause, she continues. "But people could make money, they just don't."

"How?" asks Elizabeth.

"They could smuggle things," Maryam says, "into Syria and Iraq. We're relatively close to ports here, so costs could be competitive. Then the smugglers could buy things from other people, and we'd get a local economy."

"I don't think the Israelis would like that," says Elizabeth.

"Why not?" Maryam says. "The smugglers wouldn't evade Israeli tariffs. And Syria and Iraq are barely countries. And they're officially at war any way."

"Okay," says Elizabeth. "Let's assume it works. It still wouldn't be enough to support this place."

"There are other things they could do," Maryam says. "For example, they could run news stations. Everything you hear about the Middle East is slanted: there's the Israeli perspective, the Qatari perspective, the Iranian perspective. This place could provide another perspective, one that runs across the battle lines. I think people would trust it as much as anything else. It could be a big business, especially since the people here really understand the places they've come from. You could do more than that, though. You could even expand into education. You probably have some highly educated people here. You might attract students from all over the Muslim world. Or even from Western countries interested in learning more about the Arab world. And while you're smuggling into the Arab world, you might even be able to set up markets to sell goods from the Arab world into Israel."

"You've thought about this," Elizabeth says, impressed.

"I guess so," says Maryam, with a shrug.

"Even if all those ideas are good," Elizabeth says, "there's no way to get there from here. People depend on the aid we give them, but that aid - like oil money - is cutting off their drive to produce."

Maryam answers, "Maybe, that's why all they want to do is fight. If they make their own money, maybe they'll appreciate the investments they can make – in things bigger than themselves."

"Maybe," says Elizabeth. "But that doesn't get us past the basic problem. People depend on our aid. We can't just cut it off."

Maryam smiles, again. "A smuggler," she says, "taught me something about that."

"Did he give you an answer?" asks Elizabeth.

"Not quite," says Maryam. "He had a warehouse hidden beneath the desert. It was a transit point. He fed my brother and I, and gave us water, it's one of the reasons we survived. But he also taught me something. He said if you give people money, normally, you undermine them. But if you give travelers money, like Ibrahim did, they aren't spoiled. They are just passing through, and your charity becomes an example for them, not a poison."

"That way they get the help," Elizabeth says, "but without being undermined by it."

"Yeah," says Maryam.

"But how can that work?" Elizabeth asks. "Nobody is traveling here. They live here."

Maryam just shrugs, "This place is a blank slate, and you're the expert with money. Maybe you can think of something."


Elizabeth looks at her. And then smiles. The smile is deep and fundamental. She flips around in her chair, grabs her phone from her desk, and dials a number.

She flips back towards Maryam while she waits for the ring on the other end of the line.

"A long time ago," Elizabeth says, "I had some ideas. All they were missing was a blank slate."

--

In the Sunni section of the City, Hamid – Mohammed's senior-most operative – walks slowly towards his own family's tent. It is midday, and the sun beats down from above.

Hamid pulls open the flap of his tent and steps into the shade. His wife and three children are there. His wife is cutting vegetables on a small board. His two older children are playing. The youngest, a baby, is sleeping on a small pillow.

"I have to go," Hamid announces, a quaver in his voice.

His wife looks up. "Go?" she asks, calmly.

"I have to do something, in Raqqa."

She nods, seriously. She is proud of her husband.

"Will you return?" she asks.

"No," he says, on the edge of tears, "I am not to return."

His wife rises from the floor of their tent and he reaches towards her. And they embrace.

And then, after only a moment, she steps back and whispers, "All-hu Akbar."

And he answers, "All-hu Akbar."

She sits again, returning to her vegetables.

Hamid kisses his children, one by one. He can see a tear falling from his wife's eye.

And then he turns and steps out of the tent, trying desperately to lock the images of his family in his mind's eye.

He will never see them again.

Hamid is going to Raqqa.

His orders are twofold.

First, he is to approach none other than Sheikh Abdul bin Hassan, Mohammed's father-in-law. He is to tell him that Mohammed wants something called the *Al-mi'raj*. It is the name of a fierce mystical Rabbit – a creature that strikes enemies many times its size.

And second, he is to martyr himself in the service of All-h.


Hamid does not understand.

But he is a loyal slave of All-h, and he trusts in the plans of his commander.


Without another glance, he disappears from the City.

# Crime Scene
*October 8th, 2014, Outside Qunietra*

I wake up to the sound of the muezzin. The City is still here. Elizabeth had invested another million dollars to keep it running for another week.

Before I even open my eyes, I know Elizabeth is still at her workstation; I can hear the keys clicking away in bursts of activity. As far as I know, she hasn't slept. I get up, wash and begin my morning prayers.

When I'm done, Elizabeth turns to me and proudly announces that she's finally completed the work on her new payments system.

I didn't know she was working on a payment system. But I can see that her eyes are red from a lack of sleep. She must be exhausted.

I expect her to sleep, but instead she says, "Let's go take a look at the scene of the circus attack."

"What?" I ask.

"Let's go to the site of the circus attack," she says. "I have to begin my investigation."

"You've been working for days," I say, actually uncertain whether she's slept at all. "It is still dark out. It can wait."

"No," she answers, her voice even and determined, "It can't."

I am her translator. If she has to go, then I have to go with her.

The mob crush that ended the last trip into the City terrified Ibrahim. I don't want to bring him with me. So, Elizabeth calls Steven.

Groggily, Steven's wife comes over from their neighboring caravan to watch my still-sleeping brother. Her own children will join her later.

She agrees she'll call if there's trouble.

And then, in what seems like moments, Elizabeth and I head out the door and down the slope to the City.

From a distance, and in the dark, nothing about the place seems to have changed in the last few days.

"Can you tell me about the payment system?" I say.

A smile flashes over Elizabeth's exhausted face. "Should I start from the beginning?"

"Sure," I answer.

"Okay," she says. "Twenty years ago, I was in high school, and I had all sorts of thoughts about how to change the world. Since I was six, I'd been reading the *Wall Street Journal*, the *Financial Times*, and various computer magazines that don't even exist anymore. I hadn't reached my textbook phase yet. Anyway, tax and monetary policy was splashed all over the Opinion and Business sections of the papers I enjoyed most. Everybody was talking about how lowering taxes or raising benefits or shifting this or that could transform societies and the economy. But I wasn't really impressed with what I was reading. It was like there were two groups speaking past each other, each sure that their approach fixed the weaknesses of the other group's approach, while capturing all the strengths at the same time. On the one hand, the capitalist side argued that so much wealth would be produced by an economy free of income taxes, regulation, and welfare, that even the poor would not be poor. They saw these things as hampering economic productivity. After all, if you tax or regulate something, you get less of it. Tax income, you have less of it. Subsidize laziness, and you'll get more of it. People don't work if they don't have to. The other side argued that taxing the wealthy and regulating business was the only way of stopping the richest and most powerful from squeezing the rest of the society. They also saw a world without income support for the poorest as something that created terrible and unfair risks. They saw the capitalist approach as purely dog-eat-dog. And the biggest dogs would always win. They believed that even with high taxes and lots of regulation, you could have a large-enough economy to provide, fairly, for the general good. You're following this, right?"

I nod.

"And I thought, why not try to solve both problems at once? In other words, let's try to reduce regulation and income taxes while creating a welfare system that doesn't undermine economic activity. Just like you mentioned with Abraham and the smuggler. I tried a whole bunch of ideas, in my mind, but nothing came of it. And then, one day, I was struck by a concept. You could tax revenues – the money people or businesses bring in – no matter what kind of revenue it is. If it's salary, tax it. If it is sales from a business, tax it. All of it would be taxed the same way. That would make the system much simpler. You wouldn't want the tax to discourage income, or business. That's why income wouldn't be taxed. And, if money is spent on business activity, the spender would get the tax they paid back. Understand?"

"Can you give me an example?" I ask.

"Sure," Elizabeth replies. "Let's say you bring in $100. Maybe from your job, or by selling something or whatever. You'd get to keep like $65 of it. But if you spent $100 on cash-flow generating activity, basically investments that are productive, you'd only need to spend $65 of your own money. The government would pitch in the other $35 from the tax you paid before. Basically, you'd get your tax back. Business activity would be encouraged."

"Okay," I nod.

"With this system," Elizabeth continues, "the only spending that would be taxed would be money that wasn't invested in cash flow generating activity. Investing money in gold doesn't count. Taxation would also be simplified. Because you don't care about income, all that stuff about depreciation and recognition of sales and so on would go away. Everything would be based just on cash flow. Not only that, but businesses and individuals would be treated exactly the same way. Business are just shared revenues and spending, after all."

"Okay," I say. "What about the welfare side of things?"

"Ah," says Elizabeth. "That's the fun part. Every person would have a subsidy. It doesn't matter how wealthy or poor they are. Their initial spending each month would be subsidized. And children would be included in calculating their parents' subsidy. A family might buy $100 worth of groceries, but only $10 would come from their account. $90 would come from the subsidy. When they spent their next $100, $50 would come from their account. And so on, until the subsidy disappeared, and you'd be left spending money that had already been taxed. That line wouldn't be very high. As a result, you'd need to earn *something* to get the subsidy. But not much. And you wouldn't be encouraged not to work, because everybody would get the same benefit. Unlike welfare, even if you made millions, you'd still be eligible. This approach would encourage workforce participation, while also helping the poorest buy their basic necessities."

"You'd encourage people to be productive, but they'd still have some sort of safety net?"

"Exactly," Elizabeth replies. "You'd even get rid of the minimum wage. Rather than burdening labor-intensive companies with extra expense just because they'd hired people rather than using machines, the entire society would share in the cost of the subsidies and would be neutral towards labor vs. capital-intensive business."

"What happened with the idea?" I ask.

Elizabeth gives me a wistful smile. "My mother always encouraged me to think about this stuff. To develop it. She had this idea that us kids could really change the world. But reality isn't so easy to change. There was no way to implement these ideas. There was no way to track and supplement every transaction. Also, existing tax and welfare systems were too entrenched. It couldn't work. I needed a *blank slate*. That's why I forgot about the idea. I shelved it. All I really remembered was that it was impossible without that blank slate. When I went to college, I left all my notes in my mother's house, and I basically never thought about it again. Until you mentioned that *we have a blank slate*. It triggered something in me. I called my mother then, and she found my notes. She scanned them and sent them to me. And now I know, maybe my mom was right after all."

I nod slowly. Maybe my father was too.

"So that's what I've been doing," Elizabeth says, with a happy grin. "I've been building the system. It's real, now. It will work on the payment cards – that was part of what was missing when I was in high school. Anytime you get money in your payment account, it will be taxed, automatically. And when you spend it, you just mark whether it is a business expense. The system will automatically calculate whether you get a subsidy or tax return – on each and every transaction. You won't need to file any paperwork. It will just happen."

"But people will just do business outside the system," I say, "just like they do with the cards now."

"That's the cool part," Elizabeth says. "The poor won't do business outside the system. They need to explain the money they have, so that

413

they can have their spending supplemented each month. And they'll need the people they buy from to accept the subsidies. They'll demand to be paid, and to pay for things, within the system. And that will flow up, forcing the people who are spending larger amounts of money to explain where that money came from and where it is going. There will be cheating, of course, but it will be much harder to pull off because a very complicated web of non-reporting will be needed to evade the system."

"But if they get a subsidy when they spend, they'll just spend their money and get a subsidy from the people they spend it with, and then those people can spend with them and with a little loop, they'll both get their subsidy. But there still won't be any economic activity."

"Some people might spend the money just to have the other party spend the same amount with them. But most, given the option, will want to get *something* from their spending beyond a returned subsidy. They'll buy the most they can while spending their subsidy. And the other party will do the same. Both sides will find the way to get the most from their funds. Sure, I'll be pumping money in initially. But as I remove the amount of subsidy over time, more and more economic activity will be created until the City is supporting its own subsidies."

I'm not sure that system won't be cheated, but I can't work out the way around it.

"It is sooo cool," Elizabeth says, like a schoolgirl from an American movie. "But it's only been possible for a few years. Oh —" Elizabeth eagerly interrupts herself. "And I programmed it to also give the tax back for charitable projects. If community members give charity to a disabled person or invest in a mosque, for example, they get their tax back. Of course, that disabled person and mosque are taxed just like anybody else. But the system will enable people to experience the joy of creating and then investing the fruit of their labor in the honor of All-h. Just like you described. This system is the secret ingredient."

I can't quite fathom the impacts of a tax system on social values.

"When are you rolling it out?" I ask.

"It's been done," says Elizabeth. "The City is out of money. It needs an economy, and soon. I'll keep funding the place myself, for at least a few weeks. I want to see if this works. Actually, I think I *need* it to work. Between this and the courts and actually stopping the people behind this violence, we might just make this place real."

Her voice is almost frantic. But if anybody does, she has the tools to succeed. Maybe my father's dreams can come true.

Just then, I notice the pungent smell of garbage. The hill we're walking down is upwind of it, but we'll be in the middle of it soon enough. I'd forgotten how bad the smell had become. I look around in the early morning light, expecting to see garbage everywhere. But instead I see that huge pits have been dug on the edge of the City. Garbage has been piled into it. I know what will happen next. When the winds are right, the garbage will be burned. The smell might be awful, but at least people are working to manage it.

I look around some more and realize the walls of metallic scrap that define the edges of the sectarian communities have changed. Only a few days earlier, they had formed almost unbroken masses. Only a few gaps had permitted traffic to flow in and out of the sectarian enclaves. Those gaps had been getting smaller and smaller when I'd left, while the walls themselves had grown in height.

Now, a few more openings have begun to appear. There are openings near the garbage pits. But there are others as well. Men are guarding them, some obviously armed. There is tension. But at least somebody sees some value in creating shortcuts between the sections of the City.

Before long, Elizabeth and I reach a gap in the wall surrounding the Sunni section. The guards ask us a few questions, but they know who we are. They let us pass, and before long, we're at the site of the circus attack.

There is a huge crater in front of us, but little else. All the blood had been cleaned and the remains of the tent removed. Between the Israelis and the locals, not much has been left to examine. I look around, somewhat clinically. I'm seeking clues, not that I expect to find any. But then I see that Elizabeth is shaking.

"Why are we here?" I ask, suddenly concerned. "You don't need to be here. There's nothing to find."

She looks at me, her eyes almost pleading.

"The Israelis," she says, "haven't figured out what happened. Or at least they haven't told *me*. I've been chosen by the victims' families, and I have a responsibility to them to figure out what happened. This is where it started, so I have to start here."

"Okay," I say. "But with what?"

She looks around the site. I can see her thinking. And then, far too quickly, I can see her frustration. There's very little she can use here.

"It was an Iskander," I say, trying to be helpful. "That's what the news reports say."

"Yes," Elizabeth answers, with a touch of annoyance, "I read them too. The Iskander is the newest and greatest Russian missile. People didn't even know the Syrians had them. We know they didn't shoot some old Scud, they fired something far more serious. The question is, why?"

"To get past the Israeli defenses," I say.

"I know that too," says Elizabeth. "But what was so important that they had to beat the Israeli defenses?"

"In the news," I say, "the Syrians claimed the target was a meeting of Islamic State commanders – being sheltered by Israel."

"I've read the news," Elizabeth says, almost angry. "But I was in the tent just before the missile struck, and I didn't see *any* men – let alone Islamic State commanders."

"Could they have been dressed up, in niqabs?"

"No," she says. "All the women in the tent got rid of their extra coverings. There might have been a few who didn't, but certainly there weren't any collections of them. There was no secret meeting. I know it."

We both stare at the missile.

"Somebody lied to the Syrians," I say. "They wouldn't waste *this* missile to kill a bunch of women."

"No," Elizabeth says, softening, "they wouldn't. And they wouldn't risk a war with Israel either. Or international condemnation for an obvious act of state-sponsored terror. They must have actually believed, *really believed*, that the Islamic State was here. And they couldn't use any old missile to get at them – who knows what defenses the Israelis have. That's why they used the Iskander – a high-value missile for a high-value target."

She pauses and looks around.

Then she asks, "But who would lie to them about that? And why?"

"Maybe," I say, "whoever did it lied to make the Syrian government look bad. After all, they slaughtered women and children."

"But who?"

"Maybe the Islamic State themselves," I say. "They would have wanted the Syrians to look bad. It could only help them."

"But if it was the Islamic State, they killed their own people!" Elizabeth says.

"They did," I say, "but they themselves would have died to weaken the enemies of G-d."

She looks at me, a little confused.

I just shrug. It is what it is.

"Okay, let's say the Islamic State did this. Let's say they convinced the Syrians to attack. *How* would they convince their enemies, the Syrian government, to fire the missile?"

"They must have been fed false intelligence," I say. "Either somebody left some document somewhere, or they picked up some electronic transmission, or somebody they trusted told them there was a meeting here. I think it's the last one."

She thinks about it, and she looks at me carefully. She tips her head, "Why?" she asks.

I think carefully for a moment. And then, in a slow and even voice I say, "I lied on my biography, when I came here,"

"I know you did," she says. "Your name isn't Hasna."

"I know," I say. "But I haven't told you why. I lied because I was scared. I was not a coerced wife in Deir Ez-Zur. I was actually in Raqqa. I lied because the man I was forced to marry wasn't just anybody. He was a senior weapons engineer for the Islamic State. While I was his captive, he told me he had a friend in the City. He told me his friend would use the City to reshape the world for the Islamic State. And he told me his friend was only 21."

"Mohammed?" Elizabeth asks, knowing the age of the former Islamic State commander.

"I don't know," I say. "But when I came here, Mohammed made it very clear he knew Youssef, and knew that he had died and how. Maybe it's him."

"It can't be," Elizabeth says. "I work with him, regularly. I can tell you; he isn't some double-agent. Heck, you saw him reading out the names of the dead from this attack. He isn't some stone-cold killer."

"You believe in him," I say. "I *think* I do too. But I'd bet somebody the Syrians thought was working for them was behind this. It could be Mohammed. He's convincing. And wouldn't somebody from the Islamic State capable of fooling the Syrian government *need* to be convincing?"

She just stands there. And then she says, "I'll think about it. But he's no more than a suspect. I don't have any evidence to go after him with."

"Can you track his phone calls?" I ask.

"No," says Elizabeth. "SilentVoice is totally encrypted, and everybody here uses it. Plus, if he made a call, I'd have no idea *when* he did it or to whom. It's an invisible molecule in a needle in a haystack."

I nod. And then I idly kick at a gray rock.

Elizabeth follows it with her eyes. Then she walks over to where I'd kicked it and picks it up.

"This is basalt," she says, in a matter of fact voice.

"So?" I ask.

Elizabeth walks towards the crater. "Come, take a look," she calls, when she gets there.

I walk over and look down. There's a thin layer of sand and dirt. But deeper down, there are dark grey columns of stone.

"Basalt," Elizabeth says. "Volcanic rock."

She smiles.

"Look around," Elizabeth says, pointing in every direction, "Do you see any more?"

I turn slowly. And, indeed, there are small basalt rocks scattered in a rough circle several hundred feet across."

"How'd they get there?" Elizabeth asks.

"They were blown out of the crater," I say.

"The Iskander," Elizabeth says, "comes in four flavors we know of. First is fuel air explosive, which would have sucked all the oxygen out of this place and killed people that way. But it wouldn't leave much of a crater. It explodes at a decent altitude. The second is high-explosive fragmentation. This is basically meant to kill lots of people. But, again, the focus is not on making a crater. If anything, parts of the missile would go down into the hole, not the other way around. The third type is a tactical nuclear warhead. Obviously, that didn't happen. So that leaves one type."

She trails off, waiting for me to ask.

"Which type?" I say.

"Bunker busters," she says.

"They thought there was a bunker?" I ask.

"No," Elizabeth answers. "They would have *known* if there was a bunker. They watch this border carefully."

"Then what?" I ask.

"They didn't have time," Elizabeth says, "to outfit a missile with the right warhead."

"Okay?" I say, uncertain where she's going with this.

"It narrows our window," Elizabeth explains. "The call would probably have been made within an hour of the attack – no more. Otherwise, they could have picked a more appropriate warhead."

"Can you find the call?" I ask.

"I'm not sure," says Elizabeth. "It will still be a needle in a haystack. And I still won't know what was said. But at least I might be able to see whether *Mohammed* was making a call then. It's a start, but not much more than that."

I nod. We poke around the scene some more, but we find nothing else that is interesting. Every bit of the missile has been recovered by the Israeli army.

Finally, we head back home.

--

As we draw close to Elizabeth's trailer, I see a note posted on the doorway of her house. It has my name – my real name – scrawled on it in Arabic. I open it and read it. The message is simple:

> *"You are the daughter of a traitor and an enemy of*
> *justice. You will neither survive nor succeed. And*
> *before you face the abyss of the seventh level of*
> *Jahannam, you will watch Ibrahim die. G-d is great."*

I turn to Elizabeth and show her the note. I translate it for her. She asks what the seventh level of Jahannam is. It is the only level I recognize, the bottomless abyss for those who act like true Muslims but are infidels within.

Elizabeth runs into the trailer and returns wearing a rubber glove. She carefully takes the note from me, and she promises she'll figure out where it came from.

I believe it was left by Mohammed, but I don't know. More importantly, I don't know why the note was left. It made a threat. But it made no request.

We talk briefly to Steven's wife, asking if she saw or heard anything. But she hadn't. She leaves and Ibrahim, Elizabeth, and I sit down to a breakfast of hummus and pita.

We talk, but not too much.

I glance at Ibrahim, worried about him. His parents have been dead only four months. And now, the same people are threatening him. He is incapable of harming anybody, now, or in the future.

Despite that, they want to destroy him.

It is only noon, but Elizabeth announces that she needs to sleep.

I'm not surprised.

Ibrahim and I head outside. But as he plays on the bluff, all I can see are visions of his death.

# Tunnel

*October 20th, 2014, Outside Qunietra*

As Mohammed watches his monitor, he sees a tent flap pushed aside by an extended arm. He's watching one of his men. Mohammed wishes that he could be performing the man's mission himself. But he can't. There was no way it could have happened. Even among the Sunnis, he's kept his actual mission within the City a very tightly guarded secret. The vast majority have come here with peace on their minds. Only five people in the City, the team he's personally chosen, know that he isn't all that he appears. And now that he's sent two of them away, only three such people remain. Of course, even those three know almost nothing. He gives them instructions, but they have no appreciation or knowledge of his larger strategic plans. They can't.

It bothers him that he can't tell them which of his instructions are routine and which are of deadly importance. Of course, even that basic level of information could compromise them. The way he uses them, if they are captured doing something, anything, they will have very little information to share with their captors.

It is because of these two things – his anonymity and their ignorance – that a knot has formed in his stomach. This is the most critical mission he's ever sent anyone on - even during his time as an Islamic State commander. And he can't be there to make sure it comes off well. He can't even tell the man he's chosen for the mission how critical it is.

Mohammed has done the best he could, though. He's rigged up a camera and a microphone for his agent. And the agent has an earpiece, in case Mohammed needs to use it. And Mohammed, using SilentVoice, is watching and listening as the man performs his task. The microphone is good. Mohammed could hear the rain – the first rains of the year – and the squish of boots as the man walked through the mud-filled streets of the City.

As the flap of the tent parts, the sounds shift. The wet smack of the rain is replaced with the pitter patter of that same rain on the fabric of the tent. The squishing of boots is diminished, but not eliminated. Even inside, the ground is a little damp.

There are three men waiting inside the tent. They don't look up at Mohammed's man. Not because they don't see him, but because they had already been intently watching the entrance to the tent. One of them holds a Taser, levelly facing the flap. If a visitor is unexpected, the Taser could almost silently immobilize them. Other tools, also silent, can complete the job of eliminating those who have seen what they shouldn't.

But Mohammed's man is expected. In fact, he is quite an unusual visitor. Most people can proceed no further than the first flap in the tent. But the men in the tent operate with the approval of Mohammed's larger organization. Thus, Mohammed's men can travel wherever they want. The man with the Taser nods and uses his head to gesture back over his shoulder. His Taser never stops pointing at the flap in the tent.

There is another flap there, a smaller tent within the tent. It's invisible from outside. The second flap parts, and Mohammed's man comes to a small concrete-lined circle on the ground. The small space is lit with low-amperage floodlights and the metal rails of a ladder rise up from within the hole.

Mohammed's man approaches the ladder and then lowers himself down. The camera is mounted on the man's head. Mohammed watches as the camera's perspective continually shifts between a view down the tunnel and the view of the ladder being descended. A chain of lights illuminates the path ahead.

Despite the ring at the top, the tunnel itself has almost no concrete. It had been hard to dig the tunnels. The rock is hard, and specialized diamond drills had to be used once the topsoil had been pierced. Instead, the tunnel builders had created small holes down the sides of the tunnel. They had stuck short iron bars in them and then concreted them into place. The ladder and the lights had been affixed to the bars.

Finally, Mohammed's man reaches the bottom of the tunnel. Mohammed fears that the SilentVoice signal would be lost, but surprisingly, it isn't. The tunnel builders have apparently rigged up WiFi within it. Mohammed's man steps off the bottom of the ladder and looks up - peering down the length of the tunnel. The entire thing is lit up by a string of hanging lights. It is still cut through the solid basalt. Because of this the tunnel is barely larger than a man lying down. Along the bottom of the tunnel, there is a track. Tracks are the easiest way to move substantial quantities of supplies – especially when there isn't enough space to stand. There is a tray there, mounted on to a miniature railcar. Mohammed watches as his man maneuvers himself onto it. He's lying flat. The camera peers at a small control at the front of the cart. With the push of a lever, the tiny and flat railcar slowly accelerates, traveling at a casual pace down the length of the tunnel. Eventually, the basalt is cleared. A wooden D-shaped superstructure begins to take form along the tunnel's ceiling and walls. Digging this section had been easier.

The tunnel, of course, is meant for smuggling. It travels for several kilometers and into the heart of the small town that had sprung up to service the needs of refugees awaiting their place in the City. That opportunistic village had shrunk in size during the worst of the violence; at that time, few people wanted to come to the City. But now, the place is coming back to life.

Mohammed thanks All-h for that; men entering abandoned buildings in abandoned villages with packages would be justifiably suspect, and Mohammed can't afford the suspicion of others. But if the village is full of people and activity, such men would hardly be noticed.

But Mohammed is more than thankful. He's almost gleeful. Maryam and Elizabeth are responsible for his freedom of operation. Maryam had created the courts, bringing peace to the City, and Elizabeth's new tax and welfare system actually seems to be breathing economic life into both it and the little town outside of its walls. Elizabeth and Maryam don't know it, of course, but her work has played a critical role in Mohammed's greater plans.

Mohammed's man reaches the end of the tunnel and brings his little railcar to a stop. He climbs another well-lit ladder, this one bolted onto a wooden superstructure that holds the softer earth in place. He emerges into a small stone building. Two men are waiting there. One holds yet another Taser, focused on the tunnel. The second is holding a small metal case about two feet long, two feet tall and a foot wide. The case is painted in desert camouflage and clasped together with a series of sturdy-looking locks.

The man with the Taser nods and, silently, the case is handed over. And then Mohammed's man returns down into the tunnel and back into the City.

He emerges past the three guards, stepping out into the late day light.

A few minutes later, the flap on Mohammed's tent parts, and the man enters.

Without a word or a question, he lays the package on the ground and steps back out, disappearing into the night.

Mohammed leans down, entering the codes for the case, and then opening it reverently.

The case contains the Al-mi'raj. The Al-miraj is a collection of five canisters, each connected to a pre-programmed cell phone. That isn't what's important. What's important is what is contained in the canisters themselves. They contain VX gas. The VX gas has been stolen from Syrian government stockpiles. In theory, the gas is traceable only to them.

No one will forget this attack.

No one will forget the crimes of the Shiites and their allies.

--

The next day, Mohammed is looking down at the results of his men's analysis. He realized just how bothered he was by the amateurishness of their work. For the last two weeks, they had visited the hillside repeatedly. But they had no carefully calibrated instruments, and they couldn't be seen taking notes. Instead, they recorded – within their heads – the direction and strength of the wind. Mohammed had recoded what they told him, mapping out the wind patterns by time of day.

He had collected the information they had on a series of small maps. The wind was predictable, thanks be to All-h. It swept down off the bluff in the early mornings and at night. Mohammed guessed that was the predominant pattern of the wind. But, as the heat cast itself onto the ground, thermals fought against the predominant pattern. The wind slowed to a near dead stop. But the direction did not change, only the speed.

Mohammed knew, as best as his rough calculations could allow, that his men could place the gas canisters on the bluff, and reliably have them target the Christian community.

Thanks to All-h, the Shiites could launch their most terrible attack, and the effects would be predictable.

# Cultural Relations

*October 23rd, 2014, Outside Qunietra*

Steven Gold is the first to arrive. It feels like the old days, when he showed up early at committee meetings, hoping that his example might somehow make them more successful. The way he sees it, committees suck the vibrancy out of their most driven members, turning them into zombies and creating a sluggish mass where once there had been dynamic individuals. The word itself has extra, and useless, letters.

Of course, he hadn't come to *this* meeting to participate in a committee.

He'd come only to watch one in action.

Even though he wouldn't understand the language that would be spoken, he was extremely excited by the meeting himself. He just didn't know why.

Did he actually miss the long hours under the fluorescent lights?

Hasna, the strange young girl who's come to live with Elizabeth, arrives after him. He's surprised by that. He had no idea she was involved in setting this committee up. But she must have been. Steven nods towards her, politely. She nods in return. He doesn't shake her hand or even talk to her. He's learned that's not expected.

Bishop Thoma comes in moments later. His long black robe is accented by a deep red sash and a gold cross. He wears a hat made of stacked black velvet rings. The whole outfit carries an air of ancient authority; the Bishop is not a young man. But despite his age, his eyes don't speak of authority. Instead, he seems nervous. Maybe even awed.

He sees Steven and nods towards him, respectfully. And then he sees Hasna and breaks out into a broad and welcoming smile. They begin to speak rapidly, in a language Steven can't understand. It isn't Arabic, though: Steven knows that.

Is that why he's excited? Because of the mystery of the whole affair? He's never been to a committee with a black-robed Bishop of the Ancient Church of the East.

A few minutes pass, and then the Shia representative enters. A long white robe encases his body. Some kind of thin black wrap covers his arms and shoulders. He's wearing a huge black turban over his black-bearded head. Steven had read somewhere that the black turban meant something, but he doesn't know what. The man's eyes are different than the Bishop's had been. They sparkle, but his emotions are extremely hard to read.

Two more men flit in behind him. They aren't dressed in any special clothes – just old and worn suit jackets over old and worn robes. Instead of hats, they have simple cloth wraps on their heads.

They don't talk with one another. Steven knows who they are, though. They represent the tiny Kurdish and Yazidi communities.

The various men take their seats. Aside from the quiet conversation between Hasna and the Bishop, everyone is silent. They are simply waiting. Waiting to play their part.

And then the last member of the committee arrives: Mohammed bin Hassan. He walks into the room with a flourish that belies his simple garments. He's wearing a white robe capped with a small white cap. Rather than carrying millennia of authority with it, his garments seem to demand a humble assessment. But that humility seems to raise the man himself.

Unlike the others, Mohammed is smiling.

Steven smiles to himself. Mohammed makes a heck of an entrance.

Mohammed moves around the room, greeting each of the other attendees, even Hasna. Although Hasna greets him coolly, the room warms up with his outreach. Conversation begins to flow.

Steven enjoys watching Mohammed work. He might have been an Islamic State commander once, but he has become a gifted peacemaker. He has become a blessing to this place. He has justified Steven's trust in humanity.

Steven wonders at the suspicions others have of the man. Elizabeth has told him that she suspects him in the circus attack. But her suspicion is unfounded. Mohammed hadn't used his phone for anything aside from calls to other circus organizers that entire day. That's why she decides that *that* is suspicious. When it comes to the threatening note stuck to Elizabeth's door, both Hasna and Elizabeth want to blame Mohammed. But when they reviewed the video feed, they found the note had been delivered by a man who is not in the City's database. Obviously, in both of their readings, he's somebody *Mohammed* brought in just for the task. But there's no evidence to support it. They are just targeting him because of who he was, as opposed to who he has become. Steven is confident he knows better.

He suspects Hasna does, as well. The girl is no innocent; it seems likely to pretty much everybody that she was the one who blew up the water tower. But somehow everybody allows *her* to point fingers.

Eventually, Mohammed sits at his own seat and says something. The conversation dies away. The focus turns to him. Steven can't understand a word, but he knows that Mohammed has called the meeting to order. He's seen it done enough times.

Mohammed calls out what must be a name, and then a woman enters the room. Steven's never seen her before, but he knows who she is. She's the widow of the first man killed in the spasm of violence that shook the City. She's here as a prosecutor. The whole thing seems odd to Steven, but he supposes it makes a sort of sense. This isn't a courtroom through. It is more of a Grand Jury. These men, leaders of their communities, will decide whether an arrest is warranted. They need this group. Without the agreement of community leaders, no arrest could take place, even if a court demanded it.

Mohammed asks the widow a question, and she responds with a short sentence. It must have been her name or something. He then asks her another, and she begins to speak at length. Everybody in the room watches her carefully, hanging on her every word. Even Steven is watching. He watches her body language. He watches her evident anger and pain. He can see her investment in the case she is making. She is nearly begging for the group to accept her pleas. To him, that desperation reveals weakness in the logic of what she's saying.

Finally, she concludes her speech. Her case has been made. Steven looks at the faces in the room. The Shia leader seems pleased. Thoma seems skeptical. The Kurdish and Yazidi representatives seem to be siding with Thoma. Hasna looks confused.

Steven is just watching.

Mohammed nods knowingly. And then he begins to speak. His voice is comforting and reassuring. He isn't speaking to the widow, though. He is speaking to the others. The widow nods appreciatively as he talks, and Steven realizes he is making her case. He is arguing for an arrest.

Most of his speech seems aimed at Bishop Thoma. It isn't surprising. The violence has been between the Christians and the Shiites; Thoma probably represents the man or men the widow wants to arrest. But Thoma is clearly reluctant. His eyes are sad as he carefully bats away Mohammed's insistence. The widow shoots angry glares at the Bishop. And Mohammed presses on.

And then, surprisingly, Hasna steps into the conversation.

Her voice seems measured and reasonable. It seems rational. Thoma looks at her with appreciation. The Shia man looks at her with resentment. Mohammed just smiles and asks her a question. She's baffled by it. He speaks again, a few more sentences. And then, seemingly without cause, she *explodes*. Her face reddens with anger, and she erupts in a vehement verbal assault. Her hands fly around as she gestures violently. Thoma tries to calm her, but she ignores him. She presses forward. Mohammed looks at her with concern, almost pity. He isn't fighting her; she's erupted of her own free will.

Eventually, she calms down and looks around the room and realizes that nobody is taking her side. She quiets down, reluctantly – angrily. She glares at Mohammed. There is pure hatred on her face. It all seems very strange to Steven. By looking at the others in the room, he can see that it seems strange to them as well. For Steven, this is yet more evidence of her unreasonable dislike of the Sunni leader.

And then Mohammed speaks again. He asks a question.

All the men in the room – the Shiites, the Christian, the Yazidi and the Kurd – raise their hands.

And Steven knows the answer. Whoever the widow accused will be arrested.

It is then that Steven finally realizes why he's so excited.

The point of a committee isn't really to get things done. No, committees exist so that *stakeholders* can have a voice. So that they can work together. For all the anger displayed by Hasna, *this* committee represents something fantastic. Because while Steven's highly competent team has done so much to *build* the City, all they've done is

433

build tents and walls and water supplies and logistical systems. All they've done is plant the tree the City represents. But this committee, Steven realizes, is the fruit of their labor. This committee represents the people of the region, finally working together.

It represents real community.

And Steven realizes with a smile, they *all* agreed to the arrest and trial of an accused murderer. They *all* agreed to a trial. They *all* agreed to share their justice. Nobody has been excluded.

This, Steven knows, is how a real community is built and how real peace is established. This is the bedrock of everything he was hoping for.

And Mohammed has made it happen.

All his life, Steven has wanted to truly help – not just go through the motions.

And now, thanks to Mohammed, he actually has.

--

After the meeting wraps up, Mohammed walks back down into the City. He is proud of himself. The prosecutor's evidence had been weak: just anonymous hearsay. He knew it was weak. After all, he'd provided the anonymous hearsay. But the woman had the right targets. She knew about the Christian gunmen who were responsible for the killing. Mohammed had, indirectly, told her.

When Hasna had objected, as he'd hoped she would, he'd chosen his words carefully. "What?" he'd asked, "Do you accuse this woman of being an enemy of justice, deserving of the seventh level of Jahannam?"

The line had come from the note he'd left her. The one in which he threatened to kill the little retarded Ibrahim. He knew it would trigger her anger. He'd counted on it.

And when it happened, he'd recorded it.

He smiles as he walks, idly flipping his phone in his pocket.

And then he comes to his own tent and gently pulls aside the flap. He steps inside and reaches under his cot for the small metal case. The one with the gas.

Slowly and carefully, he pulls it out. He unlocks it and pulls it open.

His eyes play over the contents. He finds they bring him joy. He wonders at the fear and the power they have inspired. They were manufactured in secret by scheming engineers. They were secured in a fortress by powerful men. They were liberated by divinely inspired freedom fighters. They were repackaged by frightened technicians. And then, they were smuggled through underground tunnels by men who knew nothing about them.

Like the mystical rabbit, like the Al-mi'raj, these canisters can conquer enemies far greater than their size would suggest.

With a final smile, Mohammed closes the case and pushes it back under his bed.

And he knows that his own salvation is close at hand.

# Deployment

*October 26th, 2014, Outside Qunietra*

Mohammed strikes a match and holds it under the first of the documents. It is the map showing the wind patterns on the hillside. The flames lick upwards, consuming the bottom of the paper. Mohammed puts the paper down on the sandy ground within his tent and then, before it is extinguished, puts the next page on the small fire.

The smell of the fire is crisp.

Mohammed wonders what the gas will smell like.

His plan is almost complete now.

One by one, his men have quickly and quietly taken the canisters from him. He had them wait until the last day because he didn't want the canisters discovered, either in their tents or on the hillside. But that day has come. The trial is tomorrow. Tensions will be high then and people will be watching. He couldn't deploy the gas then. His men might be caught.

But nobody will be watching tonight.

That's why the gas will be deployed tonight.

Actually, Mohammed realizes as he watches the paper burn, it *is* being deployed right now.

And then, within 24 hours, it will be released.

Mohammed wonders what it will smell like.

To ensure that none will blame him or his people for what is coming, Mohammed will venture into the Christian quarter tomorrow night. He will visit with the Bishop, pretending to try to mend bridges.

And then, when the gas comes, they will die together.

But unlike the Bishop, Mohammed will be greeted in heaven.

And he will be reunited with his wife and with his son.

The last of the papers is consumed and Mohammed gathers the ashes into a small bag.

In the morning, he will flush them down the public toilets.

His men are probably already on their way out of the City.

Before the time of the pre-dawn prayers, all evidence of his plot will have disappeared.

# Crane

*October 27<sup>th</sup>, 2014: Outside Qunietra*

Steven Gold watches as the gathered men call out directions. Their hands push against the sides of his trailer – his home – as a truck-mounted crane lifts it from above. This would never happen in America. Everybody would be well clear of the activity; safety regulations would require it. But the crane lifts, the hydraulics strain and the metal clanks as the trailer is lifted straight into the air.

He'll miss this spot, he realizes. From this spot, he could watch the City taking form beneath his home. He'll miss his beach chair on the bluff and his time with his wife and kids – at least when things were going well.

These last few months have been the most consequential of his life.

The crane whines, wheeling the home to the side. The men step back. The crane is moving slowly. Everything is stable. A minute later, the house is being lowered onto the back of a flatbed truck.

Then the crane is detached, and the men unstrap the house from the apparatus that had held it. Moments later, the engine of the truck is fired up. With a roar, it comes to life and the truck begins its drive; the crane following close behind.

Three weeks ago, Steven imagined this happening. But he imagined the house being empty. He imagined himself and his family fleeing from an apocalyptic ruin of scattered and flattened tents below. He wondered if his family could even survive that flight. He wondered if he could survive that kind of flight. He would have tried to help, pulling every lever he could reach, but he would have failed once again.

But today isn't like that. The truck and crane aren't going far. They're just going down the hill. Steven, Elizabeth and the others have decided to move – into the City itself.

Steven walks alongside the truck and crane, holding his wife's hand. Their children have run on ahead. They had been forbidden from going to the central playground, at least until recently. But now it is their favorite place; they're even picking up a little Arabic. With the action of the crane complete, they know where they want to be. Maggie's bright red hair marks their progress. She passes within feet of one of Mohammed's canisters. But she does not know it.

More slowly, Steven and Amy make their way down the road to the hollow between the bluff and the walls. The place is a buzz of activity. In a few short weeks, the first shoots of economic life have appeared.

It all started with Elizabeth's ideas on taxation. The idea had required an entirely electronic currency, which was why it wasn't practical anyplace else. The critical thing about the new system was that people have to bring in *something*, even if it is just charity, to get their subsidy. They have to participate in a life of productivity.

The effect had been incredible. The whole attitude of the place had shifted. Even as there was a safety net for the poor, there was also pressure to create *something*. Even the disabled could participate in the cycle of creation and the investment of their earnings in something meaningful. In just a few weeks, tax revenues had risen substantially. After all, if you wanted the work of society's most marginal people, *they* would insist on reporting their income. It was the only way to get the subsidy.

Elizabeth even created a new currency, apparently another teenage dream. Under the new currency, 100 Zuz represents an adult's median day's work. The electronic money supply is regularly adjusted to keep this true. If people start earning more, the amount of money in the system is reduced and each Zuz effectively becomes more valuable. The point, Elizabeth had explained, was that everybody would become more aware of the human activity their spending represents. And everyone would become more aware of the growth of their economy. She'd explained that other currencies are far more arbitrary, although Steven hadn't fully understood why.

The government is still providing 90% of people's sustenance. Well, Elizabeth is providing it. The productive end of the economy isn't big enough to pay for the initial monthly subsidies. But the number is falling. People are working and producing. The truck and crane moving his family are a great example. They were purchased by a local family. They had had the money for the equipment before, but they were reluctant to invest it. It had been enough money to smuggle them into Europe, if they needed to run. Now, they've purchased the equipment, they're confident and they want to be ahead of their competition.

The truck and crane themselves are licensed in Israel and the family has hired Israeli-Arab drivers who can bring cargo to them. But local men have been hired as laborers for the work within the City itself. They're cheaper. After all, Elizabeth is supplementing their wages. As the economy improves though, their spending will rise, and their subsidies will turn into taxes.

As they walk, Steven smiles deeply at the other work these men have done. The city has other trailers now, placed here by this crew. The trailers have been purchased as private homes by the citizens of the place. It is the first step in a place like this. Somehow, the City no longer seemed like a temporary place resisting an inevitable return to nothingness. Instead, it seemed like it was the nothingness that had become temporary. Nobody has broken ground yet on a proper house yet, but it is only a matter of time before they do. In the meantime, the trailers are a perfectly normal short-term solution. They no longer seem to challenge the reality of the City.

Steven passes a man on a small path between tents. He's hard at work and his wife and children are assisting him. He's assembling a lattice of wood. The City has begun paving what could be called the main avenues. The first rains have come and there is mud now. Not enough to really bother people, but now that they were actually settling here, they want it dealt with. The side tracks that dart through the camp aren't large enough, or well-defined enough, for paving. Instead, residents are paying this man – and others like him – to provide a path above the mud. The wood latticework does the job well.

A fat-tire bike speeds past Steven and his wife. Most young people use them now. They can handle the loose sand in the still incomplete roads. And the City is still too small for cars except on the largest of the paths. The rider gives them a wide berth, perhaps respecting the larger vehicles driving alongside them.

Two weeks ago, when Steven walked through it, the City had seemed dead. But now, in open spaces, there are seamstresses mending garments, handymen fixing small appliances and mechanics working on bicycles. They work in public, so others can see what they offer. There are almost certainly smugglers; paying their taxes, but their businesses are more circumspect. There have long been little bodegas, but there are more small stalls now – randomly scattered through the City. With time, they'll concentrate into markets, specializing in particular goods.

Steven realizes that his faith in these people has been justified, and that others will understand that.

As they walk, Steven smells something wonderful. That hadn't happened before. Before, the smell of the City had been one of garbage. But now, contractors paid by the City itself are driving it to the Israeli border and transferring it to Israeli landfills. The City budget, for now, Elizabeth, is covering the fees.

Steven looks down the track, curious, and sees an Indian-looking man selling spices in front of his tent. He's cooking something there. As they come up to him, Amy, Steven's wife, eagerly pulls him to a stop. The man speaks broken English and offers her a sample of his food. She tastes it, clearly stunned by its flavor. She buys a selection of spices from him. She uses her payments card, and the man smiles as he accepts her money.

And then they speed up, catching up to the trucks – and their house – once again.

A site has been cleared for them. It is near the center of the City, in what had recently been no-man's land. Maryam, Ibrahim, Elizabeth and now Steven and his family now call it home. Most of the others are still living in their old groups. But full integration isn't necessary; people just like to be with those who are most like them. As much as Steven might resist the concept, it makes sense. It is how things typically work out.

Finally, the trucks come to a stop. The men set to work again, putting the house back down. A few minutes later, Amy opens the door and she and Steven head in. They need to clean up – the dishes were packed, but not everything was. The things that have fallen need to be returned to their places.

But once they're inside, Amy just closes the door and wraps her arms around him.

She looks up, and they kiss.

It is a perfect morning.

And then, working together, they clean up the house and put things away. Steven realizes how few possessions they have here. Maybe they'll bring more, someday. Soon enough, they're done.

And then Steven heads out again. It is to be a busy day.

The very first of the trials is starting.


The courthouse is nothing spectacular. Just a triple-sized trailer. There are video feeds, so that the citizens of the place can watch the trial despite the limited space in the trailer itself. But Steven will be there in person. He is, essentially, the Governor. Of course, as the victims are accused of murder, it is assumed they will need to be convicted three times; by the court of 10s, of 100s and of 1,000s.

There's a guard at the door to the court. Not a soldier, but a civilian. He sees Steven coming and opens the door, welcoming him to the courtroom. No check is necessary.

It is hard to imagine only a few weeks have passed. It had been chaos, but now there are courts. Wasn't that what the Islamic State, Al-Shabaab and the Taliban had all offered? Al Shabaab itself was an offshoot of an organization called the Islamic Courts Union. All of them had offered courts. And now, Steven understands why. People want some sort of justice, some sort of stability. Even the rough viciousness of the Islamic State could be preferable to nothing.

Steven sits in the gallery, moments before the proceedings begin. There is a furious chatter in the room, a palpable excitement to see what is about to transpire.

And then, with a clatter, a gavel slams into the desk at the front of the small courtroom and the room falls silent.

Steven doesn't know it, but beyond the walls of the courthouse, the City itself has come to a stop.

It is a simple murder.

But the consequences of this trial will determine the fates of millions.

# Court

*October 27th, 2014: Outside Qunietra*

After receiving the note, Maryam had spent weeks worried about an attack from Mohammed or one of his men. She thought he was the friend Youssef was referring to. But, of course, she had no proof he was guilty of anything. It was even possible that she was missing the real villain.

But she didn't know. And no matter who had threatened them, she was worried about Ibrahim. As the City came to life and as people emerged from their tents, she and Ibrahim spent more and more time inside Elizabeth's trailer. They were hiding from the threat. There was nothing else to do.

Maryam went to the first "Grand Jury" meeting. She wanted to see the beginnings of the new justice system. She hadn't been impressed. The evidence had been weak, but Mohammed seemed to be pushing the case, nonetheless.

And then, Mohammed had quoted the note during the meeting. In that instant, Maryam no longer had any doubt that he was guilty. She had no doubt he was Youssef's scheming friend.

Still, she could prove nothing. Even more frightening, she couldn't understand what he was plotting.

Elizabeth believed Maryam, but that wasn't enough. All she could do was hire guards for Maryam and Ibrahim. When Elizabeth moved into the City, she left the old trailer on the hill, with the guards protecting it. Maryam and Ibrahim would stay there, in relative safety. These things helped, but even they weren't enough to make her comfortable. After all, she herself had done almost everything necessary to assassinate the well-protected Hujjatu I-Islam.

Surely, Mohammed could do more.

Elizabeth kept looking for something she could act on. She kept seeking a connection between Mohammed and the circus attack, or anything else. But she found nothing.

The man *appeared* to be what he claimed. Even though she knew he was not.

Maryam had tried to work out Mohammed's plot. She suspected it had something to do with the courts. She suspected it had something to do with the initial murders. Had he committed them? Was he framing the Christians? And if so, why?

Maybe Mohammed had bribed or threatened the judges – so they would find the young men guilty on very sketchy grounds. All the aggrieved widow-prosecutor had presented in the meeting was a note claiming the two young Christian men had been snipers in Syria and had killed the Shia man here. That was it: hearsay. Not even testimony.

Maybe Mohammed expected to undermine the whole judicial concept by forcing a conviction on weak evidence?

But that didn't seem big enough. He'd been an Islamic State commander. And he'd decided to come here instead. A farce of a trial would anger the Christians, perhaps. He might even destroy the City. But the death toll from the circus had cost the Sunnis 173 women and children. These were his people. He didn't sacrifice them just to undermine a City seemingly doomed to failure.

He had to have bigger goals in mind.

But Maryam had no idea what they were.

That was why she'd decided to go to the courthouse. She had to see what he was planning. She had to understand it.

As she walks from Elizabeth's old trailer, Maryam feels incredibly exposed. She's accompanied by a brawny South African who works for the executive security team Elizabeth hired. He seems highly competent, and he sees nothing that worries him. But he is alone. The rest of the team has been left with Ibrahim. It had been Maryam's call.

Eventually, they come to the courthouse. It is a prefab building, essentially another collection of trailers. They are very early for the trial. Her South African guard had demanded they come early. He'd wanted to check the place out before it was crowded, and he wanted to watch others as they arrived. When they get to the door, there's a guard waiting there. He was the Christian man Maryam had last seen constructing the tent for the meeting between Bishop Thoma and Hassan. He recognizes her and lets her pass. Her one-man security detail comes with her. The guard doesn't check either one of them for weapons. She isn't a threat.

As they enter the trailer, Maryam can see that it is large enough for over a hundred people.

And it is, as her guard had hoped, almost entirely empty.

The security guard recommends she stand against a wall not far from an exit. She wouldn't be able to see quite as much, he explains. But she'd be able to see over seated heads. More importantly, nobody would be able to sneak up on her, and she could escape quickly if she needed to.

As she stands there, she watches a few men lay out the tables and chairs. They put a table at the front, for the judges. And they place two others in front of them, one for the prosecutor, and one for the defendant. The men aren't working from any plan; it is probably just what they had seen on TV. They line up rows of chairs at the rear of the room; a makeshift galley for those watching the trial.

Other men rig up cameras and microphones. Video streams of the judges, of the parties to the case, and of the room as a whole, will be broadcast beyond this small space. The City will be watching. But not just the City. The whole region – perhaps the whole world – will be watching this drama unfold.

Maryam realizes that it all feels incredibly ad-hoc. Of course, it is designed to be ad-hoc. It is a new judicial system for a new reality. But she finds herself regretting the lack of form. She's worried that everything will be manipulated by Mohammed, somehow.

But she doesn't know how.

People start filing into the room. Her guard watches each of them carefully. Maryam sees Steven, who is glowing with anticipation. She sees Bishop Thoma. He's come in his formal robes, and his eyes are unusually hooded. And she sees the Hujjatu I-Islam. He looks like an excited boy, surprised that his pursuit of justice has come this far. Elizabeth comes in moments later.

And then, just before the trial begins, Mohammed enters. He's smiling confidently. She stares at him, trying to understand – if it isn't too late – what he's planning to do. But she learns nothing.

--

Mohammed sees Maryam as soon as he enters the courthouse. He can't help but smile. The girl is standing there, frightened and lost. Her own future is coming to an end. But she cannot know *how* that ending will arrive. She can't know how total it will be.

Everything is coming together so nicely.

Only a few weeks earlier, Mohammed had had a problem. He'd needed not only to destroy the City, but to cripple the Shiites – and to drive all of his enemies away from one another. The courts were one step in his delicate plan. He knew the boys were guilty. In the past two days, Mohammed had passed more and more evidence to the wife of the murdered Ali. The communities had been living together at the time of the crime. Mohammed had arranged for Sunni witnesses who could testify that the young men had left their tent during the time of the murders. When the gun was found in one of their tents, Mohammed had passed funds to her, so she could pay for a forensic analysis to compare the weapon with the bullets that had struck Ali. Naturally, it came back a match. Finally, he'd found grainy video – posted on YouTube – of the two of them fighting in Syria. They were snipers there. They were willing killers.

Putting it all together, the widow-prosecutor would be able to solidly demonstrate what she needed to. They would be unable to deny their crime.

It was what would come next that was critical.

She would ask them *who* had given them the gun, and why. That one question was to be her payment for all the anonymous help she had been given.

When the two suspects pointed the finger at the Israelis, which was all they knew, everything else would slide into place. Mohammed had made Hamid and Rashid disappear. There would be no proof they were not Israeli agents. In the conspiracy-whipped region, that would condemn the Israelis.

But that was only the beginning.

Maryam was the key to the rest. He knew now that her father had been a municipal engineer in Mosul. He knew now that she'd pretended to be a Baathist. He also knew it was a lie that everybody in Mosul pretended to believe.

It was true that Maryam's father, like his parents before him, loved Mosul. The family had been there for an uncountable number of years.

But like the 125,000 *other* Jews who fled Iraq, they should have left and abandoned everything in their flight. Instead, they became "secular Muslims." They decided to stay. They became Baathists. They took on the name *Al-Mosuli* to express their love of the City. And, dependent on the expertise of Maryam's grandfather, the local Baathist party helped them hide in plain sight.

Mohammed admired their audacity. Maryam was an Arabic name. But it was Arabic for Miriam, from the Jewish Torah. Her brother's name was Ibrahim, or Avraham. He was the forefather of the Muslims, but also of the Jews. Mohammed couldn't help but respect the courage of Maryam's father. He had been living in Mosul, with Al Qaeda, and he'd given his children Jewish names. Maryam herself pretended to pray to All-h, but he knew it was all a lie. These people were treacherous to the core.

The Islamic State had known Maryam's father was a Jew. This was why they had killed him. But when they searched his house, they found that he was not only a Jew, but a spy. Hidden beneath a floorboard, Islamic State fighters had found Israeli passports for the entire family. The consensus was that they represented the man's only true identity.

Maryam obviously hadn't known about the passports. If she had, she would have taken them with her, or at least destroyed them. But she didn't. She left them behind. Now, they rested snugly in Mohammed's pocket.

In a few minutes, he would use them to destroy her.

He had her on tape, almost screaming against what he had since made an obvious prosecution. It would look like she was protecting the Israelis from the testimony of the young men. It would look like she was trying to stop an obvious prosecution in order to protect the puppet-master Jews.

To seal the deal, Mohammed had arranged testimony from local Sunnis sympathetic to the Islamic State. These Sunnis would testify that *she* had approached them, asking them to kill other Shia leaders.

It would look like the Israelis had set the whole City up as a Christian enclave in the region. It would look like assassinating Shia leaders was part of the plan. And it would look like she was the cornerstone of the entire operation.

Mohammed knows the scandal will spread quickly; there are cameras and reporters everywhere. The world is watching this place. The City will be riven apart, and no one will trust the Israelis.

But that is only the first stage of his assault.

When the trial breaks down, Mohammed will go in front of the cameras and speak of peace and forgiveness. He'll claim, with heartfelt deception, that he wants to move forward – not back. He will show Maryam's documents and share the recording and explain that he hadn't wanted to release either one, but now he knew he had no choice.

After all, peace demanded truth.

The optics would be wonderful.

But there would be more.

The VX gas in his five canisters has come from Syrian government sources; there was no way the Islamic State, with its meager resources, could be accused of manufacturing it.

Late that night, Mohammed will pray for the last time. And then, using a burner phone to remotely activate the devices, Mohammed will release their gas. In the few minutes that remained, he would plant the phone near the Shia section of the City; he would plant the last bit of evidence. And then he would visit Bishop Thoma. He would die a victim of his own chemical weapons assault.

The press was there. The world was watching. Thousands, in front of countless broadcasting witnesses, would die. The walls and the bluff would hold the gas in. There would be no escape for those in the path of the winds. The people of the City, even some Sunnis and Shiites, would die horrifying deaths.

Mohammed himself would be among them. He would die as a martyr against Shia and Israeli oppression.

And then the world would turn against the Syrian government. They would turn against Iran and Hezbollah – the worshippers of Ali. They would even turn against the Israelis: the catalysts in the massacre. It would be like Sabra and Shatilla, where Christians had killed Muslims, and the Jews had been condemned. Only it would be far greater and far more public. Mohammed would do what his parents had never even tried to do: he would drive his enemies to fight one another.

He would reveal the true character of the oppressors. And the Sunnis, the true inheritors of the Prophet's mission, would rise once again.

Maryam, living up on the bluff, may or may not die in the attacks. It wouldn't matter. Her character would be destroyed. Her ideals, and the ideals of her father, would be forever tainted. She might have thought she would slow Mohammed's plans. Instead, she would be the fuel for their completion.

Mohammed would have his victory. And he would finally be able to join those who had died for his plans. He'd be able to join his wife and his son and his friends and the innocent Omar. He'd be able to join the women and children from the circus. He'd be able to join them all in Paradise.

In joy, they would celebrate together, knowing that a great victory for All-h had been won.

And all it would take was a sentence from two young men.

Mohammed watches as the case proceeds, perfectly to plan. The widow prosecutor presents her facts, and Mohammed watches as Mayram's face grows more and more confused. And more fearful. She knows there is a trap. The change in evidence is proof of that.

But she cannot understand what that trap is. Watching it brings Mohammed a strange sense of joy.

The prosecutor sits. The procedure is unclear. Nobody knows what is to happen next.

But then one of the young Christian assassins raises his hand. And the world turns to him.

"This," he says, in an uncertain voice, "Is not necessary. We killed the Shia politician."

Mohammed grins. He can see Maryam's eyebrows knit together in confusion.

It is going even better than he'd expected.

The widow prosecutor rises from her seat.

"Who," she asks, on cue, "gave you the gun? And why?"

Mohammed's heart races with anticipation.

And then the young man answers, "We were given the gun by two young Sunni men. They were from the Islamic State. They wanted us to kill important Shia leaders."

In a moment of shock, Mohammed shouts, "That's not true!"

And then the entire courtroom turns to him.

In that fraction of a second, Mohammed knows he's been undone. There's no way he could know whether or not the Islamic State had given the two young men their guns – unless he was somehow involved.

In an instant, Mohammed realizes he's lost his credibility. In an instant, he's lost his shield.

He imagines Syrian intelligence watching as the cameras shift from the trial to him. They'll understand immediately. They had doubts before, but now they'll know he is still working with the Islamic State. They'll know he set up the Christian snipers. They'll know it was all about manipulation. Most importantly, they'll know the circus attack was a setup, and that Mohammed was behind it.

They'll abandon him, and they'll release the recordings of his call.

*Everything* will fall apart. As he sees the future unfold, Mohammed realizes that it already has.

In that moment, Mohammed remembers his parents. He remembers them striking out blindly against their enemies. He remembers their sacrifice and their dedication. He remembers how they caused pain for their enemies. And he remembers the funeral of his father.

All eyes on him, he calmly pulls his burner phone from his pocket.

He will punish his enemies. Maryam and all the others will die.

All-h willing, the winds of daytime will still be strong enough to kill.

He unlocks the phone and opens SilentVoice. He has a pre-planned group there. The canisters, wired with their own SilentVoice apps, are awaiting their command.

He types it in, and presses Send.

And then he puts his phone back in his pocket.

Soon enough, his martyrdom will be complete.

Everyone in the room is still standing. They are in shock. But then voices begin to murmur, wondering why Mohammed had sent a text message. A panic begins to spread.

Mohammed looks at them all with the remnants of satisfaction. They are like bugs, about to be exterminated.

But then a voice rings out over the crowd. It is the voice of the Bishop Thoma. The cameras switch to him.

"You are a killer," the Bishop states, flatly.

Mohammed doesn't answer.

But then the old man leans over and pulls up the hem of his garment. Underneath, Mohammed sees a blinking green light. It is part of a phone, which is attached to a device, which is strapped to the inside of the Bishop's leg. The crowd pulls away.

The Bishop pulls the contraption free and holds it high.

And Mohammed knows what it is. It is one of the canisters. And it is releasing nothing.

"What is it?" a man asks.

"A canister," Bishop Thoma responds, "that Mohammed bin Hassan just tried to trigger. It is filled with VX gas."

In the few moments before he is overwhelmed, Mohammed looks up, across the room, and sees Maryam.

And he sees that her fear is gone.

--

In the few shorts of his life after the reconstruction of the water tower, Tadeo had always insisted that Maryam would be the salvation of the City. He told it to everybody who would listen. He spoke of it constantly. It was tiresome. But Tadeo had been respected. And he had been loved. That's why Bishop Thoma had come to trust her as well.

When Maryam had lost control during the "Grand Jury" meeting, Bishop Thoma had accepted every word she said as truth. In that same meeting, he realized that the prosecution itself must be part of a larger plot. Thus, when the young Christian men were arrested, the Bishop visited them. He asked them about their crimes. They surprised him by admitting what they had done. He'd asked them why they had done it, and they had laid out everything they believed to be true.

They told him the Israelis had set it up.

Knowing he needed to learn more, the Bishop had mobilized his entire community. With the sudden appearance of commerce, Christian men and women suddenly had legitimate reasons to enter the Sunni section of the City. So, they did. In waves, they came, selling their goods. But always, they watched Mohammed. They even filmed him. They came to Thoma afterwards, reporting what they had seen and when. They handed over their recordings.

There hadn't been much time. But, together with his priests, the Bishop quickly worked out who Mohammed's men were. And then he watched them as well.

The day before the trial, Thoma's men saw several of Mohammed's agents emerge from their community. They were headed for the hill. They stopped, each of them, and did something, somewhere along the hillside. Their positions were noted and, not long after, Thoma sent men to retrieve whatever had been buried. They retrieved five canisters of gas. The canisters had not been meant to be discovered, and so they had no fancy protections. Instead, the Bishop's men simply disconnected the canisters from the phones that were meant to activate them. And with that, they neutralized the deadly weapons.

The Bishop went back to the young killers and told them to admit their crimes, in court. And then he told them who had really sent them to kill. He told them the Islamic State was behind it.

The men believed him; he was their Bishop after all.

When the time came, they would testify with conviction. And they would be imprisoned for many years to come.

Of course, the Bishop had no way of knowing *when* Mohammed would release the gas. He had collected the canisters together and sealed them within another larger container. He had collected all of them together – all but the one he carried under his robes.

That one he wore, waiting for it to beep or vibrate. When that happened, he would know that Mohammed had launched his assault. More importantly, the phone on the canister would log the number that had triggered it. As long as Mohammed carried the triggering phone, the terrorist and his weapon would be connected. Thoma carried the canister so the connection would be clear to any witnesses he might encounter.

When Thoma came to the courthouse, the guards didn't check him. They knew he was no threat. He entered without being challenged, a canister of VX gas strapped to his leg.

When the young killers pointed their fingers at the Islamic State, Thoma was watching carefully.

Things went better than he could have imagined.

Right then and there, in view of the world, Mohammed made a fatal mistake: he gave away that he knew more than he should.

And then he made another: he tried to release the gas.

And Bishop Thoma displayed his evidence in front of millions of witnesses.


As the crowd converges on Mohammed, the Bishop looks to Maryam. She sees him and smiles.

And then he realizes, with pleasant satisfaction, that Tadeo had been right.

She has, indeed, been the source of their salvation.

The City will survive.

# Epilogue

*July 1ˢᵗ, 2064: The City on the Heights*

Forty years have passed, I realize, as I look around the sumptuous banquet hall. My brother sits next to me, a middle-aged man with a child's mind. I reach out my hand to hold his, and he reaches back. We'd experienced so much pain together, but we've also experienced so much joy. The days of shouting, of terror, and of fear have long since passed.

As I regard him proudly, I realize that he has successfully worked for almost 30 years. He maintains a community garden, dedicating all of his limited faculties to the growth and success of his plants. He earns very little, himself. But with the subsidy, it is enough to get by. He still has attacks of course, but they are rare. They are caused only by memories, not reality.

We're here to honor Steven Gold, and the fiftieth anniversary of the City itself. The man moved back to Phoenix within a few years of the City being established. He said he wanted to invest in his children. But he visited occasionally. And he always returned for the anniversaries. He has deserved the honors he has received. For a short while, he'd become a leader and he'd changed the course of a region. He'd made the incredible real. But he's 96 years old now. This is probably the last anniversary he will ever attend.

So much has changed in those forty years. My name is no longer Maryam Al-Mosuli, but Maryam Al-Golani. I've followed in the footsteps of my father and my grandfather. I've fallen in love with a place, and I've struggled to sustain it. I've made it a part of my identity.

461

In the end, I took advantage of everything Elizabeth offered. She'd adopted me. And under her aegis and with her support, I went to University. I studied and I matured. I found myself amused as the City itself was studied and debated – in classes on political science, law and even economics. I was a student of a reality I had helped create. But I didn't only study. I spent enormous amounts of time with Elizabeth herself. In many ways, that was more valuable than anything the University could offer. She became my second mother.

And then, after earning my Bachelor's degrees in the U.S. – I'd majored in Civil Engineering and minored in Economics – I returned home. I returned to the City. In those few years, so much had changed. Apartment blocks had been built; proper streets had formed. Every house had running water. All the different people who lived there mingled in vast markets. The major fault lines of the society had cracked into thousands of smaller and overlapping lines. People had not assimilated with one another, but the definition of their groups had weakened. The large clumps of flocs that had characterized our pond had broken apart into thousands of pieces. My father's dream became reality, just not in Mosul. In time, the clear edges of conflict became fuzzy and the City grew further and further from the edges of war. Tentatively, the Syrian border was officially opened to trade – not with Israel, but just with the City itself.

In time, just as I'd hoped, the City became a hub of trade and a center of entertainment and media for the entire region. Hopeful people came from everywhere, looking to establish new lives in a new reality and hoping to honor G-d in a new way.

In the main, they have succeeded, by building and strengthening the place I now call home.

I was elected mayor of the City in its first democratic elections. I was, like my father, the only person who had no people and so I was the only person who could cross sectarian lines. I'd been mayor for over a decade. I'd managed the sewers and the courts and the police. I'd helped with legislation. In some ways, I'd become the face of the City itself. But eventually, I was ousted from my position. My identity was no longer so unique. But despite all of my later accomplishments, I know I'd never done anything greater than what I had done in those early days. Sometimes I felt like I'd never done anything greater than setting the bomb that destroyed the water tank. We are defined by so few moments.

But everything I'd done had depended on others. Steven Gold liked to talk about the power of the group. And he was right. It had taken many of us to make his dream a reality.

I have family of my own now. I have a husband. I have children. And I have relatives, a huge numbers of relatives, in Israel itself. They had thought my grandfather mad to stay in Mosul. They had fled to Israel, leaving everything behind. In a way, I'd followed in their footsteps. But I am a Muslim, like my mother – but not like my father. I found my way to All-h, not Hashem. I adhere to a stream of Sunni Islam. I am drawn to its simplicity, its purity, and its unfiltered relationship with the divine.

I pray five times a day, bowing my head and praising the glory of G-d. And I no longer drink during Ramadan.

My second mother, Elizabeth, died a year ago. The City ended up being the best of her investments. In the end, she'd acquired claim to 0.75 percent of its GDP. It was not a debt the City owed, it was an equity investment she and others had made. The State of Israel itself owns a stake. Remarkably, so do the Syrian and Iraqi governments. Other governments have sold debt, investing their creditors in their survival. But we've sold equity, so that those around us are invested in our success.

But it is not only those outside who are invested. With the courts, the responsibility of justice – the responsibility of the community – has ingrained itself within the people. And debt has remained rare. People are not only responsible as judges but are invested in the success of those around them. No massive balloon of debt hangs over us, threatening to destroy everything that our people have built. Of course, there is also no flood of cash at the opening of opportunity. Our business cycle is muted.

The City is not the richest of places, but we *feel* the success we have, and find ourselves fulfilled by it. We find that All-h is honored by our work.

While the great wars of my youth have passed, and our City is peaceful, the region is still divided. It simmers with cold conflict. But open warfare has almost vanished. The shared interests of enemies, both outside and inside the City, have helped calm the winds of war. And the ideas that allow us our peace have spread, in some ways, to the surrounding lands.

While Elizabeth had donated much of her stake in the City back to its people, she did not leave me impoverished. I control tremendous wealth, and I've learned how to use it judiciously: from a master of wealth management.

I think briefly of Mohammed. In the end, he had been convicted easily. His own people had turned against him. The vast majority of the Sunni population had come to the City because they sought peace, not war. They sought to live in freedom, not religious tyranny. They too had been deceived.

In the end, the courts had decided on the cruelest punishment of all: life. He remains alive but imprisoned, watching the City flourish and knowing that he sacrificed so many he loved for nothing at all.

The lights of the room darken, and Steven Gold enters from the side of the stage.

Everybody watches, silently.

And then Steven Gold, an American Jew from Phoenix who insisted on doing *something*, begins to speak.

THE END

# Dear Reader

I live in the Middle East, only 80 miles from Daraa – the epicenter of the Syrian Civil War. Although my daily existence is largely peaceful, I have been fundamentally disturbed by the reality that has engulfed my region. Looking at the region, I can see how taking sides, invasions, "nation-building" exercises and efforts at charitable outreach have solved nothing. These responses have treated only symptoms and not the underlying diseases.

Like many others, I could see that another answer was required. That is why *The City on the Heights* was born.

Of course, I can't establish a *real City on the Heights*. The best I can do is create one in fiction, populating it with three-dimensional characters, challenging it with real issues and stressing it to its breaking point. Through this process, I have tried to establish something more than simple fiction.

In our real world, national leaders and policymakers establish their positions by appealing to a framework of shared interests, ideologies or grievances. They have a community. It is by speaking to that community, and the beliefs it already has, that they raise themselves up into positions of power.

For the *City on the Heights* to influence our non-fictional world it must have a non-fictional community. If it has a community, then the word "intervention" wouldn't necessarily be a code word for aerial bombardment or boots on the ground. If it has a community, then its tax, welfare, debt and monetary policies could inspire changes in our real-world economic systems. If it has a community, then its judicial concepts might inspire change in troubled multi-ethnic regions.

West Berlin was a heavily subsidized fantasyland, but it gained a place in the imaginations of the suffering and the oppressed. Perhaps the fantasy of the *City on the Heights* can perform the same miracle. Even as a fictional place – it can enter the discourse of a troubled region and serve as an archetype for a better future. Like Augustine's *City of G-d,* it can be real, even if only in our minds and our hearts.

I have created this world. But I cannot give it reality. That relies on *you.* For this book to impact our world, it needs champions. It needs *you.*

So, *share this book.*

Share it with your friends, review it online (particularly on Amazon) and write about its ideas when you get a chance. Bring this book and its ideas into your reality and your community. And use me. I am happy to speak about these ideas and this story and explain the reasons behind it all.

If you do this, and if those you know do this, then we will – step-by-step - establish a new and better reality.


Thank you,


Joseph Cox
cityontheheights@gmail.com
www.JosephCox.com

www.ingramcontent.com/pod-product-compliance
Lightning Source LLC
Chambersburg PA
CBHW021212260626
47172CB00002B/393